"In true Kristy Cambron fashion, *The Ringmaster's Wife* is packed with emotional depth and characters who charm their way into your heart within the first pages. But perhaps most alluring about this story is the colorful world it's set in—from England to the Chicago World's Fair to the ever-moving backdrop of the circus world, I felt fully immersed. Engaging and poignant, this is a must-read!"

—Melissa Tagg, author of *From the Start* and *Like Never Before*

"A soaring love story! Vibrant with the glamour and awe that flourished under the Big Top in the 1920s, *The Ringmaster's Wife* invites the reader to meet the very people whose unique lives brought The Greatest Show on Earth down those rattling tracks. Through each of Rosamund's and Mable's stories, author Kristy Cambron offers the rare delight of witnessing a heartrending portrayal of love in the midst of circus life . . . and how one so deeply amplified the other."

—Joanne Bischof, award-winning author of *The Lady and the Lionheart*

"In *The Ringmaster's Wife*, Kristy Cambron has created a world that sweeps readers into the circus world of the 1920s with glimpses into the earlier days of vaudeville and the Ringling Brothers. The story is poignant as it shares of breaking free from restraints in an effort to dare to live life. The story is painted with delicate strokes and broad sweeps and will leave readers entranced in the dual-timeline. I highly recommend this novel for lovers of historical romances. Open the pages and be swept away!"

—Cara C. Putman, award-winning author of *Shadowed by Grace* and *Where Treetops Glisten*

Praise for the Hidden Masterpiece Novels

"Fans of the author's first book will gravitate to this tale of the power of faith and love to cope with impossible situations, although the grim realities depicted cannot be ignored. A must for book groups and genocide studies teachers and students."

—*Library Journal*, starred review, for *A Sparrow in Terezin*

"The second installment of Cambron's Hidden Masterpiece series is as stunning as the first. Though heartbreaking in many places, this novel never fails to show hope despite dire circumstances. God's love shines even in the dark."

—*RT Book Reviews*, 4½ stars, TOP PICK! for *A Sparrow in Terezin*

"In her historical series debut, Cambron expertly weaves together multiple plotlines, time lines, and perspectives to produce a poignant tale of the power of love and faith in difficult circumstances. Those interested in stories of survival and the Holocaust, such as Elie Wiesel's 'Night,' will want to read."

—*Library Journal*, for *The Butterfly and the Violin*

"In chapters alternating between past and present, debut novelist Cambron vividly recounts interwoven sagas of heartache and recovery through courage, love, art, and faith."

—*Publishers Weekly*, for *The Butterfly and the Violin*

"Alternating points of view skillfully blend contemporary and historical fiction in this debut novel that is almost impossible to put down. Well-researched yet heartbreaking scenes shed light on the horrors of concentration camps, as well as the contrasting beauty behind the prisoner's artwork. Two stories are carefully intertwined and demonstrate that there is always hope in God despite the monstrosities inflicted by man."

—*RT Book Reviews*, 4½ stars, TOP PICK! for *The Butterfly and the Violin*

The
RINGMASTER'S
WIFE

Books by Kristy Cambron

The Hidden Masterpiece Novels
The Butterfly and the Violin
A Sparrow in Terezin

The RINGMASTER'S WIFE

KRISTY CAMBRON

THOMAS NELSON
Since 1798

Published in Nashville, Tennessee, by Thomas Nelson. Thomas Nelson is a registered trademark of HarperCollins Christian Publishing, Inc.

Published in association with Books & Such Literary Management, 52 Mission Circle, Suite 122, PMB 170, Santa Rosa, California 95409-5370, www.booksandsuch.com.

Interior Design: Mallory Collins

Thomas Nelson titles may be purchased in bulk for educational, business, fund-raising, or sales promotional use. For information, please e-mail SpecialMarkets@ThomasNelson.com.

Scripture quotations are taken from the Holy Bible, New International Version®, NIV®. Copyright © 1973, 1978, 1984, 2011 by Biblica, Inc.® Used by permission of Zondervan. All rights reserved worldwide. www.zondervan.com. The "NIV" and "New International Version" are trademarks registered in the United States Patent and Trademark Office by Biblica, Inc.®

Publisher's Note: This novel is a work of fiction. Any references to real people, events, establishments, organizations, or locales are intended only to give the fiction a sense of reality and authenticity, and are used fictitiously. All other names, characters, and places and all dialogue and incidents portrayed in this book are the product of the author's imagination.

Library of Congress Cataloging-in-Publication Data

Library of Congress Cataloging-in-Publication Data
Names: Cambron, Kristy, author.
Title: The ringmaster's wife / Kristy Cambron.
Description: Nashville, Tennessee: Thomas Nelson, [2016]
Identifiers: LCCN 2015050179 | ISBN 9780718041540 (paperback)
Classification: LCC PS3603.A4468 R56 2016 | DDC 813/.6--dc23 LC record available at http://lccn.loc.gov/2015050179

Printed in the United States of America

16 17 18 19 20 RRD 6 5 4 3 2 1

For Brady, Carson, and Colt:
Because childhood wonder becomes
the treasure of memory.

It is never too late to be what you might have been.
—George Eliot

PROLOGUE

The LORD gives sight to the blind,
the LORD lifts up those who are bowed down.
—PSALM 146:8

1929
LOUISVILLE, KENTUCKY

We only see what we want to see—in people, in love, and in life.

What we see is a choice, as is what we offer the world in return.
And it's only behind the costumes and the masks that we can be who
we truly are.

The words echoed in Rosamund's mind in a tangle of memories
collected over the past three years. She waited at the performers'
entrance at the back of the enormous Big Top, trying to ease the
racing of her heart before show time.

Waves of riotous applause ebbed and flowed with the breathtaking thrills of the trapeze act. It was a "straw house" tonight—sold
out, the bleacher seats packed and the overflow of children lining
the edges of the rings on piles of laid-out straw. Rosamund could
hear the children now through the call of horns and pops of confetti
bursts, squealing in delight at the antics of the clowns. It wouldn't

1

be long now—the ringmaster's signal for the horse troop to march in was just moments away.

A breeze caught Rosamund's attention, perfuming the air around her with the richness of caramel, mixed with the salty scent of popcorn and sweet apples from a wagonette nearby. It was a welcome contrast to the usual smell of animals and churned-up earth in their field lot. All the familiar sounds and smells, the excitement that hung on the air before a performance . . . they reminded her how the three-ring canvas castle had become her home.

The other bareback riders had ushered the troop of show horses from the ring stock tent; they were out in front now, waiting to burst into the ring.

The horses whinnied, and Ingénue, Rosamund's black Arabian lady, broke into a soft song along with them. The horse stomped her hooves, her happy jitters stirred up by the flash of lights and the lyrical cadence of the band that signaled performance time.

Rosamund stood off to the side, alone—once the glittering star of the show, but now a performer bringing up the rear of the troop in yesterday's sequins and satin. It was no longer her face splashed about on the circus posters plastering the cities and towns they visited. She wondered if the crowd would still cheer for the bareback rider with the trademark blush of English roses pinned in her hair.

Was she just an afterthought now? Someone forgotten. Perhaps never really known. Would they notice the pair of them, she riding in on her magnificent black madam horse, performing tricks from memory to enchant the crowd?

"Rosamund—here you are."

Colin Keary's Irish brogue was light, familiar, his tone of voice soft and laced with feeling.

She tilted her chin to the sound but kept her body squared to the direction of the audience. "We've had word then?" She held her breath.

"Yes. I'd read the telegram aloud, but I think you already know what it says."

Rosamund squeezed her eyelids tight and waited.

"She passed away early this morning."

It must have been tearing Colin apart on the inside. But how like him to want to tell her himself, despite the pain it would cause them both.

The Big Top rustled in the wind like tissue paper in front of a fan, as if it, too, chose to recoil from the painful news. The crowd erupted in applause just then, marveling at some grand feat of daring from the flyers, oblivious to the fact that anyone's life had changed outside the tent. The summer breeze continued stirring tiny bits of sawdust about the field, brushing the side of her face like grains of sand on the wind.

Rosamund drew in a deep breath, readying her nerve to perform. "Ingénue and I have a show to give," she said, and ran a hand down the silk of her horse's mane.

"Even if it kills you."

She shook her head, countering, "Never. The ring is home to us. We'll not fear it."

"Even now?"

"Especially now."

Rosamund felt the light touch of his fingertips against the rows of sequins at her shoulder and drew in a deep breath as she notched her chin a touch higher.

"We can't let them down now, can we?" she whispered, closing her eyes and pressing her forehead against the side of Ingénue's head.

"Rose . . ."

Only Colin called her that—a soft Irish lilt of an endearment that he'd whispered so sweetly once upon a time. She brushed the thought away, like a cobweb caught in the wind. It would do no good to live in yesterdays. Not when everything had changed.

"Listen to me." He breezed around the front of her, tilted her face to him with a butterfly's touch of his fingertips to her cheek. "You know if she were still here, she'd tell us that this life is a gift, Rose. It's given and it's taken away in a blink. It's madness to go out and perform now."

"You can't protect me," she whispered, easing his hand back. "Or fix me."

"It's not your call this time. I'm your boss, Rose, and I won't let you go in."

"The show is in my blood, Colin. Please don't ask me to be less than who I am."

He paused, as if absorbing her words and choosing his own that much more carefully. Or boldly. She couldn't be sure.

"It won't bring her back."

Rosamund felt her chin quiver. "I know that. But are you saying it for me or for you?"

They stood in agonizing silence. Her heart beating wild. Wondering if his was doing the same unrestrained somersaulting in his chest.

Their circus world toiled beyond, the tent bursting to life with the vibrancy of the band playing "Roses of Picardy," a jaunty version of the song that had always signaled her entrance.

"It's time to go," she thought aloud. "Colin, I . . ." She swallowed hard, fighting against the mental image of him standing just outside, looking on from the shadows while she performed under the bright lights.

She flipped up on Ingénue's back as she'd done countless times before.

"I can't be a caged bird with a broken wing." She wiped at tears that had gathered in secret but now threatened to tumble down her cheeks. "I know now I'd never survive that kind of love," she whispered. "And neither would you."

The band played their cue, and Rosamund nudged Ingénue forward with a gentle squeeze of her ankles to both sides of the horse's body. And forward they trotted, leaving the breath of wind toiling behind as they went in to give their last performance.

"Just like Mable said . . ." She straightened her shoulders and raised her head to the elation of the crowd. "They'll only see what we want them to."

CHAPTER 1

Three years earlier
North Yorkshire, England

Air turned to water.

It rushed over Rosamund's head in a torrent, curling and mocking as it dragged her with the current. She flailed her legs in a bevy of kicks as it rolled, fighting to keep her head above water.

Hers was a foe of muddy brown, a once peaceful brook that flowed under the old cobblestone bridge on the road to Linton. But it had swollen to a near raging river with the last heavy rain, engulfing her the instant her motor had veered off the country road and tumbled down the embankment with a great splash.

How fortunate it was that she still wore men's riding trousers. At least it afforded her some movement of her legs in the water, though not enough that she believed she could reach safety.

The current surged, plunging Rosamund into its depths again. It continued surging. Tugging at her legs first and then pulling her along like a rag doll tossed in the open sea. Her back went deeper. Then her shoulders. Her head. She felt her hair billowing around her neck like thick twines of seaweed.

The rush of water, then fear.

Her thoughts were urgent, her mind signaling the deepest

sense of danger. Was this it, she wondered, the blackness of one's thoughts at death?

Exhaustion in body, mind, even her soul, threatening to be called away.

The brown murkiness deadened the burning pain in her legs, fighting to muddle her mind and body into submission.

"Hello—*you there!*"

The shout rocked her senses.

Though still bobbing about like a cork in a bucket, Rosamund felt renewed strength to nudge her chin up out of the water. She scanned the banks on either side, frantically looking for anything that stood out beyond roiling water and dense thickets of autumn-painted trees.

"Over here!"

Another shout. This one was closer. Bold. Echoing from up ahead.

Thank You, God . . .

She'd heard the voice clearly this time and met a man's fixed stare from the bank on her right.

He'd braced himself against a felled tree, one arm hooked around the trunk and the other reaching toward her, tense and ready to grasp her as she was swept by.

He shouted again. "Take hold of my hand, all right?"

Rosamund tried to nod as a rush of the current splashed in her face. She shook her head out of it, coughing as her hair splayed across the bridge of her nose. She brushed it back with the swipe of a hand.

He seemed to pause for a second when his eyes fell upon her face up close. Yet he responded with determination, willing her hand to connect with his. Though her energy stores were all but tapped clean, Rosamund reached out and locked hands with his at the wrist. His grip was iron.

"Good. Now swim to me," he shouted, willing her to accept his word. "I'll not let go of you."

Rosamund lunged forward, falling into his grip.

The felled tree extended from a mossy bank, with water that grew shallower as it edged to shore. The man carefully maneuvered the pair of them back, trekking his free hand along the trunk.

When Rosamund felt the familiar sensation of stones beneath the soles of her boots, she lurched forward, drifting with the softening current until they were out of the water. She fell upon the bank on all fours, coughing against the ground as if mud and scrubby brush were her long-lost friends.

She untangled the long ropes of hair from one of her suspenders and swept them over her shoulder, then collapsed on the ground, relishing the glorious feel of earth beneath her.

"Miss? Are you all right?"

Rosamund felt a hand just graze her shoulder. Even over the sound of the rushing water behind them, she heard a notable Irish brogue in the man's voice. She turned to meet it, finally able to take a look at her rescuer.

The man knelt in a patch of fallen leaves at her side, his blue eyes fixed upon her. He remained calm. Quiet. Soaked to the skin himself but concerned, it seemed, only with her welfare.

"I'm fine," she answered, though fighting the ever-present burn of water in her throat. "Or I will be—" She coughed, then shook her head. "In a moment."

"Think you're keen to stand?" he asked. He offered his arm and Rosamund accepted it gratefully so he could help her rise up on shaky legs.

"Stars above . . . You got him!"

Rosamund glanced up as a second man appeared on the ridge. This man was young—perhaps not yet twenty, with round wire-rimmed glasses and sandy hair that flopped down over his forehead. He held a bundle of clothing under his elbow, but dropped it straightaway and bounded down the hill. His work boots scuffled over protruding roots and fallen leaves, sending stray trails of dirt to roll down the hill with him.

"Is he all right?" he asked, winded as he stopped in front of them.

"He is a *she*—" The man who'd rescued her corrected the assumption with a controlled whisper. "But yes. She's going to be fine."

"Miss." The young man addressed her with a quick nod in her direction, but wasted no time in continuing. "You're as crackers as they say, Colin. Jumping into the water like that!"

"You saw the motor go down the bank. What other option did we have?" He paused, softening his tone. "And please mind your choice of words in front of the woman who mightn't have been saved otherwise."

The man named Colin still stood anchored at her side, though his gaze was fixed upon the twists and turns of the water before them. With a gentle warning squeeze that he was releasing her elbow, he drew back and took several steps toward the water's edge.

"Ward, you'll have to stay with her."

"Where are you going?" The young man shook his head. "The auto's a lost cause. We'll have to hire men from the village to get it out."

Her rescuer continued scanning the surface of the water. "Not the auto." He dropped his voice. "I'm going back for the driver. Even though he hasn't surfaced, we can't leave the poor soul behind."

Rosamund had been wringing water from the tips of her hair, but snapped her head up at his words. "My driver?"

"This must all be very distressing for you," the younger of the two added, looking like he might have been able to summon just enough gumption to frown at the other gentleman for mentioning the ill-fated driver with such indelicacy. He turned to Rosamund. "Don't fret, miss. We'll see you to the safety of the village first."

Rosamund swallowed hard over the growing lump in her throat as an all-new rush of anxiety enveloped her. "Sir, I . . ."

How could she possibly explain the circumstances without giving herself away? If her parents learned what she'd been up to, she'd be locked up in the manor for the rest of her days.

She cleared her throat. "There's no one else there," she said, tipping her chin a fraction higher. "I'm the driver."

"You? Well, this English plot of ours just thickened," the younger man said, looking on with eyes wide and a charm-filled grin that washed down over his face as the truth sank in.

The man named Colin, however, gave little away.

His dark hair lay just tipping over his eyes, with which he now studied her in a most open manner. Rosamund detected the tiniest shred of hesitation as he watched her, doubt that was confirmed when he braced his arms across his chest, as if working things out in his mind.

"Miss." Colin inclined his head. "You're shivering."

Was she?

The rush of an autumn wind flooded around them then.

It carried the reminder that winter wasn't far off from their October sky. The distant rumble of thunder sent another shiver to tend the length of her spine, and Rosamund remembered all at once that she was wet, cold, and quite in need of a way out of her present mess before a storm muddled the situation still further.

"I hadn't realized . . ." She wrapped her arms round her middle, trying to calm the thoughts bouncing off every corner in her mind.

"Ward. Can you fetch my coat? I dropped it along the bank somewhere back there."

The young man nodded, then trekked up the rise to retrieve it.

He tossed the garment down to Colin, who caught it, then took a step forward.

"It'll be too big, but at least it's dry."

She accepted the coat with trembling fingers. From the events that had taken place. Or the cold. Likely both.

"Thank you." Rosamund pulled the coat up round her shoulders, trying her best to hide her hands beneath the lapels, lest her rescuer see the evidence of how shaken she truly was. "It's kind of you."

"We should see you back to the village," Colin began, his tone even. In control.

She tried not to notice his ongoing inspection of her, even with the coat having swallowed her down to the knees.

"Of course," Ward chimed in. "We can drop you off on the way to our business meeting."

"What he means to say is that after the accident you've just been through, it wouldn't be gentlemanly of us to go on without introduction and the offer of assistance home. I'm Colin Keary." He inclined his head in the other gentleman's direction. "And this is my associate, Mr. Ward Butler. And now that we know there's no one else lost in the wreckage of the motor, we'd like to offer what help we can."

"No thank you," Rosamund said. "I'm fine."

The men exchanged glances, the coy declaration serving only to pique their interest further.

"And you are . . ." Ward tipped his eyebrows in question.

"Rose," she said very simply. She wasn't sure why she'd said it, except that the pet name from childhood was the first one to come to mind.

"Well then . . . Rose." Colin paused. "We ought to be off." He held out his hand, offering to guide her to the top of the steep ridge.

"We can walk you back to the bridge, then we'll take our car to the village. We should see about getting you to a doctor first, then arrange to retrieve your auto later once the weather's cleared."

"*No*," Rosamund shot back on instinct, leaving his hand extended on air. Her refusal must have been shocking for a tiny slip of a woman to effectively halt two grown men in their tracks.

Ward's eyes grew large. He darted a glance to Colin before asking, with a tone of amusement, "No . . . ? To which part?"

Rosamund backtracked with a forced smile, hoping to cover her misgivings.

"What I mean to say is that you don't have to go to the trouble of summoning a doctor. I assure you, I'm fine. Just a bit shaken, that's all."

"Of course you are. Understandably." Colin pursed his lips as if noting something he'd chosen not to comment on.

Something told Rosamund that Colin Keary should be worthy of trusting. There was an earnestness in him that couldn't be mistaken, even if he was a stranger. He was older than his companion, Ward—maybe by ten years—and clearly in command. He had rescued her and now was steering the lot of them to calm despite the circumstances.

For that, she knew some explanation was warranted.

"I left an all-day riding party later than I should have. It set me late for an evening engagement, so I stretched the Talbot's engine in hopes that I'd arrive on time. But I misjudged a bend in the road and tumbled down the embankment instead." She squared her shoulders, trying to appear confident and proper instead of entirely aloof. "I didn't wish to bother our driver with such an all-day trip, and now I'm quite relieved he stayed behind. I know it's very untoward, but I ask for your discretion in this matter."

"You've been 'riding all day,' Miss Rose?" Colin asked, scanning the landscape around them. "And yet you have no horse?"

"Heavens. Don't tell me someone has to dive into that river after a horse now." Ward shuddered, as if the thought were too gruesome to entertain.

"My horse has been quite taken care of. I'd already hired a man to see her back to my home," she answered. "And it's not against propriety for a woman to drive through town on her own, horse in tow or not. If that is your meaning."

"On the contrary, it's impressive. It seems almost . . . How do you say it over here—*revolutionary*?" Ward broke in with an easy smile.

Truth be, he was too forward to be anything but American.

"I didn't know English women drove automobiles themselves."

"They don't. Not as a rule," Colin added.

"Are you from Linton, to know how such things are received here, sir?" she asked, hoping to keep the inquisition light while challenging his knowing tone.

"No. We're a little farther off from the English countryside, I'd say."

"Ireland then?" Rosamund responded before she could stop herself, then bit her lip.

"See?" Ward cocked a grin and tipped up an eyebrow in Colin's direction. "She noticed it. I told you the accent comes out when you're riled up."

"I meant nothing by it," she said.

"Ignore Mr. Butler and his lack of *tact*," Colin responded. "My family is Irish, but not in that way. The Kearys hail from New York. You're in the presence of a couple of Yanks, I'm afraid, in case you couldn't surmise that from this pup's rather loose-lipped manner. First trip out of the country, and he's a bit too eager."

Americans.

So she was right—about the younger of the two anyway.

Rosamund nodded as the sky once again rumbled with the threat of imminent rain. She edged forward a few steps. "My home is not far from here and my family is expecting me. I really must be going."

"Wait—you can't just march through the woods. It's going to storm," Ward blurted out, directing her to the gray-tinged sky with an accusatory finger. "And we're miles away from anything. Even Linton's a mighty long jaunt from here on foot."

Rosamund shifted her glance from him to Colin.

"Well, I'm already soaked through. A few raindrops and a walk can't possibly hurt me now."

"All right, Miss Rose. No doctor. Will that suit you?" He'd acquiesced, though something still flickered in Colin's eyes. Thunder cracked the sky closer this time, echoing behind his words. He glanced up to the canopy of trees overhead, adding, "But something tells me that despite appearances, you don't live in the village. And since that thunder sounds as though a bit more than a light shower is headed this way, you just might wish to take us up on our offer of assistance. So can I order a car to take you wherever your home is?"

"While I'm sure your offer is well intended—"

"No, it's not," Colin interrupted.

Often. And as it suited him, apparently. As brash as any Irishman she'd have expected.

"My inquisition is to ensure I'm not entangled in something sinister when I have your auto pulled from the creek bed back there. And I'd much prefer not to have an angry husband or father chasing us for compromising your reputation—on these innocent grounds or not. But if you tell me there's nothing to concern ourselves about, then I'll let the matter drop. I'm here on business, and I don't want my employer's name associated with any sort of trouble."

"Is your employer known in Yorkshire then?"

He leaned in, a twinkle flashing in his eyes, and whispered, "My employer is known everywhere, Miss Rose. Even as far off the path as the village of Linton."

"Then I'll pay you for a new suit," she offered, before thinking better of it.

He tipped up his brows, as if to ask, *Is it that bad?*

"I meant I'll pay for the *damage* to your suit. And for the obvious trouble to pull the motor from the water. I'll have a man come and meet you to retrieve it this night."

"No payment is necessary, even for a new suit." He paused, a marked lightness now lacing his tone. "Because despite my appearance, the employer I represent very likely has more money than the King of England himself. And I assure you—he likes to manage his own affairs."

He approached her with ease, looking with a direct gaze. She edged a step back.

"I'll see that the motor is put back in order—free of charge."

And with that he nodded and started trekking up the route that led back to the bridge.

Brash, indeed.

He wouldn't have heard it as a compliment, if Rosamund had said what she was thinking in that instant: Colin Keary was certainly an American and an Irishman wrapped into one.

CHAPTER 2

1885
CINCINNATI, OHIO

Ten-year-old Armilda Burton had never heard the sweet sound of a piano before.

How different it was compared to the deep-chested organ that filled the ceiling vault of their country church every Sunday. This sound was enchanting—with crisp notes that echoed through the spacious rooms and greeted her young ears the moment she stepped through the front door of the ladies' tea parlor.

Armilda had come to Cincinnati with her mother and the ladies in their parish to attend the annual Temperance League meeting outside of their small farming community of Moons, Ohio. She'd never before seen such modern brick buildings and shop after shop teeming with fashionable wares. Why, she'd only ever seen a mere handful of store-bought dresses, outside of drawings in the catalog at the Moons General Store. Stepping into the world of the ladies' tearoom, she felt small and uncultured.

And completely awestruck.

Floor-to-ceiling velvet curtains of crimson were fashioned with gold cords, pulled back like stage curtains hanging against the back-drop of white wainscoting on the parlor walls. Chandeliers twinkled overhead. The arched floor-to-ceiling windows let in an abundance of natural light. A smattering of settees—marvelous in their gold and cream brocade—adorned the front room, and clothed tables with glassware and shining china settings bedecked the garden room beyond. Both rooms carried the light scent of vanilla and lavender mixed with the sharper notes of black tea and citrusy lemon.

The ladies themselves were a vision in day gloves, hats, and their finest trappings. They had plumes in their coiffed hair and hats angled on their crowns. The most Armilda had ever seen of the soft yellows, blues, and blush-pink they wore was in the richness of the summer landscape in the fields beyond their farmhouse. But she doubted now that sky or fields could compare with the array of hues around her.

Her attention was drawn away from the ladies, however, by something in the rear of the garden room.

There stood the piano, gleaming black. Like a king presiding in court.

It was marvelous, demanding attention with a light melody over the hum of chatter and the clinking of china teacups. Armilda broke away from her mother to approach it, feeling called by a lyrical pied piper.

The pianist was a young lady of perhaps twenty, wearing a cherub-pink gown and a white felt hat with an oversized peony tipped to one side of her brow. She offered a congenial smile as her fingers continued floating over the keys. Armilda felt welcomed, but only as a guest. She was reminded at the same time that all of *this* was far beyond her grasp.

She reached out, running her fingertips against the edge of the wood.

Funny, but it felt like silk somehow.

"Why, hello." The pianist smiled at her as she rested her fingers on the keys, while the final notes echoed in the room. She tilted her head down, accepting the applause from the crowd in a congenial nod, then turned her attention back to Armilda.

"I can see that you like music. Would you like to play?"

Armilda shook her head. "No, ma'am," she answered, the words more meek than she'd intended. "I don't know how."

"But you appreciate music, which is a gift in itself. And the sound is beautiful, isn't it? This is a Steinway piano—the best. Shipped all the way from New York." Her eyes were kind but curious. "Is this your first trip to Cincinnati?"

How did she know that?

Armilda nodded. "I've never been anywhere."

"Chin up. Perhaps you'll go to New York one day and see where the Steinways come from. Mmm? Don't let that love of music leave your heart."

The pianist flipped the music sheets in front of her, moving on to another song.

Of course Armilda didn't travel. Not to New York or even Cincinnati until that day. And she didn't play a piano—she doubted she ever would. They didn't have such things at home. Not pianos with melodies like that.

Music, fine table settings, and elegant tearooms were a world away from her quiet life in Moons. Hers was a plain farm dress and her expectations of life plain as well.

She'd always believed it. At least, until now.

Seven years later
Moons, Ohio

It was a familiar memory that greeted Armilda when she blinked awake.

The piano faded away again, its song turning into the hum of crickets chirping in the fields. The view of rich taffeta gowns in her dream became the span of a blue-ink sky dotted with clouds out the open window, the velvet curtains the walls of the small bedroom she shared with her sisters. And she was no longer ten years old, but nearly seventeen—all grown up now and too old for childish dreams.

She rolled out of bed and pulled a rust-colored knit shawl over her shoulders. The floorboards creaked as she knelt, as carefully as she could manage, and ran her hands along the aged wood floor under her bed, feeling for the cigar box she kept hidden there.

Armilda tucked it under her elbow and with extra-careful tip-toed steps slipped down the stairs and out the front door. Safe on the porch, she melted down into one of the old wooden rockers. She'd be content to watch dawn escape, just as it always did, with a splash of orange painting the sky over the distant horizon. She cradled the prized O. L. Schwencke cigar box in her lap, absently running her fingertips over the raised lithography image of fashionable smiling women riding bicycles down a sunny lane.

The rocker creaked in time with the crickets' refrain.

"Armilda?"

She turned at her sister's voice. "Dulcey—go back to bed. It's early still."

"What are you doing out here, Mim?" Dulcey whispered the question, adding the nickname only the family called her.

"Nothing. Just watching the world wake up."

Dulcey eased into the rocker opposite Armilda's. She pulled her legs up and tucked them under the ends of the pinwheel quilt she'd dragged from her bed to wrap around her shoulders, then she turned her freckled face out to the span of dusky fields beyond their farmhouse. The sun peeked up between the porch spindles. "It's cold out here. Whatever happened to summer?"

Armilda glanced over at her sister and sighed. "I suppose it's gone where it always does—tucked away somewhere until it's needed for next year."

"Hmm. Next year," Dulcey agreed. "Just as long as it stays cool, I'll be happy. Last year we couldn't think of anything but melting until dusk."

How could it possibly be any different from last year? Or the year before that?

Dulcey looked down at the brightly colored box in Armilda's lap. "You're thinking about it again, aren't you? About the tearoom. And the piano."

"Nonsense." Armilda tossed the idea off with a wave of her hand. "You were snoring again and it woke me up. You really should do something about that."

"Admit it," Dulcey said. "You only get your box out when you dream. I couldn't begin to guess how many catalog clippings of Steinway pianos are buried in there."

"Shhh!" Armilda leaned forward. "Papa's probably already up and Momma's heating water for coffee, but I'd like a few moments of peace before we have to head for the shoe factory."

"Uh-uh. Not until you admit the truth." Dulcey crossed her arms over her chest.

"Fine." Armilda kicked out, connecting a light tap to her sister's shin. "But we're all allowed our secret dreams. I was merely visiting mine again. You shouldn't tease me for it."

"But we have to work today. How can you focus on your job if your mind is always flitting about in that cigar box? You're so distracted, it's a wonder you don't make shoes for a person who has two left feet."

"Oh, Dulce. I don't want to spend the rest of my life thinking about shoes—not when there's so much more out there."

"Maybe. Here there's nothing but sleepy cows and dew-covered fields as far as the eye can see." Dulcey gestured to the span of misty fields. "And when the factory moves to Chicago next year, you won't even have shoes to think about! Which is why you need to see this."

Dulcey leaned forward with a loud creak of her rocker and extended a folded newspaper clipping to her sister. "It's from the *Chicago Daily Tribune.*"

Armilda opened it and glanced at the headline: WORLD'S FAIR COLUMBIAN EXPOSITION: GROUNDBREAKING CEREMONY TO TAKE PLACE OCTOBER 21.

"So?"

"Just read it," Dulcey said.

Armilda scanned the article. Though the fair wouldn't open for another seven months after that, plans for the grand spectacle were well under way. The city of Chicago would show that it could rise from the ashes of the great fire that had felled it in 1871. And the 400th anniversary of Columbus's first landing on the continent would be celebrated the world over, with a grand showcase of technology, science, industry, and culture from forty-six different nations.

In short, it sounded amazing.

Amazing, but miles away from Moons. And a lifetime away from where she'd ever be.

"Did you read about the electricity exhibit? And there's actually a moving walkway. A *travellator*, it says. It will carry a person down to the pier without lifting a foot." Dulcey laughed. "How do you like that? With moving walkways, shoes might become a thing of the past."

"We've read exciting news stories before. Why is this one any different?"

"Think about it. It's the *World's Fair*, Mim. As close as it's ever going to be to us. It's coming to Chicago along with millions of people from all over the globe. You've always wanted to see the world. Well, it looks like the world is coming to see you."

Fashion. Art. Music. All the things she loved.

"How about that *zoopraxiscope* thing—a giant picture on the wall that moves like a photograph's come to life! Wouldn't you love to see that? And Sissieretta Jones is going to sing! Can you imagine?"

"Sounds wonderful," Armilda said, handing the clipping back. "Maybe you should go."

"Be serious." Dulcey shook her head at the folded clipping. "*You* should go, Armilda. I'm not joking. Go to Chicago. The shoe factory is moving there and you're guaranteed a job in it. And then who knows? Maybe you can go on to New York after that. Or someplace even more exciting. What else do you have in that box of yours? Maybe you could find a way onto a ship sailing for Europe."

Armilda smiled, thinking of the articles she had collected from all over, catalog drawings and fashion photos she'd clipped and saved—not even knowing why.

Venice, she thought, her heart leaping in her chest just a little bit. *Venice is in there, along with Paris. London. New York . . .*

Everywhere is waiting for me.

Dulcey wasn't finished. "You've read every book our teacher has that mentions anything about art or travel in it. And your eyes are always fixed on a point past the fields. You're special, Mim."

"But I couldn't leave, could I?" Armilda whispered, chewing on her bottom lip as the idea began to sink in deeper. "What would that do to Momma and Papa? And where would that leave all of you?"

"Where will we be?" Dulcey stood. "Right here, dear sister. Waiting for letters to hear about your grand adventures, I expect." She shrugged. "I like my life here. I know I'll be happy. But you?" She rested a hand on Armilda's shoulder. "The world is calling you,

Mim. And you should meet it head-on. You can be anyone you want to be."

Armilda took her sister's hand in her own and pecked a kiss to her palm. Dulcey was right. If she was ever going to turn her cigar-box dream into reality, reinvent Armilda Burton the farm girl from Moons, Ohio, this was her opportunity.

She leaned back in the rocker once more, the old chair showing its age with loud creaking again. *Anyone you want to be . . .*

She thought of a name she'd once read in C. M. Yonge's *The Heir of Redclyffe*—a novel in which an Irish character had the name that meant "lovable" and "dear." It was a name with star power, in her mind. With so much more unbridled strength than the provincial "Armilda" could possess. A name that should be owned by one who played Steinway pianos. And visited tearooms. Who wasn't afraid to be brave. Because that's what she'd need—the courage to walk away from everything she'd always known and step out with hopes for a reimagined life.

"I'll be Mable Burton," she whispered, the words floating out on the breeze.

Birds chirped in the loft of trees overhead, mingling with her voice. Echoing their song with her words. Her dreams. The possibilities that extended far beyond the farmhouse, beyond the sunrise over the fields.

She closed her eyes and rocked back, cradling the cigar box in her lap.

"Mable—the girl who will never be afraid to really *live*."

CHAPTER 3

1926

NORTH YORKSHIRE, ENGLAND

It was one heck of a first impression.

Colin had to admit that.

To arrive three hours late for a business meeting would have been insulting enough to the English. But judging by the butler's scowl, Colin suspected it was slightly worse to arrive at a manor in a state of disrepair, bearing no dinner invitation, on the night of a grand house party. It seemed quite enough to have been deemed utterly disastrous by the standards of the English aristocracy.

Fortunately the butler's sense of propriety also meant he couldn't leave anyone on the front step in the rain, no matter their breach of decorum. So he and Ward had been shown into the grand entry hall—for the moment at least—to await a proper announcement to the lord and lady of the manor. And with the gale building outside, it seemed a real possibility they might have to stay through the entirety of a white-tie, full five-course dinner.

Colin pictured the butler's abject horror with a suppressed smile.

The stone and wood-paneled entry of Easling Park glowed in subtle lamplight from iron-scroll wall sconces illuminating a towering wood and stylized stucco ceiling. The varying orange-yellow light of a fire danced out from a marble-faced hearth on the back wall. A gust of autumn wind drove the rain against the leaded glass panes of floor-to-ceiling windows.

Colin glanced up at the tinkling crystal chandelier above their heads, altogether relieved to be out of the storm. Putting on airs with the English upper crust he could manage. Spending a night in Linton with nothing to show for the cost and time involved he could not.

He ran his hands down the sleeves of his coal-black suit coat, shedding it of stubborn raindrops that had collected on the wool. Ward did the same with his, and when the butler left them made a feeble attempt at slicking his hair back without the aid of a comb.

"This isn't at all how it's done." He bent at an awkward angle, trying to find his reflection in a polished gold vase perched on a mahogany table nearby.

"Isn't how what's done, exactly?" Colin inquired.

"Being presented at a wealthy heiress's home, that's what." He blew out a frustrated breath. "Classic. The wind decided to wreak havoc with every effort I made."

Colin watched in amusement as Ward continued the frenzied dance.

"Something tells me it wouldn't have mattered anyway. I'm not sure working-class Americans—and circus hands at that—are high on their list of honored guests."

"Say what you want, but I heard talk from the village boys that this guy's got a daughter. An unmarried one." Ward surveyed the room, whistling low. "On top of this massive pile of bricks and estate grounds. Can you imagine the luck?"

"Bricks we've seen before," Colin reminded him, and slid his hands in his pockets with a light shrug.

"The Ringlings may live high on the hog, but not like this," Ward countered. "And certainly not with the offer of a package deal."

"Who said they're offering anything to you?"

"It's the fact that they *could* offer something, if we make a good impression. She's free to fall in love with anyone she likes, isn't she?"

Maybe Colin should have told Ward the truth, that to arrive at this very manor was the reason they'd come this far north in the first place. And she—the girl who'd called herself Rose—was the reason why.

The instant he recognized the earl's daughter in the water, Colin should have been out with it. She was dressed differently than she'd been at the Linton trick-riding competition, but there was no mistaking what he'd seen. Those green eyes had been burned in his memory. And the mare she'd ridden? Only Lord Denton boasted horseflesh like that.

There wasn't another estate in all of the North Country that could lay claim to either beauty. And falling in love with "anyone she liked" wasn't in the cards for her, of that much he was certain. The man would have to boast something far more impressive than the whole of Easling Park's estate. A cot in the corner of a circus work tent wasn't likely to be attractive to these people.

Ward was busy straightening his collar. Checking his teeth in the vase. No doubt plotting the very real possibility of a future in Yorkshire, all the while unaware that he'd already met the very lady he was hoping to impress.

He smoothed his waistcoat and added one last impassioned tug at his collar. "Well? How do I look?"

Colin cocked an eyebrow.

"I know." Ward shrugged. "But your shirt is too big on me. How's everything else?"

"Listen, Ward. About the girl—"

"Shh, shh. He's coming back."

The butler reappeared, his disapproval barely hidden below the surface. It managed to leak out, however, in his pin-straight stance and the stern glare he sent in their direction.

"Lord and Lady Denton will receive you now," he announced, extending an arm toward a long hall lined with a red filigree runner on the floor and an abundance of oil paintings bedecking the walls. "This way."

Ward nearly tripped jumping into line behind the butler, a bit too eager in his haste to get to his future. Colin, however, hung back. He squared his shoulders and, with one final indrawn breath, set his jaw for the battle he knew was coming.

CHAPTER 4

Lead weighted Rosamund's shoes with each step to the drawing room door.

By the time she arrived back from Linton and ducked through the servants' entrance, an exquisite jade-and-gold beaded gown had already been laid out in her chamber. It boasted a silk-banded drop waist fashioned by Poiret, a noted Parisian designer whom her mother had commissioned just weeks before. The gown was paired with Rosamund's finest beaded heels, a geometric-shaped trinket on a long black and gleaming gold chain, and evening gloves that added a soft pearl shimmer up the length of her arms. The final touch was a diamond-encrusted headband that grazed the chignon of finger waves her maid gathered at her nape.

The lavish ensemble foretold what awaited her—either a crowd of the most eligible bachelors her mother could summon at a single dinner party, or one carefully selected gentleman whose attentions she should properly win.

Either way Rosamund had been primped for a purpose.

The butler presented Lady Rosamund Easling and she stepped in, quite prepared to offer a cordial greeting her mother would approve of. At least that was her plan, until two gentlemen—whom she never expected to see again—appeared among the sea of faces.

Any words Rosamund might have rehearsed in her mind died on her tongue.

The two men who'd rescued her that day now stood by the hearth, observing her presentation from the back of the room. Mr. Butler owned a completely bemused look, obviously having had no clue she was the earl's daughter. Mr. Keary, however, boasted an air of reserved nonchalance. If he was surprised to see her, he covered it well.

Rosamund reminded herself to keep calm. To cross the room and not stumble. To keep her face serene, and certainly not let shock rise to the surface in a flustered blush.

Breathe in. Breathe out . . .

"Ah. And here she is. Our daughter, Lady Rosamund," the countess, Lady Denton, exclaimed in a sugar-coated welcome. She rose from her seat on the edge of the room's central settee.

Reaching Rosamund's side, she latched onto her gloved hand in a vise grip that suggested they'd be having more than a light after-dinner conversation about her whereabouts that day. And if the fear of an impending reprimand weren't punishment enough, Rosamund would now have to navigate the evening with the two Americans in the same room, and under her mother's already speculative eye.

Though separated by two decades, Rosamund knew she and her mother were pictures of the same, with expressive green eyes, dark hair, and porcelain skin. But Lady Denton was quite superior in the art of refinement. She was polished in every way Rosamund was not. The countess was able to glide across the room wearing the badge of her position, right down to the way her gold-beaded cabernet silk crepe frock floated with her every step.

Her mother was in battle mode, and that left no room for doubt in Rosamund's mind. The expectations on her this evening would be extraordinary.

"We are so pleased that you could join us, my dear." Lady Denton was generous in fawning over her daughter and absently patted Rosamund's gloved forearm. "May I present our good friend, the very distinguished Lord Brentwood, whom you'll remember last from—what was it? Two summers ago?"

"Three summers, Lady Denton. It was in London, I believe," Lord Brentwood said, inclining his head to her. "But it's an honor that you remembered me. Your invitation to stay at Easling Park once again was most kind. It's been far too long since I've visited the North Country."

Rosamund remembered him.

Barely.

As a friend of her brother's, Oliver Brentwood had been a brash lord-to-be who'd once spent time at Easling Park. He'd been cordial but had never showed interest in Rosamund as more than a young acquaintance who existed in the same social circle. In the wake of Hendrick's death, Oliver had disappeared into the drawing rooms and gentlemen's clubs of Mayfair. It was rumored he'd spent ample time in the postwar years courting women and spending his family's fortune, all quite at his leisure.

To her knowledge, he'd never noticed Rosamund before. But time had wings, and Oliver returned now as the distinguished Lord Brentwood, viscount to his vast family estates, with eyes clearly turned in her direction.

He'd filled out in the shoulders and was more polished than Rosamund remembered. He owned a thin black mustache and perfectly parted hair, and had eyes of a sharp, cool gray. They watched her with a more mature nature, the intent of which Rosamund couldn't fully make out. She could guess though, with the way he was responding to her mother's adoration, that the newly inherited title meant he'd found himself in the position to take a wife.

Please . . . don't let it be me.

"Oh yes, it was three summers ago," Lady Denton twittered. "We were so sorry to hear of Lord Brentwood's passing. Such a legacy your father left behind. And we hope to see you in this part of the country on a more regular basis, Lord Brentwood, though affairs in London threaten to keep you occupied."

He nodded. "Yes. Business of our estates is quite good, both in the North Country and in the city. But I regret that managing the duties associated with them has left little time for socializing. And my father's legacy will live on—as will Hendrick's. I mean to honor their memory while I'm a guest here."

Lady Denton offered a nod and an attentive smile, her breath hanging on the eligible lord's every word.

Rosamund watched her mother's transformation with wonder.

Showering compliments. Dripping with charm. Why, her very words could have slithered through piles of sugar. It was all, however, contradictory to the way her fingernails were digging through Rosamund's glove into her forearm.

"I'm sure you remember Lady Rosamund. She certainly remembers you."

Rosamund felt his eyes shift to her.

"It's my sincere pleasure to be in your acquaintance again, Lady Rosamund. You've certainly grown up, haven't you?"

Her mouth went dry in an instant, followed by palms that chose that moment to turn clammy in her gloves. Should she bow her head? Curtsy? Extend her hand to him?

Every shred of her mother's careful training in the art of husband-catching had flown right out of her head the instant she spotted Mr. Butler and Mr. Keary in the room. The reintroduction to Lord Brentwood would have been difficult to manage anyway, and now she had to foster small talk with their eyes boring into her back.

Rosamund swallowed hard and pressed her lips into a smile. "It's an honor to have you back at Easling Park, Lord Brentwood."

She glanced out of the corner of her eye to find Colin Keary holding a brandy glass, though he didn't look to have taken a sip. He stood tall, owning his spot by the hearth with a devil-may-care ease unusual for a drawing room in Yorkshire. And though no one showered him with a chorus of adulation, he seemed to prefer it over the attention that was being heaped on Lord Brentwood.

Colin Keary had apparently not been able to locate a razor—or a barber—on his way to the dinner party. He'd made no effort to comb his hair into submission either, unlike young Ward, whose misaligned part showed he'd at least taken some care. But Colin carried himself well, appearing polished even with his collar unbuttoned behind his tie and a tarnished gold watch chain dangling from the front of his vest. And though the other gentlemen were in white-tie formal dress, his manner was as confident as if he'd dressed in a king's robes.

Without warning, something shifted between them.

Colin had turned ever so slightly, noticing how she watched him from across the room, and dared lock eyes with her. Amusement sparkled in his, a hint of a smile not far off.

It continued as he held her gaze, heating her cheeks.

The countess's incessant flattery and Lord Brentwood's polished acceptance of it faded into the background as the events of the afternoon began to click into place. The double take when he saw her face up close. His questions by the creek. The way he'd managed to have her father's automobile plucked from the water and returned to the manor without obtaining information about their estate from her . . .

Colin was telling her, in no uncertain terms, that he'd been in view of the facts from the beginning. How, Rosamund couldn't know. But his arrogance now, as he seemingly watched the display of emotion cross her face as she figured it out . . . It set the blood to a near boil in her veins.

Good heavens . . . Why is he here?

Rosamund looked down at her hands, trying to collect her thoughts. She wished she could calm her racing heart at the same time.

Does he intend to blackmail me?

She stumbled ever so slightly off the back of her heel, but righted herself almost immediately.

"Lady Rosamund," Lord Brentwood said, "are you quite all right?"

"I am. Quite," she lied. Rosamund fought to offer a serene smile, willing courage to surface. "Thank you."

Her mother's eyes grew wide, as if her daughter had missed something vital in the conversation. She clapped her gloved hands together.

"Well, our Lady Rosamund must be tired after her riding today. My apologies, Lord Brentwood," she added between clenched teeth. "But as dinner is now served, yes—she'd be pleased to take the arm you've offered."

Rosamund shot a glance across the room one last time, read the challenge in Colin's eyes. But she agreed, adding sweetly, "Yes. Of course."

The guests flooded into the dining room, chatting and exclaiming over the grand display of towering candelabras, gold-rimmed china, crystal wine goblets, and vases of freesia and ivy that adorned the expanse of the dining table.

Lady Denton positioned herself in the center of the table and invited their most distinguished guests to sit in the seats at her side. Lord Brentwood's mother, the Dowager Lady Brentwood, and the local vicar from the peerage on the estate, Reverend Charles, were given seats on either side of her. Rosamund's father took his customary seat opposite her mother and was flanked by Lord and Lady Edwards of Brockington Hall. They owned the lavish estate of rolling hills and rich farmland to the south, and no doubt relished the opportunity to discuss their shared interest in land bordering Easling Park.

At a normal dinner party Rosamund mightn't have cared where she was placed. But the arrangement left her on the round at the end of the table, awkwardly positioned with Lord Brentwood to her right and the Americans on her left.

She kept her cool through the reverend's blessing, though her mind drifted, and she wondered just how she'd manage to talk herself out of this mess with the Americans while guests were positioned at all points around the table.

"You looked almost sick back there. No ill effects from the creek water, I trust," Colin whispered at her side, pretending to take inordinate interest in the grandiose display before them instead of looking directly at her. "Perhaps a cocktail would've helped."

"You didn't seem interested in one either."

"I'm not the cocktail type. I took the drink to be polite," he countered. "But I might have asked after your health if you'd given me the chance."

"I'm fine." Rosamund, too, kept her voice low as a footman moved about behind her.

Colin swept his napkin across his lap. She did the same with her own.

"That headband looks awfully heavy. I'm sure it's the reason for the frown."

"It is," she snapped, stealing a glance at him from the side. "And I despise this thing, if you must know. It's digging into my head."

He cleared his throat over a chuckle, noticed by Ward, who looked about as uncomfortable as she felt. He tipped his shoulders up in question, seemingly unsure what to do with the cloth napkin in his hand. He stuffed it into his shirt collar, then pulled it out again when Colin furrowed his brow and gave a slight shake of the head.

In contrast to young Ward, Colin seemed relaxed. He got Ward's attention by clearing his throat and tapped the fork that was the farthest distance from his dinner plate. He mouthed, "Work your way in."

Ward nodded, and Colin turned back to her.

"Poor chap," he said. "I remember my first state dinner. I felt like he looks."

Rosamund wasn't amused.

"What on earth are you doing here?" She couldn't believe she was actually going to say it aloud, but she added, "Do you want money?"

Colin shook his head. "I came back for my coat."

She fired him a warning look, but it only seemed to amuse him further.

"You still have it, you know. And I'm sure it's a shock to you, but it's the best I own."

Rosamund surveyed the room.

The footmen were serving the guests to her father's right first, so they'd have little time until her mother turned sides and they'd be forced to talk to the party on their left.

Realizing she'd forgotten to remove her gloves, Rosamund began hastily tugging them finger by finger until they gave way. She laid them in her lap, whispering between clenched teeth, "Talk quickly. Did you follow me?"

"No. We came on invitation."

"Why would you be invited here?"

Colin paused, then looked her in the eye. "I'm sure it's quite shocking for you to think an earl would entertain the likes of us, but we had business with your father this afternoon. I hesitate to say that we missed our meeting because we were fishing a certain automobile out of the brook a ways up the road." He took a sip from his water goblet. "You're welcome, by the way."

"It's difficult to be grateful when you lied to me."

"I didn't lie to you," he fired back, keeping his voice low. "I just thought it indelicate to mention the fact that an earl's daughter wouldn't have been caught dead in the situation you were in."

"Indelicate?" she whispered, swallowing hard on the sting of his reproach. "Is it not worse to lie to my parents, acting as though we haven't met?"

Rosamund answered as forcefully as the occasion allowed. Oh, how she wished Colin were sitting directly across from her so his shin could feel the underside of her shoe.

"As far as they're concerned, we haven't."

"If you're not here to give me away, then why have you come?" she snapped.

She thought she spied Lord Brentwood glance their way, but he turned back to Reverend Charles without a word.

"As I said, business with your father. But by the time we arrived for our meeting, we were already into the dinner hour. And due to the inclement weather, His Lordship just invited us to stay on through tomorrow night. Quite nice, actually, to meet your family and"—he paused, eyeing Lord Brentwood—"your future husband, I presume."

Rosamund ignored the barb, favoring the opportunity to still see him in the wrong.

"All that time—you knew who I was and you never said anything?"

She straightened her back when the footman approached, carrying a generously laden tray of dilled tomato mousse and asparagus feuilleté savories. They each took helpings from the tray, first Rosamund and then Colin, replacing the silver servers afterward and holding their hushed conversation until the service staff had moved on to the opposite side of the table.

"You are right about one thing. I'm not in the habit of meeting men on the side of a creek. I thought, given *my* circumstances, it would be best not to reveal who my father is."

"And though I knew you on sight," Colin whispered, leaning ever so slightly in her direction, "I thought it would be impolite to correct you when you gave your name as Rose."

"I find it difficult to believe you could be overly concerned with politeness."

"We're in Yorkshire for business. But we'll be gone after tomorrow, so you needn't worry," he said. "We'll take your secret to the grave."

Her first thought had been to blast Colin Keary for showing up at all. But now Rosamund found that she just couldn't be angry. He'd stepped in to save her. He'd made himself late for business dealings with her father—which just wasn't done when one had obtained a meeting with an earl. And now, despite her bristling, he was willing to keep the secret of their meeting, no questions asked.

Her anger faded as humility took hold.

"No, you're right," she countered, softening her voice. "I should thank you for your discretion. I asked for it and you've held up your end of the bargain. It's just finding you both here—" A faint smile edged over her lips. "It was a surprise."

Colin exhaled on a sigh. Even shook his head.

"I know. And I'm sorry. But we won't cause you injury." He picked up his fork. "We're just here to buy an Arabian from your father, then we'll catch a train and be out of England altogether. Hopefully you can put up with us through this dinner. In the meantime, I'll try to help Ward know which fork to use so we don't embarrass you any further."

"What did you just say?"

Rosamund's shock forced the question out at a decibel that drew notice from across the table. She dropped her fork, and it landed with a high-pitched *clink* at the base of her wineglass, shimmering the clear liquid, then lay still with a thud against the linen tablecloth.

"Rosamund, dear. Is everything quite all right?"

Lady Denton sounded only slightly nervous, and she maintained her mask of a serene smile, but her eyes registered horror at her daughter's behavior.

Rosamund turned to look at the stunned faces in the room, feeling like she'd just been punched in the stomach. She scanned the table, taking in the iron set to her father's jaw and the confused glances on the faces of the rest of the party.

Requiring space enough to think, she pushed her chair back from the table.

"Father, you're selling Ingénue?" she blurted. "That's why these men are here?"

"Rosamund, there is a time and place to discuss private matters, and it is not at Her Ladyship's dining table."

His voice was stern, without any wiggle room for her to continue the line of questioning. The only trouble was, Rosamund's heart was shattering in her chest. Her father had gone behind her back to sell the one thing that mattered most in the world to her—the one link their family had to the older brother she'd lost.

"We only have one Arabian left . . . ," she began.

"Come now, Lady Rosamund," Lord Brentwood whispered under his breath, trying to sate her. "Let's just enjoy the dinner. Leave the odiousness of business dealings to the men in the study afterward."

Lord Brentwood's position was quite clear.

But so was hers.

Seeing that she'd receive no answer from her parents, Rosamund turned instead to Ward and Colin, entreating them with eyes that stung with tears.

"Tell me, please—is it true what you've said? You're here to buy my horse?"

"Rosamund," Lord Denton shouted. "Not now."

Her father's breach of decorum was enough that it brought everything in the room to a complete halt.

The footmen froze behind the table, still holding trays of meat and vegetables in their gloved hands. The butler shook his head, giving the silent instruction to wait until Rosamund obeyed and the dinner was drawn back in the lines of the appropriate.

No, she thought, breathing unsteadily.

Not this time . . .

Given what he'd said to her that afternoon, Rosamund believed Colin to be the one person who would answer truthfully. He'd acted with honor by keeping their meeting a secret. If he'd thought to protect her reputation once, he couldn't deny her the truth now— even in the presence of hopelessly rich lords and ladies who couldn't care less for the impending sale of something as trivial as a horse.

She turned to him directly. "Please, Mr. Keary," she pleaded, her voice barely at a whisper. "I need to know the truth."

"Yes, Lady Rosamund," he offered with feeling, the Irish brogue suddenly weighing down his voice. "She ships out in two days."

CHAPTER 5

1893
CHICAGO, ILLINOIS

"The whole world is calling this the 'White City.'"

Sally Rivers—waitress and would-be singer—leaned her elbows back on the hostess counter at the elegant Café de la Marine, snacking on a mix of popcorn, molasses, and peanuts from a red-and-white cardboard box. She looked past Mable, out the front window to the crowds of suited gentlemen and Sunday-hat-wearing ladies who passed by over the arched canal bridge.

"And why shouldn't Chicago have a name known the world over? It's our time to shine."

Mable pointed toward the flash of midday sun reflecting off the impressive white stucco façade of the World's Columbian Exposition span of buildings.

"Look at that flood of people coming over the bridge. I predict we'll be full up later tonight."

It was a lovely sight that greeted them from the windows, with the rounded domes of the Brazilian building and the classical columns of the Fisheries building dominating the view on one side, and the bustle of the marine causeway on the other. They could even peek around the corner and see the *Viking*—a replica of the

Gokstad ship—and Venetian-style gondolas gliding majestically along the canal. The view sure beat the tangles of trolley lines and tall buildings that marred the landscape in the restaurant where they'd last worked downtown.

To work in the Café de la Marine had a certain air of romance about it, Mable had to admit. With ten finial-topped spires towering against the sky over Lake Michigan, the French Gothic–style building looked more like a storybook castle than a dining establishment. It boasted lofty ceilings with hammered gold filigree tiles, twinkling chandeliers, and awnings over the windows that soared up to the roof on each level.

Mable shook out a white cloth napkin and folded it into an elegant flat cone shape, working her way through the stack for the impending lunch rush. Before they knew it, a steady stream of patrons would step through the doors, continuing until they closed up for the night. She was scheduled to work a double shift, so she'd be chasing her tail until long after dark.

Best to get ahead while they could.

"Expecting a big day?" Sally smirked at the flow of foot traffic that had now jammed the crossway over the canal. "I suppose it looks like it from where we're standing. So many people."

Wagons stood still along with their jittering horses. Men yelled back and forth behind a wagonette that had tipped onto its side, dumping a load of food stuffs in a heap smack-dab in the middle of the walkway. The crowds parted around it, with a few young scamps making off with a pilfered treat.

Sally shoved the popcorn concoction under Mable's nose, drawing her attention back to napkin folding.

"Mable. I'm telling you—you'll love it. Just give it a try."

Mable wrinkled her nose. "You know I don't care for that stuff. Too sticky-sweet."

"Too sweet?" Sally balked. "It's incredible. Some crackerjack named Rueckheim has been selling it out of a tent down by the canal. He's had folks lined up all along the causeway. Even ran out yesterday." She tossed another couple molasses-glazed kernels into her mouth. "But I can still get it because of some gents I met last night. They liked the set I sang. All I had to do was bat my eyelashes at the right pocket and I had two bags delivered to me this morning."

Mable's friend was a live wire, even for Chicago.

Sally had stars in her eyes bigger than the saucers they set out on the tables each day and auburn hair coiffed to accent her deep gold, come-hither eyes. She sang like a lark too, and never seemed to have the slightest trouble attracting a man's attentions. It seemed to be the keeping part that caused her particular angst.

Sally wrinkled her nose at Mable's task. "Folding napkins is such a tiresome chore."

"Really? I came all the way from Ohio just to do it. It's been very thrilling for me."

"Ha-ha," Sally tossed out. "So much cheek. That's not what I meant and you know it."

"If you're asking whether I plan to be a hostess and cashier for the rest of my life, then the answer is no. But I suppose it's good enough that I know where I am right now." Mable watched as the gondolas floated by in front of the windows. "Look at our view. You couldn't ask for more than that."

"A gondola?" Sally laughed, charmed by the notion. "That's your big plan?"

"Yes! No—" Mable joined in the playfulness by tossing a napkin at her friend. "You know what I mean. Why are you laughing?"

"If that's your dream and it's floating by, then you'd better be quick to reach for it."

Sally leaned across the counter, the black-and-white piping of her dress reflected in the glass.

Mable traced her index finger along the polished edge of the counter. "I want more, Sal."

"More than what? What could be more than a life of security in a wedding ring?"

Mable knew the answer; it was a cigar box full of dreams.

"Sally Rivers! Where are you?"

Their attention shifted to the deep gravel of the restaurant manager's voice booming across the dining room. His bellow fairly shook the crystal in the chandeliers.

Sally slid down behind the counter, hiding behind the rows of cigars lining the glass shelves. "That's Mr. Morgan, and I'm late. Supposed to be waiting the high-roller tables in the dining room."

Mable exhaled. "Sal . . ."

"What?" She tapped a manicured nail against her bottom teeth, sneaking a glance out from the side of the counter. "I didn't want to have my new dress smelling like a fisherman's wharf just because he wants cocktail orders filled for a few suits. I have a set to sing."

Mable knelt down, meeting her friend eye to eye.

"You look beautiful, as always," she said. "But there's more to us than this. You know that, right?"

Sally seemed to let those words prick her heart, for she breathed deep and squared her shoulders. "I suppose those tables aren't going to wait themselves."

"Then you'd better hop to it," Mable said. She peered around the corner to see if the manager was headed their way. "The coast is clear. Run through the back dining room and come out the other side of the kitchen. If he comes this way I'll tell him I haven't seen you."

"You're a doll," Sally whispered and kissed her index finger to dot it to the back of Mable's hand. "I'll talk to you after the lunch rush. I'll have to sidestep him the rest of the afternoon if I want to keep my job."

"Good luck," Mable whispered, watching as her friend disappeared round the corner.

She stood again, just as she heard the clang of the brass bell above the front doors signaling a patron's entrance. She glanced up, expecting to find a gentleman in the same dark suit and bowler hat that the majority of men wore.

But the man who'd strolled in was tall as she—taller even, which didn't happen often. And after the months Mable had spent in the high-end establishment, she knew a tailored suit when she saw one. This gentleman was impeccably dressed in a crisp, three-piece summer suit in tan linen, with a cream-and-gray silk tie that gleamed against his white shirt, and cream-and-black wingtips that boasted a clean polish. He kept his straw hat on over dark hair that curled at the ears.

The man leaned against a gold-capped black cane as he scanned the expansive dining room.

He owned a presence that easily dominated the space. But whatever judgments Mable could make about the gentleman's dress, there was something different in the eyes. They were serious, no-nonsense, but kind somehow—and in the seconds since he'd walked through the door, those eyes had found their way to rest on the exact spot in which she stood.

They looked—and now lingered—on *her*.

He smiled.

"Good afternoon, sir. Do you have a reservation?" Mable opened the leather-bound reservation book on the counter.

"No."

She felt a twinge of nervousness creep into her midsection.

A walk-in to Café de la Marine didn't happen—no matter how

a person was dressed. The only time they'd accommodated an unscheduled guest that summer was when the youngest child of Queen Isabella II of Spain had requested a lunch there, and even that had taken some wrangling with the management.

The rule was: no reservation, no table. She'd have no choice but to turn him and his smile away.

"I'm sorry, sir. But without a reservation I'm afraid—"

"What is your name?" He cut in easily. Still politely, but with clear intention.

She blinked back, startled by the sense of familiarity in his voice. "It's Mable, sir."

"Good afternoon, Mable. I'm John."

Mable glanced from him to the dining room, finding the open connection of those eyes to hers unnerving at best.

She cleared her throat. "Well, sir." She couldn't dare call him simply *John*. "Perhaps if you'd like to make a reservation and come back on another day . . ." She took a pen out of the drawer and opened an inkwell on the counter, dipping the nib inside.

"I'd like to speak with the owner."

"The owner's not here. But I can fetch the manager for you if you'd like."

"I would."

A man of few words.

Mable nodded. "Very well. Just a moment, please."

Something told her not to keep him waiting.

Mable flew by Sally, who was chatting with a gentleman patron but looked up with a furrowed brow at her friend's pace toward the kitchen. She gave Sally a shake of the head that said, *I'll explain later* and kept moving.

She found Mr. Morgan and sent him to the gentleman at the front door, then returned to her post. Other customers streamed in the doors. The lunch rush was in full swing. Mable saw several parties to their tables, stealing the occasional glance over at "John," who was still in conversation with the manager by the door.

When she'd seated the fifth reservation on her list and come back, he was gone.

Mable felt a twinge of disappointment that he'd been sent back out the door. But the patrons kept filing in, one by one, families and couples alike, looking for a jolly midday meal during their excursion at the fair. She forgot about the encounter with the gentleman by the door.

"Mable, you won't believe it." Sally practically pounced on her.

"Believe what?" She checked off the last two names from the reservation book and bent down to arrange a stack of menus.

"That man—you know, the one who came in wearing the tan suit?"

Mable didn't try to pretend she hadn't noticed him. She lowered her voice and whispered, "You saw him too?"

Sally nodded. "Yes. And he got the best table in the house." She grabbed Mable by the shoulders, shaking lightly before letting go to cover her mouth with her hands. *"The best one.* Without a reservation. He ordered the chef's catch and the most expensive bottle of wine on the menu without even glancing at the price. His bill's already totaled a small fortune and he's still adding to it. I'd have asked Mr. Morgan who he is, but our manager is too disgruntled with me right now to answer."

Mable wasn't surprised on either count.

"We've had wealthy patrons in here before. Is this news to get so excited about?"

"You bet it is. I walked over to his table, and you know what? He asked about you."

Mable swallowed hard and glanced past Sally to the full dining room. She could just see the elbow of the gentleman's linen suit, leaning against the edge of the table.

"Me?"

Don't think about those eyes . . .

"Yes, my lovely napkin-folding friend. *You*."

"But what in the world could he want with me?" Mable whispered, trying not to tie her hands in knots at her waist.

"He wanted to know when your shift ends."

"But I'm here all day. I have to close tonight."

Sally reached out and hooked a wavy lock of Mable's dark hair behind her ear.

"You *did* have to close tonight, Mable. You're off when Mr. Linen Suit finishes his lunch. He told the manager that your shift would end the moment you agreed to take a walk with him across the canal bridge."

Mable had agreed to the walk, though she didn't know exactly why.

Everything had happened so fast. One moment she'd learned the gentleman wanted to step out with her, and seemingly in the next instant Sally was tilting a navy plumed hat on her head, fiddling with the coiffed curls at her brow, and pouring advice on her as she shoved Mable out the door.

"What would you like to see?" Mable asked, hoping to draw John into conversation.

They'd walked all the way from the café, past the lagoon, to the bright sights and sounds of the game booths and foreign attractions lining the Midway. He hadn't said much, just walked along at a steady pace, allowing her to lead them.

"What would you suggest?"

"The Turkish Village isn't very far and the admission is free. The Ferris wheel is another favorite with visitors. And there are some camels on Cairo Street right over there. They're one of the most popular attractions at the fair." She pointed to a multistory replica of an Egyptian temple just beyond the gates before them. "If you've never seen an exotic animal, they're quite a treat."

"But you don't seem very impressed," John noted, a half grin evident on his face.

Mable smiled too, noting his ability to read her thoughts. It felt as if her secret was out—she'd seen the camels a hundred times, and they seemed more like big, ill-tempered cows than anything truly exotic to her.

"I might have been impressed the first time I saw them. But I've been here on the grounds for months and, well, you get used to such things. Except for the wedding procession, of course. That's always beautiful. I try to time my breaks so I can step out and watch it."

"Hmm. I've heard about it. And you watch the same show time and again?"

"Of course."

"But what keeps you coming back, if it's not the mystique of the camels?"

"There's some razzmatazz about the show out front. The visitors like the music and the scandal of belly dancing. And those horrible spitting camels. But I like to see behind the scenes." Mable leaned in, whispering low. "You know, if you peek behind the street, just there—" She pointed down the alley behind the grand temple. "See? It's all bowler hats instead of turbans. That's where the real activity is. They've got a small army keeping everything running behind the stage, and nobody even knows it."

He smiled wide. "Is that right?"

"Of course. They also have 'The Arrival from Mecca.' They really make a show of it. The tourists just love it." She paused, thinking that she knew very little about him, except that he was smiling as they watched the hidden alleyway behind Cairo Street. Was he a tourist? What if she was telling him all about the fair and he lived in Chicago too?

"Are you a tourist, by chance?" she asked.

"I am, of sorts."

"And where do you live?"

"Here and there. I'm in Chicago part of the year."

And he left it at that.

John wasn't easy to figure out. He was quiet. Almost serious. And while she droned on about the German village they passed, the exquisite rose garden she loved, and the music lilting up from the Viennese exhibit, he said little. Just nodded or looked on as they walked farther down the Midway.

"May I ask—what did you say to him?" she asked.

Caught up in the sights around them, he asked, "Who?"

He paused as they passed the Russian furs exhibit, a long aisle with stuffed bears on hind legs and snow dogs positioned under a bower of hanging furs.

"Mr. Morgan. You must have said something for him to allow me out of my shift. He'd never agree to such a thing unless you said something quite convincing. I wondered what it was."

"Whatever it was, it's not worth telling now." John pointed his cane down the direction of the aisle teeming with animal furs and lush food smells. "And what do you make of this one? You must have an opinion."

Mable was surprised by the question. It wasn't a normal occurrence for her opinion to be sought after by anyone. She looked at the Russian exhibit and smiled. She had an opinion, all right. And since this stranger appeared to want to know, she'd oblige with an honest answer.

"I think it's fun."

"Fun?" He raised his eyebrows. "Not scary or grotesque? Those bears have fangs."

"No. Not scary. They're just . . ." She laughed. "Fun. I have the oddest idea that they'd look charming with a tutu or a suit and bright red boutonnière instead of just standing there glaring at everyone. What if they were dancing instead of menacing?"

"A dancing bear with a boutonnière? The idea has merit." He nodded, eyes smiling at the corners, giving away his amusement. He tilted his head as if considering it. "And look at the children." John took a step back as a group of eager youngsters flooded in front of them, making for a souvenir stand. "No doubt they'd enjoy your dancing bears."

"Maybe they would," she said, stepping back so the children could swarm in around the toys.

Mable watched as the children played, laughing and dancing about, and adults picked out mementos from displays of engraved commemorative glassware and rows of painted ornamental fans. The fans were inexpensive and lackluster in their artistic appeal— not like the grand Cassatt art exhibit at the fair. But still, she liked their whimsy and pointed out the bright colors and beautiful botanical scenes painted on them.

"Pick one," John said.

Mable smiled. "Are you sure?"

He was already paying the man, so he must have been. It seemed that when John made a decision, he was sure of himself in it.

Mable happily agreed to accept the gift. She chose a nature scene with palm trees, a blue sky, and a hill with colorful stucco houses built into the side. It was hot out, so she spread the beautiful gift wide and fanned it back and forth as they walked. The peace was broken, however, the instant they heard a commotion arise across the Midway.

Children bolted past them in a clattering rush.

Men in suits began to shout and point, drawing attention from the crowd and sparking gasps and shrieks from the ladies.

Over the bustle of international music and the reveling crowds they heard shouts of "Fire!" and "The Cold Storage Building is on fire!"

Mable tore her glance from left to right, searching for flames that would surely overtake them.

She'd heard too much about the effects of the Great Fire in 1871. Chicago was still rebuilding. What would happen if fire overtook the White City a second time, and in the grandest spectacle the world had ever seen? She prayed nothing like that could happen again. Not in the city where dreams came true.

The children they'd just seen—were they safe? Were all accounted for?

She glanced back at the vendor tables they'd passed.

The patrons had scattered, the children with them. The vendor was hastily packing up his wares. He didn't look up. Didn't seem to notice anything but shoving souvenirs into the crates beneath the cart.

"Mable?"

John gripped her elbow, gently but with intention, and edged her forward. "We need to keep moving."

She nodded but the action felt foreign, as if she were watching the events playing out on a stage.

The sound of clanging fire wagon bells filled the air.

Onlookers cheered for the firemen. Some hooted and hollered. The Ferris wheel had been halted, but still the patrons shouted in jubilation. Still others, like her, seemed concerned by the growing plume of thick smoke choking out the blue sky overhead.

"But why are they cheering?"

"Poor fools." John shook his head. "They don't know it's real."

Mable glanced around and saw that he was right. The faces in the crowd weren't painted with fear. Instead, she witnessed only a sense of gaiety. There were smiles. Laughter even. Fathers stood with children hoisted on their shoulders. Mothers cradled little ones in their arms, watching the phenomenon all along the Midway.

"They think it's a planned spectacle," he said, pointing to the plume of black smoke rising above the trees. "With something as grand as all this, how could they think otherwise?"

"But it's not planned . . ."

"No," he confirmed, and took hold of her hand. His fingers laced with hers, covering her palm in unexpected warmth. "This is most certainly not a part of the show."

She looked from the smoke-filled sky to meet his gaze. "What do we do?"

"It's all right, Mable." John kept his eyes locked with hers. "Trust me. I'll not let go of you."

Mable believed him. Even as an explosion rocked the ground beneath their feet. As the crowd's mood changed from excitement to agitation. As a strong breeze blew the pungent smell of electricity and burning wood to wash in over the lot of them—she kept her eyes fixed on his.

"Come on," he whispered so only she could hear, and squeezed her hand. "We've got to go."

He eased them in at a quick pace, following the throngs of people.

The masses flowed toward the colossal Cold Storage Building. And then, in a rush, Mable's heart lurched in her chest. The building had erupted into a tower of smoke and flames licking at the sky, painting their glorious White City in a wall of fire.

"But the fire . . ." Her heart raced. "All the children in the crowd."

"I've been around accidents of this sort before," he said, his voice steady and strong. "See the fire wagons? Both the Chicago companies and the World's Fair Fire Department already have boats spraying canal water to douse the flames. They'll have it under control in no time. Even though the crowd doesn't seem as concerned as they should be, they'll see to the safety of the crowds. And trust the parents to take the children in care."

"But they don't know . . . They don't think it's real."

"They will soon enough."

Mable couldn't decide what was more unexpected that afternoon: the sight of flames reaching up to graze the clouds, or the vision of this man who was so collected in the face of uncertainty.

"But how do you know they'll get things under control?" Mable searched him, her eyes taking in the depths of his.

He seemed to want to say something, but didn't. Just kept the strong hold to her fingertips.

"I'd best see you back to the café," he said, and began pulling her along with him. "You'll be safer if you're not in the middle of a mob of frightened onlookers."

Frightened onlookers? But she was one of them.

Mable scarcely remembered the way they threaded through the crowd, sidestepping scores of fairgoers who'd gathered to watch the show from across the canal. They sped down the Midway, John leading them on with purpose. And when they reached the canal at the Café de la Marine's etched glass doors, he bowed, thanked her, and quickly disappeared into the sea of bowler hats around them.

It wasn't until days later—when the smoke had faded and the building lay in charred ruins—that the fair returned to normal. The city mourned more than a dozen brave firefighters and three unfortunate fairgoers who lost their lives that day. And with every day that passed after it, Mable tried not to think about the events of that afternoon. She fought the urge to look up every time the bell rang at the café's front door, expecting John to walk through it.

She tried not to remember his eyes. The familiarity of his hand holding hers. The way he'd smiled at her as no one had before and led her through a sea of uncertainty back to safety. From loneliness to the hope of something more, even though he'd disappeared into the crowd and not looked back.

Even though she now knew who he was.

The day she'd met him, Mable had taken her cigar box down from the top shelf in the tiny rooming house apartment she shared with Sally. The fan John had purchased for her was but a penny treasure—but she wanted to save it nonetheless. Her hands had fumbled, dropping the box outright, and her catalog clipping dreams drifted down to the floor like snowflakes in winter.

She bent to pick them up, annoyed at her own clumsiness.

Clumsiness to think that a gentleman would ever be truly interested in a lowly shopgirl. Or hostess. Or farmer's daughter from Ohio. She wiped her tears, and as she hurriedly repacked her photos and newspaper clippings, something caught her eye.

Mable froze, then slid down to sit on the floor.

There before her, in an article chronicling the Ringling Brothers' circus royalty, was a familiar face. Staring back at her were the eyes that had greeted her at the Café de la Marine. The same mouth that had offered a generous smile in response to her chatter on the Midway. The same hand that rested atop a black cane in the newspaper photo before her had intentionally grasped hers and had led her to safety, away from the fire.

He wasn't just John, she thought. *He was John Ringling?*

It was the most notable thing she'd leave out of her letters to the family back home . . .

She shook her head, feeling hot tears escape to roll down her cheeks.

Mable Burton had once walked with a king.

CHAPTER 6

1926

NORTH YORKSHIRE, ENGLAND

The early-morning air was crisp and cold—just the way Rosamund and Ingénue preferred it.

A haze of fog had drifted in overnight, painting the moor beyond Easling Park in a thick layer of mist. It mingled along the tree line, curling around skinny poplars and the knobby trunks of aged walnut trees. The landscape was bathed in ink-blue with streaks of orange and yellow as early-morning sun filtered along the fields' borders.

Ingénue stretched her legs wide, pounding her hooves against the soft earth.

She was a beautiful black Arabian, with a smooth gait and low withers and a broad, sturdy back—perfect for riding bareback when no one was looking. Just as no one was looking now. Rosamund leaned into the wind and they sailed over the ridge together, the horse creating a cadence in hoof and breath sounds that ticked like clockwork.

Rosamund had slipped down the stairs before daybreak, her long waves tucked into a loose chignon, riding gloves in hand, and had fairly flown to the stables. If she hurried, one last thrilling taste of freedom could be hers. And should any other early riser happen to see her from a window, her observer would see nothing but a properly dressed young lady riding sidesaddle, with a horse moving at a permissible trot over the hill.

Underneath her wrap skirt and herringbone jacket she wore a breathable silk blouse and the trousers her maid had washed and dried. Once they were out of sight and a safe distance from the stables, she brought Ingénue to a halt. She peeled off her outer riding habit and removed the horse's saddle. Ingénue's hooves danced about, the mare just as hungry as the rider for the moments of shared bliss as they flew over the fields.

And so it was a morning like hundreds of others they'd passed before, save for the one terrible pang of hurt twisting in Rosamund's middle: this was to be their last ride.

The after-dinner conversation with her parents had proved one-sided at best. And firm. In fact, they'd known more about her riding habits than she'd realized. The motor had been returned to the manor, but it was in such a state of disrepair that she'd never have been able to keep the ruse going. Thankfully, they knew nothing of Mr. Keary's or Mr. Butler's involvement. But the horse that kept her engaged in such activities was merely the last straw, and her insubordination was to halt with its sale.

So her future was set. They'd had an offer and would accept. Rosamund was to marry Lord Brentwood in the spring. In her parents' estimation, it was long past time to put off the childishness of her riding excursions and take her rightful place in society.

Rosamund tried not to think about what it would mean to marry. To move away. To have the one limb of freedom she possessed severed from her life, and the last connection she had to the happy memories of her brother stolen away with it.

She wiped a tear that had managed to slide down her cheek, whisking it away with a gloved hand.

The day wasn't so long ago that she'd forgotten.

Even at eleven years old, Rosamund had known what was happening. It was the face of war she'd looked at, in the manner in which a child would. Not with blood and bombs. Nor with trenches or barren battlefields. War simply came and stole away the better part of one's heart, replacing it with fear. And missing. A form of missing that only grew worse with a war department telegram.

He'd been a gentleman, her older brother—quite dapper, she thought, in his captain's uniform. In his typical way of edging up against authority, Hendrick had tipped his hat just off one eyebrow to give her a comical smile the last time he climbed in the motor bound for King's Cross Station.

Rosamund had forgotten that a lady should never throw off constraint and fall into the arms of anyone before her. But perhaps she wasn't destined to become a lady. Fear had come over her with a vengeance as she wound her arms around her brother's neck, crying unstoppable tears, begging him not to go.

His words flooded her memory now, even over the pounding of Ingénue's hooves to the ground.

"But who will ride with you while you're gone?"

"I'll find someone," Hendrick answered cheerfully.

"But I'm your partner. You said—"

He'd offered a smile, a brave one, she knew.

"And you are, little Rose. You'll have to keep up your riding until I can join you again. And when I return, we'll get you a proper horse. One with enough fire to keep up with you."

"Then I won't ride until you come home."

"No, you cannot do that. I've already spoken with Mr. Archer." He winked, letting her know he'd shared the entirety of their secret with the stable master. "He's promised to look after you until I return."

"When will that be?"

He'd glanced up at their father, drawing her eyes, too, in his direction. The glare she'd met said, *Enough of that*. Lady Denton had looked on with glazed eyes and a shadow of a brave smile, but said nothing to their father's silent reproach.

"Soon, little Rose. I'll return very soon." Hendrick leaned in to brush his forehead with hers. "I promise."

And she'd believed him.

Even as he stepped into the auto that April morning of 1916. Even as the chauffer closed the door and Hendrick tipped his hat to them one more time. She and Ingénue fought the pain together now, hearts beating in sync over the fields. Forgetting. Finding their heaven in the fields of Easling Park, riding away from long-ago memories for what felt like hours.

Rosamund allowed the horse to flex her will just a bit, taking turns and galloping as fast as she cared to. Ingénue would just as quickly fall back into submission, with her power stores just restrained enough that Rosamund could lead for a while.

She'd keep her eyes fixed out on the span of fields ahead of them, balancing high on the horse's back and keeping heels lower than her toes, using her calves to hold tight to invisible stirrups. When she turned her head, Ingénue would respond by taking them where Rosamund wished to go. And when she laughed, the mare would reply with whinnying breaths that froze in the crisp air like puffs of smoke.

On a whim Rosamund reached back and pulled the long pin from the coil at her nape, allowing her hair to fall in a gleaming curtain around her shoulders and back. They slowed then, taking time to play about, trick riding in the fields.

Rosamund switched Ingénue's steps, executing lead changes that swapped the canter from the right lead to the left. She slowed the horse to quick stops, even bringing her to a rearing position, all for old time's sake. They circled and danced as the wind picked up, whipping her hair around and tousling the silk of Ingénue's mane. Rosamund even popped up, using some of their last moments together to ride standing on her mare's back. She'd jump down, then run and pull up into a mount again, unafraid because of the number of times they'd done it before.

Unafraid now because she'd tucked away old memories of Hendrick, of the rides that had brought them closer. She and Ingénue were honoring him now by making a lifetime of memories fit into one last morning ride.

CHAPTER 7

The row of leaded glass oil lamps cut a ghostly path to the back of the stable. They flickered with the gust of wind that breezed in the stable's back doors.

Colin watched as Rose peeked inside, then led Ingénue in behind her. She closed the doors again and shivered against the icy bite that lingered in the morning air.

"Are mornings always this cold here?"

She turned with a fright.

"Mr. Keary," she choked out with a hand to her collar. "You startled me. I didn't expect anyone to be out here this early."

"So I gathered."

Colin leaned back in a chair against a stall at the end of the row, the top of his vest unbuttoned and shirtsleeves rolled up on his forearms, his boot-clad legs stretched out. He bit into the flesh of a ripe Pippin apple, just as casual as he pleased.

"Found my coat." He tipped his head toward the coat he'd hung over the top of the stall door. "Your maid had one of the footmen slip it into my chamber this morning."

Rose cleared her throat, then looked to each end of the expansive stable.

"Good. Then I assume you and Mr. Butler will be about your day."

"We will. It's a bit early for breakfast, but I'd say he's already getting his fill of mealy pudding and fig jam. I believe he's taken a sincere liking to your English food. Even the kippers. Far be it from him to miss a meal in any country."

"I'd have thought you'd join him at breakfast."

"You too," he answered. "But I see your time has been better spent."

"Our last ride," she said, patting Ingénue's neck. "I wanted it to be special."

He blinked back, making no mention of it, but it piqued his interest that Rose didn't try to shadow the truth.

"So she's an early riser, is she? I'll have to remember that."

Colin surveyed the pair of them, Rose holding Ingénue steady in the patch of dawn-mixed sunlight that streamed in through the windows. He couldn't help but imagine the soft glow as a spotlight, the straw-covered ground as a circus ring, and the beamed ceiling over their heads as the vault of the towering Big Top.

He brushed the image away, remembering that Rose had no idea about the deliberation going on in his mind. Hers was a rare talent. But it was a raw and innocent one as well—one that might not be ready for the harshness of circus life. It wouldn't be drawing rooms and dinner parties anymore. She'd be toughing it out with hundreds of other performers on a packed circus train, laboring from sunup to sundown, working her fingers raw in a new town nearly every day.

If he was going to bring her into that life, Colin had to be sure she could handle it.

"Anything else I should know about her?"

"She's spirited," Rose added. "That part of her won't be broken no matter how you might try."

"Well, I don't think there will be any danger of that." He got to his feet. "What little I know of horses is that you don't break the spirit. Just bend the will if necessary. Kind of like dealing with people, I expect."

Rose had pulled her hair back, but some strands had escaped and fallen down around her face. She was still winded too, and her cheeks were red from the crisp morning air.

Colin placed his half-eaten apple on the top of the stall and reached out, easing the reins from her gloved hand.

"You're tired. Here." He nodded toward the chair. "Have a seat."

To his surprise she obeyed, tucking her skirt underneath her and crossing her legs at the ankles. Colin noticed how she studied him as he opened the stall door and led the horse in.

The mare's gentle murmuring neighs were the only sound to cut the silence that had fallen between them. Colin busied himself by easing the bit from Ingénue's mouth, then unhooking the girth and slipping the saddle from her back. He edged out of the stall, depositing the saddle on the stand near the wall.

"You must think me spoiled, to fall apart over the sale of a horse."

Colin paused, hands still on the saddle. "I think nothing of the sort."

"Ingénue was a gift from my late brother. He had her shipped to me shortly before he was killed in the war. And now you're here to buy her . . . so that's why . . ." She tore her gaze to something out the window nearby, trying to withstand the emotion that had hitched in her words. "We were very close," she added. "He was the one who always called me Rose."

Colin shook his head, bracing his hands on his hips as he stared down at the straw-covered ground. "I'm sorry."

And he was.

It wasn't her fault. The horse's either. They were caught up in the aftermath of the Great War, in which so many families were navigating the reality of grief and loss, and the tangled web of inheritances that now must go to a distant cousin in the family tree. Though he had no estate to claim, Colin knew the aftermath well. He'd been to war too. Had seen comrades fall all around him like sparrows in winter. Friends, not unlike Rose's brother, had died in the war-torn fields of France. And that reality changed more than just the men at the Front. He realized it now, watching her, as she kicked at a bit of straw under her boot.

Rose was caught up in the fray of England's more traditional world, where a patriarch's buying and selling was often done without regard to the wishes of the female members of his family. He knew it wasn't always the case, but it seemed to be the rule at Easling Park. If it wouldn't have complicated things, Colin might have liked to give the earl a swift kick in his tailored trousers for so callously breaking his daughter's heart.

Colin shook his head and walked over to pull a bucket of water from the corner of the stall. He knelt and began to bathe the horse, washing the mud from her legs up to the hock—anything to keep from looking back at the pain in Rose's eyes.

"I should have known how much you care for Ingénue. The communion the two of you have is rare, and I apologize for not realizing it sooner."

He glanced over his shoulder to see if she'd heard him.

"You're apologizing to me?" she asked, clearly surprised.

"I am. And if it were up to me now, I'd leave her right here in this stall."

"But it's not up to you."

"No. By his own admission, if your father doesn't sell her to my employer, he'll sell her to someone else. If she has to go, I'd rather she sail with me." He picked up what remained of the apple and offered it to Ingénue, who munched on it without hesitation.

He patted her nose in return, as if to punctuate his last words before turning back around. What he didn't expect to find was Rose, all five feet two inches of her, standing but a few steps behind him, blocking his path through the stall door.

She met his gaze head-on.

Few men Colin had ever worked with had issued a glare so direct it stopped him in his tracks. But she'd managed it. So much so that his knees nearly buckled.

He'd never admit to that, of course.

"Is your employer a good man?" she asked, strength underscoring her voice.

"The best I've ever known."

"And you'll send word if anything should happen to her?"

Rose's countenance changed. The light coming through the window cast shadows on the contours of her face, framing high cheekbones and a barely noticeable crease of concern that had begun to edge across her brow.

He nodded. "I'll see to it personally."

"And you'll . . ." Rose paused to pinch the bridge of her nose, her voice crumbling again. "You'll give her a taste of freedom every now and then, won't you? You'll let her roam those American fields just enough to stroke her spirit?"

"We have more marsh than fields in Florida, but yes. I'll let her roam when I can. She has spirit—that I can see. I believe it's what makes her special." He paused, choosing his words. "But we'll have to find someone else to stand on her back. I'm afraid I'm terribly unbalanced in trick riding."

Rose blinked and took a step backward into the aisle between the stalls.

"Knobby knees, you see," he teased, allowing a grin to spread wide on his face.

Rose cleared her throat.

"I might as well be honest. I was awake early this morning and saw you slip out of the manor. My curiosity got the better of my feet, so they were forced to follow."

Rose closed her eyes for a few seconds, the embarrassment acute on her face.

"How . . . much did you see?"

"From the time you rode out and took this saddle off once you were over the hill? Enough to understand why you were wearing a stable hand's clothes yesterday, and why you were so startled by my admission at dinner last evening. And when I said I knew you on sight yesterday, I meant that too. I'd come to Linton in part because of a trick riding show I knew to be there. It just so happens that an earl's daughter isn't quite as unrecognizable as she thinks she is."

Rose turned and sat again.

Instead of replying, she busied herself by removing her riding gloves. He stood still, absently running his hand through Ingénue's mane, still smiling that he'd called her on what she thought was a superior level of trickery.

"You're blushing," he said, amused by her swift change in attitude.

"It's early still." Rose fumbled with her gloves, refusing to look up at him. "I assure you it's the effects of the cold morning air in Yorkshire, Mr. Keary."

Colin had to remind himself that the years after the war had changed much. Only a few years before, this woman would scarcely have been allowed in the same room with a man who would become her husband. Now she was alone in a stable with a man of little acquaintance, talking about blushes and gentlemen's attire.

He cleared his throat, forcing the smile from his lips. They'd get nowhere if she thought he was mocking her.

He crossed to the end of the row of stalls, deposited the bit on a wall hook, and turned, stopping a few feet away from her chair.

"Mind telling me where in the world you learned to ride like that?"

She paused, thinking on it, then answered, "Hendrick."

He furrowed his brow. "And how did he learn?"

Rose shook her head. "He never did. Just said I was a natural." She sniffed and swiped at a stray tear that had eased down her cheek. "He used to goad me into standing on horseback as a childhood dare. And I couldn't let him win, so I always did it. He said I was fearless on a horse."

"Fearless," Colin repeated.

Rosamund nodded.

"Mr. Archer is our stable master here at the estate. He's taught me more in the last eight years. His father once traveled with a menagerie show, and he learned about trick riding from him. And then he worked with us until it became second nature. But no one else knows."

"How often do you ride like that?"

"Every day." She tipped her shoulders in a light shrug. "Why?"

Colin knelt down, meeting her eye to eye.

"Lady Rosamund—"

"It's just Rosamund," she cut in with a soft shake of the head. "I don't require all of what my father does. Titles don't mean anything to me. Not anymore."

"Okay then. *Rose*," he offered. "Your father is a good man. He wouldn't do this just to hurt you."

"My father is a man of propriety, Mr. Keary. Please do not confuse the two."

"Was he harsh with you because of what happened at dinner last night?"

"My parents spoke with me, yes. But they weren't cruel, if that's what you're implying. They merely stated what's happening as fact. You are buying my horse and she ships out tomorrow. That's to be the end of it."

He paused, choosing his words carefully.

"You have a good life here. People who care about you. I know I don't need to tell you how important that is."

"And you think I should marry and live happily with my wealth? I should want nothing more than a title and stacks of money?"

"Maybe, but I wouldn't have put it to you quite so bluntly."

"And what if I told you that my father is in trouble? That he's doing more than just selling a horse to you?" She lifted her chin. "He has gambling debts that are overtaking the family finances. With Hendrick's death, our estate will revert to a cousin on my father's side. He's already married, so there's no hope of a family alliance. And through bad investments and my mother's refusal to live as though we have a rapidly dwindling fortune, their only recourse is to sell their only daughter to the highest bidder. And Lord Brentwood is buying, Mr. Keary. He has quite a fortune with which to do so. Because I have a good name, that makes for a favorable match for future heirs."

"And does he know of your father's debts?"

"Of course not. I'm not even sure why I told you, except to say that I know more about how Ingénue feels right now than you might give me credit for."

Colin's jaw seemed to flex on its own. He stood and backed away for a moment, afraid if he didn't, she'd see anger seep out over his face.

He shoved his hands down in his pockets.

"One day you'll be mistress of a grand manor, and you'll be glad to revisit the memories of time spent with your brother. And with Ingénue. You'll see someday when you look back on your life that you've been given a wonderful opportunity. The kind of life most people only dream of."

Rose sat frozen for a moment, staring back at him. "And you truly believe that?"

He nodded. "I do."

"Then forgive me, Mr. Keary, as it's none of your affair, but the prospect that I could live content married to Oliver Brentwood is a fairy tale of my mother's invention. Frittering away my days with garden parties and afternoon teas at the Spencer estates may sound like heaven to some, but it will be my lifelong prison. I have no option but to accept the life they've chosen for me. So at the very least, I'd ask that you not judge me in it. As an outsider looking in, you could never fully understand my reasons for needing the daily escape of rides with Ingénue."

Rose paused, no doubt considering the impasse that had formed between them. "Tell me, what would your counsel be if Mr. Butler came to you, wishing for a different life?"

Colin sighed. Somehow he'd known that was coming.

"You couldn't stop him, Mr. Keary. Not if he knew what he wanted. He'd find his own way to get it."

"Of that I have no doubt."

Her honesty reached something inside that Colin had once felt himself. But it still precipitated an equally honest answer, one that would either dissuade her or convince her. She deserved that much.

"What would you say to him then?"

What would I say?

I'd have to be sure you want this. That you're strong enough to take this leap of faith and change your entire world . . .

"I'd say no," he whispered. Not uncaring, but firm. "That it's a big thing to give up your whole life on a whim. And if he tried to do it anyway, I'd march him straight back and deposit him on the front step of his father's estate the very same day."

He could see it in her face; Rose's heart sank.

She nodded, like she'd given up.

"I apologize to have taken so much of your time this morning. Good luck to you, Mr. Keary."

Rosamund stood, wiping the back of her skirt to free it of any straw that may have caught up on the wool, then turned to leave the stable.

Colin sighed. Ran his hand through his hair as he stood behind her, feeling the acute stab of regret as soon as the words were out of his mouth.

"Rose, wait."

He stepped up behind her.

Reached for her hand.

Never anticipating it would be the warmth of his fingers clasping hers that would draw her back. Not having expected she'd drop her gloves to the ground in the haste of his action and turn to face him with a look of true understanding alive upon her features.

Colin knew his hair must have been mussed—he'd just run a hand through it. She looked up at his brow, a tiny flicker of notice flashing in her eyes.

It spoke volumes.

"I'm not finished," he added, holding her hand a few seconds longer than he should. "I'd also say that if you're quite sure living your own life is what you mean to do, then your wish can be granted."

"My wish?" she breathed out.

"You've heard of the Circus Kings, in America?"

He knew she probably had, even as far off the path as North Yorkshire.

"The Ringling Brothers?" She narrowed her eyes in question. "I've heard of them, yes."

"My employers—and Ingénue's new owners—are Charles and John Ringling. I'm John Ringling's agent, both on the road

71

during the performance months and to recruit acts for the Ringling Brothers' show in the off-season."

"So that's why you're in England? To recruit acts for a circus?" She eased back, pulling her fingers from his.

He felt the absence of warmth when she let go.

"Yes. But in particular, I've come to make Ingénue a part of the Ringlings' world. I think she could be a high school horse, one that is so finely trained that she can perform with little to no direction. I witnessed her do so this morning, with you as her rider. If you wish it, I'll take you to see that new world for yourself."

"Why would you do that?" she breathed out.

Colin stooped and picked up her gloves, dusting off tiny bits of straw from the soft leather. He stood, then held them out before her.

"Because I know what's it's like to wish more than anything that you could change your life. And I'm here to say that if you really want it, you can see what it's like to live a different life. You can have adventure, if that's what you need, before you make a decision about your future."

She shook her head. "But how?"

"Come to America and find out."

CHAPTER 8

1904
ATLANTIC CITY, NEW JERSEY

It was hot backstage.

Too hot.

A pressure cooker, according to Sally.

Mable could feel the humidity rising, making her skin sticky and wet. Her friend's last set wasn't scheduled for another half hour, so the two sat in the backstage area of the newly built grand ballroom at the elegant Marlborough-Blenheim Hotel, baking through their break while they waited for show time.

"Remind me again why I agreed to two performances in one evening?"

Sally flounced back in a baby-blue chaise lounge, fanning her hand at her face while she laid her head back in dramatic fashion.

"You'd think sea air would be better in summer. But look—" Sally pointed to the vase of pink roses—her favorite—on the dressing table nearby. Their petals were wilted and sad, having gradually succumbed to the heat. "Even our roses lose their luster in this heat."

Mable stuck her index finger in her copy of *The Tenant of Wildfell Hall* to hold her place. She looked over the top of the binding to the withered roses, then to where her friend lay stretched out on the chaise.

Sally was staring up at the filigree ceiling vaults, with her hair pulled back in wavy tendrils that spilled about the high collar of the marvelous buttercup-yellow dress she wore. It was indeed hot, but not so much as to justify the drama Sally was making of it. Especially when she wasn't the one wearing a woolen uniform skirt in the mid-July heat.

The thought made Mable grin. Her friend certainly was suited for the stage.

"But we can't really complain, can we? It's a full house tonight." Mable winked at her. "We're poised to see some greenbacks, dearie. And if your gentlemen callers keep sending roses backstage, you can't claim the evening as a total loss."

"Don't be pert." Sally tossed a velvet bolster pillow at her. It bounced off the top of Mable's chair and fell down, sliding across the floor. "You're a cashier who's not interested in greenbacks. Who ever heard of such a thing?"

"I'm not a cashier anymore. I'm a management candidate now, remember? And maybe I'm not interested because there are more important things in life than money."

With that, she turned back to her book.

"Like what?"

Mable breathed in deep, letting out a sigh of mock exasperation. "Freedom, for one. And beautiful experiences. Like sitting in an elegant room at the Marlborough-Blenheim Hotel on the iron pier, talking with a friend. How many people would love to be in our shoes right this very moment?"

Sally attempted a laugh, though the action drove her into a near coughing fit.

"You talk of freedom? But money can buy that too," she said, wiping a hand at moisture the coughing had brought to the corner of her eyes.

Mable sighed and looked around, feeling the weight of Sally's growing bitterness against what she viewed as the confines of their downtrodden lot.

The backstage area was immaculate, as was everything in the Queen Anne–style castle of a hotel. The sheer size and opulence of their surroundings just couldn't make Mable feel anything less than grateful, even if she merely worked at the hotel instead of being a guest in it. Life hadn't issued her the same trials that her friend had been through, but still, being around the grandeur, she couldn't allow her thoughts to dip to the level of resentment that Sally had developed over the past few years.

"Money can buy just about anything, can't it? Except love, of course. The one thing it can never lay claim to," Sally breathed out on a sort of tragic whisper. "You seem to be the only one not plagued by the want of it."

"Of love?"

Mable held the book in her hands, but lost interest and gazed off into the distance, soon curling the binding under her palms. The other side of the room faded into a crowd of revelers, with the great White City behind them. And she saw in the foreground the same thing she always did: an impeccably dressed man with serious eyes, a hard-won smile, and an aura of mystery all around him. A man whose presence dwarfed any bowler-hatted suitors who had waltzed her way in the years since.

It was the vision of what might have been from many years before that still pricked her heart, asking, *What if?*

"I'm not immune to it, Sal," Mable whispered back, overcome with the vision that had already begun to fizzle across the room. She shook her head, willing the picture of the circus king to fade and leave her in peace. "But I'm also not going to wait around for it. I intend to live a full life with or without it."

Sally sat up with a rustle of crepe and lace. She braced her hands on the row of nail heads lining the edge of the chaise, staring back at Mable with a somber look painted on her face. Dark violet half-moons shadowed the underside of her eyes.

"You mean to tell me you'd turn love away if it walked in your door? What gives you the right?"

Mable felt a twinge of empathy at her friend's sullen appearance. The hollowness in her eyes spoke volumes. Still, Mable felt she had to speak truth. She'd always spoken from the heart with those whom she loved, and Sally was dear to her.

"No, Sal. I wouldn't turn it away. But I won't live in a cage while I wait for it either. And I certainly don't think that marrying for money is the same as marrying for love. I'm sorry to disappoint you, but I don't."

Sally's forearms tensed and her knuckles turned white in their grip on the chaise. She'd rebuffed Mable's view before and no doubt would again.

Mable leaned forward and placed a hand over her friend's. "You look tired," she began, treading as gently as she could. "Did you sleep last night?"

Sally tore her glance away and instead studied the spread of bottles and canisters of rouge on the dressing table. She nibbled on her bottom lip, seeming distracted. "Some."

"But you were up, weren't you? I heard you coughing again in the middle of the night, even through my bedroom door."

Sally bounced up and gathered her skirts to cross the room, then sat down on the bench at the oval-mirrored dressing table. She ran her fingertips over the ivory-handled hand mirror and horse-hair brush on its surface, staring off in the distance as if lost in thought.

"Maybe I was."

She lingered with her fingers smoothing over the top of a small group of bottles bunched together in front of the mirror. Though most were near empty, she grabbed one with the printed label *Dr. Bull's Cough Syrup* and pulled out the cork.

Mable watched as her friend put the bottle to her lips and took a long sip. She used the back of her hand to wipe her mouth and looked up in the mirror to find Mable staring back at her from behind.

"Something to say?"

"No." Mable shook her head, keeping a firm connection with Sally's golden eyes.

Sally was goading her to a quarrel, she knew. And as always, it wouldn't work.

"You may be a starry-eyed dreamer, but you're no better in that uniform than you were in any hostess or shopgirl's uniform before it. Even at the World's Fair. And you were rejected then too, weren't you? Same as me. Rejected by life." Sally spat the venom at the mirror, then curled her lips around the bottle once more.

Mable tapped the corner of the chaise with her heel, itching to cross the room to her embattled friend. But she stayed put, waiting for the outburst to subside.

Though they came more frequently now, the eruption would eventually pass.

"I'll wear any uniform I'm given—as long as I'm happy while doing it. For now, I like it here."

"What's to like about this place?" Sally pounded a fist on the dressing table, causing Mable to jump and shaking the vase of roses until errant petals drifted to the floor. "Nothing but the taffy and spun sugar you can buy on the boardwalk, if you have more than two nickels to rub together, that is."

"You're tired, Sally. This is your lack of sleep talking . . ."

"It's not sleep," she choked out, her voice cracking.

Sally sniffed loudly, upending the bottle to drink the last of the tonic. She coughed again, choking slightly over a swallow of liquid that caught on an inhale of breath.

Mable rushed to her side and knelt, placing a hand on the space between Sally's shoulder blades. She pulled a kerchief from her skirt pocket and handed it to Sally, whose chest erupted into fits again. She coughed into the kerchief with one hand braced against the dressing table.

"You can't sing tonight," Mable argued firmly. "Not like this."

"I have to. We need the money."

"Not at the expense of your health," Mable said, lowering her chin to position her face in the sightline of Sally's downturned gaze. When their eyes met, she went on. "I can take up a few extra shifts. We'll stay afloat. And in the meantime, we're taking you to a doctor."

Sally's refusal was so emphatic that she shook out a tendril from her updo. It fell down to mingle with the beads of perspiration gathering on her forehead. She slicked it back with one of her clammy hands, closing her eyes as she did so.

"Sal . . ." Warning bells were going off in Mable's head.

Something was wrong. Terribly wrong.

This was more than one of her friend's syrup-induced rages. Mable pressed a hand to Sally's forehead, feeling the heat emanating like hot coals beneath her skin. It was clear that this was sickness talking. And whatever it was, it looked to have a firm hold.

Gingerly, she took the kerchief from Sally's hand and dotted her friend's forehead, catching the wetness up in the softness of the cloth.

"You have a fever."

Sally nodded, squeezing her eyes shut. "I know."

"How long have you had it?"

"A day," she mouthed. "Maybe two."

Sally fell then, crumpling into Mable's arms.

"I just . . . expected . . . more." Sally was crying now. Unashamed. No longer angry but broken. She shook in Mable's arms. "I didn't think it would be so hard. Life is . . . It doesn't feel worth living when it's so hard."

"Hush," Mable cooed, running her hand over Sally's brow. "Hush now. It will be okay." She kissed Sally's temple and whispered calming words, gentle words, praying they'd break through the pain to reach the broken parts of her friend's heart.

"I'd always been taught that hope could ground a person. Forget dreams. Or money. Forget anything but hope, and you'll still find joy despite life's circumstances. But . . . God . . . has . . . forgotten me," Sally countered, coughing and hiccupping through every syllable. "He can't possibly redeem me now."

Mable swallowed hard, praying for wisdom. Praying for the right words to say.

"Maybe He's always been here, we just haven't really looked to see Him. Maybe there's something bigger at work than the two of us."

Sally's shoulders stilled. She trembled slightly but looked up, chin quivering.

"That's what you're really looking for, isn't it? Money. Status. Power. They're a ruse, Sally. They don't make us who we are. A person has to know who they are to start out with, or all of that will mean nothing, even if the other things are attained."

The wall clock chimed, signaling the dinner hour with a song that echoed around the room.

Sally squared her shoulders. She broke the connection with Mable's eyes and turned back to the mirror, fumbling with the trinkets on the table. She grabbed up a puff and began quickly dotting powder and rouge to her tearstained cheeks.

"I have to go onstage," she stated, her voice plain, almost emotionless.

Mable nodded.

She had the feeling her words had almost reached her friend.

They wound in, sinking deep in her own heart. But maybe that was the point. They were two girls dancing around the edges of a dream, never truly finding it. There was a place in her innermost heart that Sally kept protected. Never letting go. And never allowing anything or anyone to reach it.

"Of course," she said as she stood and turned to leave.

"Mable," Sally called after her. She flashed a ready smile—one of those heart smiles that made every face beautiful. "I'll see you after the set."

"That would be nice," Mable said as she moved toward the door. "Maybe we could take a walk down the boardwalk. Clear our heads a bit. Buy some of that spun sugar they sell on the pier."

The last thing Mable saw was Sally nodding, the smile slowly fading as she turned away. Her friend would collect her resolve, and the fever with it, and ready herself to waltz out in front of the grand ballroom and sing her set to perfection.

Mable was sure of it.

Sally was strong down to her bones, and that strength was capable of overcoming the storms life brought. But this time, despite what Mable knew her friend possessed, they'd not take their evening walk.

Sally grew dizzy and passed out midset.

The pianist picked her up, and the hotel owner himself rushed her to the nearest sanitarium in his own car. Mable wanted to go with her—she'd even opened the car door to climb in the backseat—but Sally refused a companion, pushing her back in a bemused state of feverish refusals as she was loaded into the auto.

"No. Go to the pier, Mable," she pleaded, her glassy eyes entreating with tumbling emotion. "Don't waste another minute. Make something of this night. Walk for us both."

ELECTRIC LIGHTS ILLUMINATED THE LONG STRETCH OF BOARDWALK.

The sky was ink that night, and the sea toiled in an endless barrage to meet it.

The pier was alive with tourists and laughter, and the wonderful smells of sugared pecans and hot dogs mingling in with the salty sea air. Tourists thrilled at the rides. Children ran ahead of their parents, weaving through the crowd in front of her.

Music drifted around Mable as she walked, a brass band playing lively tunes from some perch behind her.

She moved down the pier with purpose, holding fast to the old cigar box clutched in her hands. And she didn't stop until her spectator heels nudged up against the aged boards nailed at the end of the pier.

Perhaps her friend had been right.

Dream chasing was not for the faint of heart.

Losing hope in a dream could break the spirit. She questioned hers now. Mable wondered if her catalog pictures and newspaper print wishes had caused her to tread water through her life. She'd moved from job to job and city to new bustling city, but what did she really have to show for it?

A cigar box with a penny souvenir fan and a pocket full of unrealized dreams.

The wind kicked up, grazing the wisps of hair at her nape, whipping her skirts against her slender legs. She knew the wind was strong enough to carry away her dreams on this night. And with the past years of memories rushing through her mind, Armilda Burton made a decision that had eluded her for so long.

The fan she'd keep, but the box with the bicycling ladies smiling on from the cover was poison.

It had to go.

She opened it and took out the fan, clutching its now worn

edges in her palm. And with a rush of determination she extended her arms as far as they would go, allowing the searching grasp of the wind to pull the clippings, one by one, to float out across the surface of the water.

Every one of them danced . . . Photos of Steinway pianos. Drawings of pink roses. Catalog pictures of fashion models and newspaper articles from around the world: they all disappeared in the blackness of the sea.

It was a ticker-tape parade of forgotten dreams.

Mable stood there, watching the dreams float away, but she didn't feel sad.

Sally's lot only served to strengthen her resolve. From now on, Mable would say what she really felt. She'd do for others, and would never let another person in her life feel as though they didn't hold an infinite amount of value. She promised herself that she'd not let an opportunity sift through her fingers before she'd do something about it.

If she ever had the means, Mable would see to it that life had color and vibrancy. She'd not wait anymore. She'd live. And she'd help anyone else who crossed her path. It would have to be gondolas and ballrooms. Steinways and roses. Laughter and love, or nothing at all.

"Mable?"

Her name, spoken breathlessly, caught her attention.

The worn cigar box was nearly empty now, the pile of aged photos and clippings moving with the ebb and flow of the waves that crashed the pier.

She brought the box back to her chest.

"Mable. Is that you?"

She recognized the voice and turned. Slowly. Wondering if it was all a dream. And she didn't move to dry her tears. Didn't hide the fan in her hand or smooth the wildness of her hair to appear more proper. She simply turned, heart shocked but open, to see the familiar eyes of John Ringling staring back at hers.

He looked older but not old.

The eyes were the same. Perhaps wiser somehow, with tiny lines now framing them at the corners. He stood in the soft glow of lamplight on the pier, allowing the sea breeze to toy with the edges of his silk tie and linen suit.

"Mable. It is you," he said, looking from the fan and box she held in her hands back up to her eyes.

"John."

"I'm surprised you remember me," he said, his voice still deep-chested and strong, though in it she detected notes of regret.

She wiped at the wetness under her eyes, somehow unashamed to admit emotion had overtaken her. "I remember you well. We took a walk once."

"We did."

"And ran from a wall of fire, I believe." She eyed him. Openly. Without anger. But her words, too, were tinged with regret. "I couldn't have forgotten that, Mr. Ringling."

John sighed, ever so slightly.

"I'm sorry." And he seemed genuinely so. About not sharing his full name that day. About walking with her, truly connecting, and then just letting go in the span of a single afternoon. "It's been so long. Years . . . What are you doing here?"

"A friend—she fell ill tonight, and I needed a walk to clear my head. So here I am."

Mable stood still before him, wondering after his thoughts. Thinking herself that fate could be the cruelest of foes at times. It had certainly gained the upper hand on her thoughts at the moment. How could she have predicted John Ringling would show up here, now, when she'd just thought of him barely an hour before?

"And in Atlantic City?"

"I live here. For a few years now."

His gaze—eyes only—drifted down to her left hand.

"No. I'm not married," she added on a light laugh, answering the question he hadn't asked. "I'm a working woman. Not the complete ideal of a Gibson girl, I'm afraid. But I still have the hairstyle and the uniform to pull it off. And the rest . . ." She shrugged. "I'm still chasing my dreams. But you make concessions when life calls for it."

"How did you come to live in Atlantic City? From Chicago?"

"And New York, with more than one stop in between. I'm afraid I was rather spoiled with the exposition's surroundings, and I missed that life after it closed. So a pier teeming with children and happy faces is about as pleasant a place as one could find."

"So you came here." He adjusted his gaze to the sights of an active boardwalk behind them.

Mable shrugged, as no polished Gibson girl ever would. "I've always dreamed of living by the sea."

She brushed at a few stray locks of hair that the wind had wrapped across her forehead, moving them out of her eyes. Her skirt whipped in a frenzy against her legs.

"And what are you doing here, Mr. Ringling?" she asked, swallowing over the growing lump in her throat.

"Business," he whispered, never taking his eyes from hers.

"Yes. Business . . ."

Mable broke the connection, needing the space to look away.

She surveyed the pier—saw parents stopping at street vendors to buy saltwater taffy and popcorn for their children. Couples whisked by to and fro, opting for a light promenade along the pier. Even a trio of workmen had stopped and tossed fishing lines off the pier, and were now smoking pipes and chatting with lines drawn down in the water.

Everything moved about her, people happy and so far removed from the world she'd just left in Sally's dressing room. And here stood John Ringling, a man of great wealth and prestige, threatening to damage what little bit of happiness she'd still felt alive in her heart.

On instinct, Mable's feet began to move.

She edged a heel back away from him. It felt easier to be the one who'd choose to walk out this time, before she found herself in love and shattered like Sally.

Yes. Walking away . . . it was far easier than the alternative. Mable edged another step back, adding, "Well then, Mr. Ringling. It was lovely to see—"

"I never forgot you," he cut in, sharp as a knife.

The thought made her laugh even through her tears. She hadn't a clue why.

"That's nice to hear," she admitted.

And it was. Surprising, but nice all the same.

"And I've thought of you over the years, Mable . . ." He paused. "Often."

"But you never walked through those restaurant doors again." The wind toyed with a lock of hair at her brow, tossing it until it finally lay still, lingering over her eyes. She swept it away, tucking it back behind her ear.

"It would have been a pleasure to see you again," she admitted.

John sighed and looked down to the tips of his spectator shoes for the briefest of seconds, thinking over, she assumed, how he'd reply. And then he surprised her by taking a step forward. Another step. And then another, walking slowly, not stopping until the tips of his shoes nearly grazed hers.

He looked down, studying her face. And then he shifted his gaze to the cigar box and worn souvenir fan clutched in her hands.

85

"May I?" he asked.

Mable couldn't ignore the softness in his tone. She nodded, though not entirely sure why he was asking to see it.

John took the items in hand, carefully slipping the fan under the cigar box lid before he tucked both under his elbow.

"I didn't come back because I *couldn't* come back," he admitted, the lamplight illuminating his features. His brow was a touch furrowed, his mouth creased and serious. "You were the first woman who'd ever looked at me like I had the name of John, and not Ringling. And while I don't make concessions for myself in walking away that day—"

"I should hope not. I'm not sure I would allow it."

Something flashed in his eyes.

Amusement?

He nodded.

"Fair enough. But I also don't abhor wealth. My family has worked hard to build something we're proud of. Something that brings joy to a great number of people. And perhaps because of it, I am overly cautious with my relationships. *All* of them."

"I wouldn't have asked you to surrender anything, Mr. Ringling," Mable whispered. "It was only a walk." She reached for her box, eager to sidestep him and march on with life beyond the poignant exchange of regrets on a busy pier.

He eased his arm back, tucking the box just out of her reach.

"But that's where you're mistaken," he whispered above the sound of the Midway rides, jazzy music, and the delights of patrons echoing in the distance. "It was more than a mere walk to me. And I think I'd much prefer it if you'd see fit to call me John from now on."

There were differences about him, yes.

A few more years had filled out the lines of his face. But nothing had altered the smile he offered now. It was warm and unpretentious. Mable had a feeling that when a smile was granted by John Ringling, it was a special occurrence. One she couldn't ignore.

"I am not looking for a benefactor, John Ringling," she whispered, notching her chin an inch.

"That's a relief." He smiled again. With ease. "Because neither am I."

He held out his free arm. Waiting.

Mable looked down with great intention, allowing him to see the indecision before bringing her eyes back to meet his.

"Perhaps we can start again, Mable. Go on another walk? I hear there's a World's Fair in St. Louis going on right this minute. I'm sure they have any number of camels and Midway souvenirs to catch your eye. And I'd like to see them all with you."

She slipped her arm in his, stopping short of resting her hand on his arm. His eyes twinkled as he brushed a hand over hers and turned to lead them down the length of the pier.

"And what if there's a fire this time, John?"

"Then I suppose instead of running, we'll stop and put out the flames together."

CHAPTER 9

1926
London

"I think we're ready. Ingénue's settled in a car in back."

Colin nearly had to shout so Rosamund could hear the sound of screeching train brakes and chugging steam engines easing in behind them at the busy railway station.

"You can still change your mind, you know."

"I know," Rosamund answered, standing her ground.

"But you won't, will you?"

At a good ten inches shorter than Colin's six-foot frame, she had to raise her chin high to meet the question in his gaze. But look up she did, with eyes that would show only brimming excitement.

From the moment she'd awoken before daybreak, Rosamund's mind was made up: she was going to America.

She didn't question it while donning her deep-purple fox-trimmed traveling coat and silver-gray frock, nor when she'd fumbled about in the early-morning darkness, fighting to tuck her riot of waves under an ivory satin–lined cloche. And if she hadn't considered changing her mind when she'd slipped out of the manor, she certainly wouldn't do it after coming all the way to London.

She peered past the end of the wooden passenger car, then

surveyed the long stretch of tracks that met the landscape of the city's mass of buildings beyond. The brick-and-mortar skyline disappeared behind puffs of smoke from chimneys and steam from departing trains. She clutched the cider leather traveling bag tighter in her gloved hands and gave a confident nod.

"My mind's made up. I'm going."

"As if I had any doubt." Colin flipped the brim of his hat off his forehead, allowing the morning sunlight to cast a glow on a knowing smile. "I'll just go check with Ward that everything's as it should be with the accommodations for the rest of the stock. Do you have the ticket for your trunks?"

Rosamund handed over the ticket she'd received from the porter.

"I'll make sure the porter knows to transfer your trunks at the Crawley Railway Station. We'll change trains there and ride straight through to Southampton Port. We've got a stop or two to make along the way, but we should be in New York in a week and in Florida a few days after that. We'll head straight in to the Sarasota fairgrounds from there. All clear?" He waited for a nod of understanding.

She complied, biting the edge of her bottom lip over the anticipation that the biggest step of her life was but moments away.

"Good. I won't be a moment. Stay here," he ordered.

Rosamund watched Colin walk away, his broad shoulders disappearing into the mist along the side of the train.

Passersby hurried along the busy platform. They brushed by to the right and the left, and she pulled the fur collar up closer to hide her features from anyone who might recognize her there. Her mother's circles in society and her father's in business certainly extended to London. Best not to tempt fate by revealing her plan to any of the Easling family friends until they were well on their way.

Colin had offered to speak with her father, but Rosamund

knew how that would go—with the great Earl of Denton tossing the Irish-American circus agent from the mansion stoop by the seat of his trousers. She'd declined the offer and instead packed in secret the night before.

She'd taken her travel papers, enough frocks and hats to sustain her for several weeks' journey, her Bible, and a photograph of their family before Hendrick had gone to France. Everything else she left behind with a note on the fireplace mantel in her bedchamber. The note her maid was likely reading right at that very moment, with sickened heart and trembling hands.

To take in a very deliberate, calming breath took effort, but Rosamund managed it. However, putting the vision of a harried maid and furious parents out of her mind would take more doing. She adjusted her collar once more, then stared through the curling cloud of steam ahead, waiting for Colin to walk back through it.

More than anything, Rosamund hoped he was right.

Maybe the trip would open her eyes. Maybe traveling to train Ingénue in her new home would change her enough that Rosamund could return home and become the mistress of Lord Brentwood's grand estates. And, just maybe, contentment would claim her somewhere along the way.

Colin reemerged then, and her thoughts sailed back to the trip ahead.

Rosamund instinctively smiled.

That is, until she noticed that he wasn't alone, and the smile that had so freely taken over her features faded almost as quickly.

The form of an impeccably dressed woman emerged from the mist alongside him. They strolled along the platform, she a vision by his side, confidently falling into step with him. Freely. As if they knew each other quite well.

The woman was statuesque, with olive skin and ebony hair

tucked in a sleek, boyish bob under a soft blue cloche. It matched a bright-blue-and-gold embroidered traveling coat. Her lips were poppy red and pressed into an elegant smile. She walked with Colin as if floating along the platform, with a sultry grace that Rosamund had only read about in novels and seen once in a silent film at a picture show in a London cinema. Never had she dreamed that such a beauty could actually exist in real life. And never had she expected that kind of beauty to be strolling in her direction.

Colin tipped his fedora back so he could lean in and say something to his companion over the roar of the train engine. She laughed in response, with a rosy smile that showed off a slight dimple in her left cheek.

Rosamund drew in a steadying breath as the pair approached.

"*Saluto.*" The woman extended a greeting as they stopped in front of her.

Rosamund smiled through the curiosity piquing her interest, offering a congenial hello in return.

"My, my, Colin. You did not do this young lady justice. She is *bellissimo*," the woman exclaimed with a thick Italian accent. "Are you sure she's not here to join the show?"

"Not exactly. Rosamund is accompanying one of our acquisition horses to Sarasota, to see the mare is trained properly," he said.

Colin connected eyes with her, but seemed to avoid any questions Rosamund would have posed in hers.

"She plans to return to England in a few months' time."

"Will she now? What a shame. I was looking forward to becoming better acquainted."

Colin turned to welcome Ward, who'd run up behind their group with a ready smile and a half-eaten, wax paper–wrapped sandwich in his hand. He tipped his woolen newsboy cap up off his forehead and looked to Colin.

"Stock's all tucked in. We're ready to go," he said, taking a bite of his sandwich with nonchalance.

The woman tipped her eyebrows, as if she were skeptical of something, but kept silent.

She turned her attention from Colin to Rosamund, smiling down on her with lovely long lashes that framed twinkling eyes. She possessed slight lines that creased at the corners as if she'd favored others, just like Rosamund, with thousands of polished smiles before.

"Lady Rosamund Easling." Colin's voice was even, but tinged with a layer of something Rosamund hadn't noticed in him before. Indecision maybe? She hoped she hadn't judged it correctly. "This is Bella Rossi—one of the Rossi Family Flyers. They have top billing in the show."

"*Lady* Easling?" Bella questioned.

Ward took the opportunity to jump in, nodding with enthusiasm. "Right. She is an actual lady. Can you believe it? Daughter of an earl with a doozy of an estate in Yorkshire." He leaned in to Bella's side, whispering with his sandwich in hand, "That's just north of here."

Bella narrowed her eyes at him in a slight glimmer of superiority.

A piece of bread drifted from his parcel to the ground, just grazing the polished edge of her black wingtips. Bella looked down at it, then returned her glare to his face. It was subtle, but enough that Rosamund caught the instruction for him to step back.

"Uh, Ward—" Colin issued silent disapproval with a slight shake of his head.

"But it's just Rosamund now, Ward," Rosamund said, offsetting Bella's more severe reproach with an air of lightness to cut the awkwardness. "I think the mention of estates will become far less important as England fades with the train tracks behind us."

"*Buona*, dear. A pity that your title means nothing in the United States. But no doubt you'll encounter that truth soon enough when we arrive in New York. I'm sure this trip will prove most instructive."

Bella's counter was so swift, yet laced with syrup, that Rosamund was taken aback at the contradiction between her words and the inviting smile on the lips from which they'd escaped.

And in truth, she hadn't considered until that very moment how different it would be to enter a world where the title of earl's daughter carried very little weight—or none at all.

"Instructive. Yes, I'm sure it will be," she repeated, keeping her reply congenial despite the bold veil of condescension Bella had drawn between them. "It is a pleasure to meet you, Miss Rossi. I look forward to our travels."

Bella let out a lusty laugh, exclaiming, "*Molto innocente!* She's just as you described, Colin. And so English. I cannot remember the last time anyone has called me Miss. This is a treat!"

Rosamund flashed Colin a questioning glance, which he avoided by coughing into his palm.

"We're all set. Porter's got the trunks and the conductor's ready to go," he noted, steering them back to the journey before them. He reached for Rosamund's bag.

"So you are really joining us after all?" Ward piped up. "We've managed to clip you from England? Well, Florida will be the better for it when you set foot on the circus grounds. We'll have to show you around. Introduce you to the rest of the performers you'll be working with."

"It's not like that, Ward," Colin corrected. "She's not staying."

Ward's smile faded ever so slightly, showing he had been hopeful. "But I thought you said she was a bareback rider."

Bella's nose tilted up. "A bareback rider?" She wasn't interested in hiding any disdain for Rosamund this time.

"She is, Ward," Colin corrected. "Just not in the manner of a performer."

"I am a rider, but I'm only accompanying my horse to see that she'll be properly looked after," Rosamund clarified, though not feeling altogether confident about it in the moment. "Then I'll come back to my life here, Mr. Butler."

"So you're not joining up?" He looked genuinely disappointed.

"Not officially. No."

"That would've been the berries. You'd love the show. It's magnificent. The Big Top goes up in under four hours, but it can hold thousands of spectators. Can you believe it? A real canvas city moseying from town to town with animals and acts of all kinds. There's nothing like it in all the world."

Rosamund was grateful for Ward's enthusiasm, especially given the strange air of awkwardness that seemed to have overtaken the platform.

All of a sudden the trip felt like a mistake.

A step far too drastic for a Yorkshire earl's daughter. The trepidation Rosamund had buried in her midsection grew by leaps and bounds now, turning her stomach into a cascade of swirling butterflies. She stared at the backdrop of London behind them, wondering if she should—or could—possibly turn back now.

"It's time to go," Colin stated, snapping her back to the moment. "Our car's right here. Ladies? Ward?"

Rosamund watched, keenly noticing that Bella placed a hand on Colin's elbow as he led them to the train. Something was amiss, she just hadn't the slightest inclination what it was.

Her oxford heels seemed to sink into the platform, holding her back.

"Mr. Keary?"

Colin turned, almost as if expecting Rosamund to question

why the temperature around them had changed so suddenly. Bella and Ward turned too, halted, and looked to Colin. He paused long enough to whisper something, and they proceeded to the car. He waited until they'd latched the door behind them, then turned back to her.

"It's against my better judgment to tell you this, but under the circumstances, I assume you're looking for an explanation."

"Not an explanation, really. It just feels as though something's amiss. Am I wrong?"

He shook his head. "I'm sorry. I didn't mean for this to happen."

"I'm not sure I understand what *this* is." Rosamund paused, searched his face, noting the unmistakable shades of empathy that had fallen over it.

"Bella has been with the circus for several years. She's our biggest star—a celebrity in the States. I hate to say it, but that kind of notoriety means the star isn't always welcoming to a newcomer."

"A newcomer? But we just told her I'm not joining up permanently."

"Of course. There are just some business matters of the circus happening behind the scenes. It has nothing to do with you, okay? I've told her you're only accompanying Ingénue to America. But the Rossi family is notoriously private and can tend to be protective of their act. I don't think she bargained on traveling with a performer—part of the show or not—whom she'd just met."

He shifted his weight ever so slightly.

"Are you changing your mind?" she dared ask.

"No," Colin replied immediately, shaking his head. "I just want you to be sure you know what you're doing. That you're stepping on this train because you really want to, not because you're running away. And certainly not because you're walking into this with eyes closed."

Fear crept up the length of her spine. Rosamund swallowed hard, feeling the first tinges of panic she'd allowed herself now threatening to draw tears in front of him.

"I think I'm doing both, but it doesn't matter. I can't go back now. Not when I've burned every bridge I have. My world is not like yours, Mr. Keary. It's not the circus. Or America. Easling Park exists on routine and propriety. At its center is a manor fraught with rules, and as a woman living in that world, I've broken every one of them by coming here today."

He sighed. "I know."

"It took nearly every ounce of courage I have to come this far. I'll need all I have to see this through."

Colin looked from the train back to her, his speech stunted by whatever it was he wouldn't say. That explained nothing about why he was battling such discomfort in the moment.

He sighed, frustration evident.

"What Bella said is true: in America, English titles won't mean what they do here. In truth, she will continue to see you as beneath her."

The forthright manner of his admission felt like a shot of ice water to the face.

"Beneath her?"

Colin nodded, even squinted his eyes with a twinge of empathy.

"I'm sure it's not a sensation you're used to, but yes. A horse trainer, titled English lady or not, is still new to the show. And anyone new is not on the level of a Ringling Brothers star. I'm sorry, but that's the way of it."

"I see." Rosamund nodded, looking up at the train car.

She could see Bella's cloche, the velvety top just tipping up through the window.

"I'll handle Bella, okay? I promise you that. Her presence

doesn't change anything. You and I have struck a deal, that you'll accompany Ingénue to Florida and train her there. If you still wish to do that, I've a ticket here with your name on it."

Rosamund sighed, owning that her pride had been injured by Bella's snub.

True, the woman's beauty was stifling. Her manners had been unexpected, as was the way she fell into step so easily alongside Colin. And if Rosamund were honest with herself, she'd have to admit an earl's daughter would probably return the woman's barbs without civility. But Rosamund was looking for a choice in her life—an opportunity to break free and have at least one adventure before her life was decided for her.

She'd found it, and would have to accept whatever came with it.

No one would force her into the compartment unless she earnestly wanted to go.

"I don't wish to quarrel with her. If you say things will be okay, then I'll believe you. Bella is lovely and I'm glad to have met her. Truly."

"Then you still plan to go through with this? You're ready?"

Rosamund nodded. "Yes. I'll go to Florida. I'll help you train Ingénue. Then I'll spend Christmas with my aunt in New York and I'll come back here in the spring." She drew in a steadying breath. "And I'll marry Lord Brentwood, just as my parents want."

"Sounds like you have it all figured out."

"Crawley train about to depart . . ." A pause, then a repeat warning. "Crawley train about to depart."

"We ought to go," Colin acknowledged with a quick nod to the call for passengers to make their way to the train.

The station master blew his whistle with a shrill cry that cut through the air, causing an instant surge in the bustle on the platform.

"I know it's a lot to ask, but if you're up to it, I thought Bella could serve as your travel companion," he said, baring the slightest hint of a smile as he took her bag in hand. "So everything is properly done for you. Lord Brentwood would want to know his future wife was treated with the utmost respect."

It was so like Colin to have thought of such a detail, especially given the circumstances that she was expected to marry another man, yet was trusting him with her life in the meantime.

Rosamund thought of that as he led her to their train compartment and helped her step inside. Details of business. Of noticing what people said and, moreover, sometimes what they wouldn't say . . . Colin Keary was astute in the art of it.

"So the boss managed to convince you, eh?" Ward broke into her thoughts, exclaiming when they appeared in the compartment doorway.

"There was no convincing needed," Colin shot back before she could answer, then deposited her bag in the compartment above their heads. "Rosamund knows her own mind."

It was the last thing she'd imagine him to say, but she offered a soft thank-you in reply.

Ward proved positively gleeful to find Rosamund had joined the party, and patted the soft green velvet seatback next to him.

The moment she'd settled in the seat, he began rushing her through a one-sided conversation on the ills of life outside the circus world. Colin gave an exasperated sigh, then eased down into the seat next to Bella. He took out his pocket watch and began absently turning it over in his fingertips.

"The Ringling Brothers boast the greatest show known to man in a grand spectacle of exotic animals and performances by artists who defy the conventions of gravity, strength, and will." Ward perked up, nodding, hoping to engage Rosamund in his same level of enthusiasm. "It's a menagerie of men and animals creating spectacles unlike any the world has ever seen."

"Been reading the advertising pamphlets again, Ward?" Bella asked.

"But she needs to hear it, doesn't she? At least know something about the circus acts?" Ward chatted on, undaunted by the snip of Bella's remark. "So, there are baggage horses—the ones that pull the circus wagons and help raise the Big Top—and then there are the performance horses. The liberty horses run through their act without a harness. But your horse will still have one. She'll be put with the rest of the high school horses in the pad room."

"Pad room?" Rosamund asked, feeling more provincial by the moment. There was too much to learn simply to decode his last few sentences.

"Sure. Also called the ring stock tent. You'll get a bang out of seeing that. We've got hundreds of performance horses there." Ward smiled, stretching his long limbs out on the floor between benches. He folded his arms behind his head, settling in, it appeared, for a very drawn-out conversation. "Don't worry, Lady Easling. We'll get you up to speed."

It would be a long journey to New York, and Florida after that. Both because of Ward's incessant chatter and Bella's impenetrable condescension at every turn. Rosamund tried to be polite and offer smiles, even the occasional comment to Ward's conversation, but her thoughts were being carried away at the speed of the train.

Apparently, what had passed between them on the train platform had only served to root Colin's opinion of her. It seemed now that he had more belief in her gumption than she might have herself. Rosamund found her heart stirred by it, enough that her gaze was drawn to the man sitting across from her, and a growing storm that had settled in the depths of his blue eyes.

Rosamund knows her own mind . . .

Oh, how she hoped that was true.

CHAPTER 10

1926
SARASOTA, FLORIDA

Rosamund stepped from the train into the Florida sunshine, and everything came alive. Even the sky seemed bigger, an exquisite vault of clear blue, with puffs of clouds so cottony white that they seemed to stretch out with no beginning or end.

The fanning palms were so tall they'd have scraped the arches of Easling Park's fourth-floor windows. There seemed to be a world of color that opened up everywhere she looked. Bushes with vibrant pink and orange flowers, lush green foliage, white birds dotting the sky, and water so clear that Rosamund doubted anything could be closer to heaven than what was laid out before her.

It had taken six days to sail from the port of Southampton into New York Harbor. They'd stopped in New York City so Colin could catch up on business, and so Bella and Ward could catch a train north to meet up with the rest of the performers in Bridgeport, Connecticut. From there, Rosamund and Ingénue's world had passed by in a blur from port to ferry, and on to speed train rides through cities both big and modern. Finally came the ride that took them all the way south to the shores of Sarasota Bay, where

Rosamund stood with Colin now, listening as he pointed out the sights before them.

Rosamund had taken off her peach felt cloche and held it in her hand, welcoming the feel of the sun's warmth on her cheeks. She turned her face up to meet it, taking in the sight of the glittering waters of the bay and the expanse of Longboat Key bridging the horizon.

A light breath of wind caught up the tulip hem of her matching gauze frock, dancing the soft fabric about her legs.

"See that road stretching out over the water? That's the causeway. It's new, just finished in January. John Ringling was the first to drive over it. Before that you could only reach Longboat Key by boat." Colin stretched his arm out toward the edge of land beyond the bay. "And off the key is Lido Beach. Mrs. Ringling organizes picnics and games there for the local children."

Rosamund gave him a look that suggested he was in real danger of heaping extraneous details on her like Ward would.

"I know. You're new, and there's a lot to take in." He smiled, reading her thoughts accurately.

"You know Mrs. Ringling personally?"

He nodded. "Yes, I do. Have for some years now. She keeps a low profile with the media and with the performers in the show, but she's beloved in the Sarasota community. The Ringlings spend their winter months here. I hope you get to meet her while you're with us. I think she'd like you."

"I'm not sure I'll be here long enough for that, but it still sounds nice. And it really is beautiful here. More than I'd ever imagined."

Rosamund squinted, trying to picture the span of beach that hosted picnics and children's games beyond the key.

"It is that. And with the causeway, everything you're looking at is opened up now."

"Opened for what?"

"Tourists," Colin replied, allowing an easy smile to spread across his face. He tilted his head back toward the car. "Come on. There's something you'll want to see."

Rosamund spun around, taking in the beauty of the bay. "Something better than this?"

Still, she followed him back to the car, wondering what was next, feeling her excitement growing as he drove them through the heart of Sarasota.

Colin angled the car through the city streets teeming with palms and stucco buildings. They came down a long, winding dirt road that led into an open field and bumped along enough that Rosamund anchored her grip to the side of the car door.

The sky was just as blue here too, an expanse broken only by aged oak trees and palms dotting the landscape. Old plank buildings stood in a group, their exteriors long swept by the sea breeze. She could see stable houses, pens, and what looked to have once been a grandstand and moderately sized exhibit hall.

Colin brought the engine to a stop and turned to face her. "Well?"

Rosamund looked around at what wasn't there.

She saw the ghost of something—not the greatest spectacle the world had ever seen. There was no Big Top. No exotic animals or crowds of people. Just a stray bird or two flying overhead and palm trees swaying in the breeze.

"Well what?"

"This is it, the Sarasota County Fairgrounds. Ingénue's new home." He grinned. "Or it will be, when it's finished."

Rosamund could see that something had caught fire in Colin's eyes. They fairly sparkled at the sight. She tried to meet that, to see what he was showing her.

"I think Ward may have overstated the scale of the circus grounds just a bit," she said.

Colin rolled his eyes. "Your cheek is duly noted," he said, and jumped from the auto. He bounded to her side of the car and opened the door, clasping her hand to help her out. "Come on."

She left her hat and gloves on the seat and stepped out at his side.

"It's not been announced to the press yet, but the wheels are already in motion to move the circus's winter lodgings here."

Rosamund raised a hand to shield her eyes from the sun and looked over the expanse before them.

"Here?"

"We'll be in flux for a year, maybe more. But the lease for the land in Bridgeport is up come January, so the time is right for the move. We've got to form a new plan, and there are no better visionaries to do that than the Ringlings. The local economy's taken a beating here in the last year, but with the real estate opportunities that still remain, John Ringling is pressing for this to become the circus's new home. And I have to agree that winter is much more agreeable in Florida than Connecticut."

"Ward said there are more than a thousand people who travel with the show?"

"More like fourteen hundred."

She turned in a half-moon, spreading her arms wide. "So where will you put everyone? All the animals? Train cars? Everything?"

"We've got two hundred acres to work with. New buildings will go up all over. We'll have a mass of rail lines put in that come right up to the grounds. An indoor and outdoor menagerie house with elephants, apes, big cats—you name it. Dormitories. We'll even have our own hospital on the grounds. And over there"—he pointed to a great stretch of field far out in front of them—"a massive training complex for the performance horses. Enough to house four hundred or more, Ingénue among them. Everything can be done right here, from building and servicing our own rail cars to training the animals and bringing in new performers in the off-season. We can even test new acts with tourists in a two-ring circus here before we take them out on the road."

"But, Colin—there's nothing here. Well, next to nothing. Why didn't you take Ingénue to Bridgeport with the rest of the show?"

"I have my reasons. One of which is because I want to oversee her training, and I can't do that half a country away. So we'll keep her in Sarasota for now, until the show rolls. Then she'll go on the road, and by the time the season ends next fall, we'll be ready for her to come back to the new grounds with the rest of the show. We can't be sure of timing this early, but we'd like to open Christmas Day of next year."

She tossed him a speculative glance, wondering how they'd manage such an undertaking from the barren span of the grounds in front of them. "You expect you'll be ready for visitors by Christmas Day?"

"Of course," he said, scanning the fields just as she was. "We expect tens of thousands of tourists could come here year-round— maybe more. But they'll flock to see the show in the off-season, and all of that will happen right where you're standing."

"And when is the off-season?"

"The show opens in New York every March. Madison Square Garden—the greatest venue dedicated solely to entertainment in all the world. Then the train rolls out, stopping to put on shows in cities all across the country through the end of October. We stop in farming communities, manufacturing towns, and a few of the big cities, which are bigger draw opportunities for us. Then we head to Tampa to end the season. But there's talk of bringing the closing right here to Sarasota, once everything is done and the entire show can move in."

"And you'll live here too?"

Colin shook his head. "I can't say that I really live anywhere. Maybe I'll stay here during the winter season, when I'm not traveling to recruit new acts. Charles Ringling was the onsite administrator up until the latter half of this season. Since he's been ill of late, my responsibilities could increase. That makes it difficult to put down roots, even in a place as beautiful as this."

Rosamund gave a knowing smile.

The clarification made her understand Colin more. The way he'd looked after their group from England into New York Harbor. Why he'd shown no fear when he'd jumped in the creek after her that day. And why he was going to such lengths to ensure she was comfortable with the transition for a horse that most men couldn't have cared less for.

Colin Keary was the boss over thousands of lives, both of those who performed in the show and those who watched it. His were shoulders that spread wide, with responsibilities that he managed well. It was humbling, knowing the position he held and yet the time he had taken with her.

"So when Ward called you the boss, he really meant it."

"Try not to listen to half of what he says if you can help it. Everyone's got to be a boss when they're reining Ward in. Though his enthusiasm has served the circus well in the time I've known him."

"I actually didn't mind listening," she replied, smiling to remember all Ward had told her in their cross-ocean journey. In one sea voyage she learned more about the circus life than she'd ever thought possible. "He helped me to envision this place, just as you have now. I saw a menagerie house at Piccadilly when I was a young girl, right there in the heart of London. There were exotic birds and a small ape of some kind, but it was nothing like what either of you have described. I've only read about wonders like this, and here it will be real. It almost sounds like a kind of Camelot, doesn't it?"

Rosamund stood next to Colin, and in a moment of unbridled awe brushed a steadying hand to his arm without thinking. Just because she'd succumbed to the magic of what would be around her.

In it, the splendid promise of the freedom she'd sought.

She could almost see it—the vision of this grand performance glittering all around her. The old fairgrounds would be transformed, with bright red train cars and striped awnings, the sounds of animals and bustling crowds, and massive tents holding delighted men, women, and children in awe of the spectacles the various artists would perform.

Rosamund closed her eyes and could almost hear the circus band cueing up. She could see scores of children delighting over the elephants' march. Laughing at the clowns. She could imagine performers in dazzling costumes as they tumbled from bars high up in the air. She could hear the sound of the horses' hooves as trick riders awed the crowds with their bareback riding show.

It was true, what Colin had said.

Wishes for a new life could come true in a place like this. And Ingénue would be a part of that. She'd not have to be kept shut up in a lonely stable once Rosamund was married and moved away from Easling Park. She'd give enjoyment to countless people. And she'd be able to run as much as she pleased.

Her spirit couldn't be broken in a place like Colin described.

To envision it now felt like a gift.

"You see it, don't you? What it could be."

She nodded. The image stole her breath away. It needed no grand effort to do so, not when she pictured all that the grounds would become.

"Hendrick would have loved this for our horse. It's more than I imagined," she whispered aloud. "More than I ever dreamed."

Colin laughed, a slight chuckle that she'd come to know well.

"And this before you've actually seen anything yet." He tilted his head toward the old dilapidated stable nearest them. "This way."

"I have a million questions before I go back home."

"I know. And we'll answer them all. But first I'd like to introduce you to someone."

He called out, "Owen!" with cupped hands around his mouth. Once. Twice.

A dark-skinned man of perhaps fifty years finally popped his head out one of the doors, his face brightening when he saw the two of them.

He spread the stable doors wide.

"Come on," Colin whispered, guiding her by the elbow.

The man before them had deep charcoal eyes and close-cropped hair that was tinged gray at the temples. He was dressed plainly, in clothes not altogether different from those the stable hands might have worn at Easling Park—a white work shirt rolled to the elbows, canvas work trousers, and plain brown shoes that had a knot holding one of the laces together. A pair of wire-rimmed spectacles just peeked out from the top of his shirt pocket.

Colin met the man's hand in a hearty shake.

"So you're back from your travels." He welcomed them with a warm smile.

"Just today, as a matter of fact." Colin turned to Rosamund. "This is Owen Thomas, our lead trainer. And this is Lady—"

"Rosamund," she cut in. "I'm Rosamund Easling. It's very nice to meet you."

He extended a hand, which Rosamund accepted. She couldn't help thinking that her mother would have fainted dead away at any association with Mr. Thomas, but something about him triggered an instant liking.

An odd sort of wisdom seemed to radiate from him. A quiet manner. Maybe it was the humble dress. Or perhaps the kindness in the eyes. Either way, Rosamund felt instantly at home with him. What's more, she knew Ingénue would take to him, and that's what mattered most.

"Mr. Keary wired me to meet with you here. Said an Arabian is arriving today. Afraid I've been hoppin' around here like a kid at Christmas, waiting to finally get a look at her."

"She's already here, Owen. Came in on the train with us this morning." Colin cocked an eyebrow. "In fact, some of the boys are bringing her over right behind us."

A horn beeped just then, and they turned round together.

A truck with tall wooden slats lining the bed circled and came to a stop in front of the stable, its black running boards gleaming in the sun. Two men jumped out, tossing a wave in Colin's direction. He returned it with a nod of his head.

"Well, there she is, Owen. Your new protégé."

Rosamund could see Ingénue's head bobbing just over the slats of the truck. The men let down the back gate and Rosamund let out a gentle sigh of relief as they led the mare out, Ingénue clip-clopping her hooves down the ramp to the ground.

Owen took a step back, hands braced on his hips, and gazed at the horse. "She's magnificent," he breathed. "And right on time."

"On time for what?" Rosamund wondered aloud.

Colin said nothing when she sent a questioning glance his way. He just pointed to Owen—a nod to the man in charge of the moment.

"On time for what?" she repeated.

"For you to show us what she can do, Miss Easling."

"Again."

Owen's instructions were few, but the words he did say were

carefully chosen, his manner methodical. Colin had long known Owen was a trainer with exceptional skill, but it was encouraging to see him interact with a performer of Rose's unharnessed talent with both patience and precision.

Colin found a perch against a weathered wood rail and leaned against it, absently twirling his watch and chain round his fingers. He'd kept quiet throughout the session thus far, just stood watching the events unfold, checking off boxes of the pair's skill set in his mind.

"Try to stop on a dime next time," Owen instructed in his baritone voice. "And hold your balance. Concentrate. You're shifting too far forward when she stops. It makes you vulnerable to a fall."

Rosamund complied and rode Ingénue around the exhibit corral again, just as she'd done for the past hour.

Colin was quite in the habit of watching from the wings of a performance. But this time it felt different. The stakes were higher. If Rose failed, then he did too. The season was but a few short months away, and he hadn't time to go back out on the recruitment road. What's more, he didn't want to.

He needed to be right this time.

Something told Colin this bareback riding pair was the answer to managing the inexplicable problem of Bella Rossi. With every turn he watched them, kicking up dust with the clip-clop of hooves.

Come on, Rose, Colin muttered under his breath, willing her to show the same flicker of brilliance he'd witnessed at the fields of Easling Park. *Show me I'm right about you . . .*

He'd remembered to bring riding clothes, and Rosamund had changed quickly, donning the shirt and men's canvas trousers in an empty stall away from the men. She'd wound her hair in a thick braid that trailed over her shoulder now, swinging about and gleaming in the bright sun with each turn made by horse and rider.

Colin had to remind himself that this vision of the performer before him—her grit and hard work as well as the sheer beauty Rose didn't know she possessed—was business and nothing more. He was the talent scout on the road, the man who would have to mold her rough talent into that of a polished star. Somewhere deep down, he was certain Rose's will was perfectly crafted for it. He only hoped she could see it in herself.

Colin looked away for a breath. Refocusing his thoughts, lest they drift.

He kicked at a stray rock in his path.

Keep your mind on the show, Keary . . .

"That's enough," Owen shouted, drawing Colin's attention back.

Owen raised up a hand and Rosamund brought Ingénue to stop in front of him. She tugged wisps of hair behind her ears and swept the back of her hand across the beads of perspiration on her brow. Though the Florida sun could bear down on the corral like the inside of an oven, she didn't complain or comment.

She sat quietly, waiting. Absently running her fingertips over her horse's mane.

"Any experience with Roman riding?" Owen asked.

"I don't know," she said, drawing in deep breaths of air. "What is it?"

"Riding atop a pair of horses, with one foot on each horse."

She shook her head. "It's only ever been Ingénue and I, riding together."

"Aerobatics training?"

Rosamund shook her head again. "Not formally. I've done vaulting, mostly."

Owen continued, moving from one question to the next without skipping a beat.

"Vaulting. Good. The dance on horseback will be useful. Can you ride Cossack?"

She paused. After an entire training session where they'd not made eye contact, she finally looked to Colin across the corral.

He read uncertainty in her eyes, their cool green questioning him without the necessity of words.

"I've done some Cossack riding . . . ," she said.

Colin hopped up from his perch against the rail. He slid his watch into his pants pocket and strolled in their direction.

"She's being modest," he countered. "I saw Rose perform a death drag at a fair in England."

Owen's face lit up. "Did she now?"

Colin nodded.

"So you can ride with a saddle and without?" Owen asked.

Rose nodded, and a tiny ghost of a smile eased onto the trainer's lips. "Good. Very good."

"And it's more than just riding. She does backsprings. Flying leaps. And she stood up midcanter, flipping off Ingénue's back in front of hundreds. I saw it, Owen. Rose would never tell it herself, but she did it with precision and not an ounce of fear. She landed with her feet planted in that field and—"

Colin stopped a few steps away from her side, connecting his eyes with hers. Wanting her to see the pride in them. Refusing to show he'd had the smallest doubt.

"She won over the entire crowd."

Owen folded his arms across his chest. "Even you?"

Colin nodded. "Especially me."

"But riding in the ring is very different from doing it in a field," she whispered, wary of the praise.

Her caution was well placed. He knew that. But Colin couldn't look into the eyes of this English beauty who'd come so far, at his urging, leaving her entire world behind, and allow her to doubt her own abilities now.

"Rose is a quick learner," he said. "And she's downplaying her aerobatics. She can do a forward somersault on the horse's back, Owen," he said, then crossed his arms across his chest and grinned for good measure. "From her *knees*."

Colin was all too proud to put emphasis on the last word, at which Owen's face broke into an unrestrained smile.

Owen turned to Rose. "Is this true?"

"On our better days," she answered, a slight tinge of pink painting her cheeks in a telltale blush. "But I didn't know it was that special."

"Special?" Owen scoffed, looking at her over the glasses now tipped at the end of his nose. "From a kneeling position? Why, I haven't seen anyone else perform that trick in the ring since our own May Wirth debuted it in 1912. Besides, Colin knows it's a favorite of mine."

"And with all due respect to May," Colin added, sending Rose an approving glance, "Rose here is better."

"Is she?" Owen turned, shifting his attention to Ingénue.

He knelt at the horse's side, looking her over in detail. He ran a hand along her side, inspecting each leg.

"Ingénue is older than stock I usually bring in. We like to learn what a horse is good at when it's young. Its mannerisms and areas of ease with performance. It helps to know where to place it in a show."

"Rose can help with that. They've been riding together for eight years."

Owen looked up from his kneeling position. "That's quite a long time to have a partnership."

"Yes," Rosamund agreed. "My brother sent her to me months before the end of the war. We've been together ever since."

She paused then and furrowed her brow ever so slightly, as if squinting in the sun. Something melted over her features. Colin couldn't say what it was exactly. Long-forgotten memories, perhaps? Buried pain?

He fought the desire to know exactly how she felt.

Rosamund slid down from Ingénue's back. She dusted her palms on her trousers and drew in a deep breath, then offered Owen a hard-won smile. It was clear she was trying her best not to cry.

"Thank you, Mr. Thomas. I'll remember this day always."

Owen darted a glance over to Colin, giving him a scowl for good measure.

"And I will as well, Miss Easling," he said with a voice that was considerably softer than the one he'd used during the training session.

Colin stood by as she leaned in, placing her hands on either side of Ingénue's head. Rose closed her eyes. She murmured quiet words of praise against the horse's light snorts and accepted the nudging of Ingénue's nose against her palm.

She whispered one last thing to the horse before handing the reins to Colin. He took them, feeling like he'd just been punched in the gut.

"You can take her," she whispered. "With my compliments."

Rose walked away, head held high. She trekked through the field in her riding boots, then disappeared through the dusk-darkened stable.

"Well." Owen stood and shook his head, easing the reins from Colin's grip. "You want to help her?"

"I do."

"And help us too, I imagine. Because you know this show needs her."

Owen never minced words.

"Go after her, you fool."

"Right." Colin exhaled, turning in pursuit.

What could he say?

Rose couldn't have known his intentions, but she'd been recruited from the beginning. The task now was to convince her that she wanted to stay.

Colin trotted through the stable and found her standing alone. He slowed his thick-booted stride on instinct, surprised that the sight of her could hush the breath right out of him.

The Florida sun was setting low in the sky, painting the canvas off in the distance in a mass of oranges and soft pinks, as if a basketful of peaches had been tossed onto the clouds. It framed her soft silhouette. Tiny wisps of hair had pulled loose from her braid to flow against the breeze, moving in a lazy dance around her neck.

Colin cleared his throat, announcing that he'd followed behind.

He walked up to her side and she half turned, hiding the full show of her emotions from him.

"Are you okay?"

Rosamund nodded, hastily wiping under her eyes with the palms of her hands. He pulled a handkerchief from his pocket and offered it to her.

"That was brave back there."

"I'm sorry," she whispered, taking the delicate cloth and dabbing at the corners of her eyes. "It's been weeks building up to the moment . . . I was just overwhelmed that it's now staring me in the face. I didn't expect this would be so difficult."

"But it doesn't have to be."

"Colin, I'm going home soon. What could make that easy? I'm leaving my heart behind with her."

She turned to look him in the eyes, staring back with an earnestness that cinched something in the confines of his chest. "She's yours now," she said, shaking her head. "And I can't stay."

"Why not? There's a solution to every problem. This is one."

"I have responsibilities, Colin. I gave my word that I'd see this through, but only long enough for my horse to be settled. You don't know what you're asking."

Colin stopped her from spinning away with a gentle touch of fingertips to her elbow.

"I know exactly what I'm asking. And this is no spur-of-the-moment impulse. You did well back there." Colin spoke in his take-charge manner, though he looked down and rested his gaze on her much longer than he'd intended. "Just as I knew you would. And Owen's a man of few words, but he saw what I did. You should take it as a compliment that one of the best trainers in the world sees your great talent."

"You think I have talent?"

"Yes. I do," he whispered on a chuckle that was impossible to hide. "More than you know. And that's why yours is so rare. Even you don't know how good you are. You honestly don't think I'm going to let that go without a fight, do you? What self-respecting circus boss could live with himself after that?"

Rosamund looked like she'd been holding her breath until that instant. She searched his face, looking for an explanation that would make things easier.

"So you never wanted Ingénue?"

"Of course I did. I came to Easling Park to buy an Arabian. I never bargained on finding a performer—not hidden on a nobleman's country estate. You didn't know it, but you've been recruited from the first moment I saw you perform in Linton."

"Then you brought me here under false pretenses."

"You told me in so many words that you'd follow Ingénue anyway. I was just making sure you got here safely. And if you're worried about marrying to save your family's legacy, you don't have to be. You'll make enough money to send home if you'd like. You're quite capable of making up your own mind, Rose. And I'm ready to make you an offer."

"What offer?"

"I want to contract you for the Ringling Brothers' show."

Rosamund nodded slowly. "You do." Her look said she'd been expecting him to say that, but she couldn't possibly entertain the thought of staying.

"I just told you how good you are, Rose." Colin sighed, staring out over the fall of dusk on the fields where the future lodgings would stand. "There's more to it than I can go into right now. But at present, May Wirth is our bareback riding act, and she's leaving the show after this season. We're looking for a new bareback riding duo. We need someone young. A fresh face with talent. Beauty. Brains. Fearlessness. All of those things you have with Ingénue, whether you know it or not, and the crowds will love you for it."

The wind seemed to shift all around them, as if change was looming on the words he'd said.

Colin winced. He hadn't intended to include "beauty" in the list.

"How long is this contract?"

"One year," he said, turning back to her, studying her face for a reaction.

She exhaled low. "A year?"

"To start, yes. But perform well, and you'll be offered more."

Rosamund shook her head, trying to make sense of what he'd offered. "A year . . . I can't make a decision like this right now. It's too much to leave my home and commit to a year away in the same breath. May I have some time to think it over?"

Colin smiled, shoving his hands in his pockets. "That's what I told Owen you'd say."

"You did?"

He nodded. "Yeah. Rose Easling knows her own mind. But

she's also smart enough to decide what it is she wants, and when. So I'll wait. And in the meantime, you get to ride. All you want."

He knew the thought of staying on for a few more weeks—or even months—just to ride Ingénue was something Rose couldn't pass up. Instead of languishing in a stuffy manor, breathing the fresh Florida air for a little while longer . . . The thought had to pump fresh blood into her veins.

"So Ingénue and I stay here, training with Owen?"

"That's right. You need to learn to ride in a ring."

"And for how long?"

"Well, you said you wanted to spend Christmas with your aunt in New York, then go back to England in the spring. Why not give it time—make your decision by Christmas?"

It sounded reasonable enough.

Rosamund accepted with a smile. "By Christmas it is," she said, and extended her hand to shake his.

He pulled his hands from his pockets, but hesitated, falling just short of accepting her open palm. If she'd consent to stay, it had to be for the right reasons.

"Satisfy me on one thing more, Rose, and we have a deal."

"Of course. What?"

"You whispered something to Ingénue before you came back out here. What was it you said to her?"

Rosamund smiled, tipping her shoulders in a light shrug.

She leaned forward and shook hands with him, whispering, "Only what I'd want someone to say to me—I told her to have fun."

CHAPTER 11

1926

SARASOTA, FLORIDA

Evening was Rosamund's favorite time of day.

The sun would set over the bay, creating millions of tiny diamond flashes across the water. The pace of living would wind down. There'd be no more riding. No backbreaking training or worrying about tomorrow once the sun had set low in the sky.

It was her time to be still.

She sat on the dock in front of the Ringlings' yellow farmhouse-style cottage in which she'd been staying, hanging her legs over the side, swinging her bare feet in the breeze, watching fish make their intermittent jumps to pick off mayflies hovering over the water.

As soon as the training day was done, she'd come back to the cottage still wearing riding trousers and her white blouse with a wide sailor's collar. She wrapped her favorite plum, thick-weave sweater round her shoulders and went to her favorite evening spot by the water.

The telegram Rosamund had received that day she'd kept hidden from Owen's notice. She folded it gently and now held it between her palms.

The sounds of the day were all she heard, until an engine's

sputter turned her attention to the drive in front of the house. A Model T had come to a stop, and a gentleman hopped out and went up the cottage's front steps.

He wore gray trousers, a white shirt, and a jacket draped over one arm. Hat and tie, if he had such, had been abandoned along the way. The weight on Rosamund's shoulders lightened when she saw the trademark mop of dark hair, wind-tousled as it always seemed to be.

"Colin," she shouted and waved, drawing his attention to the dock.

He turned from the porch and tossed his jacket through the open window of the car, then trotted in her direction.

A slow smile built on his face as he drew near. "Owen said you'd gone back to the cottage early today."

She wrapped the sweater tighter around her middle and breathed deep. "Ingénue and I were both tired. So I came back and have been out here enjoying the view."

Colin wrinkled his nose, whether from the sunlight bouncing back in his eyes or because he didn't fully believe her, she couldn't know. He nodded and sat down, hanging his legs over the edge of the dock alongside her.

"Are you sure you wouldn't rather stay at the Ringling Hotel downtown? Or in one of their other properties? They have a bigger home on South Washington Drive."

Rosamund shook her head. "I like it here. By the water. It's so nice that the Ringlings have allowed me to stay in the cottage. I don't mind that it's small at all. It's a change from what I'm used to, and I find that somehow it suits me."

He looked out over the water. Listening. Nodding as she talked.

The setting sun edged his profile in soft light, and Rosamund tried not to think of how she'd missed him during the last couple of weeks.

She tore her eyes away, landing on polite conversation instead. "Did you have a good trip?"

"I think so. We managed to get a few things worked out for the show, so I'm glad about that. But the weather was about as good as can be expected for Connecticut in November." He grinned through a mock shiver. "Bridgeport can be unforgiving at this time of year. And to be stuck in it for three weeks. I couldn't wait to get back here to you."

Rosamund's gaze fluttered to his.

"Or to this—you know," he added, rubbing a hand to his neck. He tilted his head to the bay. "I'm just sorry I had to leave you alone so soon after you got here. But at least it was here in Florida. It's really beautiful this time of year, isn't it?"

"I can't say that I know what it's like the rest of the year, but I think I'm ready to find out."

Colin turned to her, his brow furrowed in question. The shadow of a hopeful smile seemed close by. "You've already made your decision then?"

Rosamund nodded. "I received a telegram today. From Easling Park." She stared down into the depths of the water beneath their feet. "It was quite enough to help me make up my mind."

"I see," he offered, leaning in ever so slightly. "Not bad news, I hope."

Rosamund handed him the telegram without looking up. She could hear the crease of the paper when he'd unfolded it, and the deep sigh when he'd obviously read what it said.

"He wasted no time, did he?" Colin slapped the paper against his leg. "Golly, I'm sorry."

"It's for the best, but it would've been nice to have made the decision myself."

Embarrassment prevented her from looking him in the eye. She chose the easier option of gazing out across the bay.

"But I think you did, Rose, when you got on the train at King's Cross. There was no going back after that first leap of faith. Remember that you chose to step on that train, and your life is your own from here on out."

"I never thought I'd be jilted before I even made it to the altar. But I suppose it's too much to marry a woman who's run off to the circus. How would that work in an English drawing room? It sounds odd even when I say it aloud, and I'm the one living it."

Colin squinted, shielding his eyes from the sun setting low in front of them.

"Well, forget the drawing rooms. And despicable former fiancés. You'll have men lining up to court you in every town on the map from now on. You sure you're ready for that?"

The quip made her smile, especially when she looked up and saw the twinkle in his eye.

Rosamund wasn't sure how, but they'd eased into a friendship without looking. Colin had become an unexpected source of stability and comfort. She could take teasing, even at a moment like this, if it came from him.

"You know, I did tell Bella you were innocent that day we boarded the train at King's Cross. But it wasn't meant to be an insult."

She smiled, having known that already.

"I had a bit of Italian in my tutorials as a girl." Rosamund rolled her eyes. "Enough to understand what she'd said and try not to take offense at it. It's still not the most flattering thing a girl can think to be called, though."

"I know. And I'll do everything I can to ensure things go smoothly when you meet up with Bella and the rest of the performers. We'll ease you in. That's a promise, all right?"

"Okay," she said, exhaling long and low. "So what now?"

"The show must go on. And we know you'll be a part of it.

Welcome to the family—" He smiled, then handed the telegram back to her. "Officially this time."

Rosamund's fingers brushed against his, a light touch of skin that startled her. She fumbled the telegram, almost dropped it, then shoved it down into the pocket of her sweater.

"And to the newest member of the family, I come bearing gifts."

"Gifts?"

"It's Christmas, isn't it?"

"Not for weeks it's not." She shook her head, watching as he hopped up and jogged back to the car. From it he pulled two long poles and a can, a look of victory on his face.

He walked back in her direction with the gear. "Then we're celebrating early. All the way from Connecticut."

Rosamund jumped to her feet, almost dancing at the thought of doing something as thrilling—and normal—as fishing on the bay. Never in a million years would her mother have allowed something so earthy and unrefined. She'd have been shocked out of her very fancy shoes to see her daughter standing on a dock now, barefoot, gloveless, and happy, exclaiming over the gift of a split cane rod and a can of wiggling worms.

"Ever fished before?" Colin asked.

"Hendrick used to, but I never did." She shook her head and bit her bottom lip, thinking it impossible to keep the smile from her face now.

Not when he'd brought her something so perfect.

"Then you're in for a treat. And after I teach you how to put a worm on a hook, Lady Easling, I've got another surprise for you. One I think you'll enjoy even more."

Rosamund cocked an eyebrow, feeling altogether playful now instead of heart-sore. "What could be better than this? High-wire walking?"

"Nope. Better." He tossed an easy grin her way. "Dancing."

"Dancing where? On the dock?"

He leaned down until his head was level with hers, then pointed out across the bay. "Right there. At the Cà d'Zan."

"You can't be serious. I thought performers didn't visit the Ringlings' home."

"Not usually, no. Family. Friends, yes. And now you're both. I told Mable about you, and she wants to meet you. They're planning a holiday party—the grandest this town's likely ever seen. All to open the mansion to visitors. With yachts coming up along the bay. Music and dancing. You'll be used to it, I'm sure, with the parties your mother gives."

"It sounds clever—but at the Cà d'Zan? Sarasota's a world away from Yorkshire and Easling Park. How do you even know I'll fit in?"

"You could never fit in, Rose. You were made to stand out."

She wasn't given time to consider a response. A car lumbered down the short drive to the cottage, its driver blowing the horn.

"Is there a Mr. Keary here?" he shouted. "Colin Keary?"

"Stay here," he whispered, handing her his fishing rod and placing the can of worms on the dock.

"I'm Keary," he shouted back through cupped hands.

"You're needed, sir. Right now."

Colin looked back to Rosamund.

He pursed his lips. Furrowed his brow in a manner that suggested his thoughts had transitioned from lighthearted fishing and dancing to everything related to business in one fell swoop.

"What's happened?" he called back.

"Mr. Charlie, sir. He's dead."

Rosamund's breath escaped her at the man's words. She reached out on instinct, touching her fingertips to Colin's forearm.

He didn't shrink back from the contact. Colin stood still for a long moment, then whispered a simple, "Excuse me, Rose."

Colin walked the length of the pier, rubbing a hand to the back of his neck all the way up to the car. It was painful to watch, enough that Rosamund laid the fishing rods on the dock, thinking to edge forward.

Maybe go to him.

To comfort him somehow.

She watched as he spoke with the man, saying little himself, only nodding here and there.

If Colin had traveled with the circus as long as she imagined he had, this loss would hit him very hard. No doubt Charles Ringling was a friend and mentor. They'd traveled from town to town all over the country for years. Managing the lives of animals and performers everywhere they went. And as Colin had never mentioned a family of his own, she suspected the Ringlings were the closest thing he had to it.

Now that delicate world had shattered; Mr. Charlie was gone.

"Rose—I'm sorry," he called out to her. "I have to go. But I'll come back for you as soon as I can."

Rosamund nodded understanding, even as he hopped in the car with the gentleman and they sped down the road.

And just like that, she was left alone again.

Even the sun ducked behind the horizon, leaving reaching streaks of orange and ink-blue to paint the sky. The fish had calmed. The wind stilled. As if nature itself knew an ill wind had just passed over them all.

She looked down, watching the water again. This time not feeling so afraid.

It felt easy to take the telegram from her pocket and, without an ounce of regret, allow it to slip from her fingertips.

The telegram floated down to kiss the water of the bay. Drifting out from where she stood. Leaving her behind.

No need to watch it, she thought.

Rosamund walked back up to the cottage, keenly feeling the filter of dusk that had fallen over the bay. And all thoughts of fishing and dancing—and even of a home and former fiancé very far away—were forgotten.

So was the Western Union telegram that read: LORD OLIVER BRENTWOOD, VISCOUNT SPENCER, MARRIED TO LONDON HEIRESS LADY VICTORIA NORTHAM. NO NEED TO RETURN.

Rosamund was ready to let go.

For more reasons than one, everything was about to change. And the great John Ringling was now the last of the Ringling Brothers, and she was to perform in the Circus King's show.

CHAPTER 12

1905
TRENTON, NEW JERSEY

If Mable were to rank the experience, her afternoon at the Ringling Brothers' circus was more amazing than any visit to the Chicago World's Fair. Here, in a once lonely field outside Trenton, was a makeshift world within a world, one in which the inhabitants of a rural community could step through the gates into a collection of wonders the likes of which only J. M. Barrie could have dreamt up, for one of his Neverland plays.

A rainbow of balloons pointed to the sky around sundry wagonettes. The singsong melody of chiming bells filled the air, mingling with children's delighted laughter. These were echoed by the errant roars and deep-chested grunts of exotic animals that weren't far off. Dazzling sequined costumes caught the sunlight, flashing as performers passed by. Carnival game masters shouted through the crowd, inviting guests to stop in and show their strength at the high-striker game or their skill in toppling a tower of milk bottles in a single throw.

This was her introduction to John's world—a remarkable oddity of sights and sounds, tinged with the sweet smells of candied apples and the molasses popcorn Sally would have favored. Tents with intricately painted façades lined the field path along which they now walked, drawing curious minds into their innermost canvas rooms with promise of the mysterious and strange.

"Have your eye on something?" John asked. She was gazing at the image of a snake-charmer painted in a leafy-green jungle vignette spanning the length of a nearby façade.

Mable was intrigued, but not by the sideshow oddities. Not primarily, anyway.

"I might." She laughed. "But not here. I want to see the gears turning, Mr. Ringling. Show me how it all works."

The shadow of a grin spread on his lips and he nodded, pointing the way with his cane.

They waltzed in the autumn sun as he granted her wish, leading them to the behind-the-scenes action of the back lot. There Mable could ask questions and see every detail of the performers and animals in the show, including clowns without makeup and the unglamorous cleaning up after animals on the lot.

The Midway was full of delights—games, treats, and a sideshow that held some interest—but all that paled in comparison to the cogs and gears that kept running behind the Big Top's drawn curtain. Mable much preferred watching the making of fun, in all of its raw nature, versus watching the fun itself.

They passed a considerable wagon—the largest she'd seen yet—vivid in red, yellow, and white paint, with gilded lion engravings peeking out from the base. It was painstakingly detailed, with carvings all around an inner, iron-barred cage. There were rich filigree designs and painted discs that covered the spokes on the wheels.

"This one is for the lions," she guessed, looking up to see John's reaction. "Yes?"

"How did you know that?"

She pointed to the lion engravings. "Gives it away every time, Mr. Ringling."

"And that one?"

Mable shook her head. "Easy. Rhinoceros." She pointed out the carved designs of turban-wearing hunters and the engraving of a large rhino head bursting through grasses shining out from the edge of the iron bars.

A canvas curtain shielded the animal inside.

"Would you like to see her?"

Mable laughed. What an oddity. He talked about rare animals as one would a member of the family. "Her?"

He nodded. "Yes. Mary is her name. She was our first rhino. We acquired her just two years ago. Can you believe it—all 4,800 of her pounds are supported by that wagon."

"I think we should leave her in peace, poor Mary. No doubt she's got a long evening of delighting patrons in the menagerie tent. She'll need her rest."

"Too right. But our animals are treated well. She's not overworked, I assure you. But since you prefer to judge matters for yourself, I'll take you to the menagerie. Try to prove me wrong if you'd like."

"Now there's an idea." She found herself smiling. Too much. Even biting the edge of her bottom lip like a schoolgirl every moment or so. The sights were too much. Too exhilarating. And she had to admit—it was wonderful to see it all with him. "But I would like to see the birds if we could. I've always had a fondness for them and have yet to see any truly unusual ones."

"We'll look at anything you wish to see. We also have zebras. Kangaroos. Royal Bengal tigers, which are a favorite among the circus guests. And of course, Prince—our lion. I doubt Noah himself had finer stock. Though I must confess, we didn't wish to manage such big animals—the ones that carry a burden of liability with them."

"Perhaps not, but Noah certainly had more," she teased.

"All right, Mable Burton. If you're so clever, what about that wagon over there? With the canvas covering the bars. There are no engravings to give it away. Who lives in there?"

"If there are holes in the roof—which I cannot see myself—the giraffes. If not, I'd say you are hiding a hippopotamus. The more exotic the animal, the closer you watch it, and the more *we* pay for the pleasure."

"Very astute," he noted, tipping his hat to her. "I bow to your knowledge of the game."

"I admit—I read it in an advertisement. I saw an additional charge to see those animals. You keep them out of the parade because of their rarer nature."

"I am glad to know someone reads the advertisements we spend so much money on," said the man approaching them. He was tall in stature, with a smart suit, dark hair, and matching thick mustache. There was no doubt about it. He must be one of John's brothers.

He smiled at Mable. "It makes smart business sense, doesn't it? Our brother Al's idea. But since I'm charged with the army of advertisements for our promotion, I'm mighty glad it's paying off with our customer base."

"She's not a customer today, Charles. This is Mable Burton." John paused. "She's my guest."

A look of understanding passed between the brothers, though Mable wasn't sure what it meant.

"You must be a good friend indeed, Miss Burton. John seldom takes walks through the back lot—at least not for leisure. And I don't believe he's brought one of his friends home to meet us yet. This really is a pleasure."

Had she heard him correctly? She was the first girl he'd brought home? Even if "home" was most unconventional, with thousands of workers and guests, and animals who'd eat them for lunch, it still spoke volumes that he'd invited her into the thick of it.

"Thank you," she replied, glancing at John out of the corner of her eye.

He'd grown quiet, a measure of retreat evident on his face. Perhaps there was some sibling rivalry behind the show. Or perhaps not. John was, by his own admission, careful with all of his relationships.

"Well, I'm off." Charles lifted a large leather case in his free hand. "I play the horn once or twice a season, and today's the day." He nodded in farewell. "Make sure my brother here finds you the best seat in the house, Miss Burton. The big show's about to begin."

THEY DID HAVE PERFECT SEATS.

Mable chose them.

John had begun to lead them to the bleacher seats near the front, to really feel the action in the ring. But when Mable clamped eyes on the scores of children, all with such looks of enchantment covering their faces, sitting on straw bales along the outside of the performance rings, she knew exactly where they should sit.

Mable edged her way down the bleachers to the children, waving for John to follow.

She moved ahead and found an open seat, then planted herself right in the midst of a Wonderland of the Ringling family's making. She sat on a straw bale, surrounded by squeals of delight and little pairs of eyes that brimmed with excitement under the immense canvas sky.

Mable chatted with the children around her.

They shared their peanuts with her, calling her a nice lady. They munched on popcorn and spun sugar candy in a bevy of rainbow colors. A little boy spilled chocolate ice cream on the hem of her dress.

She didn't blink an eyelash, for all of it proved magical. Even the ice cream.

The music began—deep, booming tones of brass playing together, lively tunes to christen the show. And then the ring-master stepped out, in a top hat and bright red coat that made him look like the captain of a great ship. He announced the acts as they came, but Mable didn't hear a thing but the wonder of childhood.

Laughter at the antics of the clowns.

Oohs and *aahs* at the feats of the aerial acrobats.

Riotous giggles when they watched the dancing bears . . .

"Remember them?" John leaned in, whispering in her ear.

She'd forgotten he was there. In truth, Mable had been lost for some time. Happily so, but lost.

"Dancing bears?"

"You remember," he said, pointing to the furry animals. "At the Exposition? You said dancing bears were fun. Not scary or men-acing. Just fun. I thought we could use some of that in our show."

A flood of recollection washed over her. It was something she'd said and only vaguely remembered. But not John. He'd made it a matter of remembrance and put action to it.

"How did you . . ."

"How did I remember?" He smirked, a gesture she thought not commonplace for him. "I remember everything you say, Mable."

"You do. Why?"

"You have good ideas. You could be very helpful around here. You know, keep us men in line. Challenge us into new ways of thinking."

She nodded, feeling her heart sink a little.

The children still laughed all around them, oblivious to the heavy words of adults in their midst. But she wondered why he'd complimented her by remembering such a nominal detail, then brushed over it so nonchalantly.

"John Ringling, I have a job. I'm not sure I'll be available to come share ideas with you and your brothers. Besides, you seem to be doing quite well without my help."

"Mm-hmm," he said, nodding. "Yet you've come all this way at my invitation."

"It's been breathtaking to see everything today, but I really couldn't—"

"Then it's settled. We must find you a new job that's more suited to your talents."

The children laughed, well timed to his comment, though they were reacting to the pratfall of a clown in the ring.

"A job?"

It can't be why he's asked me here . . .

"Yes. A job, of sorts. One I hope you'll consider."

She felt all of the excitement deflate out of the moment.

They'd shared dinners. Seaside walks on the boardwalk in Atlantic City. John had even agreed to meet Sally, and had gone with Mable when she'd sought to help her still sick friend get a rare day out of a sanitarium. He'd brought a car so they could ride around, letting the wind hit her face so she could breathe in the salty sea air.

All of it had been pointing to something, hadn't it?

Love, Mable had hoped, for she so enjoyed her months with him. John's quiet way really was a compliment to her bustle and brash.

But now . . . a job.

That was his offer.

Mable sighed into her response. "While I'm flattered, I like the job I have. I told you—I've always wanted to live by the sea. I get to do that in Atlantic City. There's no job here that could truly satisfy me more than that."

"Yes. I thought that might be your answer," he countered softly.

"And that's why it must be you, Mable. Because you're genuine. You're not after fortune or notoriety. You don't ask for a thing in return. You're just . . . *you*. And the only job you could fill is in my heart."

She turned to him.

Not sure she could have heard him correctly.

Cymbals clanged somewhere off behind, followed by the roar of applause from the crowd. The circus band cued up for a riotous melody. Something marvelous must have been happening in the ring, but she didn't see it.

"I think I'm the one who should be applying for a job with you, Mable Burton." He paused, looked out over the activity in the circus rings, then turned back to her with a gleaming smile. "Marry me? Let me tag along on your adventures?"

Her smile came easy.

It was a moment Mable never expected. One she'd not forget. With the Circus Kings' exhibition of wonder all around and the children presiding in their court, Mable's world changed forever.

She nodded, tears in her eyes, agreeing to become a circus queen.

CHAPTER 13

1926

SARASOTA, FLORIDA

Wind agitated the waters of the bay, though Rosamund couldn't feel a victim of its onslaught. Not while standing on the upper deck of the Ringlings' massive yacht, the *Zalophus*. It cut through the water toward the Ringlings' new home with ease, moving along as if waltzing on dry ground.

The party to open the newly christened Cà d'Zan and celebrate John and Mable Ringling's twenty-first anniversary hadn't been canceled in the wake of Charles Ringling's death, though it was scaled back to a much smaller affair.

Rosamund wore her black chiffon and pink-gold gown, the one with a delicate scalloped hemline and intricate botanical-themed beading along its front and back panels. She'd wound her hair back in a bevy of twists at her nape, framing the sides with finger waves and a simple peacock plume band tipped low on her brow. Gone were the diamond-encrusted headbands and elaborate gowns her mother had always insisted she wear for a big event. Her dress and trinkets were of nominal value—ones she'd bought for herself, with money she'd earned in signing a contract to appear in the Ringling Brothers' 1927 circus season.

For that, Rosamund felt dressed as a queen.

Colin stood by her side, clad in a three-piece suit of very distinguished black pinstripe. Like the family, he wore a black armband on his left arm, indicating they were still in mourning. And as was customary for Colin, he hadn't bothered to dress in white-tie formal. He seemed at ease no matter the setting and didn't waver as he stood by, pointing out the party guests from a small group tippling cocktails by the yacht rail.

"The one on the left is William Pogany. Willy, he's called. And the gentleman with him is a business acquaintance—an animator from California. I believe his name is Walt." Colin craned his neck just a bit to see past a few guests who had stepped into their path. "Willy's an artist too, so I suppose that's how they know each other. He designs sets for an opera company in New York."

"The Metropolitan Opera," Rosamund breathed out.

Colin crinkled his brow. "You don't know him, do you?"

Rosamund gave him a look that suggested he was the innocent one for a change.

"I know *of* him. My mother's talents in rearing cultured children are quite legendary, I'm afraid. She sought to ensure we knew all of the *important* things." She sent him a coy grin. "Mr. Pogany is a friend of the Ringlings?"

Colin leaned against the yacht rail, watching her with keen interest. "You seem impressed."

"We have a copy of *The Welsh Fairy Book* in the library at Easling Park. It was a favorite of mine as a girl. And that gentleman illustrated every picture. I can't believe he's standing there, right in front of me." Her lips melted into a smile. "Is it like this all the time here?"

Colin tipped his shoulders in a shrug. "I'd assume so. The mayor of New York is a frequent guest at parties. As are the Ringlings' friends and business partners," he added.

"But not performers."

"Not as a rule, no." He paused, shifting his stance to look at her more pointedly. "But they're just people, Rose. Like you and me. Remember that, and no matter who you meet in this circus world will be a friend instead of a celebrity."

"I hadn't thought of that."

"Well, time to start. Rosamund Easling will be looked at the way you're looking on Mr. Pogany now. But you're probably used to a bit of that, aren't you? As an earl's daughter?"

"I suppose. But not to the extent you're suggesting."

"It can't be that different." He nudged her side ever so slightly. "Come on. I'll introduce you to him if you want."

It was the first time Rosamund had to equate her new world as more than just bareback riding. There was an entire public image of her that had yet to be born. One that Colin Keary and the Ringlings would fashion for her.

Colin introduced her to Mr. Pogany and then to others, including an entertainer named Flo Ziegfeld and his wife, Billie. She had bouncy brunette hair and a strikingly sweet, high-pitched voice, displaying both in animated fashion as she exclaimed over the floral beading on Rosamund's gown.

And on it went. The circus boss presented their new talent, Lady Rosamund Easling, to the crowd of guests. She smiled and greeted them, but worried that she'd have trouble keeping their names straight. By the time they were approaching the shore, Rosamund's head was swimming with countless names and faces.

What would it be like when she finally met the Ringlings?

The buildup was adding a thick layer of anxiety to her middle.

Colin stood by her side, pointing out a bright light set much higher than the other flickering lights on the shore. It illuminated a stucco tower standing tall and distinguished in the distance.

"Is that it?"

He nodded. "Yes. That's the Cà d'Zan."

The moment proved as magical to Rosamund as if she'd been brought to a real Venetian tower along the Grand Canal.

Colin offered her his arm and she accepted it, anchored at his side as she took her first steps on the mezzanine. Her heels clicked against the intricate design, pieced in herringbone rows of pink, black, gray, and white marble to form an exquisite outdoor dance floor.

Sarasota in December was vastly different from Yorkshire. Here the women wore dresses of airy gauze fabrics and light, beaded designs without suffering ill effects of the elements. Rosamund passed groups of them in dresses of liquid gold, creamy ivory, and seafoam green, with multiple layers of silk and beaded overlays, all twinkling in the glow of twilight. They danced about with elegantly dressed gentlemen, enlivening the outdoor ballroom under a rich canopy of stars.

Money and privilege Rosamund had seen before. It was the manner of her entire life at Easling Park. But here? She felt like turning circles the instant she stepped on the mezzanine.

"Well?" Colin asked.

"It's . . ."

Freeing, she wanted to say. *So different from the life I've led up to now.*

A cascade of colored glass windows ran the length of the mansion's west façade, with tall arched doors that had been spread wide, allowing the breezes of the bay to mingle with plush red curtains on their borders.

"It's enchanting."

Colin led her through the kaleidoscope doors to a two-story central room with gleaming marble floors and a lofty, gouache-painted cypress ceiling. Rosamund wasn't surprised by the sounds of chatting guests or the lilting notes of a piano, but she hadn't expected the sound of chirping birds echoing off the tall ceiling.

"Are there birds in the great hall?" She looked up, scanning the second-story balcony for the source of the sounds.

"It would be called a great hall if you were back in England. But here this is the court," Colin said. "It's a common space in Italian homes. And the birds you're looking for are finches caged in the foyer. There's even a German-speaking African gray they keep in the kitchen."

"Truly?"

Colin nodded, humor dancing in his eyes.

Rosamund could see the fondness Colin had for the Ringlings—for both their home and their way of life. It made her smile to see lightness come alive in him.

"The Ringlings always have animals in the house. Their dogs—miniature pinschers and German shepherds—are given freedom to roam the first floor. They even have two chimpanzees and a gorilla right here on the grounds."

Rosamund glanced around them, thinking of the splendor of the animals boasted by the Ringling Brothers' show. She could only hope nothing too exotic—with big teeth or sharp claws—would come bounding around a corner to greet them.

"Don't worry, you're safe," he added, reading her thoughts. "They don't roam the house during parties."

She believed him, but made a mental note of the nearest exits just in case. She wasn't sure what to expect next, with the oddities of the circus world blooming all around her.

Colin eased a hand under her elbow to lead her deeper into the court. "Come on. She'll want to meet you."

A mansion-size estate Rosamund had lived in before, so

affluence wasn't a shock. But the Cà d'Zan was about as close to touching a dream world as one could get. Colin was right: it was like nothing she'd ever seen.

The interior was meticulous in its design, boasting traditional elements of gilding and fine art partnered alongside playful designs of a Masonic pavement floor in black-and-white-checked marble and hand-painted botanical designs on a lofty two-storied ceiling of wood and colored-glass panes.

Everything was new, yet so full of the hints of history. Each corner seemed dusted in elegance, even down to the painted baseboards and gilded sconces. The wonderful contradiction of whimsy and lavishness gave the new home something of an old soul. And in the center of it all, a woman stood—stunning. Drawing attention, though she hadn't any need to demand it.

She was nearly as tall as Colin and dressed from head to toe in yards of elegant black satin, the drop waist of her gown gathered in a front seam with an eye-catching diamond buckle. She laughed easily, having found humor in something one of her guests said, easing her deep red lips into a generous smile. They were the same hue as the embroidered crepe shawl that draped her shoulders.

Clearly, this was the enigmatic Mable Ringling, for she owned the spot in which she stood.

"Mable," Colin greeted her, smiling widely as they approached. He welcomed her embrace and pressed a light kiss to her cheek.

"My dear Colin. Welcome."

She embraced his hand at the wrist, giving a gentle squeeze that Rosamund judged as an acknowledgment of the family member they'd both lost.

"Charlie would have been glad you've come. And Mr. Ringling will be as well."

Colin responded with a nod and a flat smile, wordlessly accepting her condolences and offering his own.

"We have a guest tonight." He turned to Rosamund, and she let out a breath she hadn't known she'd been holding. "Lady Rosamund Easling, this is our hostess, Mrs. Mable Ringling."

Mable's was a presence that warmed and welcomed at once. She tipped her head down in a nod, smiling generously.

"*Lady* Easling, is it?"

Rosamund nodded in return. "Yes, Mrs. Ringling. It's a pleasure to meet you."

Rosamund hadn't the presence of mind to recall what her mother's teaching would have dictated at a moment like this. To curtsy or nod didn't matter. Mable Ringling may have boasted one of the most elegant homes Rosamund had ever seen, but the welcome inside it was real. The kindness genuine. And propriety faded behind it.

"A titled young lady in this house? What a treat. We'll have to talk, my dear. But first Colin must show you off to our guests. I'll not have you as a wallflower at our Cà d'Zan. Please enjoy yourselves. Take a turn on the dance floor too, hmm? If only to humor me."

Mable reached out to clasp her gloved hand. "Of course. Thank you, Mrs. Ringling."

Any tremble of nervousness that may have overtaken Rosamund's hand melted away with the embrace. And it wasn't the great name of Ringling or the list of distinguished guests that made the moment so meaningful. This was her first genuine welcome into the circus. It was a woman of uncommon kindness and a home with lasting heart that had been her induction. And as Colin slipped his hand in hers, any unease was kept at bay.

Colin led her to the outdoor mezzanine with the rest of the ladies, to turn circles in her whimsical new world.

THE PARTY HAD DWINDLED AFTER THE ELEVEN O'CLOCK HOUR, but the lyrical sound of Rosamund's playing on the golden Steinway drew the remaining partygoers' attention from the ballroom to the activity in the court.

Applause erupted with the final notes of her song.

Rosamund had to admit that the night had proved most enjoyable—and very much in contrast to any party she had attended before in her life. Easling Park wouldn't have seen such revelry. But here? The playful tone wasn't just in the Cà d'Zan's bones around them. It was reflected in easy smiles, contented laughter, and genuine acceptance in the eyes of the guests who'd gathered around the Ringlings' piano.

"You play exquisitely, my dear!" Billie Burke exclaimed, then turned her attention to the entry. Her gaze settled on the archway that joined the ballroom with the dimmed foyer.

Rosamund turned with her, finding Mable there. She stood silent, shrouded in the cover of the entry, watching as their small group smiled and laughed around the piano.

"Mable, come." Billie waved their hostess over. "Come. Mr. Ringling said she could play it."

"I'm pleased that he did," Mable breathed out. "And if he'd dared to say no, I'd have openly defied him and allowed it anyway." She eased into the light. "I heard it from the ballroom. Yours is a level of proficiency I've not heard in some time."

Mable walked through the heart of the court to their corner. With quiet smiles still pinned on, the group parted to make an open space for her on the side of the piano.

"Your playing reminds me of another piano's song I heard once." Mable looked as though she was recalling something sweet and personal. "It's a long-ago memory of a young girl's enchantment with a melody played in a Cincinnati tea parlor."

"A tea parlor? How lovely!" Billie leaned against the piano, cupping her chin in her hand. "Well, I asked Rosamund to play something, and she's just delighted us all. Why, I have a mind to order Flo to steal her from you. The Follies could use a talented young pianist like her. We have a show premiering next year at the New Amsterdam Theatre in New York City."

Mable's gaze flitted over to where Colin stood.

Rosamund noticed something silent pass between them. He shook his head, ever so slightly. His eyes shifted from Mable back to Rosamund's piano bench for the briefest of seconds, but she still caught it. She wondered what it was that neither had said aloud.

A smile pressed Mable's lips.

"I believe she's already spoken for, Billie. But Mr. Ringling and I are of course flattered by the compliment."

Billie threw back her head and laughed.

"I had to try, you understand. Far be it from us to steal from our friends. Why, I very nearly walked off with that Italian beauty the last time Colin brought her to a party. But lucky for you, he convinced her to stay in the Big Top. It's no surprise he could talk our Lady Rosamund here into the same delicious fate."

Billie chirped the comment with such lightheartedness, it was clear she hadn't a clue what she'd said.

Rosamund looked to Colin, feeling the misstep like a stolen secret that drew the breath out of her. He wasn't in the habit of bringing performers to any of the Ringlings' parties, or so she'd thought. But maybe it wasn't such a rare occurrence after all, especially if the guest was Bella Rossi.

Colin gave little away. He stood, blue eyes stormy, watching her from his perch across the room. It set her heart to wonder what he wasn't telling her.

Billie tapped her fingernail to the piano's top.

"Let Mable choose one, hmm? To christen this lovely home with music!"

"Yes, of course." Rosamund nodded out of her momentary stupor and managed to keep her voice steady. "Shall I play something for you, Mrs. Ringling? Something special, to celebrate your anniversary."

Rosamund studied Mable, noticing that something seemed to have genuinely touched her. There was the evidence of moisture in her eyes. She was quiet. Thoughtful, even. And taken with a sense of melancholy that didn't fit with the general gaiety of the rest of their party.

Perhaps it was the loss of Mr. Charlie. Or Billie's contrary tongue. Maybe something else entirely . . .

"Do you know 'Roses of Picardy'?"

A twinge gripped Rosamund's heart. "I do," she whispered. "It's a favorite. It reminds me of someone who was very dear to me."

"Is that so? Well, 'Roses of Picardy' it is, then. And roses are a reminder of someone who was very dear to me as well. We have something in common, Lady Rosamund."

Something twinkled in Mable's eyes, and she nodded.

Rosamund had played for her mother's parties many times, but this was different. This was the first time she'd not been ordered to play, but asked. Nudged into it by kindness and genuine affection.

She glanced toward Colin and saw him shift his stance, directing his gaze away from the party room to fall instead on the bay's dark toils outside.

Rosamund sang.

Softly in the beginning, but with bolder conviction as the notes continued on. The party stood by, fading into gold-outlined silhouettes from the warmth of the Cà d'Zan's crystal chandelier overhead.

A cool breeze swept in to envelop the audience.

The gentle gust caught up wavy locks of Rosamund's hair, releasing them to dance against her brow. It felt soft as a caress and eased the anxiety around her heart, making the circus world seem open somehow, as though she could belong in it.

Rosamund closed her eyes as she eased her fingertips down on the keys to play the song's final notes. She hesitated there, finding solace in the gentle moment.

She opened her eyes again to find that the party—Mable, Colin, even the audacious Billie—had grown quiet.

"Well. There you have it, Billie. She can command the attention of any crowd," Mable said, a satisfied air in the upward drift of her chin. "I think we can most certainly say that this English Rose is quite spoken for. She is circus now," she added, smiling in Rosamund's direction. "Through and through."

CHAPTER 14

1927
NEW YORK CITY

They arrived in New York City on a Sunday afternoon.

The wind had kicked up between the buildings on Eighth Street, sending an icy chill to blast Rosamund's face the moment Colin opened her car door. She stepped out and shivered, pulling the fur collar up tighter against the underside of her chin.

She stood on the sidewalk between Forty-Ninth and Fiftieth Streets, staring up at an enormous lit marquee announcing *Ringling Bros. and Barnum & Bailey Present: The Greatest Show on Earth.* The new Madison Square Garden had been dubbed the grandest building in the world that was dedicated purely to entertainment, and looking at the side of it now, she understood why.

"Well, this is it." Colin paid the driver and hoisted their bags in his arms. "But we'll have to keep you under lock and key so the Ziegfelds don't try to recruit you while you're here."

Rosamund rolled her eyes at him. She looked to the left and the right, seeing a large span of shop windows facing the street, but no entrance for the circus.

"So where do we go?"

"Straight in through the front doors," he said, smiling. "Like you own the place."

If it was a moment of confidence to walk through the Garden's front doors, the moments that followed had the exact opposite effect. She obeyed, but nothing could have prepared Rosamund for what she saw.

They ventured down to the lower level beneath the Exhibit Hall, past an enormous ramp on which circus wagons were being wheeled into the building. She tried to follow close behind Colin, but everything hit her at once. Outside it had been a busy New York City street in winter. But inside lived a world within a world. She realized how little Ward had managed to tell her about the circus. Or rather, how much there really was to know. It seemed she'd have an education starting from belowground up.

Everywhere she looked, men and women stopped Colin to ask questions. He answered rapidly, being both quick in decision and intentional in reply. He looked at clipboards with interest. Listened attentively as issues were posed, gave thoughtful answers to each. He even patted what looked like a baby ape as a handler carried it past. It seemed he noticed everyone and everything around him, placing equal value on all.

A loud screech pierced the air, stopping Rosamund in her tracks.

"What was that?" she mouthed, unable to get the full question out before Colin was at her side.

"Ah. Those would be the chimps," he said, letting out an exasperated sigh. "You'll get used to them. They always do that when they're agitated, and a train ride will do the trick every time."

Rosamund nodded, trying not to jump when another screech threatened to split her eardrums. She'd not even realized she'd been gripping the front of her coat until the leather of her gloves began cutting off the circulation in her fingers.

"Come on. Nothing to worry about."

She shook out her hand and quickened her steps, following behind as Colin's broad shoulders cut a path through the crowd. They moved through the underground area, past the most curious sights she'd ever seen.

Men bustled back and forth, moving wagons with animals and great metal poles that looked like giant plumbing pipes. She heard strange sounds—including what had to be the roar of a big cat somewhere in the distance, sending an errant chill throughout her body. Rolling racks of costumes whizzed by. A woman sauntered past in a gold belly-baring ensemble, carrying an armful of long, curved knives. A group of acrobats even flipped in front of their path, nearly knocking the hat from her head.

Rosamund jumped back with hand to hat just in time to avoid a collision. She had to run several steps to catch up with Colin's long strides.

They passed rows of wagons holding animals of all kinds. She walked past, trying to make out the animal in the shadows in each. One had leathery skin, bunched up in a heap in the back of the cage. A rhinoceros?

Her pulse raced.

To see such wonders . . . up close. As plain as day, as if it were commonplace to walk amongst such rare beasts.

In the next cage, a leopard. Rosamund was sure of that. But oddly enough, he wasn't alone. It was most curious to see a man sitting on a chair smack-dab in the middle of the cage, reading a book. He was using the big spotted cat as a sort of footstool, rubbing the animal's underbelly as one would a tabby cat on a rug by a cozy fire.

The man smiled at her, a large handlebar mustache tilting up at the corners of his mouth. Rosamund would have thought to return the gesture if she weren't so shocked. He didn't seem frightened at all. In fact, he'd already gone back to the book in his hands, turning one page to the next, with the cat happily toying with his leather slippers like a housecat playing with a ball of yarn.

"Rose?" Colin tipped his head for her to keep up.

She ran on ahead, her heels clipping the floor.

"Is it always like this?" she nearly shouted, drawing the attention of several ladies scooting by. They giggled and kept on their way.

He nodded.

"Somewhat. We're not always crammed indoors. And on the road is a little different. But it's controlled chaos, I assure you." Colin nodded in greeting to one of the men who'd waved from the lot. "This way. We'll get you settled in."

It wasn't until they came to a row of makeshift horse stalls that Rosamund could finally breathe. She saw Owen bent over a horse's hoof, talking as another man inspected its shoe. She hoped that somewhere in that row of fine horses was her Ingénue.

She craned her neck to see if she could find her.

"Rosamund?" Colin said, drawing her attention back.

He presented a tiny sprite of a woman with blond hair in pigtail buns set high upon her head and cheerful violet eyes. She smiled in greeting, welcoming Rosamund with genuine warmth.

"This is Annaliese. She's in the horse troop too and has a little experience under her belt, so she'll give you the lay of the land."

"*Enchantée*," Annaliese said, nodding with a little flip of the chin. She bowed into the depths of a ceremonious curtsy.

"Oh yes. And this one's French, so at least once a day she'll try to tell you that Paris is the greatest city in the world."

Annaliese looked delighted at the prospect of such a conversation.

"*Mais, oui!* It is the greatest city. I used to perform with an acrobat troop in the shadow of *la Tour Eiffel*. With flowers blooming all around. They perfume the air . . . I don't see that in Manhattan. It is too cold here for any such splendor."

Colin rolled his eyes. "It's cold in Paris too, and you know it."

Annaliese smiled back at Rosamund with a light pink flush to her cheeks and a youthful sparkle in her eyes.

Relief flooded into the confines of Rosamund's chest. It was a comfort to have found a genuinely welcoming face amongst a sea of strangers. She was ready to cling to it.

"You already know Owen. He runs things over here, and he'll make sure you have everything you need. He's got your training schedule, so make sure you check with him before you leave to go back to your hotel tonight. Okay?"

Rosamund took in a deep breath, offering him what she hoped was her bravest smile.

Colin turned to leave, then stopped short, something drawing him back. He leaned in and tipped up his hat, whispering so only she could hear. "It's a long way from Easling Park, isn't it?"

"And quiet docks in Sarasota," she agreed.

"The trick is, Rose, never show them you're afraid."

"Animals or people?"

"Both. Equally."

She nodded.

"I'll see you later?" He returned her smile, then turned to Annaliese. "Take care of this one for me?"

"*Bien sûr*, Boss," she confirmed in her sweet French accent, making Rosamund think of the colorful macaroon cookies Hendrick had once brought her from a Paris patisserie.

Annaliese was the epitome of colorful, sugar-sweet Parisian charm. She popped her heels together to stand at attention and issued a pert salute at their boss's retreating back.

Colin moved on to greet a group of performers who'd gathered in front of them. Rosamund saw a flash of the same ebony hair she'd seen from the train platform at King's Cross. She didn't need to be told who they were, but asked anyway.

"Are those the flyers?"

Annaliese looked up, wrinkling her nose when she saw them.

"*Oui*. The Rossi family. See the tall man standing behind with the graying hair and mustache? That is Marvio. Their uncle. Leader of the troop. He brought them from Tivoli some years ago. They also have two cousins who left the troop after last season. They are still stars of the show, but mostly it is Bella who draws the crowds. She is quite famous for her—how do you say it in English—*mystique*?"

Mystique. Rosamund was sure she didn't know.

A cool blonde with long, slender legs and a pair of icy blue eyes sauntered up to the group. She might have been lovely, if not for the glacial air about her.

"And she's a flyer too?"

Annaliese let out a long sigh.

"*Oui*. Frances Knight. Or Frances Rossi now, but she goes by Frankie. Her *mari* is Enzo. Just there," she whispered, pointing to a man of medium build standing off past the horse stalls. He boasted the same dark hair and Mediterranean good looks as the others. "Bella's brother. Rumor has it that Frankie's father is in prison for rum-running in Chicago, but who knows if there is any truth to that. She's one of the troop now, and they keep to themselves."

"You don't get to know a lot about the people you work with?"

Rosamund toyed with the button on her coat, thinking how little she actually knew about anyone there, including Colin. In all the months they'd known each other, he'd not once mentioned anything about having a family or a life outside of the circus.

"*Oui*, you do, especially if you're in close quarters like we shall be. But not with the Rossi family. They stick only together."

Rosamund watched as Bella turned to find Colin standing with the group. She seemed cool as ever, but greeted him by pressing a welcoming kiss to his cheek.

She doesn't seem to have trouble sticking to Colin, she thought.

"*Célèbre.* Maybe one day we will be stars too." Annaliese shrugged, a layer of longing thrown into it. "But they are today. They have a private train car and their own tents when we travel."

"We don't get our own tents?"

Annaliese shook her head.

"Not unless you count a tent full of horses. But I traveled with a riding troop from Marseilles, so it's really no different here. You do the show."

"I made Bella's acquaintance in England," Rosamund whispered, thoughts trailing off as she watched the group. Colin greeted Enzo and Marvio with steady handshakes, then hurried off somewhere, disappearing into the activity before them. "We, um . . . we traveled into New York Harbor in October. Along with Colin and Ward."

"So I have heard. Or so everyone has heard."

"Heard what?"

"You were recruited all the way from England with your Arabian in tow. And you are replacing May Wirth, *non*? You're the next big thing around here. And whether that information is from Ward's wagging tongue"—Annaliese cocked her eyebrows and offered a dimpled smile—"or from the preparations Colin made for you both, that is tantalizing. *Potins!*"

Rosamund had taken enough French to know exactly what that was: *gossip.* And by the look on Annaliese's face, it seemed Rosamund was topic number one.

"But no one even knows me, Annaliese. What could they have to gossip about?"

Annaliese shrugged her shoulders, as if the answer was easy as pie. "You're the English Rose, and you're going to be a star. That is quite enough."

Rosamund shook her head. Politely, but firmly.

Joining the show was one thing. Being told she'd be a star was something entirely different.

"But you mustn't worry about that now. We shall be sisters." Annaliese bounced, pecking a kiss to Rosamund's cheek. "We have a show to give! And you, dear, need a new costume."

"I suppose I do."

Annaliese hooked her elbow around Rosamund's. "Yes. I will introduce you to Minnie, our costume mistress. And as the way of things in the circus, the unexpected has happened. She needs to see you to take your measurements."

Annaliese had an almost sinister tilt to one eyebrow, like a petite detective ready to scope out her next suspect for a crime.

Rosamund almost laughed. "The unexpected?"

"Minnie designed a costume for you already—a lovely satin number. Satin and tulle in canary yellow. And you would have looked like *soleil* in the ring. Truly. Every bit of sunshine."

"*Would* have looked? You mean the costume . . . Something happened to it?"

Annaliese nodded. "I thought you knew," she whispered, daring to look over at Bella Rossi before continuing. "More gossip. We found it hanging in the costume wagon, cut to shreds."

CHAPTER 15

1905
HOBOKEN, NEW JERSEY

Mable had never worn a wedding dress before, and certainly not as she walked through the halls of a sanitarium, trying to angle stiff crinolines and yards of lace around the metal wheels of hospital beds positioned as fabric traps the length of the walls.

The staff at St. Mary's Hospital bustled about in the care of their patients. Mable ignored their curious looks, holding her head high and continuing on as though it were the most common of occurrences.

"It's right here, Miss Burton. Room 24," the nurse leading her advised.

"Thank you."

Mable stood just outside the open door, perched in the confines of the hall.

She exhaled a breath she'd been holding since she'd stepped from John's car and crossed the threshold of the sanitarium's front doors. And of all times to find herself afflicted, she stood frozen now. Unwilling to turn around and leave, but unable to take a step forward.

The effects of influenza had forever weakened Sally's heart. No longer able to sing, she was in and out of the sanitarium regularly. And though drinking cough syrup had been an aid to Sally's frayed sensibilities for years, she'd transitioned to find open comfort in strong drink for the many months that had followed her collapse during a set at the Marlborough-Blenheim Hotel.

Now Mable's friend languished in the sanitarium, humming tunes under her breath while she stared out the window, watching the sky float by.

Meanwhile, John had breezed back into Mable's life. And he was staying. The exquisite lace dress and pompadour hairstyle she wore were evidence of that now—it was her wedding day, and her groom cared enough to make this stop on their way to the Hudson County courthouse. Yet there she was, hiding in the hallway of a busy hospital in a perfectly elegant gown, reluctant to face the possibility that the moments ahead might very well be the last she'd share with her friend.

She rapped lightly on the door.

Sally turned from the bower of winter clouds outside the window and smiled, seeing her friend in the doorway.

Mable moved to walk in.

"No," Sally said, raising a hand to stop her. "I want to marvel at you from there. Can you spin?"

Sally's auburn hair, so rich and fiery once, hung in lifeless tendrils about her shoulders. The porcelain complexion Mable had always admired had now dimmed to a soft gray, one that colored the skin on the underside of her eyes with dark, sunken-in patches of purple. And she was terribly thin. Why, it looked as though a light wind could blow her from the surface of the bed.

Mable swallowed hard, pushing down the emotion that welled up from the confines of her chest. "Oh, what good would spinning do but make me dizzy?"

"Humor me."

Mable sighed in mock exasperation and did as she was asked, turning in a quick pirouette on the edge of her heel.

"A thirty-year-old woman just danced like a grammar-school ballerina in your room. I hope you're happy."

"I am. And let me guess. You're on your way to vote? Or to sit for a Gibson magazine cover shoot?"

"You know very well that if women had the vote, I'd have worn twice the amount of lace." Mable smiled, cocking an eyebrow at her. "I'd want to dress the part—Gibson magazine cover or not."

Sally's face warmed in a smile.

The kind that Mable had always admired about her.

"Come," she invited, waving Mable into the room. She patted the side of her bed. "Sit with me. We'll watch the world fly by outside the window. Unless you have somewhere else more important to be today?"

Mable shook her head and edged into the room, taking slow steps that clipped her heels against the linoleum flooring.

"Nowhere more important than here. Than right now," she answered, and swept her long skirt underneath her to sit at Sally's side. "Well, look at us. Both dressed in white." She winked.

"White . . . Yes. There's a lot of white around here. Everywhere you look. I wish they could see fit to introduce another color . . ." Sally's voice faded away for the briefest of moments. Then she seemed revived, saying, "They say my heart is giving out, you know."

She refused to look at Mable as she bluntly changed the subject, instead opting to twist the edges of a white cotton blanket on the bed round the tip of her index finger.

"Sally . . ." Mable sniffed, wiping her nose on a handkerchief.

"All of them say it." Sally attempted to tease, rolling misty eyes to the ceiling. "I could have told those doctors it gave out a long time ago. What girl can keep a ticker in her chest when it's ripped out time and time again?"

"Don't talk like this," Mable urged. "I'll be back soon. Very soon. And we'll take another one of our walks along the pier. You'll see every color in the rainbow then. There's a Ferris wheel now—just like the one we saw at the Exposition in Chicago ages ago. Even the Marlborough has added a new wing. It's the crowning glory of the steel pier. John and I will take you to see it all."

Sally looked like she almost believed her. "A walk on the pier would be lovely." She closed her eyes. Shutting out pain, squeezing a tear between her beautiful long lashes. "Tell me, Mable Ringling—what will you see on your honeymoon?" she asked in an embattled whisper.

"We sail for Europe this evening."

"And will you visit the Venetian opera house we once talked about?"

"Perhaps." Mable nodded, licking her lips and blinking over tears that fought with her own lashes too. Even though she'd promised herself she wouldn't cry. Had promised them both she'd be strong if this was good-bye. "If I find it. I'll go there and bring you back some memories."

"Tell me again? About the opera house. The one you saw when you walked into the Shamrock Club in Chicago?"

"Hmm." Mable laughed. "My memory is a bit hazy, but I recall it had something to do with a stylish young stage-stealer who could sing like a lark. I was transfixed—an Ohio farm girl who walked into a Chicago club looking for a job, and instead was taken halfway round the world by a friend's gift of song."

"Keep going," Sally whispered, laying her head back on the pillow.

"I saw a singer—Sally was her name. Standing onstage, wearing the finest silk this side of the Orient. In her very favorite shade of pink. And her voice? It carried up to kiss the gilding on the grand auditorium's ceiling. That girl reminded us all that having a dream is a special thing. She reminded me that it's okay to carry a cigar box around, as long as you don't live in it."

Sally opened her eyes to gaze back at Mable. "And what do you carry in it?"

"A lifetime of memories," Mable mouthed, having lost her battle with her tears, which had begun a trail down her cheeks. "They're what dreams become."

"Yes. Memories. That's what you need to keep building in that cigar box of yours. Do you hear me, Mable? You will never take this for granted. You know why?"

Mable shook her head. "Why?"

"Because you found something more precious than gold," Sally said, reaching her hand over to hold her friend's. "You found love. It's genuine and warm and everything I'd always looked for. And I know that God has shown you favor, because you prized something far more worthy than the rest of us."

"I've done nothing, Sally. Nothing but dreamed of what I wanted my life to be. That's all. Having a dream is easy. It's being brave enough to walk the journey every day that sets you apart from the crowd."

The clock on the far wall chimed low, ringing with the call of midday.

They both turned to it.

"It's time for you to go, isn't it?" Sally asked.

Mable nodded. "John's waiting in the car downstairs."

"Those are your wedding bells, friend. You go answer their call." Sally patted her hand, nudging her on.

Mable rose, finding it easier to turn and go quickly rather than linger in the moment. She told herself that they were being silly. That Sally's illness was temporary. That it was December now, but surely the warmth of the coming spring would help her condition. And the sea air would enliven her again. She'd be back onstage to sing a set in no time.

She told herself that this was just good-bye for now. So she could gather more pictures in her cigar box and bring them back home to share.

"Mable Burton?"

Mable stopped in her tracks, one hand braced on the door-frame. Realizing it might be the last time she'd hear that name, save for when she'd speak her vows.

She held up the side of her dress, keeping the yards of lace away from the danger of her heel. She turned, head held high, taking the sting of death like a Gibson girl would—with strength and poise and not an ounce of regret.

"Yes, Sally?"

"What kind of bouquet will you carry? I want to picture it."

"Our favorite, of course. Pink roses." She lavished a smile on her friend. "I promise I'll always have them around. I'll have a rose garden for us. And I'll tend those blooms with my own hands. There will never be a rose that comes into my life that will be over-looked. Not on my watch. Not if I can help it grow. I promise you that. There will never be a single dream lost in any garden I tend."

"You know what? I believe that. And I'm not angry anymore. I've had a lot of time to think about it," Sally whispered, wiping a tear from her cheek with a graceful hand. "I think I was shown favor too. God hasn't forgotten me. Not in Chicago, and certainly not here. Something was always at work behind the scenes, because He brought me a friend like you."

Mable took an instinctive step forward, but Sally shook her

head softly, as though she were the bearer of wisdom and not the other way around.

"No, Mable Ringling. You go board your ship of dreams. Go to Venice. See everything your heart has been waiting for. I'll want to hear about it when you get back."

"I KNEW I SHOULD HAVE GONE IN WITH YOU," JOHN ADMITTED, shaking his head when she joined him in the backseat of the car.

"No. I'm fine." Mable waved him off, flipping her wrist as if she hadn't any tears still glazing her eyes. She fought with the rows of lace on her gown, pulling and smoothing to ensure it was all inside before the driver closed the door.

"How is Miss Rivers?" John asked as the car began lumbering down the half-moon circle in front of the sanitarium.

Mable glanced at him out of the corner of her eye.

John had turned toward her, those eyes she'd always remembered serious and empathetic at the same time. Mable liked to believe he'd only ever show that look to her, and no one else. Knowing his reputation for indifference and a staunch level of seriousness in his relationships, she was warmed to see that he could debunk that myth with a single glance her way.

She leaned in, dropping a soft kiss to his lips.

"Let's go get married," she whispered, grinning wide.

"Driver," he half shouted, tapping his cane to the floor of the automobile. "You heard my fiancée. To the courthouse."

"But we have one stop to make along the way."

John turned to her, an easy smile tipped on the lips she'd just warmed with her own.

"Already it starts. Every man is driven by the woman behind him."

"Ah, but that's where you're wrong, Mr. Ringling. I shall never interfere with your business dealings."

His eyes widened, heavy brows lifted in a look of genuine surprise. "Is that so?"

She gave a quick nod. "Of course. The circus is your world to manage, and I'll leave you to it. But I will always walk *beside* you. That I can promise. I'm not a walk-behind-anyone kind of woman."

"I see."

Her soon-to-be-husband was indeed a man of few words. But it was his actions that could speak louder. He surprised her by pulling a bag from the floorboard on the other side of the car and placing it in her lap.

"Then what in the world will I do with this?"

Her heart could have burst right there. "What is it?"

He lifted his shoulders, tipping the wide collar of his wool coat as if he hadn't a clue.

Mable bit the edge of her bottom lip on a rush of excitement that tumbled in all at once, making her feel like a child at Christmas. The package was wrapped in pink tissue paper, which she delighted in tearing into.

And there in her lap, shielded by a bevy of airy pink tissue, was an oilcloth briefcase of meticulous tailored design. It looked handcrafted. And what's more, it was stamped with the initials MBR in gold leaf, plain as day on the front.

"I thought you'd like it." He placed a hand atop hers. "When I saw your cigar box that day on the pier, I thought you'd need something better to carry your treasures in."

Mable smiled, delighting in the quiet ways he managed to compliment who she was.

It was as if he alone knew what had been in her heart, even as far back as the memory of a tea parlor in Cincinnati. And now he'd bought a satchel for her dreams from that point on. The dreams they'd share together.

"Look inside."

She opened the flap and, with a gloved hand shaking ever so slightly, plucked an old, worn souvenir fan and two ocean liner tickets from the inside pouch.

"The boat won't wait. So, my dear, where are we stopping on our way to this wedding?"

Mable wiped at her eyes, laughing to think of how her afternoon mixture of tears had likely damaged any paint on her face beyond repair. But it didn't matter. Wedding days were made for smiling and tears. They'd welcome both.

She hugged the briefcase to her chest.

"We have to find a flower shop. I should have a bouquet, shouldn't I? Pink roses. That's what we need now. Pink roses to say 'I do.'"

"You may have all the roses you can carry, Mable. And collect all the dreams you want," John whispered. "We'll live them together."

CHAPTER 16

1927
NEW YORK CITY

Crowds had never bothered Rosamund.

Though she had only performed at small street fairs and local village carnivals, some were large enough to amass an audience of a hundred or more, and she'd performed well each time.

This was very different.

The roar of the crowd was like nothing she'd ever heard.

It was a sea of thousands, shouting and clapping through every spectacle before them. The vault of blue sky she and Ingénue were used to performing under had been transformed into a bower of rope, steel, and electric lights, every bulb flashing down on the great circus rings like spotlights on an immense stage.

She waited in the wings with Annaliese and Owen, watching the Rossi Family Flyers thrill the crowd with spectacular feats of daring through the Garden's iron sky.

Frankie and Enzo had been perfectly paired, soaring in ice-blue sequined jumpsuits that flashed with each toss and catch of the bars, the spotlights following their majestic dance through the air. Marvio, too, was distinguished in his performance. He led the troop with gusto, tossing and catching the magnificent Bella Rossi as if she were a weightless bird. And the crowd was mesmerized.

Even Rosamund found herself watching, her jaw dropping at the artistry and absolute flawlessness of Bella's performance.

Bella soared. Smiling. Dancing on air. Proving she was the queen of the center ring. And even down to her final flips through the air it was clear as day: the star had drawn a line in the sawdust, proving her worth.

Bella bowed low, accepting the thunderous applause, fawning under the adoration of the crowd. She turned luxurious circles in the ring, still pandering with bows as the next act began to move in.

The cue of the circus band couldn't drown out the roar.

Rosamund stood waiting in the wings, transfixed, as Bella exited the ring and sauntered in her direction.

"Where is your costume, dear Rosamund?" Bella tossed back over her shoulder, freezing Rosamund with her glare. "You were supposed to be in yellow, were you not?"

Rosamund's heart catapulted in her chest, throwing her mind into a bevy of destructive thoughts. She watched Bella disappear into the shadows beyond the performers' entrance, swishing the blue satin cape she'd pulled across her shoulders.

"Rosamund!" Owen shouted, snapping attention away from the icy vision who'd just left her gaping in her wake.

"Get your head out of the clouds. That's us!"

Annaliese had pushed her mount forward at the band's cue and was already following a line of liberty horses trotting out under the lights.

"Right." Rosamund nodded, seeing the gap she'd allowed, and nudged Ingénue forward into the spotlight.

"Ring three," Owen called out, then left her as he led a group of liberty horses out to their place in the center ring.

For the possibly thousands of times she'd ridden bareback before, this was the one time Rosamund was most keenly aware of every step her horse took. Their trotting was clipped and rough. She noticed a tenseness to the muscles in Ingénue's back, could feel the rise and fall of her thighs with the horse's shallow breathing.

Ingénue jerked her head up after every few footfalls, fighting against the bit in her mouth.

"I know, lady," Rosamund whispered between her teeth, trying to show a smile to the face of the crowd. "I know. I'm just as scared as you are."

Rosamund smoothed her hand against Ingénue's back, rubbing in a circular motion by the withers, trying her best to keep her horse calm. Even if her own heart was thundering in her chest. She breathed in and out, fighting for focus as the lights bore down.

"We can do this," she said, as much for her benefit as for the mare's.

They moved through the motions, rolling through the act Owen had choreographed for them in the months they'd spent training in Sarasota.

First, riding round the ring balancing in a standing position. She'd raise her leg to a pointed perch while Ingénue soared, turning them into ballerinas dancing in circles.

Rosamund stooped, kneeling for her forward somersault.

It was a trick she'd never worried about before. But this time— her breathing was choppy. Her legs shaking. She flipped up and over, grateful when her feet found Ingénue's back again instead of finding that they'd tumbled to hard ground.

The crowd responded with applause. They roared, mesmerized to a fever pitch.

Rosamund might have liked it, even might have had time to notice as Bella did. But her palms were growing moist, slipping against any hold she sought. She felt her legs grow even shakier with each trick, her confidence more and more unsteady. Until the moment arrived for a backbend, in which she'd stand and fall back in an arch midstride, then carry through with a backflip dismount.

She told herself to focus.

To put Bella's performance and the veiled malice she'd shown out of her mind.

Rosamund tried to envision the fields of Easling Park instead of the sea of faces whizzing past. But the lights and the show—her every thought—jumbled together in a fog, muddling her senses until her focus finally snapped and she felt her arms unable to hold fast any longer.

Without warning her hands slipped from the bridge of Ingénue's back and she fell from her backbend down to the sawdust beneath the horse's hooves, jarring her head against the ground.

The crowd released a chorused gasp.

Rosamund shook her head. She tried to see through the fog that had overtaken her vision. Everything was a haze of color and sound. And though Rosamund had several more tricks to run in their routine, nothing made sense except to crawl on all fours to find what safety she could at the side of the ring.

A pair of arms wrapped around her middle.

Dark arms, belonging to Owen, picking her up from the ground. He shouted at her to get out of the ring before she was trampled.

It took but a second to fall from Ingénue's back. Another to stumble out of the ring with the knowledge that Bella Rossi had proved her place in the show.

Winning the crowd as the "English Rose" wouldn't happen on this night.

Any star power she might have possessed wilted before it had been given the chance to bloom.

~⊃

"You decent?"

Colin rapped his knuckles on the side of a trunk before step-ping into the backstage dressing area. He found Rosamund sitting on a crate, holding a poultice of ice against her elbow.

She looked up, nodding him in.

"Decent? I suppose that's relative to whether you were seated in the audience tonight."

"Well, I agree it could have gone better," Colin admitted, folding his arms across his chest. "Minnie told me there was some damage to your costume. Did that shake you up before you went out there?"

"That was nothing. Just something that happens from time to time. She got me a replacement."

"Okay. But that wasn't the same Rose I've been watching train for weeks. Something shook you tonight. What was it?"

Normally Rosamund would have welcomed him to sit, as she had at the cottage in Sarasota. But now? He watched as she drew in a deep breath. She looked as though she was willing herself to keep from crying in front of him.

"You've done that backbend and dismount hundreds of times. You want to tell me what happened out there?"

"I don't know . . ."

"A jittery horse is to be expected in her first show. Was it Ingénue?"

"I'd never blame her."

He whistled low. "So who's responsible for your near death out there? If Owen hadn't dragged you out of the ring, I would have done it for him. You were nearly trampled to death."

"Colin, I don't even know what I'm doing here. There's no way I can win over that crowd. It's impossible."

"Not true. And the crowd is the last thing you should be

worrying about right now," he added, trying to make light through the pain of her bruised ego.

Colin couldn't shake the instinct that he was right about Rose. She could be a star. He'd already seen it in her. He just hoped she'd realize it sooner rather than later, or things could get mighty ugly for him in the process. He had a feeling that if Rose failed, it could spell disaster for them both.

He walked over, scraping a stray crate across the floor to a stop in front of her. With a sigh, he sat down.

"The crowd isn't why I'm here, Rose. We need to talk."

Rosamund looked up.

Despite their growing friendship, Colin knew he had to play the boss now, and from the evidence flooding over her face, he could see that Rose recognized the change.

"Are you hurt?"

She gingerly rubbed her elbow, but shook her head.

"I can't show any special treatment to you, Rose. We both saw what happened out there. But I'd wager your view of it looked worse while sitting in the sawdust."

"I've never fallen before. Not like that. I don't know what happened."

"Every performer falls now and again. And it might surprise you to know that my view of it includes offering grace when it's warranted. Despite a failure." Colin grimaced, reminding himself that he wasn't above feeling as she did now. For how disappointed he was, Rosamund surely felt ten times worse.

He kept his tone firm, but not so much as to damage what pride she had left.

"But you were looking up, Rose. Owen warned you about that. And so did I. You forgot everything he taught you."

"But you don't know what it's like out there. There were

thousands of people. Lights in our eyes everywhere we looked. Ingénue and I are not used to that! You can't expect me to march out there and perform like I've got years of experience under my belt. Not when this is all brand-new."

He shook his head.

"Years of experience . . . ," he started, then stopped short of adding *like Bella* at the end of it. He didn't need to.

It all made sense.

The showstopping star had given a flawless performance. The interaction Rose had with Bella on the London train platform might have been worse for her than he'd initially thought. Or maybe there was something more going on behind the scenes. Perhaps Bella had gone out of her way to make Rose feel every bit the newcomer, despite his expectation that she act in a professional manner.

Colin squeezed his eyes shut on a drawn-out exhale, wanting to curse. Maybe to punch something. Certainly to fire someone, if necessary. He'd never had to do it with a top star in the show before, but he was confident he could warm up to it if need be.

"What did she do?"

"Who?"

Colin sent Rosamund a direct look, one that he hoped would show her he didn't want to fight. All he wanted was the truth.

"You know who. Bella."

I just want to help, he willed, keeping his eyes connected with hers.

Rosamund kept her head up, still meeting his gaze, but she looked utterly miserable.

Colin knew she wasn't spineless—quite the contrary. He had the utmost respect for the way she'd been brave already, stepping out of the life she'd always known and daring to dream something different. But in the moment, doubt crept in.

Doubt for the instincts he'd had back in England.

Maybe Rose wasn't ready. And maybe she never would be.

"I'm on your side, Rose."

"I know," she started, then paused to tuck a few stray locks behind her ear. "But this time I can't blame anyone but myself."

"But something had to happen. You didn't look like you do in practice, not from the moment you led Ingénue out there in that ring." Colin shook his head at her. "On opening day. At Madison Square Garden. With the Ringlings in attendance. Rose . . ."

"The Ringlings were here?" Rosamund eased her forehead down in her palm.

"Yes. They're in New York for business and stopped in to see the show."

"I'm sorry for that. I really am. But maybe I'm not supposed to do this. Maybe you thought you saw something in me that you really didn't. Ingénue and I, we're made of flesh and bone. We'll make mistakes. Neither of us can expect perfection in our first or even tenth performance."

"But it's what this show demands. It's perfection or someone gets hurt. Everyone here does their part. We're a team. A family traveling on that train we're loading. Whether a person performs under stage lights or not, whether man or beast, if just one performer fails, then we all do. It's a balance, Rose. And I'm sorry, but you fell flat with it tonight."

"Up to now, I've been a joy rider doing tricks in a field. I'm not a professional, Colin."

"You became a professional the moment you signed the contract we gave you. And don't discount your abilities. You've done much more than riding in a field. Owen went down to Florida expressly to work with you. For months. Please don't tell me that his time was wasted. Yours either. Don't tell me any of it was."

Rosamund bit the corner of her lip and looked down to the sequin-sparkling tips of her riding slippers.

They'd worked hard for weeks, Rose and Ingénue, with Owen guiding them. She'd performed the tricks hundreds of times. And yes, Colin had to admit she'd looked ready. But it took about five seconds of introspection to realize that though he wanted her to succeed, it wouldn't be accomplished on skill alone.

"Here's what I saw: you were watching the flyers, weren't you? You had your eye on Bella before you ever set foot in that ring. You forgot everything you've been working for, Rose, and you handed her your performance tonight."

"I know I did."

Rosamund clamped her eyes shut, sending a fresh pang of regret to burn the inside of his chest. She was broken and bruised, and he hated to feel the cause of it.

"But . . . ," he added, with the compassion he knew Rose needed in the moment. "Little-known secret: everyone is a disaster their first time in the ring. It's not fatal, Rose. I just want you to remember what you have to prove—for yourself and everyone out there in that ring—you can do it."

"Shall I go down fighting then? I'm overjoyed that no one from Easling Park came over for my debut. At least I can hold on to that, hmm?"

"You didn't tell me you'd invited your parents."

"I sent them a wire."

Rosamund's shoulders dipped. The backstage light was dim, but Colin could see enough through the shadows to note the unmistakable trembling of her chin.

"I'm so sorry they didn't come."

"It's a long voyage for one routine, isn't it?" She paused, toying with the end of a sequined length of satin from her skirt. "The truth is, I don't know if I can do this. And it wouldn't matter if they'd chosen to support me, not if I really believed in myself."

"You can do this, Rose."

"How? How do you know that?"

"Because I believe in you. And *I chose you*, Rose."

Colin stopped, shocked that he'd actually said the thought aloud. The sentiment was one of familiarity—one that couldn't rely on a platonic relationship between show boss and employee forever.

He wanted—no, *needed*—her to know that her presence there wasn't a mistake.

Rosamund remained silent.

She blinked, an earnestness covering her features. It was enough that he pulled back from the connection of her green eyes to his.

He clapped his hands against his legs and stood to leave.

"Remember what you said to me in the stable at Easling Park? It was your wish to live a new life. Well, this is the life. And if you could forget what you *think* you're supposed to do for one minute, you just might ride out into that ring and have the most fun you've ever had."

Have fun.

He reminded Rose of the words she'd whispered to Ingénue after the first ride they'd had in Florida. He hoped they were well placed now.

"Stay here, okay? I want to send the doctor in to check you over." When she opened her mouth to counter, Colin raised a hand to stop her. "And no disagreement this time. We're not standing on the side of a creek. We've got a process to how things are done here. Anyone falls in the ring, the doctor is sent in. No arguments."

She nodded understanding. Even graced him with the hint of a thankful smile as she readjusted the muslin pack of chipped ice on her elbow.

"Chin up, Rose. The show rolls in two days, and we'll start again." He turned to leave. He wasn't sure he could stand another moment of watching the pain flooding those beautiful green eyes . . .

"Colin?"

He turned back. Was jarred by the welcoming green once again. "Yes?"

She drew in a deep breath, then offered, "Thank you."

"You're still my star, Rose. I know I'm right about you. But we can't work with anything less than your whole heart out there. You've always known your own mind. So get out there and prove it to everyone else."

CHAPTER 17

"May I join you?"

Rosamund recognized the voice immediately.

She turned, jumped, and nearly overturned the crate she'd been seated on in her haste to pop up to a proper standing position.

"Mrs. Ringling . . . I—"

"No, no." Mable shook her head. "No need to get up. And please, call me Mable."

Rosamund did as requested, settling back down on the crate with a swoop of sequined ribbons flouncing about her lap. She chewed the edge of her bottom lip as Mable sat before her.

"I'm sure this visit is an unexpected one. In truth, I hadn't anticipated it myself. But, well, here we are."

The alcove in which they sat was dim and shielded almost entirely from view.

Rosamund had never been more grateful for the haven of anonymity. Here they could talk. Unnoticed. Watching the circus pass by beyond their hidden corner without anyone else seeing the bareback rider who was poised to receive a reprimand from Mrs. Ringling herself.

"This is all new, you know, this location for Madison Square Garden," Mable began, quite differently than Rosamund had expected.

She'd expected the conversation to begin with *You're fired*.

"Yes." She paused, uneasy. "I did hear that."

"The city heads got it in their minds to widen Madison Avenue some time back. My favorite part of the old building was torn down."

"What was your favorite part?"

"All of it." Mable laughed. "It was a lovely piece of Venice right here in the city. But time marches. Changes are made. Everything has to be bigger and better . . . Flashier, including the Garden. But this underground area is nice. Much larger than I'd thought."

The barrage of normal chitchat proved too much, and Rosamund interrupted, squeezing her eyes shut as she blurted out, "I'm so sorry, but I can't bear it any longer. Are you here to fire me? Please tell me, and I'll just get my things and go."

Rosamund cracked open one eye, feeling but an ounce of courage to do so.

Mable appeared taken aback, both by the question and by the honesty of Rosamund's distress so readily on display. It felt safe then to open both eyes and hope for the best.

"Fire you? I have no call to do anything of the sort," Mable replied. "No power to do so either. Only don't tell that to Mr. Ringling. He'd never let me live that notion down."

Rosamund's trepidation eased, her shoulders lightening with it.

"No, I'm here for another reason."

"Did Mr. Keary send you?"

Mable shook her head. "That would not be in keeping with our Mr. Keary's nature. I expect he'd fall into a very manly swoon if he knew I was here talking to you right now."

"Why is that?"

"Because I've never done this before."

Rosamund stared. "You've never . . . what?"

"Gone backstage to talk to a performer." Mable confirmed it

with a light shake of her head. "Not once. The circus is my husband's world, and I do not intrude upon that. I stick with the fun and just watch the shows. But I did venture down to the performance floor. Just once, years ago. I stopped by to chat with someone who was not altogether unlike you—new in his role. Figuring things out. Maybe on the verge of making a mistake or two along the way."

"So you're here now because of what you saw tonight?"

Rosamund rubbed a hand against her chin. Her performance must have been the worst in the Ringling Brothers' history if it brought Mable all the way underground, to places she'd never thought her boots would tread.

"No one's given a performance that bad?"

Mable laughed at that, a hearty chuckle that brightened her entire face.

"Of course they have. You know, Mr. Ringling tells of a snake-charmer act they once had in the early days. A very exotic woman from the Orient. And though she was quite skilled, a python got away during her first performance and tried to have one of the dog act's schnauzers for lunch. You can imagine the friction that caused, both with the crowd and the schnauzer."

"And what happened?"

"She married one of the clowns, and their family toured with the circus for years."

Rosamund let loose with an easy smile. "Really?"

"Yes. Really. I won't pretend to know what it's like out there in the ring. But I felt a tug on my heart after I watched you at our party this past December. It's brought me down here now, to remind you that you weren't acting that night. You played the piano for us, allowing music to flow from your heart. And you won over every person in that room because you swept in there like a fresh breeze, simply by being who you are."

"I'm not sure who I am anymore. Certainly not in that ring. Colin—"

Mable cut off her argument with a swift interruption.

"Please forget Mr. Keary for a moment. This has nothing to do with him. Circus boss or not, that man needs a little shaking up. If your performance jolted him, then I say good. He'll be the better for it."

Rosamund nodded. Listening keenly. Noticing how Mable's eyes twinkled ever so slightly, adding little touches of encouragement to her words.

"It's a common thing for a woman to doubt her place in life. Do you consider it an abhorrence to marry, to have children?"

Just what the subject had to do with her performance that night, Rosamund hadn't a clue. She shook her head slowly. "Of course not."

"And if that was what your life was—no performances, no name up in lights . . . no circus at all. Just Lady Rosamund Easling living her days as a wife and mother. Would that be enough?"

"I never wanted my name in lights. I'd have been quite content with being a wife. A mother someday. But I wanted to choose it for myself. I think a woman's place shouldn't be thrust upon her. It should be her decision whom to marry, or to marry at all. And if I wanted more, that should be my decision too, shouldn't it?"

Mable paused. Nodded. She absently smoothed a hand over the span of ivory silk beading of her dress peeking out from the fur spread across her lap, considering the idea.

"Yes, I agree. It should. But do you know how remarkable, how brave it is that you've stepped forth in spite of all that, risking everything for the reinvention of who you are?"

It didn't feel remarkable.

Nor brave.

From where Rosamund sat, her faith leap had resulted in a

bump on the head, a terribly raw elbow, and a helping of pie that was both humble and bitter at the same time.

"No. I hadn't thought about it like that."

"But I think it is brave. It reminds me of a young farm girl who once left home. She was scared too, but more afraid of life passing her by than of what it might cost to step out and really live. She even carried an old cigar box around with her dreams hidden inside, planning, one day, to experience every one of them."

Mable pursed her lips.

"You know, you're not so very different from the ringmaster's wife who sits in front of you, Rose. She's gone from farm girl dresses to Paris couture. From a horizon of plowed fields to the seaside backdrop of Sarasota Bay. But she's also gone from feeling discontent to finally breathing in freedom. In that way, you and I are alike."

For the first time, Rosamund saw the connection between them. And Mable was right.

"You may not have set out to be a star, my dear, yet here you are. Under Mr. Ringling's Big Top. Name flashing and colors flying from atop your horse. You may not have come here for the glittering life in that ring, but now you've got it. And so I ask you . . ." Mable leaned in, staring deep into Rosamund's eyes. "What do you plan to do with it?"

She produced a blush-pink, long-stemmed rose that Rosamund hadn't noticed and twirled it in her fingertips. "I was thinking of my garden at the Cà d'Zan tonight. Did you know that we had it built long before the house was ever dreamed up?"

Rosamund shook her head.

"It was called Palms Elysian then. We bought the property in 1911, and after we closed the verandas to keep pesky mosquitoes out of the house, it was the very next thing I had built. You would have still been a child then, like the young ones sitting on the straw bales tonight. Marveling at the sights and the sounds. Getting your fingers sticky with cotton candy and caramel corn." She chuckled. "I never did like that stuff."

Laughter at Mable's teasing came easy. It broke into Rosamund's thoughts on the matter of the circus life. Of children. Of dreams and living through the outcome of decisions.

"I had dreams. And my rose garden makes me think on them. Often."

Rosamund pictured a young Mable Ringling with stars glimmering in her eyes and smiled.

The vision suited her.

"What were your dreams?"

"Oh, same as yours. Love. Freedom. Something up in lights—didn't have to be my name. Just something to make the journey sparkle a little." She leaned in, winking on the words. "And if you can look past the exterior of a dream, what's buried deepest is always the most rewarding. My Cà d'Zan has a grand exterior. It's playful—the way I wanted it. But if you look past the house, you'll find that the rose garden has been tended with far more care. By my own hands, for a much longer time. So you see, it's the journey we're all after—not the reward."

"I don't know what my dreams are anymore," Rosamund said. "I thought I did, but then I came here and . . . everything changed."

"Bravo then," Mable countered. "This building up of what we want doesn't have to be a tearing down of who we are. It's the worst kind of extravagance to think we're above adversity. Isn't that what God calls of us, to acknowledge that we are moving with this undercurrent of something that is always at work around us? Something bigger than we could ever be as just one person?"

"I hadn't thought of it like that. I thought my big faith leap was boarding a train at King's Cross Station."

"But it wasn't?"

Rosamund shook her head. "I think it's been in the days in between then and now."

"Rosamund, we only see what we want to see—in people, in love, and in life. It's a choice, my dear. That's the point of all this. You choose the face you offer the world. And it's only behind the costumes and the masks that we can be who we truly are."

She extended the rose.

Rosamund took it with gentle fingertips, clasping the stem as if it were made of the finest porcelain.

"I think you are like this rose—beautiful, and with all the sweet potential in the world. Pink is your color, and roses are your perfume." Mable stood. "Use them to show the world who you are."

CHAPTER 18

1906
NEW YORK CITY

"One more step up," Mable whispered, her hands covering John's eyes from behind.

He obeyed and stepped up gingerly.

The tip of his shoe hooked on the last step and they stumbled together. He righted them with a firm grip to the rail on the back platform of their custom-built Pullman train car, saying, "Honestly, Mable. I'm going to break my back for a car I've seen a hundred times already."

She'd spent the last months designing their train car, dubbed the *Wisconsin*, making it their lavish home on iron wheels. If she had a mind to surprise him with the outcome of her efforts, Mable decided he'd simply have to play along—broken back or not.

"You've seen it, but not like this," she countered, despite his attempt at sourness for having to succumb to her childish games. "Not when everything's finished just so. You'll have to endure my notion of fun, Mr. Ringling."

John stepped through the mahogany-lined threshold into the observation room, the large open space where they'd entertain their on-the-road guests.

"Okay," Mable said as she pulled her hands away, though instinct drew them back to her mouth. She half covered her bottom lip, excitement spilling over. "Open."

John complied and opened his eyes, adding a tiny huff for good measure.

There was a grand spectacle of wagons and animals outside the car windows, but it delighted Mable that John didn't seem to notice.

In the moment, he was effectively captured.

He turned in a semicircle, scanning the space.

She, too, gazed around the room, its gold-tipped ceiling, stained-glass windows, seat cushions of tufted green velvet, and rich mahogany walls all singing in unison. It was late evening, so she'd switched on all the lights for effect, and every surface appeared to have been dusted in a warm gold glow.

John glanced down the hall that ran the length of the car, leading to the kitchen on the end.

"The staterooms and dining room are just down there, remember? All polished and perfect, down to the very last nail."

Movement out the windows caught her eye, and Mable saw the great gray bodies of a line of elephants lumber past. Their eyes were level with the glass and they seemed to peek in, the electric lights casting a shadowed glow on the side of each wrinkled visage.

The circus was preparing to head out on the road for the 1906 performance season, and there was the customary hustle-bustle about the train platform. It wasn't a mundane sight to see a menagerie passing by outside the window. Yet John hadn't noticed. The space inside the train car held him captive, and that felt like a win for her decorating prowess.

"I regret that we couldn't fit a Steinway in this room." She pointed at the Victrola against the wall and leaned in to whisper in his ear, "But we could dance in here if we had a mind to."

"We could that."

"Well then, Mr. Ringling. You've had a nice long look. What say you?" She tipped her chin up. "Will it do for our travels?"

"Will it do?" He turned, bestowing upon her a rare, full-toothed, only-for-Mable smile. "Of course it will do. You're here in every detail. That will make the months of travel seem far less daunting."

"Don't tease me. You love the road. But it's still settled." Mable stood to the side, acknowledging his praise with a satisfied nod. "We always travel together. I won't push into the business of your circus world. I'll just enjoy it as long as you promise to spend time here, in mine."

"After all this, I'm almost afraid to ask," he said, settling into a brown leather armchair against the wall. "What's your next project? I'm wondering how you'll manage to top this."

Next project?

Mable hastened to admit she hadn't considered what would come after. She'd simply thrown herself into the goal of outfitting their travel home.

The first day John had taken her to see his circus drifted into her mind without warning. Mable saw the young faces of those she'd sat with on the straw bales lining the ring. Children, delighted. Parents, proud. Proud that they could give their young sons and daughters a glimpse of whimsy under the Big Top.

She remembered that first trip to the Ringlings' circus world—the world in which she now belonged—and wondered . . .

Were the memories of a child's wonder in their future?

Our next project, she thought.

Would they add the sounds of delighted laughter and the pitter-patter of tiny feet to echo against the mahogany-lined walls of the *Wisconsin*?

"Mable?"

John's voice snapped her back to attention.

"What?"

He sighed.

"I said, are you hungry? It might be nice to have one last dinner while we're here in New York. How does Delmonico's sound?" He pulled the pocket watch from his vest, checking the time. "We can still make it if we hurry."

"Yes," she breathed out, adding a light roll of her eyes. No sense in opening up a conversation they hadn't time to delve into at the moment.

But later, perhaps. When the train rolled and the lights were dimmed . . . When they were alone and the rest of the world was passing by outside, Mable would tell him she wanted a child of their own.

1911
SARASOTA, FLORIDA

"AND THE ROSE GARDEN WILL GO RIGHT OVER THERE," MABLE said, spreading her hand wide across the span of yard in front of their new winter home, the Palms Elysian Estate.

She knelt and dug into the oilcloth briefcase at her feet, thumbing through fabric samples and photographs she'd collected from another one of their trips to Venice the year before.

Mable had seen fit to drag John away from the pressing matters of business dealings littering the desk in his office and take him for a light afternoon stroll round the estate yard. And if they'd happen to stop and plot out her garden in the middle of it, that was exactly what she'd set out to accomplish for the day.

"Ah, here it is," she added, plucking the photograph of an Italian villa garden out of the bag to hand over to John. "Right there is where it will go. And we've got twenty acres to work with, so I think we can duplicate the traditional Italian wagon wheel motif. What do you think?"

"You plan on a twenty-acre garden?"

"Perhaps," she said, imagining a bower of blooms exploding in color before her eyes. Lining walkways. Stretching their leaves to be kissed by the warm Florida sun. The roses were everywhere in her mind, perfuming the air with their scent and frosting the landscape in vibrancy.

Mable stood in her bright white day dress covered with a bevy of botanical blooms, surveying the span of land at their disposal. If this was to be their winter paradise, it couldn't be such without the one thing she knew it needed—a spectacular rose garden. One she'd tend herself. One she'd dreamed about since the day she'd become Mrs. John Ringling. And one that was necessary for her now.

"I am amazed," he said.

"Really? Then you like the idea?"

Ah. Success! Mable gave a satisfied nod.

"Amazed that the first thing you decide to do when we finish repairs to the house is build a rose garden. You've had your nose stuck in books for days, looking for who knows what kind of ideas. I knew a project was forthcoming, but I thought surely you wanted to talk about building a new estate house on the grounds," John revealed. "You mean to tell me all you want is a garden?"

"That's right. But not just any garden—a *rose* garden, Mr. Ringling."

"And that's it?"

"Your pocketbook is safe for now," she declared, returning a wicked smile to his quizzical one. She felt the light tease adding a little pick-me-up to her excitement. "Maybe we'll start with Old Garden roses on the borders. Then rows of hybrid teas, because their pink is so vibrant. I'd also like ivory floribundas and red grandifloras. And we must have miniature roses and shrubbery to create elegant walls."

John listened. And as usual, quiet was his way. He paused for several long seconds, thinking on the idea.

"Well?" Mable nudged, eyebrows arched.

"Mable, I want to ask you something before I agree to this."

Her excitement was tempered a bit, brought into submission by the serious tone of his voice. "Of course."

"Is all this because of yesterday? What the doctor said?"

She tried to shake her head, but he cut off her reply before she could speak.

"The truth," he demanded. "Why do you want to be surrounded by roses all of a sudden? You could have any size estate you want, and instead you're asking me for a few flowers."

"I love roses. I always have."

"But you haven't asked me for roses in some time."

Mable looked down at the tips of her shoes. "Not since our wedding day . . ." Her voice trailed off as she remembered it. "You bought them for me. Took me to Venice for our honeymoon. And when we got home? You had a lovely Tiffany vase waiting for me. Another gift, Mr. Ringling. You shower me with them."

He paused. Waited. Perhaps fighting inside to choose the right words—any words that would heal instead of hurt.

"I know what you're thinking. You don't want roses to fill your vase. Not really. You want laughter to fill our home." He tilted his head, watching her. She noticed it out of the corner of her eye, but kept her gaze fixed to sweep out over the landscape. "We need to talk about this, Mable. It's on your mind. Always. And now we know for certain that we won't have our own children."

It was so like to him, to understand her heart before Mable had herself.

And yes, it made sense now.

To have received the news that she would never bear him children, that the smiling little cherub faces in the Big Top's crowd would never include one of their own—it had indeed sent twinges of pain to her heart. But she'd not shared that with him. Maybe she'd been too afraid. Too ridden with guilt over the entire matter to ask for anything but the simple gesture of flowers.

Had she failed him as a wife? Did he believe so?

I won't let this limitation define me, she'd thought at hearing the doctor's summary of her medical condition. *I'll still tend a rose garden.*

Mable cleared her throat before speaking. "I am a strong woman, John. I will not fall into tears over this. I will simply find something else to do."

"I know you're strong. But you also have a heart, Mable. And right now, I think it's broken." John reached out for her hand, gently lifted it, and opened her palm to the sky. He placed the wagon wheel garden image in it, curling her fingers around the photo. He kept her hand in the warmth of his.

"Tell me the truth," he whispered. "Is it troubling you?"

"Addison's disease is a death sentence."

"It doesn't have to be." John shook his head. "And not in this case. We'll manage it."

"Adrenal gland insufficiency? Too little cortisol?" She waved off the diagnosis with a flick of her wrist. "That's just fancy physician talk to explain the bouts of weakness. The faint feelings and the lack of appetite. If it were those things alone, I could manage them. And they wouldn't matter one bit if we had some hope. If there were a chance for a child, I could accept it all. I could weather any diagnosis but this one." She stiffened her spine, willing courage to keep hold of her. "This is heart failure, John. *My* heart."

He exhaled low.

Not in frustration, she knew, but rather in a show of solidarity. Perhaps he suffered from heart failure now too.

"I didn't marry you for the children you'd bear me."

"And I didn't marry you for your money," she fired back, unconscious tears glazing her eyes. "You know that. But I must be of some worth as your wife. Where will the sound of laughter come from, John? Who will fill our halls with it now?"

John was always strong. Tall and solid.

Mable had always loved that about him. But for the first time, his shoulders seemed to slump. He reached for her. As if he realized it was a problem he couldn't think or buy his way out of. One they'd weather, but would never be able to fix.

She buried her face against the lapel of his suit coat, hiding her tears from the sun.

"We can still have the sound of children here," he whispered. "Do you hear me? The circus is full of laughter. And didn't Ralph Waldo Emerson say that the earth laughs in flowers?"

Mable nodded against his chest.

"Well then, I ask you—why would you ever doubt my answer about a garden full of them? Mable, we have a million children all around the world, and we're making them laugh every day. We take them on every adventure we have. How many couples can say that?"

"Few, I know."

"None that I know of. And you've sworn to stay out of my work boots, haven't you? You pledged not to get involved in the circus, but here you are, building gardens only to bring happiness to everyone who comes here."

He paused. Reached a hand up to caress the side of her brow. She felt the heat of his palm warming her skin.

"Will you look at me, Mable?"

She raised her eyes up to meet his, unashamed of the evidence of tears she'd shed onto the collar of his coat.

"Don't ever try to go through anything alone again. Understand?"

"I do," she breathed out. "I really do understand you, John."

He nodded. "Good," he said, clearing his throat over a hitch of emotion. It was replaced quickly, customary strength returning to his posture even then. "Now, Mrs. Ringling, is that all you wanted? A rose garden?"

"As I said, Mr. Ringling." She swept her fingertips under her eyes, ridding her cheeks of stubborn tears that had gathered there. "That's all for now. But you've given me the idea for an estate house . . ."

Mable stood with her chin in her hand, mulling over the prospect of building a new house in the place where the white clapboard Palms Elysian now stood. "You have to admit, the idea holds merit."

"Your ideas always seem to hold merit," he sighed, feigning annoyance. "Well, what will this grand estate house look like? Should I expect the usual grand undertaking?"

Mable felt the smile return to her face. She stooped and retrieved her oilcloth briefcase, hugging it in her arms.

"I suppose we'll have to collect some more ideas to find out. I think it would be lovely to build a house that's born of laughter. With a rose garden. A wonderfully tended rose garden. Perhaps we could bring a little bit of our beloved Venice to Sarasota. What do you think?"

"Whatever you think." He nodded, agreeing to the idea. "Maybe we could name it after you."

She shook her head.

"No. I may design it, but an estate like that sounds like an enchanted castle and should be named for a king. We'll call it *Cà d'Zan*—the House of John."

CHAPTER 19

1927
NEW YORK CITY

"*Voilà*. You see? Those are the animal stock cars. And behind them, the flat cars with the Big Top equipment."

Annaliese pointed out the steel-faced cars close behind the locomotive. She drew a gloved hand up to her brow, the purple leather shielding her eyes from the early-morning sun streaming in on the train platform. She and Rosamund watched as workmen loaded circus wagons onto the steel flat cars farther down the line.

They'd awakened early and packed light—taking only what they could carry from the hotel to the train. They stood off to the side with the rest of the acrobats and horse showmen, Rosamund's fox-trimmed coat complementing Annaliese's purple-and-gold one. Their show trunks were already loaded on the train, and within the day the circus would arrive at their first scheduled stop in New Jersey. Their eight-month-long nomadic life had begun.

"The stock cars will be packed with the elephants, big cats— any of the larger animals in the menagerie."

"And Ingénue will be loaded with them?"

Annaliese nodded.

"The liberty and high school horses are loaded in the cars

immediately after the big stock. See? And the baggage horses go in the cars behind that. Those are the horses for work. They set up. Tear down. Help with the Big Top. They pull the equipment wagons down from the flat cars, so they are always kept close."

"And what about all the animals? Is it . . . safe for them?"

"Of course. The elephants go two to a car, facing each other. So they do not get lonely," Annaliese advised, her playful French accent adding a light singsong to her voice. "That way, they have plenty of room and access to water and food through the night. The big cats are caged in their own cars. And the handlers are always nearby—even for the *petit* ones. The monkeys, dogs, birds . . ." Annaliese's energetic nature carried through in her dimpled smile. "So it's safe for us too—in case you were wondering."

Dogs and birds were one thing. But Rosamund couldn't help thinking about the scary possibility of a lion or tiger getting loose, and just what that would mean for a circus grounds teeming with people. It was a lot of trust to put in a great number of people—that every precaution was taken for safety and for the best care of the animals.

"It's hard to believe everything could fit on one train."

"But we have near a hundred cars now, so it's quite possible."

Performers weaved in front of them, lugging suitcases and colorful carryall bags in their arms.

It never ceased to surprise Rosamund now, how normal the sight of oddities in dress and mannerism had become. There were sideshow performers who mingled in with the rest of the circus crowd as if there were nothing out of the ordinary about them at all.

Rosamund had been quite shocked when she'd first laid eyes on the many peculiarities of the circus. A tall man of more than seven feet could be seen walking alongside his friend—a man of a probable four-hundred-pound girth. They wove through the crowd, drawing no particular attention on the way to their assigned train car.

Rosamund saw Rebecca Lyon, a bearded lady who was following close behind. It was odd that the first thing she'd ever heard about the woman was not that she had the mature whiskers of a man, but rather that she was widely regarded as the best cook traveling with the show. She was often found in the dining tent, instructing the cooks on ways to improve their served meals. And Edith, another in the sideshow, boasted elaborate tattoos that snaked up her limbs to her neck. She was quite a sight to behold, though when Rosamund knocked over a trunk at the Garden and hands belonging to tattoo-covered arms reached out to help her pick up the spilled wares, she had found Edith sweet and perfectly normal.

Edith spotted her now and waved from across the platform.

Rosamund lifted her gloved hand in response, smiling and thinking all the while how peculiar it was that her surroundings weren't so peculiar after all. They included real people. With real hearts and giving natures few ever saw.

The circus was a world within the world, and the packing of it into a train really was one of the most thrilling things she'd ever been a part of.

"You see, everything runs like a machine. It has to if we're going to raise the Big Top night after night. Everyone pitches in."

"We travel every day?"

Annaliese nodded, adding, "Most days. *Oui*. We move from city to city, sleeping on the train and waking in a new place. The Big Top goes up and we chase thrills. Then it comes down again after the show. That's almost more impressive than watching the tent city go up. All of it goes back on the train—fitting in like a jigsaw puzzle. Then we speed away with a few stray programs left behind in the fields as the only evidence that we were ever there. We are performing ghosts now, Rosamund. We even have agreements with the towns we visit to remove the advertising posters when we roll out. A week later, no one would ever know we were there."

A crowd of workmen passed by then, moving to and fro, each seeing to his job loading the flat cars.

"See him?" Annaliese pointed out a tall man with a lanky build, white hair, ample beard, and kind eyes behind wire-framed spectacles. He stood by the side of the nearest flat car, tinkering with something on one of the wagon wheels.

"That's Jerry. He's the head machinist. Works with the men on the train cars. He also helps with the wagons. They say he can take just about anything and make a tool out of it."

Ward wandered in from somewhere along the tracks, then hurried over to Jerry with a toolbox in his hands. He winked at Annaliese and shouted, "Good morning, ladies!" as he trotted by.

Rosamund grinned in spite of herself.

"Jerry's very kind, which is much to his credit since he's charged with keeping young men like Ward Butler in line." Annaliese waved at Ward, adding, "Oh, that handsome devil."

Annaliese brought a gloved hand to toy with the amber stud in her earlobe. The sun caught the gold glint of it out from under a violet cloche that perfectly framed her heart-shaped face and eyes that twinkled in Ward's direction.

"How long have you been with the show?"

Annaliese wrinkled her nose, thinking on it. "Two years, I suppose."

"And you learned all of this in two years? It seems like you know everyone here."

"You will too," she said, and slipped her arm through Rosamund's elbow. "Just wait a few weeks. You'll feel right at home."

Rosamund peered down the line of the cars on the tracks. There were so many, it seemed she couldn't see an end. They extended back, disappearing into a thick layer of spring fog that the morning sun had yet to burn off.

"Attention, *chérie*," Annaliese hummed, drawing her back.

She tugged Rosamund by the elbow, halting her steps. And the instant Rosamund looked back down the line, she knew why.

For every child who'd thought the circus held a certain amount of fairy-tale enchantment, the moment would have solidified it for them. Down the line, elephants marched along the tracks, appearing through the mist as if they'd just been dropped out of the clouds. They lumbered in a single-file line, strong and steady, with trunks holding tails. Their handlers led them straight as an arrow, bound for the stock cars in front of where they stood.

"It's not a stampede, but I wouldn't want to explain to Mr. Keary that you were flattened by a line of elephants on the first day."

"Thank you, I'm sure."

Rosamund edged back as the great gray animals approached. She watched, noting how strange it was to be so close to an animal she'd only read about in storybooks.

Leading the procession was a large one, with thick leathery skin and spots on its head. It had an abundance of wrinkles overlapping around large, expressive eyes. And as the animal was led by, Rosamund was surprised to see depth in those eyes. Truth be told, Rosamund thought she detected a softness in them that belied the build of such a beast.

"That's Nora out in front."

"Nora?"

The handler slowed the line for a moment, bringing the elephant to a stop at their side. The elephant stood still and calm.

Rosamund's eyes widened when its trunk curled, reaching out near them.

"*Oui.* This is Nora. And it seems you've made a friend of her."

Rosamund raised her hand, reaching out with fingertips that trembled ever so slightly. "May I?"

"Of course," Annaliese answered cheerfully.

Rosamund pulled off her glove, wanting a real touch to Nora's skin. A breath escaped her lungs and a smile burst forth on her lips when the elephant's trunk curled round her hand. The skin wasn't as hard as she'd imagined. It almost felt like an eraser she'd used in her studies as a child, with a funny wet snout at the end that tickled her fingertips.

"Oh, are you hungry, Miss Nora?" Annaliese giggled. "See? She's gentle. Just looking for a treat, I think. Everyone loves her. She may be an elephant, but she's the real pro. You have questions about anything on the lot, you might ask her. Been around the longest. Almost as long as the Ringlings themselves."

Annaliese winked and leaned in until she was side by side with Rosamund, looking down the line. "And see the little one who stands shorter than the rest?"

There was indeed a smaller one, with a notch in the ear that faced them.

"Yes."

"That's Mitra. He was born from Nora."

The thought made Rosamund smile. It was an enchanting idea that the circus really was a family, as Colin had claimed. What a beautiful way to see it.

"Mitra," she breathed out. "What does it mean?"

"It's Indian for 'friend,'" Annaliese said, and leaned in to Rosamund's side, hugging her elbow. "Which we are to be as well. *Allons-y,* eh?"

"Let's go," Rosamund repeated, proving she was learning more of Annaliese's French colloquialisms every day.

"*Oui*, because our car is down the line and the boss will have our hides if we miss the train. Let's make tracks."

"ARE YOU LOST?"

Rosamund stood at the top of the metal steps, wedged in the space between two cars. She whirled around to find herself face-to-face with Enzo Rossi. He stood with arms crossed over his chest, looking down on her with the unwavering glare of a security guard watching a vault of diamonds.

"No, not lost. I—" Flustered, Rosamund dropped her satchel in her haste to keep both it, her coat, and her suitcase bundled in her arms. "I was looking for my car."

Rosamund glanced behind her, looking for Annaliese to follow as she had said she would. But it appeared as though the holdup was Ward's doing, as he'd pulled her friend off to the side, holding her hostage with an animated tale of something they both found amusing. Because of that, Rosamund was left alone with the looming figure blocking her path and her satchel on the step at her feet.

"You're new," Enzo exhaled, and bent to help her collect her bag. "And you are lost if you're standing here."

He had the classic good looks of his sister—dark hair and eyes, a firm jaw and slender build. Except for the fact that he wasn't given to the narrow-eyed greetings Bella now preferred when she saw Rosamund, they might've been twins.

"Yes." She took the bag, grateful that though he was direct, Enzo's manner didn't seem to indicate blatant unkindness.

He rose to standing again, tilting his head toward the car behind him.

"These are private cars, miss."

Rosamund looked past, just able to see through the frosted

glass door into the compartment. She saw their uncle, Marvio, sitting at a card table in the center of the room. He smoked a cigar while playing cards with two other men. There was ample space behind them, with a wooden desk mounted on the far wall and two green velvet benches on the opposite side. She could see through to what looked like a sleeping compartment, lit by exquisite, Tiffany-style lamps hanging from the ceiling.

"I'm sorry," she offered, pulling back out of view of the gentlemen in the car. "I was looking for the shared passenger car."

"Which one?"

"There's more than one?"

A svelte figure appeared in the doorway, slinking past.

Rosamund recognized her as Frankie because of both her exquisite beauty and her aloof, chin-up attitude. She wore an elaborate beaded gown in lavender and silver, with a luscious head-to-toe mink draped over her shoulders.

"You bet there's more than one," the icy blonde cooed, pecking a kiss to her husband's cheek before stalking past into the confines of the car. She left the door open, hanging there so she could drop the mink from her shoulders and smooth it into her hands. "You'd best march right down those stairs and get back to your car before we shove off. The train won't wait."

"You're Enzo," Rosamund said, attempting a familiarity. "And you're Frankie? It's nice to meet you both. I'm Rosamund. I traveled with Bella on our passage from England."

The blonde stared through her introduction, offering the warmth of a glacier.

"My name is Frances Rossi—to low-rungs," she asserted. "And you really shouldn't be here."

Enzo cleared his throat, leaning into the private car enough to whisper something in his wife's ear. Whatever he said had enough bite that she closed her mouth and moved deeper into the car. She eased into the background, peeling the gray leather gloves from her arms with jerky movements, looking incensed.

Enzo turned back to Rosamund, pointing down the steps to the train platform beyond.

"What she means is, if you go down the stairs back to the platform, the shared passenger cars start two back from this one—directly behind the privileged car. You'll find other performers back there who can show you to which one you're assigned."

He nodded, as if that were that, and stepped back into his compartment. He clicked the door closed and, without missing a beat, pulled the shade in her face.

"Thank you," she added under her breath. But he'd already gone.

The thought occurred to Rosamund as she trekked down the stairs that she could have given them a piece of her mind and been in the right place for it. Had they been in England, the tables would have been remarkably turned. She'd have been recognized as Lady Easling there, the wealthy daughter of an earl with vast holdings. And as the daughter of a rumrunner, Frances Rossi would have been seen as unfit to polish her boots—according to the pecking order Rosamund's mother would have outlined in the moment.

But she sighed, thinking that wasn't who she was. Or not who she wanted to be now. Her old life had faded away, and if this was the new social order of things, then Rosamund decided she'd just have to get used to it—unwelcome airs or not.

She blew out a breath on the busy platform.

Rosamund scanned the crowd of people and animals hurrying toward the train, looking for Annaliese's petite figure. She walked alongside the cars, looking up to see the Rossi family through the windows, moving about in their private car while she walked with the low-rungs out on the platform.

Enzo looked to be engaged in a passionate exchange of words with Frankie. Marvio stood behind, hand raised to defuse whatever had passed between his nephew and his wife. And though Rosamund hadn't known she was in the car at all, Bella was tucked away in the window of their private car's sleeping quarters. Rosamund could see her reflection through the glass, light hitting her jet-black locks and olive skin with a warm glow. She gazed off in the distance, eyes fixed on nothing or no one in particular.

Rosamund lowered her head and kept walking.

So much for the family atmosphere Colin had advocated.

It wasn't the sweetness of friends like Annaliese or kind, lumbering beasts like Nora that Rosamund recognized as family-like. This time it was the boiling over of family dynamics in the Rossi car that took center stage. The jockeying for position was familiar. As was showing off wealth and privilege to anyone with a pair of eyes . . .

That was the world of Easling Park, and she understood it well.

Rosamund gripped the rail two cars down and climbed the steps up to the shared passenger car. She stood behind several other performers, all waiting in line to find their fold-down cot space on the sleeper train.

It was with arms full and aching from the load she carried that Rosamund promised herself one thing—she'd be different from that day on. She wouldn't let the pecking order of the Rossi family or anyone else define her. And if she had to, she'd work harder than any other performer in the show.

If that's what it took, she'd prove her worth.

CHAPTER 20

1927
Youngstown, Ohio

This was poised to go badly.

As sure as he had instincts about anything, Colin knew how it would play out.

Enduring a conversation to tell Bella her contract wouldn't be renewed was about the last thing he wanted to do that day. He almost wished he was headed to the big cats' wagon rather than walking into a den of lions bearing the last name Rossi.

Colin trudged up the stairs to his wagon.

It was dark still. Early enough that all the lights were out, and the enameled metal coffeepot stood cold and untended on a back shelf.

Figures.

It was one of Ward's simple tasks to fetch the coffee. One he never seemed to remember on the best of days. And this—a rainy, unseasonably cool summer morning—looked to be among the worst.

And on the morning I really need a cup . . .

He crossed the wagon in a huff and flipped on the desk lamp.

It illuminated Mr. Charlie's old desk, casting shadows on every nick and crevice in the aged wood.

The administrative wagon was the way the Ringling Brothers' operating manager had always preferred it: clean and orderly, minus superfluous detail. It was the same now, save for the stacks of mail and the endless paper ledgers Colin despised gathered in a haphazard pile that spilled out from the bin on the desk.

He'd squeezed a canvas cot up against the wall in the corner, his if he slept at all. He traveled with his stacks of books too, just like John Ringling and Mr. Charlie had. And the case for the prized violin Colin now owned held its perch with a worn leather strap keeping it secured on a high shelf. An oversized map of the United States hung on the wall, pins marking all of the circus's show stops through the end of the season.

These were all his worldly possessions, squeezed within four walls. He couldn't help but wonder what it all amounted to.

The brass wall clock ticked, drawing his attention.

Nearly seven o'clock.

Within minutes, four passionate personalities would be in his wagon, all more than ready for a fight. Best to clear the desk now and remove anything that could become a flying missile aimed at his head.

Colin spotted a peach crate under the desk, the one he'd emptied and refilled dozens of times for his travels through the years. It was sturdy and dependable, and would no doubt travel with him again— this time when the circus moved to winter lodgings in Sarasota in the New Year.

He pulled the crate up to the side of the desk, then upturned the mail bin, sending the load of paper fluttering down inside. It piled up like a small, daunting mountain asking for a lighted match instead of a reader.

"Caffè?"

Colin looked up.

Bella leaned against the doorframe, lifting one ankle in a sultry tilt. She held out a porcelain mug, extending the peace offering of a cup of coffee as the rain fell behind her.

"It's miserable out," she said, brushing raindrops from the cap sleeves of her dress. "I suspected you wouldn't have any, so I brought you some."

Bella was indeed beautiful, but calculating. It wasn't about rain or coffee. She wanted something and brought sugar to attract it.

Same as always.

"Open or closed?"

Colin eyed her dark silhouette in the doorway, wondering how much she'd already guessed about their meeting.

"Closed."

Bella clicked the wooden half door closed and waltzed in, alone. Her face serene. Her lips painted in a garish red and her hair already coiffed and tucked under a hat—both odd for the early hour.

She set his coffee cup on the edge of the desk and eased into the leather-and-wood swivel chair tucked beneath it. She crossed her legs at the ankle and sat up, poker-straight.

Colin wasn't about to give her the satisfaction of sitting on the cot below her level, so he leaned against the wall. The wagon creaked with age—the only sound to cut through the pitter-patter of raindrops on the roof.

"Thank you for the gesture. Ward seems to have forgotten the favorability of hot coffee in the morning instead of cold coffee in the afternoon."

He held back on drinking and instead eyed the door. No one else came stepping through it. He paused, crossing his arms over his chest.

"No Rossi Family Flyers this morning?"

"Oh, they found their *caffè* somewhere else today." She paused, stopping to tap her nails on the armrest. "And I thought our conversation was best had alone. We were able to talk once, weren't we?"

Bella's words sliced through the air.

She was confident and without an ounce of fear—at least not that she was likely to let him see.

Colin could keep just about anything from showing on his face as well. He owned a poker face better than most. But he'd need all of his wits about him if he was going to win the next round with Bella, and she looked ready to play.

"You're sure you don't want the rest of your family here right now? Marvio will want to know what's been said."

"And I can take whatever you wish back to my uncle," she said, her tone silky. "Or don't you trust me, Colin?"

He opted to leave that question alone. "Fine. Here it is: we're not renewing your contract."

Bella noticeably stiffened, despite the layers of garments she wore. Her jaw formed a tight line.

"Unless"—he paused, giving her full disclosure that water was about to be poured on her flaming ego—"you can guarantee no more drinking. We'll renew the rest of your family for two years, but you'll be left out. I hate to put it so bluntly—"

She cut in. "Oh, but you know how I appreciate your frankness."

"You had to know this was coming, Bella," Colin fired back, keeping his tone stern. In control. "This is a business."

"Oh, it's business, is it? You're already out recruiting new acts should I have a complete fall from grace. Taking them to meet the Ringlings for a little Christmas party, hmm? You didn't think I would hear about that? I own respect in this show and I have earned loyalty enough to stay informed when I need to."

Colin wanted to sigh. Curse loudly. Or light something on fire. It would have felt good, given the veiled reference to his recruitment of Rose. This was a meeting about Bella, and Bella alone. The last thing he could do was appear frustrated, especially when he needed to retain the upper hand.

"We recruit new acts all the time. It's part of the show. You know that. We're here to talk about that stunt you pulled in the ring at the end of the season. Do you realize what might have happened if that net hadn't been under you?"

"Have a problem with failure, do you?"

Colin swallowed hard.

The sting of her venom cut deeper than Bella might have intended, had she known what she was truly saying. If pasts were anything to be considered, he'd risk his future to make up for his own shortcomings. But to make excuses for Bella now? It felt weak. And clumsy.

"Failure? Not so much. It's the scraping performers up from the sawdust that turns my stomach a sight more."

"Flyers fall all the time. It's part of the job. You know *that*."

He leaned forward to look her in the eye, the wall creaking behind him.

"I'm not judging you, Bella. What you do in your off time is up to you. But when you represent the Ringling Bros. and Barnum & Bailey, any illegal activity—especially when it's been addressed before—will precipitate one of these conversations. The Ringlings are very firm on this. It's a family show."

"And I am the star of their show!" she snapped, slamming her gloved palm against the chair's armrest. Her lips looked brighter in the lamplight, as if she'd drawn blood with the ferocity of her words.

"One of them. You are one of many, all of whom can be replaced if need be."

She stared back. Seething.

"There are Prohibition laws, for goodness' sake! Bella, you can't keep this up. You're not immune to losing your job. Or prosecution, even. The circus is not above the law. It goes with us to every town we stop in."

"It's not illegal to consume alcohol—just to make or sell it. I'm not doing either. And don't try to tell me that Irish blood of yours doesn't have you taking a sip now and then, hmm? So righteous." She blew out her breath. "Americans. Always in a fluff about something . . ." She flitted her wrist in the air. "Today, *vino*. Tomorrow, who knows?"

"But this is a family show, so that's the law around here and we have to live under it." He pulled the contract from the inside pocket of his vest and walked over from his perch, sliding the paper across the desk. Next to it he laid a pen. "Now, do you want to sign this first, or do you want to tell me what's going on?"

"Tell you?" She leaned forward, anger flashing in her eyes. "I'd sooner talk to the backside of an elephant." Bella shot to her feet.

"It's a contract for the next six months. But if there's any more of this behavior, you're out. I'm sorry, but that's the way it has to be. The decision's in your corner."

He watched as Bella removed the glove from her right hand, unscrewed the cap of the pen, and scrawled her name across the bottom of the contract. She tossed the pen across the desk without recapping it, surprisingly in control with every movement.

"Is that all, Your Majesty?" she added.

Colin reached for the coffee cup, the contents still releasing tiny swirls of steam. He took it in hand, swirling the liquid around the inside of the cup. Fully debating whether to drink it. Only half in jest, he wondered to himself if she might have laced the liquid with something. At the very least, it gave him something to stare at while he framed his words.

"I'm sorry, Bella. For everything that's happened." He looked her in the eye. "I'm here to help if you need it, but I have to do my job."

"Sorry? You're sorry. How dare you talk to me about being sorry and the cutthroat business of this circus in the same breath! This conversation is over."

She turned to leave, her composure firm as concrete as she headed for the door.

"One more thing." Colin cleared his throat and took a step toward her, softening his tone. "I need you to be kind to her, Bella."

Bella turned. Slowly. As if she had all the time in the world to blast him with an icy reply. "Who?"

He wanted to forget he'd said it the moment the words were out. Maybe find an extra second or two to convince himself it really was only about the show. That Rose's success in it was just smart business, and whether Bella was truly kind didn't matter beyond that.

"The English brat?"

"The show needs her," he reasoned. "You know we're losing May Wirth."

"Sounds as if she is escaping tyranny."

"She's just moving on. She wants to tour more of the country fairs and smaller, indoor circus shows. So we need Rose to stay. Just as we need you to. And whether Rose knows it or not, she's got the kind of talent that will sell tickets. Just like you."

"And now I am to be flattered so you can get what you want."

"No," Colin answered. "I just want you to know I'm putting her in the center ring. Soon."

"And does she know this?"

He shook his head.

Rose didn't know it, but she'd slowly eased into a flow of excellence in the ring. There wasn't any place she could go now but under the spotlight.

"I see. It is a sacrifice I must make for the show then, hmm? I must play nice under the Big Top," Bella breathed out, slithering through a cool smile as she stepped back to the stairs. "No, Mr. Keary. I do not think so. You do not want me to be nice to her. You want me to fall in love with her—just like the crowd. *My* crowd. But there's something you seem to have forgotten. The people belong to me, and I will not share them."

CHAPTER 21

1912
NEW YORK CITY

Mable had noticed the young man some weeks ago.

He'd casually brush against a gentleman in the crowd as he offered to park cars outside Madison Square Garden, with a ready apology for his clumsiness. He'd then scamper off into the nearby park, blue eyes twinkling, with a wallet in his hand and a victor's grin splayed wide across his face.

Shrouded in the darkness of their Rolls-Royce, Mable waited in the backseat while John engaged in an impromptu conversation with a business colleague. And there he was again—the young man on the street corner, tooling the crowd. Up till now Mable had been content to observe and not intervene, but now he edged too close to her husband's place on the sidewalk.

Mable knocked her gloved hand against the inside of the door, drawing the driver's attention to the backseat. "I'm getting out," she advised, and opened the door without waiting for him to hop out and do it for her.

She stepped out, lowering her head to clear her fur hat under the doorframe. The driver met her on the sidewalk, having darted from his perch in the front seat.

"I won't be a moment," she stated, her breath freezing in a fog. "Please wait here for Mr. Ringling. And if he should return before me, tell him I'm about circus business."

"Very good, madam." The driver nodded, albeit with a quizzical expression. Even the staff knew Mable avoided her husband's business dealings. But if he thought anything of the comment, he kept it to himself, clicking the door closed behind her.

Mable marched down the sidewalk, eyeing her target.

She'd have to time her approach perfectly. Too early, and he'd shy away from the deed. Too late, and her husband's wallet would be lost.

The young man tipped the edge of his cap back off his forehead and in a split second of acting bumped John in the side. Her husband turned immediately, his eyes furrowed to the boy's profuse apology.

Perhaps John's size was overbearing. He stood tall at an even six foot four inches—and with a hat adding a few more to the top of his head, he proved quite an imposing figure. Mable saw something flash in the young man's eyes, as if he knew this moment would come one day and it could now be time to pay for past debts.

In his haste to turn he experienced a genuine fall this time, a near collision with a couple who had just exited the Garden's front doors. John may have known exactly what had happened and might have even offered grace at watching this turn of events—Mable couldn't know. Because the instant she saw a flash of gold hit the pavement and the young man scoop up the item to quick-step it to the park, Mable approached, slipped her arm under his elbow, and whisked him away from the crowd.

"Mable? Is that you?" John saw her breeze by and called after her. "Where on earth are you going?"

She waved him off with a gloved hand. "Just for a turn around the park, Mr. Ringling. We'll return momentarily."

"What? Who is that?"

The questioning voice faded away behind them. The young man grappled with the viselike grip she'd placed around his elbow. Though nearly dragged, he kept pace as Mable tugged him along.

Good thing he was more wiry than strong, and she was far more determined with her muscle than he'd likely have allowed for a woman in a fur coat and heels. She was quite able to keep him attached at her hip until she was willing to let go.

"Who are you, lady?" he groused, trying to wheedle away from her grip.

"I'm the woman who may have just saved your life. And the woman who's going to testify at your trial unless you cooperate and follow me away from that group of gentlemen," she snapped. "Now, keep walking until I tell you to stop."

They stood at the corner of the street, waiting for several carts and horse-drawn buggies to pass by before crossing over to the park. Once there, she turned him round to face her.

She held her gloved hand out, palm up, and sent him the most no-nonsense glare she owned. "Give it back. Now."

Mable could see him shiver under his light tweed jacket. He crossed his arms across his chest, trying to trap as much warmth as he could.

"Give what back?"

"The watch you stole from my husband."

He began shaking his head, but stopped the instant Mable cocked an eyebrow in his direction. She tapped her foot, waiting for him to decide that she wasn't bluffing.

"It's cold out here," she huffed. "And it makes no sense to stand arguing in the elements. Please save me the trouble of having to walk you over to that policeman across the street, and give the watch back now."

The young man cupped hands with fingerless gloves around his mouth, blowing air into his palms. He looked over in the direction of the street corner. Surely he'd seen the uniformed officer there, smoking a cigarette under the light of the streetlamp.

"Well?"

"If I did have a watch, how do I know it's yours? I might have one of my own."

She glowered at him. "Because there is an inscription on the inside. A quote by George Eliot. I ordered that watch from Tiffany and Company last year as a Christmas gift."

He eyed her warily. She could see the shades of indecision etched on his face.

"Go on," she prompted. "Read it for yourself."

The young man looked at her, the blue of his eyes suddenly sharp. He reached in his pants pocket, retrieved the watch, and slapped it into her outstretched hand.

If it was possible, a wave of understanding made the watch burn through her glove. The watch chain dangled, flashing in the dim light of the streetlamps. She gathered it up in her fingertips, seeing that the face was now blemished with a crack across the glass, and curled the chain into her palm.

"Oh, I see." She exhaled. "You can't read, can you?"

He said nothing, only narrowed his eyes.

"Well, I still have a mind to turn you in," she said. "But I won't."

His shoulders eased ever so slightly.

"If"—she pointed a finger at him—"you promise never to do that again."

"To anyone? Or just the tall man?"

Mable shifted her pose, cocking one hip.

"The 'tall man' is my husband. And I've seen you before. It was weeks ago that I noticed your undignified profession being employed on the sidewalk over there. I let it go because I thought it was just boyish folly. But now I see that it has become a nasty habit."

"It's not a habit. I'm good at it."

He straightened the brim of his cap. Stood a little straighter. Probably trying to appear older than the thirteen or so years she'd have guessed he could claim.

"Boyish folly indeed," she huffed. "But you are not a boy, are you?"

"I'm fifteen."

Fifteen? And he couldn't read? She paused, considering.

"Then you're a young man. And you ought to think about how what you're doing only spells trouble. May I trust that this moment of forgiveness will change your mind? If not, we can summon that officer over there and be done with the matter altogether."

She raised her eyebrows, punctuating the point. The cold was getting the better of her, so she gave a nod and turned round, intent upon fleeing home to their warm apartment in the fastest manner possible.

"Ma'am?"

"Yes?" She turned toward him again.

A slow smile eased over his mouth, spreading the spray of freckles on his cheeks wider across his face. "The words on the watch. What do they say?"

"It says, 'It's never too late to be what you might have been.'"

The young man chuckled, his breath freezing on air.

"Is that funny to you?"

"No." He shoved his hands into his pockets. "I was just wondering what I might have been—especially since I'll have to look for a new street corner, thanks to you."

"Is your life all played out then—at fifteen?"

"I'm old enough to know there's not a feast of options in this life, not for someone like me. I bet *you've* never had to think twice about where your next meal will come from. A watch would buy me too many to count. And I wouldn't have to return to the Garden for some time. Maybe not until spring."

Mable could feel the watch ticking in her hand.

The wind breezed in, reminding her that John was waiting for her in the cold, with the minutes passing by.

"Six thirty-six Fifth Avenue," she replied, pressing her lips into the hint of a smile. "Noon. Tomorrow. Be there and you can find out for yourself."

He drew back a step. Eyes searching for any signs of deceit he could find in the contours of her face.

"You'll have the police there."

She shook her head. "I will not."

"How do I know you're not lying?"

"You don't. I suppose you'll just have to put your faith in something bigger than yourself."

The young man turned his attention across the street. The police officer was now strolling down the sidewalk, baton twirling in his hand like he was on a carefree stroll through the park.

"And who do I ask for?"

Mable let the warmth of a smile ease fully over her face. "Mr. John Ringling."

His eyes widened. "The tall man?"

"Yes. He'll put you onto an honest job here in the city, if you're up for it. One that carries three hot meals per day." She gave a proper nod and a gentle pat to the watch in her hand. "He'll expect you tomorrow then. And be smart about your time. Nice doing business with you."

He almost smiled.

They parted ways, and Mable was nearly back to the car when she felt a tug on the sleeve of her coat.

"Excuse me, Mrs. Ringling. Give this to the gentleman your husband was talking to?" The young man held out a leather wallet.

Mable took a step backward. This young man might be rough and riddled with thorns, but she had a feeling he had more to offer in life, if only given the chance.

Her thoughts turned to Sally, and the promise she'd made to her dying friend the day of their last visit. *There will never be a single dream lost in any garden that I tend.* The fact that this young man had brought the wallet back showed there might be hope for him yet. Mable felt a sudden compulsion to find out what that hope might become.

"Wait!" she called after him. "Your name, young man?"

He turned and flashed a quick grin over his shoulder.

"Colin," he shouted back, heading for the darkness of a nearby alley. "Colin Keary."

CHAPTER 22

1927
SPOKANE, WASHINGTON

Rosamund sat on a straw bale with her hands cradled in her lap, listening to the soft patter of rain against the Big Top's roof.

Her palms were blistered and raw from the days she and Ingénue had trained. The muscles of her back and legs burned nearly every time she walked. And her body seemed to ache all over—no doubt from learning to sleep on a cramped train car and the grueling training schedule they'd undertaken in between performances.

Never before had Rosamund been so exhausted that she crumpled down right on the spot, content to stay put for more than an hour after they'd finished. She'd fallen against the straw bale, not caring that it poked through her cream silk sleeveless blouse and high-waisted riding pants. Just to rest and recover was such a luxury that she couldn't be bothered by the small inconvenience of a few prickles to her skin.

The show had rolled in March, Rosamund and Ingénue with it.

They'd gone out in front of crowds of thousands for months now, executing—but barely. Theirs was the bare-minimum per-formance, with both of them struggling each time. Rosamund no longer looked up to the flash of blue sequins and the smiles brought to the crowd by the spectacular Rossi family. Now she looked to the crowd. Wondering what they were thinking. How they'd receive the jittery Arabian and the automatic routine of the petite brunette in ring three, with the lack of charisma and the blush of English roses laced in her hair.

"I thought you would have gone back to the ring stock tent by now."

Colin appeared at a side entrance to the tent, leaning against the edge of the wooden bleachers. A flash of lightning illuminated the sky behind his shoulders.

Rosamund was surprised to see him, but determined not to show it. She curled her fingers into her palms and pulled her hands in closer to her waist, hiding them from his view.

"I was waiting for you, but you never showed."

She rolled her eyes to the direction of the rain dancing on the roof. "The rain. I couldn't go back to a busy tent just yet. It was too peaceful here." She leaned against the bale of straw behind her. Tiny stalks poked her shoulders again, and she readjusted until they finally left her in peace. "What time is it?"

He didn't reach for his watch. Just noted, "It's late."

"I was too exhausted to move," she admitted with a light smile, rubbing the ache out of her arms. "Even to go to the dining tent for a cup of coffee. You know it's serious when I'll forgo that."

Colin nodded. As though he'd expected her to say something like that. "Lucky we don't have to roll tonight. One more day staying put can be a blessing sometimes."

He stepped inside, hands buried in his pockets as he walked toward her.

She could see the rain-dampened hair hanging low over his forehead. His striped work shirt was speckled with drops at the shoulders and collar.

"May I?"

Rosamund nodded, scooting over to share the straw bale with him.

She could hear the sounds of men tinkering somewhere off behind them, with hushed conversation, arbitrary clinks of metal, and the occasional laugh or two as they finished their tasks for the night. Other than the far-off company, they sat alone in the dim light of the Big Top, side by side. And she felt better for it.

She wasn't certain she could collect her thoughts if she had to look straight at him.

"Owen is a good man. I've worked with him for years. I can attest to how well he treats the performers in his charge—both people and horses. He makes no distinction between them. But he'll put you through your paces to get a performance that's up to his standards, and I can't fault him for that."

"Neither can I, to tell you the truth."

He pulled something from his pocket—a small glass jar that was half full of a cloudy, sticky liquid. "Here," he whispered, and twisted off the lid. "Give me your hands."

Rosamund felt her pulse quicken, as it had the night of the party. "How did you know?"

He shrugged. "Been around the lot for a long time. You're not the first bit of raw talent to come waltzing through our doors."

They hadn't spoken much in the past few weeks.

She'd seen him around the lot, muscling wagons onto train cars at depots, standing guard in the wings during every performance, with an intense glare and arms folded across his chest as she and Ingénue rode into the ring. Those flashes she caught of Colin Keary had been of Colin the boss. He was always watching. Managing every detail. Ensuring that the Circus King's show went off without a hitch.

But it was not the same man who'd appeared in the stock tent now.

This man was relaxed, sitting with his palms out, waiting to accept hers. He was the same man who had once brought her fishing rods at a Sarasota dock. The one who had taken her hand in his and led her around the outdoor dance floor at the Cà d'Zan.

Colin had keenly avoided her since the show opener. To give her space as she trained. Maybe to give them both a bit of it, being boss and employee. But now those winds had shifted, and the old Colin had breezed back into her path.

He waited, his quiet way punctuating the sudden silence between them.

A familiar longing squeezed in her chest. Rosamund realized now how much she'd missed him.

"May I?" He was asking rather than telling this time, his tone layered with sincerity.

She nodded, wincing from the sting that shot up her arms as she stretched her palms wide. "Yes."

Her hands felt warm in his fingertips. Then cool, when he rubbed balm over the painfully inflamed parts of her palms.

"The flyers swear by this stuff." He spoke over the rain, taking time as his fingertips brushed across her palms. "Been using it for years. Trust me—you'll have new hands by morning. And try using more talc between sets. You need to keep your palms dry or you'll find yourself nursing hands like this all season."

Rosamund kept quiet as he worked.

Except for her heart. That began beating louder, so much so that she feared he'd hear it over the pattering of rain overhead. She watched him work, felt the balm soothing every rough edge out of her day, wondering why it was that his very presence could stir and soothe at the same time.

He ran a finger over the base of her wrist, having noticed the scar there. "Where'd you come by this? It doesn't look like a riding injury."

"Evidence of a stubborn nature, I'm afraid."

She almost laughed to think on it now. Those youthful days of running from her tutorials, hiding in the rose garden to avoid getting caught.

"I'd been hiding in the rose garden. Hendrick found me there and took pity on me. He seemed to think that a diversion might lessen the sting of a thorn that had badly pricked my skin. That was long before he went to war. Before Ingénue, before everything changed. And it left a scar, right where I can always see it."

Colin seemed to understand that there was more to the story, but didn't inquire further. He merely nodded as she talked, listening as was his way.

"This has been hard on you, and I'm sorry for it."

"I know. But you've done what you had to in order to get a performance out of us."

His eyes shot up, connecting with hers. The blue in them was open. Stormy. Searching the contours of her face.

"Is that really what you think of me?"

"Well . . . the circus has to come first, right? The balance. Everyone doing their part around here."

"Not always, Rose." He shook his head ever so slightly. "We do have our parts to play. I know that. In fact, I live by it. But I thought if I left you alone, you'd fare better. So they wouldn't think I'd shown any favoritism. I was worried that some of the other performers might have been . . . uncivil."

"Uncivil about a privileged lady trying to squeeze into the ranks? Never."

She allowed a bit of a laugh to escape the gentle part in her lips. That was the understatement of the year.

"It's good to hear you laugh again," he said, a noticeably quieter note having taken over his voice.

He released her hands and screwed the lid back on the jar, then placed it on the bale between them.

"Let that dry. Then put on another layer first thing in the morning, okay?"

"I will," she promised, trying not to look him in the eye for very long. Staring down at her hands seemed easier, and so she did.

Rosamund expected him to leave. He'd apologized. Checked on her. And surely there were a hundred things he could have been doing at the moment, rather than wasting time with her. But instead of standing, he leaned back against the bale behind them, content to stay put.

His shoulder grazed hers.

"It's nice in here," he whispered, looking up at the vault of the tent ceiling as the sounds of the pattering rain eased off. "I don't come in when it's empty like this. I used to. But not anymore."

She gazed around at the hushed atmosphere, with rows of empty bleachers and corners shrouded in shadow. It was almost as if the giant tent were asleep, and they'd lowered their voices so as not to disturb its gentle slumber.

"I hadn't thought it could be like this either."

"Even in the number of years I've been here." Colin shrugged. "You still can't get used to seeing it like this."

"How long has that been?"

It was, Rosamund hoped, an appropriate time to ask the question.

She knew very little about him. It seemed few knew about his past. And as he'd come to her now, so open and very much the man she remembered from Sarasota, she hoped it would be enough for him to stick around a little longer.

"Fifteen years, give or take," he answered, sighing into the words. "Feels like a lifetime."

"I can understand that. For me now too." She kicked at a piece of errant straw in the path of her riding slipper. "I wonder what my mother would think of me. I wear trousers now more than dresses."

"The circus will do that to you." He chuckled. "You know, I met Mrs. Ringling before anyone else. And for how she's content to stay out of the limelight of Mr. Ringling's business affairs, she's the one who first brought me into this circus world. It was an adjustment for me too."

"I think I could believe that." Rosamund smiled. "How did you meet her?"

"I stole a watch from Mr. Ringling, and she caught me in the act. I was young. A scrappy Irish lad. Thought I knew it all back then."

His voice faded on the memory and Rosamund sat up a little straighter, her attention piqued.

"Much like your hiding in the garden, it was not my proudest moment. But I was living by my wits back then, and a gold watch was quite a meal ticket for a youth like me. The New York City streets get pretty cold in winter, so right or wrong—you do what you have to in order to survive."

Colin watched her. Searching her face. Maybe looking for any sign of pity now that he'd shared some of his scars with her.

"But didn't you have any family? A home?"

He didn't hesitate—just pointed up to the maze of rope and poles and stringed lights crowding the ceiling overhead, as if the answer were simple.

"This became my home. John Ringling gave me a job, and that was it. I left behind anything I'd once had in New York and joined up."

"What kind of job?"

"Nothing as glamorous as you've got going on here. I started out selling programs in the crowd outside Madison Square Park. But I wanted to go on the road with the rest of the show. And as soon as Mr. Charlie found out I had a past that could be useful, they put me to work with the Pinkerton detectives, ferreting out pickpockets on the circus Midway. I don't think a single dime was lost by a guest that year."

"So you used your powers for good."

"Maybe. God knows. But I worked my way up from there. Not with any great intention—just because I'd found my niche. Or rather, it found me. It's what I'm good at. And now it's all I know. This tired old canvas held up by rope and wood . . . it's my home."

Home.

The word begged remembrance.

"It's a home on wheels."

"Home can move," he answered. "As long as your heart goes with it."

The sudden turn in the conversation reminded Rosamund that hers was a life still in flux. She felt a sudden chilling breeze and shivered, drawing her arms around her middle to pull in her warmth.

"Rose, tell me something. When you were back home, what did you hear when you would ride?"

It was the last thing Rosamund expected him to ask, especially given that he'd managed to read her thoughts in earnest.

She swallowed hard, avoiding his eyes. "I didn't hear anything. I was out in the fields."

"Not true. I think you heard something. What was it? Birds? Wind? Ingénue breathing? Tell me. I know you're holding something back."

"Yes. I could hear Ingénue," she whispered. "She's always been with me."

"But that's not all, is it?" He turned suddenly, locking eyes with hers. "When I saw you riding at Easling Park that morning, you were a million miles away. What took you there?"

She shook her head, as if she didn't understand.

He wasn't buying it.

"Close your eyes," Colin whispered. "Go back to that day at Easling Park, when you thought it was your last ride with Ingénue. Tell me what you hear."

Rosamund obeyed, aching for remembrance. To get lost in the childhood memories that she'd not shared with another person before. She went back, living in them for the moment. Relishing the opportunity to revisit the hidden parts of her heart.

"Music."

"What music?" he prompted.

"Hendrick's."

"He played music for you?"

"Yes," she breathed out, trying to avoid allowing tears to fall in front of him. "On a violin. Did I ever tell you that?"

She heard him exhale. Maybe chuckle just a bit.

"No. You didn't."

"He stood in the fields and played his heart out for me. Fun tunes. The kind my father never would have allowed in the manor. It really was his gift."

"Playing the violin?"

"No," she answered, shaking her head. "Giving to others. And I haven't thought of that in so long. I think I made myself forget that part of him."

Her pulse beat faster with the shock of feeling Colin's palms cup her jaw. Then feeling his thumb tenderly wiping a tear that had escaped to dampen the edge of her lashes. It brushed against the soft skin under her eye, lingering there against the apple of her cheek.

Rosamund couldn't open her eyes. Didn't dare look at him. Surely he'd see the inner workings of her heart revealed there.

Her hands trembled in her lap.

"So you hear him when you ride."

"Yes. It was my freedom. The only kind I knew. And those moments became the memories when everything was right. When we were a family. There was no bitterness. No loss. Just . . . music." She paused, swallowing over emotion that was trying to get the better of her. "Remember the song I played at the Cà d'Zan? 'Roses of Picardy.' It was published during the war, and it was the last song he played for me. Looking back now, those are the only moments that are all mine. I don't have to share them with anyone."

She felt the shock of his lips, whisper-soft as they grazed hers.

"But you just shared them with me," he said against her mouth.

Rosamund blinked her eyes open and met the cool blue of his eyes, still revealing an openness before her. But it didn't last. He eased away, dropping his hands in an instant and turning away as if he'd been burned. The action left a cold void between them.

"I'm sorry. I shouldn't have—"

He stopped short.

Let out a rough sigh, rubbing a hand to the back of his neck. He gazed out over the span of the ring in front of them for long moments.

Saying nothing of the line they'd just crossed.

"You have to show that to the crowd, Rose. Those memories? They're powerful. And they make you the woman that you are." Colin stood, turning to face her. "You need a day for your hands to heal, then I'm putting you in the center ring."

"No." She shook her head emphatically. The stakes were too high. How could she convince him he was wrong? "We're not ready. You know we're not."

"You are. It's time, Rose. And during your performance,

let down your hair. Get lost, just like you did at Easling Park. Remember what you just told me and live it out in that ring."

How had he remembered that day?

The notion that he must have thought about it too—maybe more than she'd realized—struck Rosamund with great force. And it was telling that despite the obvious warring with the weight of his responsibilities, he'd kissed her anyway. He'd made the decision to cross the line drawn in sawdust between them.

She stood too. And, shaken by what he'd done, took a hopeful step forward.

"How can you be sure?"

"Trust me. I know what I'm saying when I tell you to go back to a time when your memories are sweetest. Live there while you can." His voice held a note of softness to it, his Irish brogue edging out more than usual. "You've already got all the tools you need to win the crowd. And if you go back to those rides, if you forget anyone's watching and just perform with the music you hear, something special will happen."

Colin took several steps back, putting more space between them. "Do that, and the crowd will be yours."

ROSAMUND GATHERED UP HER THINGS IN A DAZE.

After such a lengthy near silence from Colin, the last thing she'd expected was to journey into new territory as they had under the Big Top.

She wrapped a sweater round her shoulders and pulled on her leather riding boots, grateful now that she had them for what could prove to be a trek through rain-dampened fields.

Rosamund slipped into the canvas neck that connected the Big Top to the menagerie tent. She'd swiped two extra apples at dinner, hoping to bring one to Nora after the show. The other she'd gift to Ingénue for their pre-breakfast ride in the morning.

She poked her head into the tent, waved to the animal care-takers. She held up an apple, and when they'd nodded her in, she slipped inside.

It wasn't too late after all.

Rosamund greeted Nora and smiled that a life with exotic animals as friends was commonplace now. She held out the apple. Nora curled her trunk around Rosamund's hand, taking the apple to drop into her open mouth.

"You're welcome, pretty girl." She smoothed her hand against the elephant's trunk, patting with affection. "You know, you're one of the very first friends I made here. Remember that? But I think you were looking to fill your tummy even then."

"You just make friends everywhere, don't you?"

Rosamund jumped and turned around. She was taken aback to find the red-lipped Bella Rossi, of all people, standing behind her. She wore an elegant silk dressing robe tied over her performance costume, with puffs of camel-colored fur lining the wrists and wide collar.

"Bella . . ." Rosamund caught a hand at her chest. "I'm sorry. You startled me."

It wasn't in the flyer's nature to mix with man or beast outside her private tent. Rosamund didn't want to judge why—but it was commonplace that this star wasn't in the habit of trekking through the fields like some of the other performers were. Not in her stylish T-strap heels and Italian dresses, and certainly not right after the fields would be covered in mud from the steady rain.

She held an elegant garment of blush-pink silk and gauze fabric over one arm.

"Minnie was looking for you," Bella announced. "She finished sewing your new costume tonight. She wanted you to try it and make sure it fits before tomorrow's matinee performance. I hear you're taking center ring once we reach Vancouver."

"News travels fast. And we're still two days out," Rosamund noted, wondering how in the world Bella could know that already. "I just learned of it myself."

"Well, that's to be expected around here. And as I was in the costume tent for my own fitting, I said I'd come and find you."

Rosamund hated to suspect that there might be more to Bella's appearance than just extending a new costume and offering kindness. But still, she'd offer the same gesture of charity back, no matter what the other woman's motive.

"Thank you." She reached to take the costume, only to find that Bella artfully drew her arm back.

"Why not come to my tent and try it on? It's closer than the pad room."

Rosamund cleared her throat. "Well, performers don't change in the pad room anyway. Because . . . it's for the performance horses. We change in Minnie's costume tent."

Bella waved her off, as if the reply were a frivolity of some sort. "Yes, of course. But why walk all the way back in this weather?"

"It's no trouble," Rosamund said. "It's not far."

"Nonsense. I insist."

Bella nodded as if that sealed the matter, and stepped from the tent with full expectancy that Rosamund would follow. So she did, sending one last look to Nora, wishing altogether that she'd waited until morning to gift her friend the apple. Now it felt like she'd be paying for the gesture.

The cookhouse and nearby dining tents were still lit.

As they passed by, Rosamund noticed men seated inside at the bench-style tables. She scanned the tables, looking for Colin's face. He was nowhere in sight, though she did spot Ward playing cards over the red-and-white-checked tablecloth, sipping drinks with the rest of the men as they sat in the lamplight. Someone must have scored a hefty haul with a winning hand, sending a general ruckus of hoots and hollers up from the other men. She smiled as the sounds faded behind her back, wondering if Ward had somehow been the cause.

Now that the rain had stopped, small campfires with performers circled around them dotted the landscape.

Rosamund wondered if Colin was out there somewhere, perhaps sitting around one of those fires, talking and laughing too. More than likely, he was shut up in his private wagon, drinking cold coffee while mapping out a strategy for the next stops of the show. She doubted he slept much at all. Doubted even more that he'd have been trekking through the fields now, looking for her in every tent he passed, thinking about their kiss for far too long afterward, as she was.

She noticed that she'd pressed her fingertips to her lips, remembering, and dropped them at her sides, trying to force the memory out of her mind.

They crossed the field until they came to the private tents for the show's stars.

It was written in her contract that a private room in a train car and private tent on the circus lot grounds would be provided once she'd earned top billing. Up to that point, she'd been barely hanging on the bottom rung to keep her job.

Stepping into Bella's tent now felt like a reminder of just who and what she was.

Bella Rossi's tent was lavish—even for a traveling entertainer.

She had a beautiful dressing screen in shades of wine and black set in the back, with a gold-filigree rose pattern along the top and sides. The grass and earth field beneath their feet had been covered with an ornamental rug, and Bella slipped her toes out of her heels to walk around on it barefoot.

Open trunks laced with her trapeze rigging, studio photographs, and publicity stills covered one side, along with an oversized cot with satiny throw pillows and a brocade coverlet in rich tones of red and gold. And while that may have been quite enough to intimidate Rosamund, the other side of the room was entirely fashioned to amplify Bella's star mystique. There stood an enormous dressing table with a gilded mirror and a tall standing trunk with elaborate costumes of all kinds.

Bella sat on an X-frame wooden stool at the dressing table, her back to Rosamund.

A single electric light glowed from its perch at the top of the mirror, creating soft shadows on the contours of her face. She looked at Rosamund from the reflection cast in the mirror.

"Not exactly like the pad room, is it?"

There was no point in advising Bella a second time that the pad room was for horses. She knew the difference, Rosamund had no doubt.

"No," she confirmed. "Not like the pad room at all."

"The screen is behind you," Bella advised, without looking up. She'd occupied her hands with sorting through a tray of costume jewelry on the tabletop.

The tent was intended for Rosamund to see. That was very clear. What she wondered then, as she crossed to the screen in the back, was why the invitation had been extended at all. Why would this woman go to such lengths to establish her seniority in such an ardent way?

"You were rehearsing late again?"

Rosamund swallowed hard and fumbled with the buttons on her shirt.

Please . . . don't let her have seen me with Colin.

"What time is it?" she edged out, nearly squeaking on the words.

"Late enough, I suppose. But not too late for your riding."

Rosamund thought of the same question she'd asked Colin. For some reason, he'd not answered it either. Did no one recognize time unless it was show time?

"Yes," she called out from behind the screen. "As you said, we go in the center ring soon. Ingénue and I want to be prepared."

"And Colin? Does he think you're prepared?"

Rosamund yanked the fabric over her middle with the surprise of such a question. A tiny thread came loose at the seam of the corset-waist, splitting by more than two stitches. It made a tiny rip, causing her to grimace.

"Um, I wouldn't know. You'll have to ask him." She ran her fingertips over the split seam. "A stitch came loose," she called. "I'll have to take this back to Minnie tonight."

The wooden stool creaked, indicating that Bella had eased her weight off and stood. And then her voice was directly across from Rosamund, on the other side of the screen.

"Toss it over the top. I can repair it."

Rosamund obeyed and slipped out of the costume, tossing it over the screen as instructed. By leaning back ever so slightly she could see the standing trunk in the shadows, past the side of the screen, boasting all of the elegant clothes Bella owned. There was more than one fur coat. Several hats. And too many elegant frocks to count. The sight of them all made Rosamund abhor the riding clothes she'd been forced to slip back into.

She came round the screen, pulling a suspender over her shoulder.

Bella was bent over the fabric, a needle and thread in one hand, a golden thimble on her index finger, patching the seam of the garment.

"Sit," she offered without looking up. "This will only take a moment."

Rosamund found a second X-frame stool not far from the dressing table and sat.

Awkward seconds ticked by. Wind grazed the sides of the tent every so often. And the faint sound of laughter and harmonicas still drifted in the background.

She watched Bella with sudden curiosity.

Each stitch she made was with precision.

After Rosamund's long history of her mother's required dress fittings and couture wardrobes for each season, she'd seen enough of tailoring to know an expert when she saw one. Bella was a learned seamstress.

She finished the last stitch and tied it off, breaking the thread away from the needle with her teeth.

"Never look directly in the lights. They'll blind you."

She held out the costume.

"All right." Rosamund took the silky fabric in hand, adding, "Thank you."

One look over the seam confirmed Bella's skill. It was better than perfect, with no evidence that any rip had even occurred.

"Don't eat a large meal before you perform. It will sit in you like a stone and will show in your performance. And if you lose any part of your costume, you keep going with the act. That goes for slippers, hairstyle—anything."

Rosamund didn't quite understand.

Bella was elegant and refined in her condescending quips, but was bestowing actual advice on her. Rosamund found that the oddest contradiction.

"Why . . . why are you helping me?"

"Every new performer needs something. Some kind of help."

Bella paused, tipping her head to one side. She ran the golden thimble over the tips of her fingers as she talked, her hand moving absently while she collected her thoughts. "You know, you might think about cutting your hair. It is awfully long, isn't it?"

Rosamund brought up a hand, unconsciously patting the thick coil at her nape.

Hers was nothing compared to the stylish bob that Bella wore so well.

Bella's was sleek and sophisticated, with blunt-cut bangs and soft curls that framed her cheekbones on each side of her face. It was striking how much she favored an Italian version of Louise Brooks—a stunning film actress Rosamund had seen in a show at the cinema. The look was seemingly effortless for both women, but would have proved a major feat for any normal woman to have achieved.

Bella notched her chin, having noticed Rosamund's inspection of her.

"Long hair isn't really the fashion in Europe any longer. Nor in the States."

Bella rose, slipping the thimble in the pocket of her robe as she walked over to the spot where Rosamund sat. With gentle hands, she ran her fingertips over the waves framing Rosamund's face and, finding a pin, slipped it out. Slowly. Allowing Rosamund's hair to come loose and then tumble about her shoulders.

"Every woman has short hair now," she whispered. "Except for you."

"My mother insisted on keeping the length."

"But your *madre*—she isn't here, is she?"

Rosamund shook her head. "No. She's not."

Bella didn't wait for an answer to move behind Rosamund. She placed her hands on the top of Rosamund's shoulders in a gesture of veiled dominance.

"No one is here to give you advice, are they? Because I have so much more experience, I feel it incumbent upon me to do it." She reached into her pocket and retrieved the thimble, holding it to expose it to the light. "Do you sew?" Bella asked.

"No." Rosamund shook her head, her hair waving in a light dance about her shoulders.

"But I assume you've seen one of these before?"

"Of course. It's a thimble."

"It's a thimble, yes. But see this?" Bella ran the tip of her index finger around the thick golden rim. "It's meant to be cut off. When a young seamstress marries, this etched gold band becomes her ring."

"I didn't know that."

"It's a working girl's trade secret. Something an earl's daughter couldn't know. A thimble with the rim attached means the seamstress never married. It's rare to find one intact."

Rosamund's heart fluttered.

Bella's words were spoken softly, but their meaning was no less cutting.

"The circus will travel on. We'll go from town to town, and you'll find that you have become a social pariah. *Rimonta* they'd call you, in my country. Here, you're a vamp. And that's if the townspeople are in an agreeable mood. Men will whistle. They'll look at you as one of the lions would their supper. They'll gawk at the tiny costume but never propose marriage. And the women they do marry? They're much worse. They look straight through you. You'll be cast off everywhere you go. You don't need to be in the sideshow to be excluded from the parlors or quilting circles of any town in which your poster hangs. They'll see you on the street corner and walk to the other side just to avoid the scent of your perfume. And all the while, you will lose your innocence. You'll eventually cut your hair. Shorten your skirt. And one day your star quality will fade. But the thimble will remain in your pocket. Tarnished and unused. You'll become as rare as me, Lady Easling."

Rosamund could feel her heart racing, feel the blood pumping faster through her veins. But she'd give no indication of it. She merely swallowed, keeping her chin high as she stared back at their reflection in the mirror.

"He'll hurt you, you know."

"I don't know what you mean."

"Don't you?" Bella stepped around to face her, staring down. A sudden harshness had taken over her features.

The lamplight still glowed, but shadows had bled into the contours of her face. Making her look worn under the layers of powder and rouge. A primped star with exhaustion in life marring her perfectly coiffed crown.

"Circus is all Colin Keary knows. It's all he cares about. There have been many long-haired poster beauties before you, and there will be many more after. And it doesn't take long for a costume's seams to fray and sequins to lose their sparkle. Not here, and certainly not in his eyes."

Rosamund shot to her feet.

It no longer mattered whether Bella had seen their kiss under the Big Top. There was a line drawn in the sawdust at her feet too. It separated the childlike wonder of the circus from something harsh. Unfiltered. A world that was crass and bawdy, in which the center ring's star had grown all too bitter. Bella Rossi's was a line drawn between light and darkness, laughter and pain.

Rosamund wanted no part of it.

"Thank you for the fitting," she shot out in a hasty whisper, offering a polite nod before spinning on her heels to flee the tent.

"Your hairpin," Bella called after her.

Rosamund padded across the oriental rug back to Bella's side and took the oversized hairpin in hand. She tried to leave again but felt the grip of cold fingers catch the underside of her elbow, drawing her back.

"Take this too," Bella offered, pressing the thimble into her palm. She curled Rosamund's fingers over the flash of gold. "I don't need it anymore."

CHAPTER 23

1927
VANCOUVER, CANADA

The center ring had been a source of much angst for Rosamund in the months since that first disastrous performance at Madison Square Garden.

But not this night.

She told herself they'd not fear it.

Even with Bella's ominous words still ringing in her head. Instead, she'd focused on the rose she'd been given. The gift had given her the idea of taking Mable's wisdom into the ring. And so Rosamund had brilliant blooms laced all along the nape of her neck, English roses intertwined with long ropes of her hair twisted round their stems. She wore her new costume of pink, a sweet corset design with layers of gauze and gold sequins falling down like colored air about her waist. Tiny slippers, sequined in gold and blush-pink, adorned her feet. And even Ingénue was bedecked for the occasion, with English roses braided into her mane and a harness that flashed with gold ribbons dancing.

Never in one of her mother's couture-designed dresses had Rosamund felt as beautiful as she did in that moment. The costume and the ethereal magic of riding out on a dream made everything she'd ever worn pale by comparison.

Rosamund's hands had indeed felt better by morning. And even the sting of the encounter with Bella the night before was forgotten when she gripped the reins. Her hands felt sure. Her heart ready.

Owen approached their side.

"Annaliese will ride into ring one with the liberty horses. And you go on to your place in the center ring." He let out a deep sigh, one tinged with a smile. "There you'll shine. Go dance, the two of you, for every eye in the house."

Rosamund nodded, biting the corner of her bottom lip over the emotion she read in his face. It was almost paternal in a way, a sense of pride that she hadn't seen anyone use when looking on her in quite some time. Maybe even since Hendrick.

But it was there in Owen's eyes; he believed in her. That was enough.

"And you've got something special for the act tonight? Colin wouldn't say what it is, just that I should be ready for it."

"Just that we plan to march into the center ring and take the Big Top by storm," she confirmed, patting Ingénue with a soft rub of the neck. "We're ready."

"It's your time then," he said. "And you'll make us proud."

The ringmaster signaled their entry, and Owen nodded before hurrying out in front of the troop. And with that, the horses rode out and began their part in the show.

Annaliese was pert and engaging as usual, stirring the crowd with tricks and delight, flitting about like a fairy as the liberty horses clipped around their ring in precision. Children marveled as she whisked about in front of her horses, dancing light as air as she ran through the act.

Rosamund would have liked to stay and watch, but the center

ring was calling. She nudged Ingénue forward at a light, high-stepping trot. They'd circle the ring to come to center on the opposite side.

Maybe it was the dimming of the lights over the bleachers. Or perhaps it was the spotlights that shone down, tracing their path. Rosamund was more inclined to believe it was a combination of that and the moments she'd shared with Colin in that very spot the night before. But whatever the reason, fear dulled. And in its place was joy.

Rosamund hopped down and discarded the long tails of ribbons from Ingénue's harness, leaving nothing to the Arabian's costume but the bower of roses braided in her mane.

They began to run through their act, she thinking to guide Ingénue through. But it became clear, as they performed one trick after another, that Ingénue required no firm hand and no calming of nerves. Sawdust became the field grasses at Easling Park and the Big Top no longer canvas, but the North Yorkshire sky. And there they rode together, having lost all notion of anything but dancing in the fields that for years had been their haven.

Rosamund didn't notice the hush that had fallen over the crowd until the halfway point in the act. But the circus band had faded into silence, replaced by the sounds of Ingénue's hooves hitting sawdust and their cadence of breathing in tune.

Not knowing why the music had stopped, and unable to see past the bright spotlights shining down, Rosamund's only thought was to continue.

Then, without warning, life came back with the gentle cry of new notes.

The amplified sound of a single violin cut through the tangles of rope and wire in the vault above their heads, owning the air with the most beautiful music she'd ever heard. Rosamund recognized it at once as "Roses of Picardy"—her beloved British wartime song.

She looked from left to right, still nearly blinded by the spot-lights. She wondered as they rode—*Who? Where?*

Someone was playing the violin under the Big Top, and playing it for her. It sang out, its rich tones filling the air. Coursing through them, sending her heart to soar higher than their canvas sky.

Together with Ingénue, she was lost. Just as Colin predicted and Owen had hoped.

As she popped up to stand tall on Ingénue's back, she reached up and unthreaded the string of roses from her hair. It fell in a dark curtain against her back, soaring out behind her, mixing with the sweet notes of the violin and falling rose petals.

She performed vaulting—the elaborate dance on horseback—while Ingénue cantered round the ring. Her balance was flawless. Her limbs fluid. Light as air. Supporting her through her somer-saulting, giving her wings. And her signature move—the backbend to backward flip from Ingénue's back—she flew through without an ounce of trepidation, her feet planting in the center of the ring, the dismount the perfection Colin had always known she could display.

It wasn't until the performance had ended that Rosamund real-ized they were still in front of the crowd.

Thousands of hands clapped.

Voices erupted with unencumbered shouts and applause, thundering like clouds pouring rain.

Rosamund eased Ingénue to the side of the ring and stood there, arm braced under the horse's head, cradling her nose to bring their foreheads to touch. And together, they took a bow, with Rosamund's hair spilling over her shoulders and happy tears run-ning down her face.

She pulled roses from Ingénue's mane and tossed them to the children in straw alley.

It was then that she dipped her head enough to catch the glow of another spotlight. It was positioned in front of the crowd, shining down on a man who'd been shrouded in shadow until that moment. He, too, was used to the ring, but never before as a musician.

There stood Colin Keary, with a violin and bow in hand.

The behind-the-scenes lifeblood of the show, the Irishman turned ringmaster, was staring back at her now with pride alive in his eyes.

He nodded once, slowly. A gesture of respect.

For the courage to go back in the ring when she'd once failed so miserably before him. And for family even, for the ring had become their home and the performers in it part of their heart, never to go back.

Colin swept an arm out in her direction, presenting the Ringling Brothers' English Rose, and the crowd erupted in adoration. There was nothing to do but laugh. And cry. And take in the glorious moment that she knew would forever be engraved upon her memory. Hendrick had once played for her; it was Colin who'd taken the reins now.

She'd be Lady Rosamund Easling no longer.

She'd found her home as the Ringlings' English Rose.

ROSAMUND BOUNDED OUT THE BACK ENTRANCE OF THE TENT, somehow knowing that he'd be waiting. She fell into Colin's arms, and he picked her up, twirling around with a smile of pride upon his face.

"You did it! I knew you could do it, Rose, and you did."

"But how?" She covered her smile with her hand, fingertips shaking. Feeling her heart could burst. "You never said anything. Not even after what I told you about Hendrick."

"Would you have believed me?" he asked, the most genuine grin she could imagine spreading wide across his face.

"Probably not."

"And what a performance you gave in there. You've got them eating out of your hand. As they will in every town we stop at from now on."

"I don't know about that," she said as she bit the corner of her bottom lip. "But I do know that it felt wonderful, just as you said it would."

Colin stopped their circular dance and stood still, holding her in his arms.

Then, perhaps remembering that he was the boss and they were embracing in the entrance within view of any number of circus hands and performers, he dropped her feet back on the ground and took a step away from her.

"Where did you learn to play like that?"

"Mr. Charlie taught me. All the Ringling brothers were talented. They played instruments and performed in the show in its beginnings. John Ringling was even a clown in the early days—and a good one, I'm told. But Charles traveled with every show and continued performing with the band on occasion. He took time with me just because it was who he was."

"But when?"

"There's a lot of time to burn when you're traveling on a train, Rose. And sitting around a campfire."

"But don't you—" Rosamund paused, shifting her words. She looked him in the eyes. "I mean, didn't you sleep?"

"Sleep is overrated when you've got a show to plan."

At that moment she didn't see him as the show boss standing in front of her. Not with the openness with which he was looking at her now. And especially not after what he'd just done for her.

She flashed a grateful smile. "I don't know how to thank you, Colin. You made me feel at home in there, and that's something I never expected."

"Just doing my job, Rose." He whispered her name, the name no one else called her, lacing it with feeling. "Now get back to work, eh? We've got the rest of the show to get through."

He offered a hint of a smile before turning to stalk off through the tent alley.

He'd go his way, no doubt answering questions and lending a hand wherever needed so the show would roll without a hitch. She was sure of that. Colin was a man of uncommon kindness, willing to do what was necessary for the good of others, even up to surprising a bareback rider with a special gift under the Big Top sky.

"English Rose?"

It hardly seemed possible anyone knew to call her that already, but Rosamund turned.

A young girl of no more than six or seven years bounded up behind her. She trotted along with bouncing braids of gold and a smattering of freckles dotting the bridge of her nose.

"Hello, darling." Rosamund stooped down to her level. "And what can I do for you?"

"This is for you—the English Rose."

She held out an envelope with a delicate rosebud design penned on the outside.

"Thank you, dear. How sweet."

Rosamund ran her finger through the edge, splitting the envelope open. She took out the heavy cardstock paper from inside and unfolded it.

A single word was scrawled in the center: *Morte.*

She turned the paper over.

Blank.

Just the one word, and it was meant for her. The English Rose.

"I'm sorry, but who—"

Rosamund glanced up, but the little girl was skipping away

through the crowd. The few instinctive steps Rosamund took weren't likely to be enough to catch her, so she shouted out, "Excuse me," drawing the eye of several onlookers down the alley. "Little girl? Where did you get this?"

"Some lady." The child shrugged with a jostle of the braids on her shoulder. "She said to give it to the English Rose. And she gave me this!"

She held up a silver five-cent piece, flashing it between her finger and thumb before turning back to run off.

The little girl fled to spend her spoils, disappearing into the sea of performers and circus-goers swarming beyond the tent alley.

There was no opportunity for Rosamund to ask more questions. No chance to find out if her instincts were right.

Bella Rossi wanted her out of the show. And she wanted it badly enough to send Rosamund the omen of a single word.

Morte. Italian for "death."

CHAPTER 24

1927

SARASOTA, FLORIDA

They'd made it through the end of the season, with Rose a shining star in the center ring.

The winter lodgings were just as Colin had predicted they would be—expansive and bustling for the grand opening celebration on Christmas Day. There was ample room for performers, their charge of exotic animals, and the crowds of eager tourists who had come and now jam-packed the lot.

The wind blew, carrying the scent of popcorn and cotton candy. The palms fanned in the breeze. They even had the old Ringling Brothers' 1892 bell wagon drawn back and forth through the streets, chiming out with the happy tunes of the circus. And the animals sang out all around, roaring or neighing just as loud as they pleased.

It was a resounding success. A grand opening that should have catapulted Colin into a sense of satisfaction at all they'd accomplished.

Instead, he was on edge.

Colin stood with Owen at the back of the ring practice area, watching from a distance as a long line of eager children and parents snaked along the side of the horse training barns. They seemed content to wait for their chance to meet with the popular English Rose.

Little girls of all ages were gathered around Rose. They absorbed every smile from the bareback riding star, laughing and asking for autographs in a delighted swarm of swishing skirts, ankle socks, and black buckle shoes.

She took time with every one, patting heads and letting little fingers touch the long sequined ribbons of her skirt. She handed out roses from a basket near Ingénue's hooves. And she knelt at their level, making it a point to value each little face, dotting a few button noses with her fingertip and lavishing smiles on each little girl who breezed through the line.

Rose would flip up on Ingénue's back and hoist a young one up with her, holding tight as they learned to stand just like a real bareback rider.

The sight was impressive, though not altogether surprising.

In the last months, Rose's star power had grown seemingly without effort. And by the time the show closed in October, it was the young bareback riding star who had helped to pack the Big Top to capacity for each performance.

"Look at her—Rosamund's enchanting them." Owen cut into his thoughts. "Watch out, my boy. Or she might do the same to you."

Colin coughed, suddenly aware that his attention was far too fixed on Rose, instead of just in the general direction of paying tourists.

"She is enchanting them. I've no doubt. She's doing her job."

"Colin. Look at them. They're all waiting. In the hot sun. Wild animals all around, yet they're waiting to see *her*. That's more than just doing a job, and you know it." Owen motioned to the line of patrons waiting to greet the circus's newest star, the long display wrapping around the side of the stables to the road. "It's time to tell her. She's the star of the show."

"It's a heavy burden."

"Yes," Owen agreed, tapping a finger against his chin. "But I've seen everything I need to since she first stepped off that train. She's proven herself. It's a burden she's able to carry."

Colin shook his head. "I just don't want to jump at this."

"You're not having doubts now, after you trained her up, brought her this far?" He wrinkled his forehead in an all-knowing, almost paternal glare.

Colin huffed. "Don't look at me like that."

"Someone's got to do it. Now, I know you're circus first, Colin. But there comes a point in every man's life when he realizes what really matters. And I don't think it's a canvas tent that holds the most interest for you."

Colin had willed that night under the Big Top to leave him alone. That moment, that one memory of crossing the line to do what he'd imagined so many times before . . .

Rose had never mentioned their kiss to anyone, he was sure.

Nor had he.

How in the world could Owen know?

"I'm just thinking of her, Owen. It's a lot to shoulder. I worry that she's too kind for it. Maybe too generous to be a showstopper in this life. I've seen it before—the rise. The fall. It happens with stars all the time. I just don't want it to happen to her."

Owen studied his face. "You're worried about how Bella will take it?"

Colin nodded. "I am."

And he was. More than he cared to say at the moment.

The Rossi family had kept packing in the crowds through the end of the season. And though Rosamund's act had settled into a routine that was gaining notoriety in the towns they'd visited, the Rossi flyers remained a steady draw. Still, after the doubt surrounding Bella's future in the show, the family had opted to keep an even lower profile on the lot than usual. They'd circled the wagons, sticking close to their tents. Even kept the shades drawn on their train car most of the time.

Bella seemed the most out of sorts. Her beauty had been eclipsed by tired eyes and a despondent nature that even Colin could see from the ground floor of the Big Top. There was just no spark in her performances.

Colin watched as Rose propped yet another little girl on Ingénue's back. She laughed aloud when the girl threw her arms up over her head in a pose worthy of the center ring itself.

He ran his fingers through his hair, indecision boiling over.

"You might know—we've had some trouble with Bella in the past. Alcohol."

Owen nodded.

"I'm worried it's plaguing her again. And I'm not sure we can risk the show by renewing her contract for another year."

"And you're afraid that if you don't, the fallout will affect Rosamund."

"It's complicated," Colin said, offering his friend a slap on the shoulder. "Nothing to burden you with now. Especially not on Christmas."

"But you'll tell Rosamund what's behind the shift in the show's billing? She deserves to know."

Colin noted the subtle deflection at his change of subject.

It was one thing to offer Rose a contract for top billing. But it was quite another to open wounds that had been sealed up long before she came into his life. He wasn't sure he could tell Rose about his past. About Bella. About everything that had been built up and then crumbled down again in their relationship.

"Fine. It's settled. I'm giving her top billing."

"No." Owen shook his head. "It's not settled until you tell her everything. If Bella's poised to become an enemy, then Rosamund has a right to know why."

"I'd already planned on it. Tonight. We've got top billing business to discuss about the New Year. And God help us—maybe some of this will be behind us by then."

Rosamund sat on her bed in the freshly painted dormitory, flipping the envelope back and forth between her fingers. She shook her head, feeling fresh tears sting her eyes.

"You are in here."

Colin's voice floated in from the doorway. She had her back to him and quickly slipped the envelope under her pillow. She dabbed at the tears in the corners of her eyes before turning round to face him.

He'd cleaned up. No work shirt and suspenders like he usually wore on the lot. He wore a suit and crisp linen shirt, and had even managed to tie a respectable but slightly loosened knot in the striped navy tie around his neck. He'd even wrestled his hair into submission, combing it into a sleek part at the side. He didn't use the sticky pomade that other men favored, though, and it was likely that the unruly tousle would be back in his hair the instant they stepped out into the heat of late afternoon.

"Minnie will have your hide if she catches you in here."

"Her bark is worse than her bite," Colin said, shrugging as if he couldn't care less that men were not allowed in the female dorm. He'd set the rule himself and now, it seemed, he was quite content in breaking it.

He stepped in, crossing the room she shared with Annaliese.

"In truth, she knows I'm in here. Scared the wits out of this Irishman. She's waiting at the end of the hall. Gave me two minutes to appear at the door with you, or she said she'd come back up the stairs and turn the fire hose on me."

Rosamund couldn't help but smile. "She must have thought you were up to no good."

"Maybe, but I told her it was Christmas and she let me pass." He furrowed his brow just a touch. "Hey—are you okay? Was it too much today, all the people?"

"No. I loved seeing the children. It's just—" She rolled her eyes to the ceiling. "Old ghosts, I suppose."

"Old ghosts, huh?" He paused, as if trying to read her mind for the trail of thoughts she wouldn't share with him. "Well, no more haunting today. I've come to escort you to dinner."

Rosamund glanced out the window.

The sun was still high in the sky behind them. It couldn't have been four o'clock yet.

"It's a bit early, isn't it? The Christmas party isn't until six."

"I know. But I thought maybe we could duck out, if you're game for a little road trip." He tossed her a smile layered with mischief. "Well, a short one anyway. We have an invitation from John and Mable, if you want to accept."

"We?"

He nodded. "There's some business at the Cà d'Zan. Then a Christmas party at Lido Key after."

She was confused. What business could possibly demand her attention at the Ringlings' mansion on Christmas Day?

"And you're quite sure they know I'm attending?"

They heard the echo of a throat clearing out in the hall. Minnie was apparently making her rounds.

"I'd better go," Colin said, walking back to the door. "I'll let you get changed. Meet me downstairs. And it's not formal. A family dinner on the beach."

"Family . . . ," she whispered after he'd patted the side of the doorframe and disappeared down the hall.

Family, was she?

Rosamund closed her eyes and dropped her head in her hands.

All of a sudden it appeared she had two of them—one in Sarasota, who'd invited her for dinner at their estate, and another very far away at Easling Park. She wondered if the latter would accept her if she had to come crawling home.

She eased her fingers under the pillow and pulled the envelope back out into the light.

Another note had been left for her—this one slipped under the pillow on her bed. It, too, bore a warning message, folded in the same card stock as before. But this one was different. No scrawled words. No veiled threats. Just a strip of canary-yellow satin tucked inside.

She'd almost convinced herself that her first costume had been destroyed by accident. But now that lie faded.

Someone wanted her out of the show, and they wanted it badly.

"Bella . . . ," she breathed out, squeezing the satin shred in her palm.

CHAPTER 25

Colin turned the Capitol Roadster toward the gated entrance to the Cà d'Zan.

He drove past the gate and whizzed down the lane, not stopping until he'd brought them around the circular drive that hugged the front of the mansion.

"You've got a lot of nerve, tearing down my drive like that."

Mable stepped out of the field of palms and tall shrubbery that led to the rose garden, a basket of woven sea grass draped over her arm. It was overflowing with a riot of blooms: roses in shades of bright bubbly pink, ivory, and deep crimson.

It made Rosamund smile to see her, wearing gloves and carrying shears like a gardener while dressed in an elegant dress of gray crepe suited for a night at the opera. The fabric shimmered in the shades of twilight that were poised to fall around them.

Colin seemed to know it was cheek Mable offered, and grinned in response. He jumped from the pickup and rounded the back to open Rosamund's door, then extended his hand to help her out.

"Mable," he said, smiling ear to ear. He took Mable's hand, greeting her with a light kiss to her cheek. "Merry Christmas."

"Colin, you think it appropriate to drive like that with a titled lady in the car?"

He cleared his throat. "Well, I didn't want to be late. Not for this."

Mable arched her eyebrows up at him, sending him a disciplinary glare. She then turned to Rosamund, greeting her with a smile while she pulled off her gloves.

"And that is exactly why I don't have a driver. If I want to go somewhere, I hop in the motor myself. That way, I control the madness."

Rosamund was so taken with the idea that she smiled and looked from Mable to Colin. He shrugged and raised his hands in submission.

"She's telling the truth. She drives her purple Pierce Arrow all over the county." He leaned in to Rosamund's side and whispered in her ear, "Stay off the roads when she's tearing them up in that limo of hers."

"Colin, stop trying to start trouble." Mable shoved her basket of roses into his arms. "Take these in for me, hmm? Give them to Tomlinson, and tell him I want to take them to hand out at the beach tonight. And be sure to ask our butler about your guest. I believe he arrived some time ago, and I had Tomlinson invite him into the court. He'll be waiting for you there."

Colin did as he was told and swept the basket of Mable's roses into his arms. He trotted up the front steps and headed through the front doors, not waiting for the butler to admit him.

Rosamund turned back to her hostess. "Thank you for having me back to the Cà d'Zan, Mrs. Ringling."

Mable held up her hand in response. "No. Call me Mable, remember? I insist."

Rosamund thought that for anyone on the outside looking in, Mable Ringling did not seem like a woman of untold wealth. She was genuinely kind and as unpretentious as a great lady could be, even standing in the shadow of her mansion.

"Well, thank you then, Mable. And Merry Christmas."

"That's right. This is the second Christmas you've spent with us, isn't it?"

Rosamund nodded, scanning the vast landscape of palms and the water of the bay behind them. "It's hard to believe it's been that long since I've seen England."

"Well, walk in with me," Mable directed, holding her arm out to link with Rosamund's. They walked slowly, easing along to the side entrance of the mansion. "Colin has a surprise for you. A Christmas gift from all of us. You'll be pleased."

"I'd almost forgotten it was Christmas until this morning. It seemed so far away last year when we were planning for the opening of the show. And now the winter lodgings have gone up and we're accepting tourists."

"And has a lot changed since you were here last?"

Rosamund thought on it.

The last time she'd been at the Cà d'Zan she'd been a reluctant performer. She'd played the piano in front of a small party of ten. And now? She was used to performing in front of thousands.

The threatening notes burned a hole in her thoughts again, reminding her that those performance days might be numbered.

"Some. But I think *I've* changed more," she answered, forcing a smile. Hoping Mable couldn't see anything through it.

"Well. That's what's important, isn't it?"

Mable opened the door to the solarium and held it wide, inviting Rosamund into the sun-swept room. It boasted familiar views of the bay through the colored-glass windows. The ceiling was a cool blue, with whimsical baseboards and a painted medallion around the Venetian-style lamp hanging from the ceiling. Sconces were aglow in the foyer, illuminating the wonderfully lavish works of art and antique furniture they walked past.

Rosamund could see Colin standing in the court, chatting with a man who boasted height similar to that of Mr. Ringling, but had chestnut hair and glasses perched on his nose. The men were engaged in conversation as two miniature pinschers yipped around their feet.

The dogs bounded across the foyer when Mable entered, and she stooped to rub their ears.

"Don't worry, they won't bother you. There's also a German shepherd around here somewhere. He's called Tell. He likes to bound through the kitchen, though, and it doesn't sit well with our cook." Mable pointed to an intricately scrolled black iron gate that cut off the alcove containing the lift and the marble staircase. "So we put those gates in. You can just move them out of the way if you need to get through."

Mable nudged her toward the court. "Come in, my dear. You and Colin have some circus business to attend to. I'll return shortly and we'll go on to Lido Key. I just want to go see that my roses get water."

Rosamund followed Mable into the room.

"Good evening, Mr. McCarty," said their hostess. "We are glad to have you back at the Cà d'Zan."

The man inclined his head, offering a polite, "Mrs. Ringling. Lovely to see you again."

Rosamund noticed only then that there were three easels set up by the hearth, each one with a sheet of white linen drawn down over the front.

"Here she is," Colin said, perking up at her entrance. "This is Lady Rosamund Easling. Lady Easling—this is Ron McCarty."

"It's a pleasure to meet you," the man said, his eyes kind.

"Likewise." Rosamund nodded in greeting. "And what's all this?"

Colin's eyes danced in a way she'd never seen before. "They're for you."

"What on earth?"

Colin wasted no time. He walked over to each easel, pulling at the cover and allowing the linen to float down to the marble floor, never taking his eyes off her the whole time.

"Merry Christmas, Rose."

The sight took her breath away.

"Ron is here on commission of the Ringlings to help with the museum that's going up here on the grounds. He's a celebrated artist, and we thought we could kill two birds with one stone. So he's been working on marketing materials for the upcoming season." Colin braced his hands on his hips.

"But they're all . . . me."

"That's right, Lady Easling," Mr. McCarty noted, smiling. "These will be put up in every city from here to the West Coast. They'll be published in newspapers and magazines. And on the canvas covers lining the wagons. They're the hallmark for our marketing campaign for the entire 1928 season. But we've still got time to make small changes, so go ahead." He ushered her forward. "Have a closer look if you'd like."

Rosamund approached in wonder, gazing over the posters that depicted a bareback-riding beauty in various graceful poses. She had long hair that streamed out behind her shoulders in a cascade of chocolate that curled around the gold filigree borders. There were great blooms of English roses trailing behind, falling down like soft pink rain against the deep black of Ingénue's gleaming coat.

The title splashed across each poster's top read THE ENGLISH ROSE in bold block letters.

"It can't come as that much of a surprise to you," Colin said.

"You misjudge me then," Rosamund said, searching for words that would seem adequate. "Because I'm completely shocked."

"Surely you aren't surprised that you're getting top billing, Rose. You've earned it."

It was surreal to stare back at her own image, looking so ethereal.

So beautiful. It humbled Rosamund to know how others might perceive her. And could she live up to that standard?

"You'll have your own train car. A private tent on the road. And you'll be paid handsomely. It's all set."

Colin pulled a swatch of folded paper and a pen from his inside jacket pocket and held them out to her. "All you have to do is sign."

The shock of his words sank in.

She reached out, just edging her fingertips over the surface of the artwork, but recoiled almost as quickly, as if the paint had burned her skin.

The threats came back fresh in her mind. Bella's confrontation at the Garden. The shredded costume. Her first triumph in the center ring, and the subsequent realization that Bella wanted her out of the show. The threats seemed so loud that not even the beauty of the posters could drown them out.

Rosamund took a step back, shaking her head slightly. "Colin, I need to speak with you."

"Now?" he asked, confusion marring his brow.

"Yes," she said, taking another step back. "Right now."

"Come on," Colin said, leading Rosamund up the stairs. "We can be alone here."

He'd taken her by the hand and led her to the top of the Cà d'Zan's five-story belvedere tower.

She climbed the top stair after him and came out to an open-air overlook, with Venetian arches and ornate stucco creating the canopy of a domed ceiling over their heads. It boasted a view of the water on one side and a wide span of palms and Mable's rose gardens covering the estate's acreage on the other.

Rosamund turned away from him, finding the view of lights across the bay easier as she tried to compose her thoughts.

"What happened down there? I thought—" Colin's voice turned softer. "I thought you'd be happy."

"I am happy."

She heard his shoes scrape the floor tiles, knowing he'd come behind her and was but a breath away.

"But I need to go home," she blurted out.

"What?"

Rosamund turned around to face him. Her breaths were uneven, emotion having tripped them in her chest.

"I need to go home. It's been a lovely year, but I can't sign on for the new season."

It was the first time she'd ever seen Colin Keary speechless.

He nodded. Just once. And shoved his hands into his pockets— the gesture she knew so well. It was his telltale sign that his mind had clicked two steps ahead and he was already working things out, looking for a solution to the problem at hand.

"Top billing isn't enough for you then?"

"You misunderstand," she whispered. "I'm honored that you have the faith in me to believe I can handle top billing. But I just can't stay."

"What's changed, Rose? Did your parents write to you, tell you to come home?" He ran a hand over the tie at his collar, tugging to loosen it as he turned away.

"No."

"Then what?" Colin leaned over the rail, resting his elbows against it as wind kicked up off the water, mussing his hair to tip down over his brow. He lowered his head for a moment. "Is this because of what happened with us?"

He raised his head then, turning to look at her. The depths of his blue eyes had turned stormy. They seemed to look through her, right to her heart.

"No. It's not," she lied.

It had everything to do with him.

That Bella had slipped a golden thimble in her hand and told her that the man standing in front of her could never truly love her back. That he was incapable of it. And despite threats or ruined costumes, the thought of falling for Colin and then losing him scared her more than anything.

"Look, Rose. You haven't signed a new contract, so I can't stop you if you want to go. But it's not a crime to want to live your own life. I wish you could see that. I saw a young woman at Easling Park, and I know she was scared, but she still boarded that train. She still stared fear in the face and took a chance on living."

"They're beautiful," she said.

Colin narrowed his eyes. "What?"

"The posters. They're so beautiful," she whispered. "I should have thanked you for them. I'm sorry."

His sigh came easy. As did the shrug of his shoulders.

Rosamund walked toward him. Not stopping until she was at his side.

"Why did you bring me here tonight, Colin? We both know you could have shown me the posters at the winter headquarters. So why now? Why here?"

Colin's eyes searched her face.

The glow of the tower light overhead illuminated his features. She could see something there—pain, maybe. Questioning, definitely.

"Because I wanted to show them to you away from everyone else. Rose, I saw how effortless your beauty was with those young girls today. This is where you belong. I didn't want you to look back anymore. Not when you can really live. And I didn't want to elevate you to top billing because the show needs it. None of that matters now. Despite what the pressures are around us, I only wanted it for you."

"Then you want me to do this—be your star?"

He shook his head. "Be yourself. Stay if you want to."

Everything about Colin said he was holding something back. His gaze was intense, but battling somehow. He seemed on the edge of wanting to tell her something, just as she was with him.

Did they both have secrets?

"Dance with me," he whispered.

"Here? But there's no music." Rosamund looked around their empty dance floor, the only sound around them the wind whipping off the bay and the gentle sway of palms fluttering behind them.

"I hear music."

Colin stood before her, arms extended. Waiting. Seemingly content to leave the conversation for the moment. She accepted, stepping into his embrace. He rested his chin on the top of her head as he held her, together swaying to the dance of the wind.

"Colin, I . . ."

He eased back, looked in her eyes.

Bella was harmless. Rosamund had been sure of it that night in the star's tent.

The shredded costume and the note—they were empty threats from the bitterness of a life worn. Nothing more. But Rosamund feared that if she revealed Bella's actions now, Colin would disagree and send her home on the next boat. And she couldn't bear the thought of leaving him. Not now. Not when they were moving in step with one another.

"I think I hear the music too . . ." A tear fought its way down the side of her cheek. "It's telling me to stay, that the rest of this will work itself out somehow."

Maybe they'd talk after dinner, she thought. Or maybe Mable was right. People only see what they want to, and perhaps Rosamund never wanted to see the truth in Colin Keary or, more importantly, in herself.

She escaped into Colin's arms, and for tonight at least, it was enough.

CHAPTER 26

1920
NEW YORK CITY

Mable eyed their new understudy for Manager of Operations, who had proved his industriousness by fashioning a makeshift desk in a lonely corner of the Garden, tucking an upturned peach crate and folding chair alongside the performance floor.

Colin looked prepared to carry the weight of leading the circus's hundreds of performers and crew on his wide shoulders. His tall frame was hunched over a stack of papers as he contentedly worked long hours after the arena had all but hushed for the night. The teardown after the last show had been swift. Only workmen lingered now, clanking metal to wood in the background, readying the inner structure of the Big Top's bones to go back under canvas for the upcoming season. The train was to pull out in two days' time with man and beast, stopping in more than a hundred cities and towns through October. And Colin would go with it just as he had in years past.

Only this time, things were different.

He'd matured from his many months in the war. Mable couldn't help but think Colin was bowed down at the shoulders, and quite older than his twenty-three years should have allowed. He sat there running a hand over his chin, lost somewhere in the depths of his thoughts. And now, once back to the circus life after more than a year away, he'd stepped into the shoes of Charles's right-hand man in a steadfast transition that would keep him a fixture in the Ringling family.

Colin was content with very little. A small stack of books. A black violin case slightly worn at the edges—probably one of Charles's old ones. A small carpetbag of red-and-orange paisley, with the clothes he'd packed for the coming months, all leaning against the side of the crate in a tidy line, his hat sitting on top.

And the watch. Always Colin carried the watch, weighing down his pocket.

Mable knew he'd not leave it behind.

"Am I disturbing you?"

He looked up, turned, slightly jarred by her voice. He jumped to his feet, scattering the top sheets of paper on the crate until they fluttered to the ground.

"Well, it looks as though I am."

"Not at all, Mrs. Ringling. Just some last-minute matters of business to attend to before the show rolls. It's just details," he said, extending a hand, offering his small wooden chair. "Sit. Please."

"Thank you."

Mable obeyed, watching as Colin cleared the wares from the crate. He swept the papers away, along with a fountain pen, collecting them in a pile to tuck in his bag.

"It's late," he added, sitting atop the crate as a stool. "I hope we haven't disturbed you. I'd hate to think that we'd kept Mr. Ringling about at all hours."

"Not tonight. It's the closing of the show at Madison Square and the opening of the season for the world, so John also had some last-minute business. We start for home this evening. I could have gone ahead, but the apartment is lonely without him. Besides, I wanted to talk to you."

"You're breaking your rule, aren't you, by stopping down here? Mr. Ringling assures me that his wife prefers not to step into the business side of the family name—though between you and me, I think you could take charge of the lot of us." He leaned in and whispered, "Don't tell him I said that though. Might not bode well for my career."

"Rules?" Mable flitted the idea away with a characteristic flick of her wrist. "They're made to be broken on occasion. But then, you're not a performer, are you? And there's no show left here. You see, it's not that I entirely keep an oar out of Mr. Ringling's business affairs. I simply know where I'm needed. There's a difference."

The tinkering workmen behind them dropped a stack of poles, creating a clatter of some substance. Colin edged off the crate, as though he'd wanted to leap into action at the mere hint of disorder.

He tilted his head up, looking off in the distance. Watching with a keen eye.

"You conduct yourself like a leader already, Colin," Mable noted. "You have the instincts for it. I know you see this as a big responsibility, and I wanted to wish you well."

"Do you have advice to offer? You have spent more time with the leaders of the show than anybody else around here."

Mable had a purpose in the visit to the performance floor. It wasn't to banter about titles and shows, or lines that sometimes needed crossing. Not that day. Instead, she'd come because she'd missed him, and it felt right to show him somehow. To acknowledge—if only in the smallest of ways—the value placed on the position he held within the Ringlings' circus family.

"No advice today. A bon voyage, rather. Mr. Ringling and I intend to spend the latter part of the year here in New York. Then we sail for Venice to christen the New Year. I wanted to see you off."

"This new post is a far cry from my days of watch-hunting on the street corners." He furrowed his brow. "Are you checking up on me? You're not worried that I'll take up my pickpocketing ways again, are you?"

"Not at all. In fact, I think you have the only watch you'll ever want right there in your pocket."

Colin studied her.

Saying nothing, save for a slight nod to confirm her comment, he eased back onto the crate.

"I gather it might take some time to become acclimated to civilian life again. You didn't expound in your letters, but I pride myself on reading between the lines."

"I told you enough that you know who I am."

"And I can't ignore that, no matter how much you'd prefer I do."

He laughed lightly. "Yes. And I'll probably jump at every sound for a while. But I can't complain. At least I came home. There are too many boys who died in France and won't see our shores again. Who won't marry or have children of their own to bring to the Ringling Brothers' show."

"Does it feel like giving back? To take what life hands you and make the best of it that you can?"

"Yes," he confirmed. "It does feel like giving back in a way. And I know you understand why I say that."

Mable flitted her glance to the small pile of Colin's belongings stacked by the crate.

Dear Colin.

Always paying penance.

Never finding freedom, no matter how many lives he attempted to help. He seemed eager to prove his worth, even now, despite rising to the occasion time after time. And now, back from war, he was unchanged in that regard.

Colin still carried that small amount of baggage everywhere he went.

"And that's all you need? You could have a home, Colin. An opportunity to change your life. Is traveling with our show how you want to live it?"

"I have no home. Not anymore. Being in New York again reminds me that those bridges have long since burned."

"I just want you to be sure it's what you want. Because you've become a fixture around here, Colin Keary. Circus is in your blood, isn't it?"

He scanned the vast arena, looking around at the stadium-style bleacher seats that cast shadows in every corner.

Mable watched the shades of remembrance wash over his features, as if he could see the circus lights and the flyers bounding overhead. No doubt he could hear the band cueing up, with clowns and animal acts moving about the rings in front of them.

"It is. This life is right for me. It's all I know now. And if it's paying for the sins of my past to want to help others, then I accept it."

It was no wonder Colin had sentenced himself to a life of servitude for the mistakes he'd made in his past. And the dreams that couldn't be fulfilled.

She was reminded of her first trip to the circus grounds. All those years before, John had whisked her into his world, and it had felt right. The rigging lacing the arena above their heads and the span of performance rings in front of them—they'd become home to her too.

"I think it's in my blood too, Colin. We're alike, you and I. Transplants into this glorious world. Seeing where a measure of charity is needed. But that's the easy part, isn't it? God willing, we're brave enough to take the next step and offer it. And that's your strength. It's why this is your job now. You have the courage to offer absolution to others, especially when it's not deserved. There can be no better leader than that."

Her voice sounded far off. Dreamy, even to her. Thinking of regrets she had. Of the days before she'd met John and become the Circus King's wife. She was reminded of Sally. Of time that marched on and dreams that could go unfulfilled. She didn't want that for Colin, not if she could help him.

"Well. Those animals will be looking for their breakfast early, and I'm sure you'll want to be there to supervise it." Mable clapped her hands together and stood to leave.

Colin stood when she did, offering his arm should she wish to take it and navigate around the obstacles of bleacher seats and hardware waiting to be loaded onto the wagons.

A crash resounded from across the arena, this one much louder than before. Colin crinkled his brow and firmed the line of his mouth into one of politely subdued concern.

Mable could see his feet were itching to jump in and take charge. She knew the instant she left, he'd be running in that direction.

"I can see that you're needed, so I'll let you get back to work," she announced, bestowing a light double-tap to his forearm. "We're all quite proud to have you back as a member of the Ringling Brothers' family, Colin. I hope one day you'll be ready to give up that watch. And I'll be rejoicing from the sidelines when you do."

CHAPTER 27

1928

ALTOONA, PENNSYLVANIA

There was a chill in the night air . . . early spring's last cool breath before summer.

Rosamund pulled the sweater tighter round her shoulders in response. She walked past an old barn behind the back lot, gazing at her poster image layered several times over against the planks of aged wood on its side.

It had taken some getting used to, seeing posters with her image plastered in railway stations and on country outbuildings everywhere they went. The circus's advance team would always move into a performance stop to advertise days before the train pulled into town, papering every flat surface within a several-mile radius of the station. By the looks of things that night, they'd done their job with fervor.

The English Rose was everywhere.

Even in the shades of darkness that blanketed the back lot, the smiling and serene poster beauty floated through the air as Rosamund walked by.

A twig snapped behind her, drawing her notice from the span of poster art to the deserted back lot.

She stopped, half turning, feeling an edge of uncertainty creep up her spine. She heard distant cries from the animals and the far-off chug of the train whistle. No doubt the men were loading the Big Top pole wagons on the flat cars by now, and the show would be rolling out before too long.

Quickening her step toward the performers' tents, she considered her nerves to have been pricked only by exhaustion after the show and long days and nights with little sleep. The sound of a twig snapping out in a tree-lined field was nothing out of the ordinary.

Until it happened again.

And she heard voices. Male voices that she didn't recognize, muttering words she couldn't quite make out.

"Hello?" she whispered, looking past the long trail of canvas to one side and the deserted back lot of field and trees on the other.

A gust of wind swept by, rustling the grasses of the field and whispering through the trees.

Instinct prickled at the hairs on the back of her neck, screaming at her to run.

She turned to sprint in the opposite direction, but something yanked on her sweater, pulling her from behind.

Rosamund knew she should have cried out, knowing that help couldn't be too far away. But the sharp pain of an unexpected blow to the back of her head came so suddenly that the only thing she could do was fall to her knees. She punched out at air, trying to fight off whatever or whoever had attacked. As she gasped for breath, her vision blurred, sending her eyes to flutter closed on their own.

Blackness invaded like a wave and sleep became her friend.

~⌒

"Where is she?"

Colin stormed into the tent, anger seething with every breath in his chest.

Rose looked up, meeting his glare from her sitting position on her cot. She tipped her head down away from him, trying to hide the fact that she was holding a linen cloth to it.

He'd had no idea what to expect when he got to her, but certainly not what he saw.

Rose had blood matted in her hair and dark smears of dirt caked on her costume and face. Her knees were cut so that they looked scraped raw. Even the woolen blanket that had been draped over her shoulders like a shawl couldn't hide the fact that she shook uncontrollably.

"*Bien*, Colin. She's okay," Annaliese whispered to him, then patted Rose's hand before stepping back out of the way.

Colin filled the void she'd left, kneeling down at Rose's side. "What happened?"

"I'm all right," she said, trying to produce a meager smile for him. "Truly."

Colin reached out a hand and pulled down the linen, revealing a round circle of bright red. He clenched his jaw at the sight of it.

"You're not. Nothing about this is all right," he said, using his thumb to brush at dirt on the underside of her chin. He noticed the gentle trembling of her shoulders. "Are you cold?"

He pulled the blanket tighter round her collar and rubbed her upper arms to generate warmth.

"I'm not now," she breathed out, offering him the tiniest smile.

It shredded his restraint.

Colin shot to his feet, blasting the audience in the tent with a furious glare.

Enzo and Marvio held back, silently eyeing him from the safety of the shadows. And Annaliese stood with Ward, wringing her hands as she looked back and forth between Rose and the men, positioned on opposite sides of the tent.

"You'd better have an explanation that will satisfy me," Colin shouted, bounding forward to stand up to the younger of the two flyers, "or I'll have you thrown behind bars for attempted murder."

"We saved her! Found her and brought her here." Enzo's temper flared back. "You can't accuse us of anything."

Colin shook his head, fury barely restrained in balled fists at his sides. "I know what I see!"

"And what is that?"

"Do I need to spell it out for you? Someone is trying to put her out of the show."

"Why would any of us do that? It hurts everyone if the show fails to bring in the crowds. If she's out, then so are we."

"Stand down," Marvio said, easing in before tempers exploded and fists began to fly. "Both of you. This isn't helping anything."

"It'll help me if I can put a fist through his jaw," Colin shouted back.

"No," Rose called out, silencing the tent. "No, Colin. Please. They helped me. They found me and brought me here."

It couldn't be. Not possible.

Annaliese stepped forward, bobbing her chin up and down. "Ward and I were walking back from the dining tent. We saw them pick her up and carry her across the lot. They found her knocked out in the field behind the performers' tents."

Ward stepped up next to Annaliese. "It's true, Colin."

Colin exhaled low. He kicked the straw at his feet, taking his anger out on the tip of his boot.

"I think you should tell him now," Annaliese squeaked out,

drawing the ire of Rose's furrowed brow. She shook her head ever so slightly, trying to button Annaliese's mouth before she said anything further.

"Tell me what?"

Colin's anger subsided only long enough to show Rose the shock that he knew must have covered his face.

Enzo and Marvio stood back, looking genuinely surprised.

Ward closed his eyes and sighed over Annaliese's admission. He slipped an arm over her shoulder, trying to edge her to the exit.

"Tell me what, Rose?"

She didn't answer. Just looked at the rest of the faces in the room, then returned her eyes to lock with his.

Right, he thought. *You want to be alone.*

"Everyone out," Colin ordered, not even looking over his shoulder to see if his demand was being carried out.

He heard shuffling feet. Annaliese whispered some cooing words before Ward dragged her away.

Colin stood still in the center of the tent, his hands braced at his hips until the sounds subsided and he was sure they were alone. He plucked a stool from Rose's vanity table and pulled it up next to her place on the cot.

He sat, elbows resting on his knees. "What's going on?"

In contrast to his stance when the others were in the tent, he knew he couldn't show her the rage pumping through his veins. If he wanted the truth, she'd have to feel safe enough to tell him.

He lowered his voice to a rough whisper. "You can tell me, Rose. We're alone."

"I don't know," she started, chin quivering ever so slightly. "I was walking at the back of the lot, and I think there were some men from the village . . . I heard voices. I don't know who they were, but they seemed to recognize me from the posters."

"Why didn't you run? There are men everywhere who would have come to your aid. Jerry and Owen are always tinkering with wagons and things at the back of the lot. You could have gone to them."

"Colin, I tried. I was hit from behind." She shook her head, trembling washing over her like a wave. "And I wanted to fight back, but I didn't know who or what had hit me."

Colin swallowed hard, willing like wildfire that anger wouldn't get the best of him. At least, not until he learned who was responsible.

"What else do you remember?" He encouraged her to keep going with a brush of his index finger over her hand that held the blanket over her shoulders.

"I shouldn't have been walking through the back of the lot alone. It was stupid. I'd gone to check on Ingénue before she was loaded on the train, and I was trying to save time by cutting behind all of the activity. I wanted to get back and board without any fuss of having to ask someone to go with me."

"But why would someone need to go with you?"

Unless you were already afraid . . .

The answer popped into his mind.

"What are you not telling me, Rose?"

"I didn't want you to worry," she whispered.

"I'm more than worried now."

"It's just—" She paused. Embattled. Looking back at him with as much pain as he'd ever seen. "I thought you'd send me home if you knew. It's why I considered going back to Easling Park at Christmas. It seemed easier for everyone if I did," she whispered, tears clouding the green of her eyes. "But I couldn't bear the thought of leaving . . . my life here."

"What are you saying?"

She swallowed hard. "You were not wrong. Someone does want me out of the show."

Colin's shoulders slumped at her admission. He dropped his head, running a hand through his hair, then exhaled in frustration. His eyes searched her face, begging her to refute it.

"It started with my costume the first performance. Remember? At the Garden?"

"But I thought you told me that was nothing. Things get damaged all the time."

She shook her head. "It was done on purpose."

"How do you know?"

"Because the same day you gave me the posters at the Cà d'Zan, I received another note threatening me if I stayed on for the 1928 season. A cut shred of the fabric was inside."

"You should have told me, Rose! How do you expect me to keep you safe if I don't know what's going on under my nose?"

"You don't have to keep me safe. I can take care of myself."

He did a double take, feeling the sting of her words deeper than he'd thought possible.

"Not by the looks of you right now. For God's sake—you're bleeding, Rose," he fired back, not giving her an inch of leeway. "Where are the other notes?"

"They're in my tent."

"I need to see them," he answered automatically, sounding all business. "And I'll report this to the local authorities. But I can't do much more to help if I don't know what's going on around here. You keep things like that from me and you put not only yourself at risk, but every person and animal in this show. Rose, I don't need to tell you what could have happened to you tonight."

"I know." Tears formed on her lashes. "But I don't think they meant any real harm. They seemed to want to frighten me."

"They?"

She nodded. "I heard men behind me. Two or three, maybe. And one of them whispered something and that's the last I remember."

"What did he say?"

Her voice hitched ever so slightly, but she whispered, "I couldn't make it out . . . Just footsteps. Voices."

Rose's bottom lip finally give way, and her eyes released the tears she'd been fighting to hold at bay. Colin responded by reaching out, resting the warmth of his hand on hers.

"I hope to God it's not who I think it is. But trust me, I'm going to find out," he vowed, wanting to show the same solidarity he had with promises on the first day they'd met. "I don't know how yet, but we'll make sense of this."

"But it doesn't make any sense."

"I'm going to the authorities," he began, causing an automatic shaking of her head. "But we'll have to keep this quiet until we know more. Can you do that?"

Relief was medicating in the moment.

They had no answers. And she must have been on edge for weeks—months, even. Why? Because of Bella? Because Rose wasn't certain she could trust him?

Colin exhaled. It felt like a sword to the chest.

Rose nodded. Weakly. He knew she'd given every effort to accept his promise. Then, finally, when the white-knuckled grip she'd kept on his hand proved ineffective, she fell against his shoulder, burying her face against his collar.

Colin cupped a hand to the nape of her neck, holding her still. Letting the release of tears come.

"Rose? Do you want to leave? Tell me the truth."

"No." The answer reinforced by a firm shake of her head against his neck.

"Good. That's all I needed to hear. So promise me one thing?"

"If I can," she answered, her lips moving against the linen of his shirt.

"I can't do what I need to if I'm worried about you. Until this is sorted out, I need you to go back to the ring stock tent with Owen and wait for me there after your performances. I'll walk you back to your tent every night. And I'll make sure we have trusted eyes on you at all times. If I can't be there, then Jerry or Owen will. I'll even conscript Ward into security detail if I have to, though I worry he'd give up his post if it ran over into mealtime."

She gave a faint smile. "It's not necessary, Colin. You have enough to do without watching over me."

"It is necessary, Rose." He leaned back to look in her eyes. "I need to know you're safe. And I need your promise that you'll do this for me. If anything happens on the lot, you'll go back to that tent and wait for me."

"If you really want me to."

"I need you to," he countered, the words soft. Entreating her to listen.

"Then yes. I will."

It was the only promise Rose had made to him that Colin feared she couldn't keep.

The threats were real.

And Colin had to consider who, of the circus family all around, was behind them. He now knew that if someone wanted Rose out of the show, they'd stop at nothing to accomplish that goal.

"Come on then. Let's get you to the train."

He helped her stand, bracing her elbow until she nodded that she was okay.

"I don't want Bella punished for this."

"Bella?" Rose's statement could have knocked him over with the brush of a feather. "What about Bella?"

The first thought in his mind was, *Why ever not?* Followed closely by every scenario in which he prayed it wasn't Bella Rossi's doing. He didn't want to imagine a star in their show could be so calculating. So callous and cruel as to strike a woman from behind.

"What are you saying, Rose? That you know it's her?"

"Not for sure. But I can't see it any other way. The first note I received, Colin . . ." Rose stared back, regret illuminating her eyes. "It was written in Italian."

CHAPTER 28

1928
PORT HURON, MICHIGAN

Storm clouds rolled in across the vast fields in which they'd put up their tent city.

The sky was more than menacing, with a straight line of purple-gray that spanned the city's horizon and added a wide shadow behind the tips of the tall trees. Coupled with the kick-up of cool wind off Lake Huron and speckles of raindrops that sent intermittent pricks against Rosamund's skin, it created a sinister backdrop for the impending evening performance.

They were minutes away from show time.

Rosamund and Owen stood in the backyard area behind the tent, which was reserved for performers in the show, taking in the scene from the alley hidden away from the public eye.

The entire backyard area seemed shrouded in a blanket of darkness that had fallen without warning. The sun wasn't set to go down for another couple of hours, yet it was far too dark already to signal anything but a deluge headed right for them.

"I don't like the looks of it," Owen said, reading Rosamund's thoughts.

The horses, too, seemed uneasy. They picked up their hooves, jostling about as if they were taking turns stomping at ants on the ground.

"Shhh. Shhh," she soothed, taking Ingénue by the bit. "Calm down, lady."

"I think we should prepare for this," Owen whispered, his eyes scanning first the line of ominous clouds, then the span of the tent city before them.

"You're thinking of the people."

He nodded. "The animals too. Crowds can be directed. But big cats and elephants can be tricky to manage on the best of days. Even trickier when storms roll in. I'd rather we not take any chances with them."

"I can already tell with the horses," Rosamund muttered, adjusting a surer grip on Ingénue's bit. "They're far too anxious. I wonder if we should call it off tonight."

"A little late to cancel, seeing as the show's already begun. But it'd be Colin's call to shut things down now. You seen him?"

Rosamund scanned the bustling back lot, looking for their boss's mop of dark hair standing out against the crowd.

"No. Last I saw him was more than an hour ago. He was pulled away to deal with something on the Midway. An altercation with some boys from town, so he shoved off to handle it. Said he'd stop in to check on us after the performance."

"We ought to find him. And soon."

Owen's forehead revealed a slight crease at the brow, and hard lines chiseled the skin around his stern mouth.

"You don't think we have that long."

He shifted his glance her way, shaking his head. "We've seen storms on the lot before, but never like this. That sky is black as death."

Rosamund swallowed hard, not liking his choice of words. "Okay. What should we do?"

"Batten down the hatches, I'd say."

It looked like they already were.

All around her, the back lot bustled.

Rosamund saw Jerry trot by with a couple of men in tow. They'd obviously found the machinist to work out some problem with the circus diner concession wagon nearby, its goods quickly being caught up in the mounting gusts of wind. The men battled together, working to pull down the raised panels on the back while the concessioner tried to keep his stacks of popcorn bags from flying away.

Across the yard she could see Minnie's costume wagon and changing tents, the costume mistress gathering up brightly colored taffeta gowns, plumed hats, and sequined leotards while stealing glances up at the line of thick clouds. Clowns, too, were gathering their props and pulling down the rolled sides of their tents, should the sky open up while they were waiting for their part in the evening performance. A train of elephants ambled by, their trainers casting nervous glances at the storm clouds overhead. The lumbering beasts didn't look as surefooted as usual, and that was always cause for concern.

Rosamund couldn't see the lines at the main entrance from where they stood, as it was on the other side of the Big Top. She could, however, hear the generous roar of the crowd inside the tent. If they hadn't sold out that day, they'd come very close to it.

"How many do we have tonight?"

Owen clicked his tongue against his teeth with a *tsk tsk* sound, then said, "By all accounts, we're full up."

The Big Top could accommodate up to fifteen thousand people. *God help us . . .*

She shook her head. How could they find shelter for that many?

"Colin needs to know about this."

"He already does, Rosamund. All he has to do is look up at

the sky. That man is two steps ahead of everything concerning this show. But I'd feel better if we were certain as to what he wants done." Owen ran his hands over the nose of the horse nearest him. "We have protocol for this, but I'm not at liberty to set the wheels into motion without his say-so."

"So what do we do?"

"Get these animals under cover. Now."

"What do you say we get the horses in the back entrance of the Big Top? There's enough room. Once the flyers go into the last part of their set, we can march into the ring a little early. That way, we'll free up room for the elephants behind us, and no one will have to be left in a downpour. They'll still hear the storm, but at least they won't have to see what's happening. That would buy us some time, wouldn't it?"

"Good idea. I'd feel better knowing the elephants weren't watching the sky."

Rosamund nodded and pulled the horses toward the Big Top, just as thunder rolled in a gentle rumble overhead.

"I wish we weren't either."

THE BIG TOP WAS JUST AS LIVELY AS EVER, WITH ROARING LAUGHTER as the clowns ran through their act.

Rosamund sat on Ingénue's back, scanning the crowd. She looked from the span of people to the openings in the tent in the back and the darkening sky behind them. It had begun to rain by then, a steady crying down of water that charged the atmosphere with growing anxiety. She felt a prickle in the hair on the back of her neck, as if a blast of cool air had just swept in to tease it.

She clicked her tongue against the roof of her mouth, trying to keep Ingénue as calm as possible.

A sharp crack of lightning shook the canvas vault overhead, making the crowd gasp in unison. It seemed they'd been oblivious to the onslaught of rain and wind up to that moment. But any oblivion shattered after that. The air began to sizzle with nervous energy as the sky sent another crack of lightning to earth. And then another, the last one stirring the horses enough that several of them reared back.

Rosamund managed to calm them down, hushing them with soothing words and the steadiest tone she could manage.

The band still played, though the roar of wind outside battled for its own attention. It agitated the crowd enough that some patrons stood. Even edged toward the exits. And the band suddenly stopped, all of the instruments shrieking to an off-key halt.

Alarm bells sounded in Rosamund's head the moment she heard the new tune.

Every performer knew that the playing of "Stars and Stripes Forever" indicated a matter of urgency under the Big Top; it meant something was terribly wrong and was a cue to put everyone on full-scale alert.

She looked from her left to her right, scanning the walls of canvas and the growing agitation in the crowd.

There was no way they could perform now and do it safely. Not when the storm was causing such a stir. Parents were tugging frightened children along, clogging the exits as the band continued to play.

Rosamund glanced up ahead, struggling to see where Owen stood, looking for direction.

He'd raised his hand out in front of their troop.

She caught his gaze but Owen shook his head, telling her to hold fast.

In the many months she'd traveled with the circus, Rosamund's strength and intuition had grown. From unwelcoming crowds in some towns, to sick animals and the unfortunate accidents that could plague a traveling circus, the unexpected had become quite commonplace. There were injured men. Illness. The responsibility to care for animals and watch for abuse, even in the actions of friends who worked around you.

And then there was the coil of nervousness in Rosamund's midsection, ever-present as she remembered the threats that had been aimed directly at her. Any strength she'd built up seemed fleeting now as the sky bled ferocious tears.

The wind tore at the tent like a child throwing a toy. At that moment the interior lights failed. In an instant the Big Top became a prison for frightened performers, with the fierce trumpeting of alarmed elephants and the horrifying shouts of guests trying to flee for their lives through a pitch-black death trap.

CHAPTER 29

Blood covered Rosamund's hands.

It was sticky and wet, causing her fingers to slip as she kept fabric torn from her costume in a tight compression on the girl's thigh.

"You're going to be all right," she cooed, brushing strands of mud-caked hair back from the little girl's brow.

Rosamund tore her eyes away, looking up and down the back lot alley.

It was still dark, the skies echoing gray overhead. It was no longer the line of deep purple and black they'd seen before the storm rolled in, and she took that as a good sign.

Performers had scattered. Guests ran past the tents anchored at the far end of the alley. All were soaked and most were terrified, though some had the presence of mind to stop and loot from damaged tents.

Rosamund cried out, calling to them. Desperate for help.

"Rosamund?"

She looked up, relieved to find Jerry crouched at her side. He turned his head down, keeping it out of the wind, and looked her over.

"No." She shook her head. "It's not me. It's her."

He pulled the blood-soaked fabric back, inspecting the wound.

"She's bleeding and . . . not crying anymore . . ."

282

Jerry unbuckled then tore off his belt. "Help me lift her," he instructed, pushing his glasses back on his nose with his index finger.

Rosamund nodded, slipping her hands under the girl's leg as he eased the thick strap of leather under it. He pulled hard, seeing that the leather was taut.

"I've got her," he said, scooping her up in his arms. "If you find her parents, say I've taken her to the hospital tent."

She knelt in the mud, the wind spattering her cheeks with rain, and watched as Jerry ran off with the child bundled up in his arms.

Dazed, she looked around. Canvas and steel anchors of tents had been torn to bits like they were made of rice paper and string. They marred the landscape like casualties of war. And the animals—who knew where they all were—made horrific, guttural moans and cries in the distance, followed by human shrieks and cracks of thunder.

Please, God. Don't let the lions be loose. She got to her feet, limbs shaking. If the big cats smelled blood . . .

Leaves flew past, mixed with circus programs and rain-soaked popcorn bags, littering the air like butterflies tossed in the wind.

"Rose!"

She turned, hands shaking, the rain spreading the blood from her hands to stain the front of her costume in crimson.

Colin emerged from the chaos, rushing through a line of people like a warrior tearing through battle. He was without his vest or hat, his shirt covered in mud and clinging to his skin, taking in heaving breaths with a rise and fall as though he'd been running for miles. His arms were braced at his sides, his hands balled up in tight fists as if he'd been ready to fight the storm with his bare hands.

He locked eyes on her, and immediately the tension eased from his stance.

Rosamund ran to meet him at the entrance of the ring stock

tent as water dripped from the overhang and gathered in puddles between them.

"You're hurt?" he said. Words clipped. Eyes begging for an answer.

She shook her head. "No. There was a girl. She was injured and . . ." She ran her hands down the front of her costume on instinct, as if she could simply brush the blood away. "I'm okay. Come in out of the rain. You're soaked to the skin."

Colin obeyed, moving past her as a roar of thunder clapped behind them. He stepped into the tent with her, easing into the opening by the horses.

"See? I'm fine." She shook her head, then wiped the dampened hair that had fallen down in her eyes. "What happened after the lights went out? I heard the elephants . . ."

"Lightning struck just outside the Big Top, and Nora went mad. Tore through the side of the tent." He shook his head. "She's . . . she's dead."

Rosamund's hand flew up to her mouth. "No . . ."

Not the kind-eyed mother elephant that she'd first met on the lot.

"The police followed her as she rampaged into town. I tried to get there in time. They put her down, Rose. Right there in the middle of the street." He slapped his hand on his leg. "What a waste. She must have been terrified—she couldn't have known what was happening."

Rosamund's heart squeezed in her chest as she watched the anguish on his face. Behind them, the rain was now coming down in sheets.

"And then I came back to this—disaster everywhere. Some are badly injured."

"God in heaven . . . ," she whispered. "How could this happen?"

"It just . . . happens, Rose. I've seen every kind of accident you can imagine. This is the life. Don't you remember me telling you that?" There was frustration, even anger, in his voice.

"Of course I remember!"

"Do you also remember the deal we made after you were attacked? If anything happened on the lot, you'd bring the horses back and wait for me here? I came back and found this tent empty, Rose! All the while, we've got a tornado blowing through the Big Top and wild animals running loose, and I'm trying to track down a lost bareback rider like a needle in a haystack. Because she's too willful to do anything I ask of her."

"Owen and I—we did come back. We had to get the horses to safety. And I did wait here at first, but there were frightened people everywhere, running all over each other. And when the little girl fell and cut her leg, I couldn't just stand by and do nothing."

"I looked for you in every corner of this tent, and in the Big Top. I crawled through piles of overturned chairs and sawdust on my hands and knees in the dark, looking for you. Scared I'd find you with another knock on the head, or worse this time."

"But I've been here, Colin." She exhaled the breath she hadn't known she held, incredulous. She held her arms out at her sides, the wet sequins pricking at her skin. "Look at me. I'm . . . I'm fine. See? Nothing's happened."

Colin shook his head. "I pulled you out of a raging river once before," he told her, hands clenched at his sides, emotion barely restrained. "Remember? And I won't do that again. Do you hear me? I can't do my job if there's any chance you're in danger. Love does that to people, Rose. It takes over every part of you so that you can't think straight. Everyone out there is demanding answers from me about what to do, and all I can think about is finding you! So yes—I think I am entitled to be a little angry right now."

Rosamund froze.

She blinked. Hearing only the sounds of her own breath and the intermittent neighing of the horses behind them. Replaying what she thought he'd just said in her mind.

"What did you just say to me?"

Colin ran a hand through his hair—his telltale sign of acute frustration.

He exhaled. "I'm trying to tell you that I love you. That your safety means more to me than anything or anyone."

The same instinct that had frozen her feet in place only moments before now prompted her to take a step toward him.

He did the same. Looking at her. Searching her face for a reply.

"It's why I stand by to watch every performance. Why I played for you in the ring that night last season," he said softly. His brow was furrowed. Almost pain-wracked. His stare ardent. "It's why I'm standing here right now."

"And I told you I'm here," she whispered. "See? I'm fine, Colin."

"Yes. I see you, Rose. I've always seen you."

He lowered his voice to a rough whisper, just low enough that he'd have to step closer so she could hear each word over the pattering of rain on the roof.

Colin looked up. "It seems like we're always surrounded by storms, doesn't it?"

"But we don't have to be."

He stepped toward her, then edged the hair back from her forehead with his palm. Looking over her face, wiping at a smudge on her cheek. Looking down on her the way no man ever had, and she was sure no one would again.

"When I saw you riding in the field at Easling Park that day, I thought my heart was going to burst right out of my chest."

Rosamund fell into his embrace, forgetting about the storm or her fear or the crumbling show around them, and accepted a kiss that was long overdue. She wanted nothing more than to hear him say those words again, and to return them with her own.

With a stomping and splashing of puddles, Ward suddenly burst into the tent, soaked to the skin and covered in mud up to his knees.

Colin and Rosamund broke apart and she turned away, shoulders shaking.

"Thank God I found you, Colin," Ward exclaimed. "We've been looking for you everywhere."

She looked up to find Colin's gaze still lingering on her. He kept the connection with Rosamund's eyes. "Please, Ward. I just need a moment," he snapped.

"No—you need to come quick, Boss," Ward ordered, urgency weighing his voice. "It's Bella."

CHAPTER 30

The thought of popping by Bella's tent after what had just happened between them wrenched Rosamund's breath away. She had no idea what she and Colin would encounter, or whether the flyer would be in top form to offer her usual helping of condescension. But when they reached the private tent, Rosamund's concerns were silenced.

Bella was on the ground by her dressing table, curled over and coughing in mad fits. She lay on her side, an oriental robe of red silk over her flyer's costume, her hair laced with straw and patches of dirt. Frankie knelt behind her, trying to pull her up to a sitting position.

Colin tore in, rushing to kneel at her side. "Bella?" he whispered. He patted her face, trying to get her eyes to focus on him.

The beautiful flyer's complexion had dimmed to a pale gray. She continued coughing, deep rumbles that rattled low in her chest, shaking her entire body. She fought to cover her mouth with a kerchief clutched in her hands.

Its edges were tinged with the bright, shocking color of blood.

Colin took the kerchief and dabbed at the spot where more drops had gathered. He pressed his hand to her brow.

"She's burning up," he muttered. "How long has she been sick?"

Frankie stood back, wringing her hands. "It wasn't quite this bad yesterday." She held up a near-empty bottle of tonic. "I thought it would pass if she drank more cough syrup."

"That stuff? It's pure alcohol, Frankie! How did she even get it? You forget that she's not supposed to have any?"

"A doctor prescribed it for her cough a couple stops back."

"You mean she's been performing like this?" Colin demanded, glaring. "Why didn't anyone tell me?"

"You're not exactly a confidant at present, Colin. She swore me to secrecy. I didn't want her to go out and perform either, but she insisted. I would have come to you after the show. But then all this happened with the storm and no one could find you. We looked everywhere."

He stole a quick glance at Rosamund.

"Well, your promise may well have killed her. Back up," he ordered, slipping his arms under Bella's legs to scoop her up from the ground. He moved past Frankie and gently laid Bella down on the cot in the corner of the tent.

Rosamund and Ward stood planted in the doorway, watching.

Ward shifted nervous glances from Bella back to Rosamund, perhaps processing what he'd just witnessed—or almost witnessed—when he'd found them together.

"Somebody get her some water," Colin ordered over his shoulder.

"Got it, Boss."

Ward disappeared in a blink, sailing out into the deluge without stopping to inquire about any details.

Colin patted Bella's cheek. Her eyelids fluttered, then opened. A smile eased over her lips when her eyes focused on him. He seemed to pull his emotions into check then and softened his features considerably.

"How do you feel?"

"Like I've just been hit by a tornado."

"Very funny," he whispered, the hint of a laugh escaping at her attempt to find humor in the moment. "But this is more than a tornado, Bell. You should have told me."

"I used to make you laugh like that. Remember?" she asked, then fell into a coughing fit. "Before you became so serious. No time . . . for laughing . . . these days."

She rose up on the cot to a near sitting position. Colin braced a hand at her back, helping her through the worst of it.

"What can I do?" Rosamund asked. "Shall I fetch the doctor?"

Frankie blistered her with an icy stare. "The doctor can't help her, you fool."

"Frankie." Colin cut her off. "You're not helping."

"But this is all her fault! Bella was so worried about losing her place in the show that she wouldn't tell you how sick she really is. She's been drinking again to cover it."

Colin shook his head. "To cover what?"

Frankie gritted her teeth. "She has consumption."

Rosamund's mouth fell open.

Tuberculosis? It could spell a death sentence.

"And don't act like that means something to you," Frankie said, turning on Rosamund. "You swooped in on that horse of yours, with your sweet little smile and your pink roses plastered on every poster from here to the coast. You came into this show like a princess, and there you stand, a sprite with a knife, ready to stab people's backs. You should have blood on your hands."

Frankie scowled, hands planted on her hips.

Her words penetrated deep. Cutting places Rosamund never knew existed.

"You walked over Bella on your way to the top, little girl. How pious of you to come here now, wide-eyed as can be, asking if you can *help*. When you were brought into this show as her replacement."

Rosamund looked from Colin back to Frankie. "But I didn't—"

"You didn't know?" Frankie shot an accusatory glare over at Colin, burning his back with a piercing stare. "And you didn't tell her? You romanced this little girl, and she had no idea that she's just another in a long line of unfortunate stars who have crossed your path?"

"Frankie, you don't know what you're saying," Colin said.

"I do. I know exactly what I'm saying," she spat. She turned back to Rosamund. "Bella doesn't need your help. All the while you're trying to steal the show and her fiancé out from under her feet. Haven't you taken enough from her already?"

Colin lowered his head. And Rosamund knew it was true.

It made sense now.

Bella's immediate dislike of her in London. The way she'd abhorred Rose's presence from the very first show at Madison Square Garden. The threatening notes. Even the attack when she'd been struck down from behind.

She shuddered now, thinking how right Mable had been.

Bella's mask had been fragile, but she'd covered her true colors well.

Whatever had been there between Colin and Bella, she couldn't see it. Didn't want to see it. But it was there now, clear as day. Colin's shoulders were slumped with it. Bella's eyes locked with hers now, the fever amplifying the color of bitterness in them.

Rosamund stood stone-still, her heart shattering under the double onslaught of Bella's hatred and Colin's silence.

"Get her out of here," Bella mumbled.

When Rosamund made no move to go, she called out louder. "I said leave! Get out!" She fought to come up off the cot.

Colin tried to push her down at the shoulders. "Bella, you're sick. You don't mean it." He brushed a hand over her face, trying to soothe her.

"I do. If she'd had any decency, she'd have stayed away. She'd never have climbed on that train in London . . ."

Bella fell back in his arms then, her limbs slack and powerless.

"Rosamund," Colin whispered, even as his arms braced the broken flyer.

It was the first time he hadn't called her Rose. The meaning behind it was painfully clear.

"Maybe you should go."

"Colin . . ."

"Please," he said, entreating her with sympathy in his eyes. The emotion she saw in them penetrated deep. "Just go for now. We'll talk later."

There was nothing left to say.

Her chin quivered through the single nod she could muster, and she turned, stepping back out into the rain. She passed a confused Ward, who'd returned, running down the backyard alley with a bucket of water balanced in his outstretched hands.

"Are you going for the doctor?" He did a double take when she ignored him, then called after her even as he rushed into the tent. "Rosamund?"

She kept her feet moving, one in front of the other, until Ward's voice faded in the patter of rain to earth. She heard a lion's roar off in the distance. And the yard moved around her with the sounds of workmen bustling to the train cars, pushing wagons of tent poles and bailing rings through the mud along the tracks.

She didn't stop until she'd reached the safety of the ring stock tent.

Owen wasn't back yet, but she hardly noticed.

The English roses that had been laced up in her hair were wilted and sad now, falling from the chignon of rain-dampened hair at her nape. Their fragrance was still sweet, but now the scent filled the air with an angry sting, like alcohol poured on an open wound. She thought of the first time she'd worn them in the ring for Colin.

Rosamund tore the roses from her hair and threw them to the soft earth at her feet.

It wasn't until she'd crumpled to the ground on top of them that she let the tears fly.

CHAPTER 31

1928
VENICE, ITALY

Mable sat at the window of their room at the Palazzo Contarini Fasan, gazing out at the sunlight caught up in the water of the Grand Canal.

She and John both loved the Gothic architecture of the hotel, and when in Venice stayed there often. It shared Old World romance with the weary traveler, so much so that Mable had fashioned the Cà d'Zan's Venetian guest room and balcony after the water view that was lavished upon them now.

They'd opened the window, welcoming the softness of the breeze to drift in. It played with the pink chiffon neckline on her dress and the side-swept waves across her brow. Gondolas and other boats passed by with travelers in tow.

"Do you suppose it's any coincidence that Venetian legend says this building was the home of Desdemona?"

"Hmm?" John grunted, only half listening. "Do we know a Desdemona?"

Mable drew her attention away from the streaked sky painted by the setting sun, redirecting her gaze to John. Her lips curved into a smile.

John sat at the desk, mulling over contracts or ledgers of some sort. He fluttered paper back and forth, turning from page to page. It was so like him to take her literally, especially when he was focused on something entirely different from what occupied her mind.

"No, we don't know her personally. She's a character in Shakespeare's *Othello*."

"Ah, yes. The Venetian beauty who gave up everything to follow her heart. She married the much older Othello, and I believe some epic drama ensued?"

"As only Shakespeare can tell it," Mable answered, playing with the end of the sash around the dropped waist of her dress. She ran the light fabric over her fingertips. "She was killed by her estranged husband in the final act of the play."

John looked up, raising an eyebrow. "Is that something you've been concerning yourself with, alone at that window over there?"

"No," she said, smiling easily. "Not today. I'm just tired."

They were to attend an auction the next morning. One in which they hoped to acquire more art for the John and Mable Ringling Museum of Art—the massive museum and art school they were presently breaking ground for at the Cà d'Zan complex.

There were eighteenth-century "courting" fans listed, one of which was strikingly similar to the souvenir token John had first bought for her all those years ago in Chicago. He had already promised to buy her the "Bird Catcher" fan so she could hang it on the wall in the guest room, to remind her of their trips to the Grand Canal.

She should have been happy with the next morning's promises. Instead, her heart was heavy, and she was feeling the full weight of travel. Severe fatigue. Blurry vision. Weight loss and fainting spells that could buckle her knees without warning.

John must have detected the sadness lingering in her voice. He lowered the paper in his hands to the tabletop and leaned back in the desk chair, meeting her gaze. "What's wrong, Mable?"

"I'm unwell, John. We both know it."

It wasn't customary for her to show cracks in strength. But emotion lay raw under the surface now. It was the unspoken companion in every room in which they stayed. Her chin threatened her composure by quivering on its own.

"We know you've been tired. Overly tired lately. That's all. Travel will do that to anyone. And you are a most traveled woman."

"I am tired," she said aloud, thinking of how she felt too weary to pull her body off the mound of pillows she'd braced behind her on the room's gold-gilded chaise lounge. "Bone-tired, though, and there's a difference. Especially when it comes with the weight loss. And the dizziness. I could hardly climb the stairs this evening."

"The doctors said they can't be sure just yet. Let them do what they do best. Hmm?"

"You said that once before, remember?"

He tilted his chin, questioning. "When was that?"

"Our first walk together. There was a fire at the Exposition, and you stayed calm. You said to let the firemen do their jobs. That they'd handle it. And they did. The fire was eventually put out."

"It's a lot like the circus, then. Every man and woman and animal knows their job. And they do it well. So we must let the doctors have their say."

Mable nodded.

But the outcome they wished for now wasn't the wide-eyed wonder of children eating cotton candy and popcorn. This wasn't clowns or animals. It was real life. It was the freedom they enjoyed possibly being stolen away by a serious illness.

"But they said diabetes."

"They said *maybe* diabetes," he corrected. "There's a big difference."

"And Addison's disease, with diabetes? What of that?"

"That we will not worry about until the time has come to do so. If everyone knows his or her job, then yours is to not worry."

Mable thought on it a moment. Then, after clearing the emotion in her throat, she whispered, "I don't want them to know. Not my family or yours. Not Colin or any of the performers. Especially not the public. This is our secret, as long as we can make it such. I think there's a fight ahead for me."

John's reticence was a mannerism that Mable had grown quite used to over the years. She was the talker, he the listener. It was just their way. But sometimes he could surprise her, complimenting with few words or silent action. It was the little things, the ways his heart understood hers so thoroughly, that spoke volumes.

And it spoke loudly now.

He stood and dragged the desk chair across the center of the room. It scraped the floor, echoing against the lofts in the ceiling.

"What are you doing?"

He crossed in front of the fireplace and didn't stop until he'd pulled the desk chair right up next to her chaise. He then eased into it, content to sit at her side.

They gazed out at the Grand Canal for long moments, letting the soft spring breeze usher in evening around them. Finding that words weren't necessary. The sun dipped, fetching night from below the horizon, painting the sky in darker shades of orange and deep blue.

"Nice view. Is this what we pay for?" he asked. He extended his hand.

Mable nodded, accepting it. She laced her fingers with his. "Yes. This is what we pay for."

"Hmm," was his reply. "Well, it's beautiful. Not Sarasota-beautiful, but it tries."

He squeezed her hand, pulling her tear-glazed eyes over to meet the depth in his.

"Do you remember what I told you once? That it made no difference to me whether we had children?"

"I believe your exact words were, 'I didn't marry you for the children you might bear me.' And you, Mr. Ringling, were angry when you said it."

He nodded. Even let a hint of laughter escape his lips.

"I was a little angry. Because I love you, Mable Burton Ringling. And I told you we already have a million children. God gave us quite a gift in them. And we have our show. Our family of performers. Colin will keep all that in working order."

"He has been a gift, hasn't he? And we haven't asked him to be perfect."

He nodded. "Certainly not. It's too unpredictable a life. I told you I received a telegram about the storm damage. Colin confirmed the media reports. Guest injuries, though none killed, thank God. But we lost an elephant."

Mable sat up straighter. "Which one?"

"Nora," he said with a rough sigh.

Because loss troubled him, she knew. That's what it was—a great loss of something beautiful.

"I hate to shorten our trip, but would you like to go with me?"

"So you think it best to join them. Where is the show?"

"Michigan now. Indiana soon. Not far from Chicago, if you'd like to stop in there. Either way, this is serious enough that I need to be on hand."

Mable gazed out over the Grand Canal, watching the flicker of tiny diamonds across the surface of the water. It glinted with a warm rose-gold that reflected off the porticos of the warehouse-and-merchant-combined fondaco houses across the way.

"I don't think you do need to go, John. Not this time. Colin must learn to handle being a leader. The only way he can do that is if we allow him the opportunity."

"It's like your rose garden then, isn't it? You insisted on tending it with your own hands. You gave it love and care all these years. What if a storm blew in? Would you ignore the roses now? Would you leave them to fend for themselves?"

"No," she breathed out, pleased that he could see her side of it without a moment's hesitation. "I'd never leave a rose without helping if I could. But I don't think we need to go this time. It helps Colin—and the show—more if we allow him to make his own decisions. We won't be here forever, John. Someone has to take up the sword."

"And that is why we—and not you alone—will share our view from this and every window. Do you understand me, Mable? There are times when making decisions alone is to a person's advantage. But not in a marriage. Not for us. We carry the same sword, you and I."

Mable's thoughts drifted to Sally, the friend who'd passed more than twenty years before. She'd been alone for much of her fight. And Colin, too, battling out his past in every relationship he had. And what of Rosamund, the young bareback rider whose taste for freedom so mimicked Mable's own?

They all had one thing in common: faith that when one has no control, there is One who does. It was comforting that God had sent John Ringling at a time in her life when Mable had really needed him. And after the fulfillment of many dreams that had been hidden away in her treasure box, she still possessed that most precious gift.

She looked from the earnestness in John's eyes back to the canal, scanning the rows of gondolas lining the Gothic buildings across the way. The boats bobbed there, attracting lovers for the nightly tours that would flow past all the bridges of Venice.

"It is very beautiful here, John. And I do love the view," she said, turning to face him.

She gave him a genuine smile, meant to show her gratitude that he understood enough to come and sit by her side.

"But I want to go home. To our home. I want to see my garden. And if we have to tell Colin, I want him to hear it from us. Take me to our Cà d'Zan?"

CHAPTER 32

1928
CHICAGO, ILLINOIS

Flames licked up from the campfire, chasing the night sky overhead.

Someone had made coffee, and Colin's stomach tightened with the sweet smell.

He hadn't eaten. Had barely slept. His razor had been forgotten days ago, as had any basic comfort like coffee by a campfire. The need for anything normal had simply been chased out of his mind with the duties of the cleanup and dealing with the revelation of Bella's deteriorating health. They'd lost both the Fort Wayne and South Bend shows due to the storm and the media coverage of Nora, and he'd had to jump in and pick up the wrecked pieces in the aftermath.

Colin could see that Rosamund had accepted a mug but had set it in the grass at her feet, uninterested. She'd opted instead to watch the fire flicker, getting lost in its inviting orange-and-yellow dance.

"Rose."

Colin eased down next to her on the pinwheel quilt spread over the ground and braced his arms on his knees.

He reached toward her, freezing an outstretched hand on air.

Rosamund remained quiet, not looking up to see what he

offered, until a glint of gold flashed in the firelight. She watched him as a clink of metal fell upon the quilt at her feet.

It was his old pocket watch and chain—the one he always carried. She'd probably noticed it before, as he had a habit of turning it over in his fingertips when he was deep in thought. What he needed her to understand now wasn't why he had it, but rather why he was now offering it to her.

"I told you about this watch once, remember? I tried to steal it from Mr. Ringling long ago. I dropped it on the sidewalk that night and the glass cracked. So Mable gave it to me. Seemed to think it could be a marker for the start of a new life."

"You wanted a new life?" she whispered. "Why?"

"At Easling Park, I told you I knew what it felt like to wish more than anything that you could change your life. Well, this represents the difference between us. You deserved a new life. I didn't."

He could feel Rosamund surveying his profile, staring back. Waiting for him to continue.

"You asked me one time if I had a family. I did."

"Had . . . a family."

"Yes. It was broken. I was broken. Everyone has their secrets, Rose. Your family and mine both. We're not so different. You're an earl's daughter. I'm a steel magnate's son. Both born wealthy, from fine family histories. But I was illegitimate. I had no name. My father never claimed me, and my mother was forced to marry a man she didn't love. A fisherman. A good father to a son they eventually had together, but a man who hated the very idea of me and everything I stood for."

"Why couldn't you tell me that before? It wouldn't have changed anything."

"Because I've never told anyone. Owen knows a bit of my past, but only Mable knows who and what I really am."

"And what is that?"

"I'm a man who can never change the lives he's ruined," he began, pausing to blink back at her for several long seconds.

She said nothing. Just looked on, inviting him to continue.

"In my youth, the streets became a haven for me. Avery, my stepbrother, used to trail after me when I'd run off. And though I told him to stay out of it, he'd follow me anyway. Idolizing an older brother, I suppose. It was an attempt at pickpocketing gone wrong that almost got me caught one night. Avery saw it, ran from the alley out into the street to free my collar from the grip of a policeman . . ."

His voice trailed off and he dipped his head, staring at the ground between them. It seemed safer than being forced to read the pity he'd no doubt find in those green eyes.

"Avery was struck and killed by an ice wagon. And it was because of me."

Rosamund turned to look at him, and he met her gaze, instantly sorry to find a mask of horror there.

"He was six years old. My mother could never forgive me. I left home that night and lived on the streets. And by then, I was numb. Drifting from one misadventure to the next. Stealing to stay alive. Not caring about anyone or anything. Until I stole a watch from the Circus King, and his wife refused to give up on me. I sometimes wonder if that was my second chance, to make up for what happened."

Tears were trailing down Rosamund's face. Her hands trembled softly, as if she yearned to reach out to him. To ease his pain somehow.

"My past mistakes can never be undone. I can't change them or the man I've become because of them. I went to war. I fought and never should have come back. I didn't deserve to, when so many good men died in the mud, blasted to bits. But I came back to the only home I'd ever known, one that travels on a train, never putting down roots. And that's why I refuse to give up on anyone else. I need you to know that. This watch is a daily reminder of where I've come from. It's my penance to carry it."

The watch glowed on the ground between them.

Rosamund reached out, fingertips grazing the metal first, then picked up the watch.

She turned it over, winding the chain around her fingers. She opened the gold cover, ran her index finger over the cracked glass and the words engraved on the inside, as he'd done thousands of times before.

"Colin, I'm sorry you've had to carry this with you every day. But you can't fix what's happened," she whispered, shaking her head in the flicker of firelight. "We can't do anything to make up for our transgressions. There must be grace to cover them—no matter what they are or how deep they run within us. Grace has to be stronger."

Colin turned to face her, feeling an extension of the reprieve she'd offered.

He took up her hands in his. She kept them balled in a fist around the watch but still he held them, brushing his thumb over the back of her hand.

"I need you to know that what I told you after the storm—I meant it. God help me, Rose, I meant every word."

"I know you did," she said softly.

"And what happened in Bella's tent was meant for me, not you."

"I know that too. Owen may not have understood all of the reasons why, but he told me about Bella. About me being her replacement, and how you didn't know what was happening to her."

"Then you know we're no longer engaged—or never really were. It wasn't love, what we had. I was trying to fix something that had been broken in her. Maybe broken for me too."

"And now? What will happen to her?"

"There's a sanitarium in Kentucky—Waverly Hills. The Ringlings will pay for her treatment. They have doctors who will . . ." He cleared his throat over emotion that gathered there. "They'll know what to do to help her. She'll bounce back. Bella always does. But it will spell the end for the Rossi Family Flyers as we know them."

Rosamund nodded, watching the dance of the firelight.

"I know what Frankie said was in anger, because if Bella was forced out of the show, the Rossi family would lose the act altogether. She was speaking out of fear. I have no bitterness toward her or Bella." She paused, then turned to him. "Or you."

"Then you forgive me?"

Rosamund fell into the embrace he offered, wrapping her arms around him.

Colin buried his face in the crook of her neck and threaded his hand through her hair, drawing her close. Unable to think straight. Thanking the Almighty that he'd been given the mercy of a second chance with her.

"You don't need my forgiveness," she said. "But I hope you can forgive yourself one day, because you are a good man, Colin Keary. Do you hear me?" She eased away until his eyes met hers. "You gave me a chance at a life of my own, you and Mable both. You've changed everything for me, and I could never forget that kindness."

"It wasn't kindness. It was more than that—"

"Please, wait." She shook her head, edging back away from him.

He felt a chasm open up, creating a void of doubt between them.

"Colin, I've had time to think . . . And no matter what my heart wants to feel right now, there's always going to be this between us. Like the watch—there's too much that's been broken. I didn't understand that before, but I do now. Even in my own life. I was running away when I left Easling Park. But healing was always there for me—I just had to take it in hand."

He searched her face, eyes narrowed and brow pinched with a deep, almost painful furrow. "What are you saying?"

Rosamund reached out, opening his hand. She dropped the watch in it, then curled his fingers around it with a gentle squeeze.

"I'm saying that everyone is broken in some way. And we can't fix ourselves, Colin. We can't keep running away," she breathed out, whispering through tears. "That's why I'll finish out the season. I'll work through my existing contract, but I'm leaving the show at the end of October. I'm finally going home."

CHAPTER 33

1928

SARASOTA, FLORIDA

There would be two shows at the end of October at the winter lodgings, both on the final day of the season.

Rosamund walked from the back entrance of the stables with Ingénue in tow, passing through the palm-lined streets to the ring practice area.

With Bella gone, the Rossi family was without the biggest crowd draw in their act. Marvio, Enzo, and Frankie had continued, but their star power had faded without Bella. And without her, they'd not be signed to a new contract for the following year. Rosamund, meanwhile, had blossomed in the center ring as the top-marketed act for the remainder of the season.

But the rest of the performers had no idea their final performance of the season would also be her last with the circus. She and Ingénue had performed at the matinee and now were taking their last walk from the stables to the performance ring.

"Rosamund! Thank God you're here."

Annaliese came running toward the stables. She stopped and bent over to rest her hands on her knees in between sucking in heaving breaths of air.

"What's wrong?"

"Look," she said, pointing to the sky at the opposite end of the complex. "The menagerie house."

A thin line of smoke curled up in the sky, dancing like black thread woven through the Sarasota sunlight.

"A fire? Here?"

Annaliese nodded. "Hurry. I came back to get you, and we have to go right now. We're being evacuated to the entrance, just as a precaution. Owen sent me for you. All of the guests are being escorted out too."

Rosamund knew Owen meant well, but her first instinct was to protect the animals. What if the fire were to spread?

"But what about the horses? We can't leave them behind."

"They'll be fine." Annaliese waved a hand for her to follow her ginger steps on the road. "The fire is nowhere near the stables. Owen wants to account for everyone first. He'll go back with a few once he knows everyone is safe outside."

Rosamund wanted to obey. Even eased Ingénue forward, thinking the last thing in the world she wanted to do was make Owen worry. But her steps were halted by the memory of a promise she'd once made.

Colin.

If anything happened, Rosamund promised she'd go back to the ring stock tent and wait for him there. She'd left him the night of the storm and couldn't bear the thought of doing that to him a second time. Especially not if he would have to search all over the complex for her. He'd go to the stables. She was sure of it.

"No, I'm going back. I'll stay with the horses until we hear the all-clear. And if we need to evacuate the animals, Colin will come and make sure we do it together."

In one fluid motion, Rosamund swept up on Ingénue's back and turned the horse in the direction of the stables.

"Rosamund, you can't! Owen sent me to come and get you. I cannot go back alone. He'll have me for dinner!"

"You can," she said, shouting over her shoulder as she pulled Ingénue into a steady run. "Don't worry about me. Tell Owen that Colin knows where I am."

It wasn't but a moment of Ingénue's galloping before they found themselves at the stable complex. Rosamund eased them around to the back, avoiding tourists as they hurried down the road in the direction of the train tracks and the safety of the front entrance.

She slid down from Ingénue's back and eased them in through the back door, walking past several rows of stalls. It was eerily quiet. The horses were stilled. There was no breeze to brush against the walls. Even the building seemed hushed, for Rosamund could hear the sound of water dripping into a trough in some stall nearby.

"Hello?" she breathed out. "Owen?"

Her words echoed through the empty stable. And then a strong odor began to float around them, blasting Rosamund in the face with each step deeper into the building.

She slowed Ingénue to a halt.

Kerosene?

Rosamund's breathing shallowed out in a blink, suspicion overwhelming her that something wasn't quite right. Her eyes had only just begun to adjust in the dim stable light around them. She scanned the expanse of stalls, counting the horses along the way.

She saw nothing but the backs of horses mingling in with the shadows inside their stalls. But then a sudden movement caught in her side vision and Rosamund froze, her eyes fixed upon it. She exhaled lightly, her breath shuddering over parted lips.

The last thing in the world she'd expected to find in the back of the stable was the tall form of Marvio Rossi, bent over a pile of mounded straw with a kerosene can in one hand and a lighter fixed in the other.

He stood and flicked the top of the lighter, exposing a flame to the air between them.

"I knew you'd come back."

"Mr. Rossi?" She fought to keep her voice calm. "What are you doing?"

The strong patriarch of the Rossi family stood before her, the muscles in his arms taut and the lighter fused in his grip.

God, no . . .

"Did you set fire to the menagerie house?"

He shook his head. "A small fire in a trash can. Just a diversion."

"A diversion for what?"

"For you, Miss Easling. As I said, I knew you would come back here. I heard you make that promise to Colin the night you were attacked. But you didn't come to the ring stock tent the night of the storm, did you? I thought that was my chance then. But he had eyes on you every moment after that, so there was no opportunity. Until today."

Rosamund's thoughts slammed about in her head.

"It was you all along," she breathed out, hands gripping the reins until her knuckles were white and her wrists shaking.

The notes. The threats. The attack that could have done so much more than simply knock her out for a few moments . . . All the while she'd thought it was Bella who had tried to scare her out of her place in the show—not the man who'd been kind. He'd been the voice of reason between Colin and the Rossi family. He'd even helped her after she'd been attacked. It was he and Enzo who had picked her up in their strong arms and carried her back to safety.

"But why did you stop? The notes . . ."

"You already thought Bella hated you. And that made it easier to plan in the event Colin wouldn't listen to reason. I tried to
convince him. Gave him every opportunity to support Bella. But
he decided to travel to England instead and recruit someone to take
her place. To take our entire family's place. And he came back with
you. He threw Bella away. Discarded all of us like we didn't matter."

"But it was a woman . . . The girl said a woman paid her to give
me the envelope."

"I paid a woman to do it. It was not difficult. And the men I
hired were supposed to put you out of the show. Not slide you right
into the star spot with a sympathy wound to the head. They didn't
do their job. And I was forced to clean up after them, just like I'm
doing now."

"You don't understand." She found herself pleading against the
ghostly indifference she saw on his face. "I'm leaving. Today's my
last show."

Marvio shook his head, scoffing. "You're lying. Colin would
have announced it if that were true. You're his star."

Rosamund looked from the bed of straw in the center of the
stable back to the lighter in Marvio's hand. The horses jostled
around them, some bobbing their heads with soft, murmuring
neighs. Ingénue had taken to clip-clopping her hooves in place,
showing her growing sense of agitation.

It seemed even the animals could sense the threat.

Rosamund gave a gentle tug on Ingénue's reins, thinking to
walk her backward through the doors. She glanced over her shoulder, realizing the path to freedom was too far. If Marvio had doused
the ground with kerosene, everything would become a firestorm
that would engulf them in a matter of seconds. She couldn't possibly
turn and climb up to ride them out in time.

"Please," she entreated, looking around at the scores of horses that would perish if he dropped the flame. "You don't have to do this. Bella can still recover. She can come back. And I won't be here when she does."

"You're right," he whispered, holding up the lighter. "You won't."

"Stop." A voice carried across the length of the stable.

Rosamund spun her head around to the opposite end of the stall row, looking for the source. Her breath caught in her chest and relief flooded over her. Enzo stood in the archway, his hand anchored to the side of the door that had been cracked open.

He took careful steps forward, walking in his flyer's costume with leather slippers crunching on straw, until he stood directly in front of them. He stopped, bracing his feet apart and holding balled fists at his sides.

"You won't hurt her, Uncle."

"Move, Enzo. This has to be done."

"Then you'll have to go through me." He stood firm. "I won't let you do this. It's not what Bella would want, and you know it."

Marvio shook his head, arms trembling with pent-up anger.

"I did all of this for Bella. For us! We're family, Enzo. That goes deeper than this show."

Enzo stared back. "You didn't do this for me or for her. I may have wished things to end differently for Bella, but she has a chance now. It's a slight one, with consumption, but that's something. And I won't let you harm this girl, no matter what's happened. It doesn't justify what you've done."

Rosamund's fist was tightened around Ingénue's reigns.

"You can go, Rosamund," Enzo said, keeping his voice deadly serious and his eyes affixed to his uncle's.

Marvio squeezed his hand around the lighter even before she made an effort to move. She fought to keep Ingénue still, making *shh* sounds.

"Rosamund, back away slowly," Enzo instructed. "Go ahead. It's okay."

She obeyed, feeling her throat drying up. They edged backward, she and Ingénue together, taking each step at a slow and intentional pace.

"What about all we've lost? What about your sister, Enzo? And your wife. You'll be left with nothing!" Marvio shouted at his nephew.

Rosamund gave a light tug against Ingénue's reins and turned to look back at how far they had yet to go. Her breath caught in her lungs.

"Colin . . . ," she breathed.

He was edging closer across the stable from her, shaking his head with a finger pressed to his lips. Her eyes darted back and forth from Enzo and Marvio to Colin, who was shrouded in the shadows.

"I'll still have my name," Enzo answered, the calmness in his voice unwavering. "This isn't the way it has to be, Uncle. And I know you don't want to do this either. You can choose."

She couldn't risk saying anything. But Rosamund's heart felt as though it could have burst from her chest when she saw Colin crouch down behind the stall slats, moving in closer behind the unsuspecting Marvio, ready to spring.

She blinked back with glazed eyes and gave a faint nod, hoping he knew what she meant by it. She knew he'd remember where to find her. And he'd kept his promise to always come back.

Marvio shook his head and allowed his shoulders to drop, as if his decision had been made. He flicked the lighter, bringing back the flame.

Without warning, Colin darted in a flying leap from behind, jarring his shoulder into the thick of Marvio's broad back. The lighter pitched from his hand, landing in a bed of straw farther down the line of stalls. It caught fire, sending a rush of flames up in the air, crackling against a wooden support column near the mound of kerosene-soaked straw.

Enzo raised an arm up, shielding his face from the burst of flames.

While Colin worked to subdue Marvio, Enzo ran to the corner of the stable where stacks of fire-proof canvas lay mounded in heaps. He tugged at one pile, gritting his teeth at the weight until one strip finally gave way, then ran back toward the growing fire with the canvas in his arms.

"The horses!" Enzo roared, slapping at the flames with the shield of canvas. "Get the horses out, Rosamund!"

Rosamund edged around the scuffling Marvio and Colin. If Enzo couldn't control the fire and the stable went up in flames, she'd free as many horses as she could before the building was consumed.

"Go on, girl!" she shouted, sending Ingénue in the direction of freedom in the afternoon sun.

She ran to the end of the stable row and wasted no time, pulling open the stall door of a chocolate mare. Rosamund slapped the mare's hindquarters, sending her from the stall.

"Out you go!"

Down the line she went, throwing open stall doors to free as many horses as she could. She crossed over to the other side of the stable, working her way back up the line, coaxing each jittery horse to freedom.

She turned back to calculate the distance of the flames. To see whether Colin had managed to wrestle Marvio into submission. And whether Enzo was still battling the fire.

What she saw was three men battling the flames together.

Colin stood out in front, smoke and soot having painted the skin of his face a sweaty black. Enzo and Marvio slapped canvas at the flames together, the smoke, too, coloring the light blue of their flyer costumes a charred, sickly gray.

She didn't understand why Marvio was now helping to subdue the flames he had ignited, but the sight of the men working together charged her back into action. The back row of stalls had caught fire, and there was one horse left to set free.

The air in the stall was littered with ash and tiny sparks of orange, causing Rosamund to cough with each drawn breath. She raised her elbow to shield her nose and mouth, praying the light cover of fabric from her costume would filter enough air so she could breathe.

"Come on," she yelled.

The mare resisted, retreating back against the inside of the stall.

"Out!"

The horse reared with a surge of frightened energy, throwing Rosamund back against the plank edge of the stall. She met it with a jolt of pain at the base of her head, stunning her enough that she crumpled against the wooden wall.

The view of the stall row and the cloudy sky beyond the doors became a fluid vision, dissolving into a jumble of hazy silhouettes and melting colors. She shook her head against it, having the oddest sensation that the fire, the shouts of men, and the mare that had bolted past her were all moving about in slow motion. Embers floated like fireflies around her. The sounds dissipated as though she'd been dropped through a tunnel. She felt dizzy and nauseated as she tried unsuccessfully to get to her feet.

In a flash of stirred memory, Rosamund was pulled back to the field at Easling Park.

Her face was in the soft grass. The scent of dew and earth filled her nostrils. And two polished riding boots stepped into her line of sight.

Hendrick crouched down with a violin and bow tucked in his arms, a concerned brotherly frown marring his brow. He was young. Alive. And she gasped, wishing she could speak to ask if it was really him. If he was truly there.

"Are you all right, little Rose?" he asked, tipping his head to one side.

She'd fallen from her horse that day. Badly. She'd been so small and the fall from the horse's back so far that she thought she'd never reach the ground.

"Get up, Rose."

She fought to obey, feeling the sensation of warmth filling her limbs, but no pain. No fear. She just listened to his coaxing, swimming in her thoughts.

"Get up," Hendrick insisted, his green eyes staring back at hers. "You're not afraid."

Rosamund braced a leg in a kneeling position, hooking her arm around the stall rail. She pulled herself up, still reeling from the blow, but determined to defy it.

It was important to stand on her own two feet, she knew. She scanned the stall, it, too, feeling like a tunnel built around her. The mare had run out, leaving her behind. She leaned against the rail, drawing in deep breaths with her eyes closed and face lifted to the ceiling.

"Rose?"

Arms came around her, enveloping her with strength.

Were they Hendrick's?

Rosamund could smell the smoke on his shirt as she buried her face against his shoulder. He breathed quickly, nervous energy sending breaths in and out in a fervent pulse.

"Are you all right?"

He braced his hands on either side of her face, and she opened her lids, finally able to focus back at the blue eyes entreating her to answer.

It wasn't Hendrick, but Colin.

She willed her mind to focus. Focus on him alone.

Colin. She could feel his hand patting her cheek. *You're here.*

"Rose?"

The first thought that came clearly tumbled out her mouth. "Is Ingénue okay?"

"She's fine," Enzo called out. "I have her here."

Rosamund shook her head, still feeling the room spinning around Colin's face.

"What happened?"

"We got the fire out," Colin answered, staring back with intensity. He rubbed the back of his wrist at the beads of perspiration on his brow. "The fire marshal is here with the police. They've taken Marvio into custody. Did you fall?"

She shook her head, licking her lips against the dryness the smoke had caused. "No, the mare. She just reared up and I was thrown back. I'm all right."

"Enzo, go get the doctor. You need him too."

"No. I'll be fine."

Colin ran a hand over the side of her face. "Are you sure you're okay?"

She shook the cobwebs of dizziness away, then placed a hand over his, patting it against his fingertips.

"Just shaken a little. But I'm fine."

She turned back to Enzo, who stood behind Colin with one arm cradled in his other hand. His forearm was inflamed to a bright pink, a burn puckering the skin from elbow to wrist.

Ingénue bobbed her head when Rosamund approached. She cupped her hand, filling it with Ingénue's nose, giving her a gentle pat.

Rosamund reached out to take Ingénue's reins from Enzo's grip. "And you?"

He shook his head. "It's not bad. I'll mend."

She looked around and saw two uniformed policemen walking a handcuffed Marvio out the far end of the stable.

"And your uncle?"

"I don't condone what he did. Or tried to do." Enzo raised his head, strengthening the line of his jaw. "Not everyone thinks you stole something from us. He realized what he was doing and tried to put out the flames. But not soon enough to avoid walking out like that."

"Thank you, Enzo. If it weren't for you . . ." She shook her head. "Thank you very much."

She turned back to Colin, seeing the fear and relief beneath the smudges of soot that covered his face.

"It's our last show together." She stood as tall as her frame would allow. Praying he'd see the resolve in her face and not question what she knew she had to do.

She slipped her arm around the side of Ingénue's head, giving her a loving pat. "We're going to perform."

THE RING HAD BECOME HER HOME.

Rosamund felt welcome there under the flood of lights and sky of canvas and rope. And for her last performance, it was no different. The smudges of soot on her costume and the hastily tied-up chignon of roses at the base of her neck made no difference. She'd not think about the fire. Or Marvio. She'd ignore the leftover haze of dizziness that had claimed her before, choosing instead to focus on the show. She was a professional now, just as Colin had said. No excuses for a lack of balance, no matter what had happened in the stable.

Though it was a much smaller crowd than they were used to, the audience welcomed them home as stars, showering applause as the overhead lights dimmed and they high-stepped into the ring.

The music enveloped the inside of the practice tent—the circus band playing its usual rendition of "Roses of Picardy." And together, Rosamund and Ingénue allowed themselves to be quite lost in it. The spotlights found their focus, and they went to work. Happy in the dance, of course, but Rosamund was still filled with the bittersweet knowledge that it was the last show they'd give.

They moved through the act, starting and stopping with precision. Rosamund performed mounts and dismounts. She knelt on Ingénue's back, stretching the length of her leg back in an elegant extension midride. They turned. Absorbed the applause of the tourists. The opportunity to stand a final time came at last, and Rosamund unlaced the bower of roses from her hair.

It wasn't until the lights around them fizzled and faded out that she realized something was happening. Something that wasn't right. The crowd did not cry out in fear when the lights dimmed. Nor did Ingénue stop in her gallop around the ring.

Rosamund fell to her knees, nearly toppling off Ingénue's back in her haste to grope for the leather harness. She slipped her hands underneath the cool leather, tugging, fighting to keep her balance when the distance between Ingénue's back and the ground below was unknown.

She pulled Ingénue to a stop, unsure whether she was in the center or at the edge of the ring. There was nothing to do but grip the harness and slide down to the side, feeling for the touch of ground to the bottom of her slippers.

The crowd responded—some shouting, "Is she all right?" while others grew silent.

The mixture of concern and question floated around her,

causing her head to spin. She leaned in to Ingénue's side, melting there from fear and disbelief.

"Rosamund?"

She heard Owen's voice, drawing her to turn her head to the left.

A hand eased over her shoulder. It surprised her how she was shaking. How quickly fear had swooped in, crippling her in the ring.

"Rose."

Colin was there too. She recognized his voice.

"What's wrong?"

"I . . ." She breathed out, shaking her head through the muddle of black-and-gray shadows dominating her vision. "Colin?"

He slipped his arms under her knees, scooping her into his arms.

The crowd had grown silent. Owen, too, made no sound. Even Ingénue seemed to have faded somewhere in the background.

Had the roses fallen from her hair?

What was happening?

Her heart willed the question. Wondering why she could feel Colin's every running step, why she was bundled in his arms and saw nothing flying by as he carried her away from the ring. She could only feel the touch of air against her face, the speed of his steps causing it to stir around her.

"Colin . . . ," she said, voice cracking as she looked up, trying to fix on his face. "I can't see."

CHAPTER 34

1929
NEW YORK CITY

The nurse popped her head into Mable's room, announcing in a cheery voice, "Your visitor has arrived, Mrs. Ringling."

Mable peered into the hall, then, seeing their guest, sat up straighter against the mound of pillows at her back.

She turned to look at John, who'd been occupied with staring out the second-story window of the Leroy Sanitarium to the street below. The narrow art deco building overlooked the business sector off Madison Avenue, and he'd passed the time by watching it for two days.

"John," she whispered, trying to draw his attention to her bed in the center of the room. "Our visitor is here, John. Would you see her in?"

He pulled his attention away from the honking horns and street sounds below, turning to gift her the warmth of a smile. "Of course."

John met Rosamund at the door and placed her outstretched hand in the crook of his arm. With his other hand he leaned on his walking cane.

Mable was altogether relieved that if Rosamund could see anything in the room, it wouldn't be the tears that had formed in her eyes.

The young bareback rider was still striking in beauty; the loss of sight couldn't mar that. She was dressed in a pale-pink and nude dress of beaded silk, with a soft gray cloche that she'd removed and held in her hand. A youthful glow of natural blush brightened her lips and accented her high cheekbones.

Mable watched as John carefully led her to a cushioned chair at the side of the bed.

Rosamund felt her way around the obstacle of armrests with her fingertips and searched the depth of the cushion. She eased down into it, sweeping her skirt under and then folding her hands against the cloche in her lap.

"She's right in front of you, Rosamund."

Rosamund lifted her hand. John led her fingertips to graze the blanket on the edge of the bed, helping her to get her bearings.

"And now, Mable dear, I will leave you ladies to visit."

Mable watched as he gathered the things he'd brought with him that morning—a newspaper, his cane and bowler hat—and moved to leave. He passed by the bed and swept his fingertips across the back of Mable's hand.

"I believe this room could use some pink roses," he said, putting on his hat. "There's a flower shop nearby. I won't be long."

Rosamund tipped her head to the sound of his shoes clipping the linoleum floor, and a smile swept the corners of her mouth.

"Thank you, Mr. Ringling."

Mable watched him pause on Rosamund's words. He looked over the back of her head to Mable, meeting her gaze with pursed lips and narrowed eyes.

"You are most welcome, young lady," he whispered back.

Mable watched him go, forcing himself out of the confines of a room they'd been in together for the last two days. He'd never left her side. And now, feeling the need to give her a private visit with Rosamund, he was stepping out to buy her flowers. Just as he always did.

She sighed, turning her attention to Rosamund.

The young lady stared ahead blankly, her green eyes stunning but fixed, not moving from their attention on the far wall. Mable felt the same regret that John seemed to feel wash over her. It reminded her why she'd asked Rosamund to visit her in the sanitarium.

She swallowed over the emotion in her throat, hoping to add cheer to her voice. "Well, this is not the Cà d'Zan, I can tell you that. But they are being kind to me."

Rosamund's lips eased into a faint but polite smile. "I didn't want to pry and ask how you are."

Mable flitted the idea away with a light shrug. "Diabetes is not strong enough to take the spring out of my step," she said.

She wasn't walking then, of course, but illness wasn't something she had time for—and she certainly would not give it ownership of her thoughts. She allowed a smile to warm her voice. "You know, I visited someone in a sanitarium once."

"I imagine they're not the most endearing of places to go."

"I agree. They are not. But I was visiting a friend and I wanted her to see my wedding dress. So I marched through the halls in my satin and lace, staring down every doctor who dared to give me a sideways glance."

Rosamund's chin tipped ever so slightly. "You visited a sick friend on your wedding day?"

Mable nodded, then realized Rosamund couldn't see it.

"People have done crazier things on a wedding day, I'm sure." She cleared her throat. "But yes. I did. Her name was Sally. And believe it or not, you remind me of her just a bit. Though not in your coloring—she had hair red as fire and a temper to match."

Rosamund's face broke into an unconscious smile. "I must admit to having a temper as well."

"And you'll be better for it, my dear. I'm sure of it. We have to get riled every now and then. It reminds us that we're still alive."

Mable watched Rosamund's face, seeing each polite smile. Noting the way she sat pin-straight in her chair, with posture that held strength despite the affliction of near-blindness.

"There's been no change in your condition?"

The smile dropped from Rosamund's lips.

"No. The doctors are optimistic that my vision could improve with time, but they caution me against setting too much hope in it. I can see some light though. Shadows around objects. Enough to avoid bumping into anything too dangerous. But as for perform-ing . . ." She shook her head. "I'll never see the ring again."

Mable sank her tone to one of seriousness. "This spring was the first time in two years the circus opened and you weren't with it."

Rosamund nodded, adding a soft, "Yes."

"Rosamund, I realize accidents are a circumstance of the job. Performers know the risks they undertake in the ring. They've fallen before and it's likely to happen again. But this is different. It's something that's been done to you. It wasn't by your choosing."

"No, it wasn't. But they're not certain it was a result of the acci-dent in the stables or even the attack in the circus back lot. The doctors believe the damage to my eyesight may go as far back as the fall I sustained in my very first performance. Either way, it's happened."

She held her head high, but Mable saw the shreds of vulnera-bility as her eyes glazed.

"You're not going home?"

"Not for the moment, no. I . . ."

Mable watched as Rosamund grimaced, finding pain in what she was trying so hard not to say.

"That's all changed now. And I fear, to be blunt, I cannot go back and be the blind spinster haunting the drawing room of Easling Park. Even if they'd extend forgiveness and take me back, I won't do that to my parents or to myself. My aunt in New York is being exceedingly kind. She's allowed me to stay with her, ensuring I'm taken care of. While the doctors look after my progress."

"I see." Mable looked over Rosamund's face, searching it without the young lady's knowledge. She sighed, keenly feeling the weight of sadness at what had happened. And if there was anything she could do now—even from a hospital bed—she meant to make things right for the beauty who sat before her.

"Rosamund, it takes a special kind of courage to dare to dream of a different life. Of something extraordinary. I thought I had that courage in spades when I was young. I was born in a small farming community to good parents and a loving family. It's important that you know I could have had a wonderful life had I stayed there. But I felt called to more. Not to wealth or privilege, and certainly not to power or success. I didn't flee a normal life. I know now that I wasn't running away; I was running toward something. But what I had to learn was the difference between having a dream and cultivating the courage to live it out day after day."

Mable reached across the bed, extending her hand. "Give me your hand, please."

Rosamund obeyed, reaching out with her fingers splayed on air.

Mable took her hand, turning it over until her palm faced the ceiling. In it she placed a watch and chain, gleaming gold. Mable watched as Rosamund felt the coolness of the metal on her skin, saw how her fingertips trembled.

The younger woman closed her fingers around it. "What's this?" she asked, chin quivering ever so slightly.

"It's a gift for Colin. A new watch. One that isn't broken."

Mable watched as emotion flooded the graceful lines of Rosamund's face.

She didn't hold back.

In fact, Mable watched in wonder as the young lady before her embraced the depth of feeling that leaked out in soft tears, melting in trails down the porcelain skin of her cheeks. It was graceful to watch empathy weep straight from another's heart—not in wracking sobs, but in a gentle embrace.

"He told me about Avery," Rosamund said, brushing a fingertip to a rogue tear that had caught on the edge of her lips. "About the accident and how he came to meet you. Everything."

"I thought he would. It's his way. He feels regret very deeply. And though he's made mistakes, he's not unlike any other person in having a past."

"Mrs. Ringling—"

"I've asked you before, dear—please call me Mable. You don't know this, but we're not so formal when I'm sitting in front of you in a dressing gown and robe. It is from Paris," she said, trying to make light, running her hand down the soft silk fabric. "But that doesn't make it any less a dressing gown. When you're looking out from a sickbed, you only find friends there to speak to."

"Mable . . . ," Rosamund began, apparently searching for the right words to say. "If you're asking me to give this to him, I'm not sure I can do that."

"Yes, I am. And you can, my dear. You can go back. Because this watch is a promise I need to give to Colin. I'm not able to take it to him myself, and I couldn't trust it to anyone else." She eased her hand over Rosamund's. "I don't know when I'll get out of here, so I need you to take it to him. John will ensure you know where to go. And your aunt can accompany you. You'll travel in our private train car all the way to the circus lot. And after that, you are free from any request or further obligation. I'll just consider this a favor between good friends."

Mable watched as Rosamund paused, rubbing her fingers together over the watch, moving through an internal deliberation over whether to accept.

She took a deep breath and asked, "What do I tell him?"

"I need him to know it's a gift. That I want him to have his time back. He's spent far too much of it grieving. He needs to know he is what he wouldn't allow himself to be long ago—forgiven."

Rosamund sniffed over her tears. She clasped the watch in her hands, hiding it away like a treasure in her palms.

"And is there anything else?"

In that moment, Mable thought her heart could sing.

It had been so long since she'd thought of her old cigar box—the place where she'd hidden away the tender dreams of her youth. But it bled into her thoughts now, prompting her to recall the memory of that Cincinnati tearoom from childhood. She'd wanted to hear the sound of the piano lilting through a brilliant melody. And she'd wanted adventure. To really live. But now, many years and many experiences away from that old cigar box, she saw something that was infinitely more dear. From the inside of a hospital sickroom, it became clear: the great adventure was love. There was freedom in it like nothing else. And that's what mattered in that moment. Not wealth. Not prominence or prestige.

"Love is patient, Rosamund. It has to be. It is kind. And never self-serving. And because of that, we can't expect everything to be in our timing. What would be the adventure in that? Instead, it is in the knitting of lives and hearts together. It's why you're sitting here with me today." Mable drew in a deep breath. "You love Colin."

Rosamund had been staring straight ahead. But on Mable's last syllable, she squeezed her eyes shut, as if confronting the truth beyond the confines of her heart for the very first time.

She nodded. "Yes. I do."

"And that's why this is so difficult."

"He wouldn't want me now," Rosamund cried, clutching the watch to her chest. "Colin would think he does. But I'm changed by what's happened. He's changed. And he'll feel responsible for everything. That's why I left Sarasota after the accident. I couldn't let him love me out of pity. And what if we married? I'd tie him down to a life of his same penance. He'd see Avery and Bella every time he looked at me, and he'd carry a broken watch for the remainder of his days. I won't do that to him."

The air between them fell silent.

Maybe it had to. Matters of the heart required patience, just as she'd said. They demanded pauses at times, allowing the right words to come.

Mable folded her hands in her lap, composing what she hoped would be comforting thoughts wrapped in the truth this girl needed to hear. It had to be an infusion of courage that would carry her to board a circus train and go back to Colin's side.

"Do you remember what I told you once? We only see what we want to see. In people. In love. And in life." Mable repeated the words she'd shared with Rosamund after her first performance at Madison Square Garden. She added a hint of a wink in her voice, whispering, "Tell him that, and I think he'll figure out the rest on his own."

CHAPTER 35

1929
LOUISVILLE, KENTUCKY

The band played their cue and Rosamund nudged Ingénue forward, leaving the breath of wind toiling behind her as she went in to give her last performance.

"Just like Mable said . . ." She straightened her shoulders and raised her head to the elation of the crowd. "They'll only see what we want them to."

The crowd was not indifferent to Rosamund's blindness; they didn't know about it.

She'd left Sarasota as soon as the doctors confirmed her sight had been irreparably damaged, before the 1929 season even took shape. The circus posters depicting the bareback riding star had faded into the background, and to the reveling circus-goers, new stars had simply been slipped in to take her place.

She knew she might not have been missed in their eyes, but Rosamund rode out with her head held high, decrying any disability whatsoever.

"I'm trusting you tonight, lady," she whispered, feeling her way through each step of Ingénue's trotting to the center ring. "Your sight will be mine. Let my eyes see what yours do."

They high-stepped around the canvas arena, heads cocked high before the crowd, their every sound echoing with chords of cheers and applause.

The band continued to play as they trotted to position.

Rosamund could sense the lights gleaming down over them, shining in the eyes of children in their straw seats. Sawdust would cover the ground like a blanket. And the firmament overhead would be filled with ropes and trapeze riggings, the kind the Rossi family would have used to pierce the sky overhead.

Rosamund slowed her horse to a stop, ready to roll into their act before the thousands of eyes watching. But the melody of the band began to fade, and the crowd grew quiet. She heard only her own breathing, mixed with Ingénue's, and she felt for the first time a sense of fear that she'd tried to undertake something so risky. Something that only the sight in her hands could possibly lead her through.

She prayed silently. Prayers that tumbled from her mind.

Rosamund needed the strength from them now. She knew that courage was possible—Mable had made her believe it. It wasn't in the initial faith leap to chase a dream; rather, the magic was in the day-to-day living and breathing and choosing to be courageous when common sense told one otherwise.

She gripped the reins tight, feeling her hands begin to shake.

Listening for the silent crowd to make a breath of sound in reply. She heard nothing, until . . .

The soft cry of a violin sang out against the canvas vault overhead.

It echoed deep in a powerful cadence over the crowd, singing "Roses of Picardy." And every memory flooded back. She and Ingénue had gone through their act too many times to fail. And so they fell into step with one another, dreaming and dancing in one accord before the crowd.

Rosamund closed her eyes. Not needing showmanship, but release.

She drew in a steadying breath, and they went to work.

It was her gift to Mable. And to herself maybe, showing Lady Rosamund Easling that she was more than the sum of her hurts. So much more than failures or limitations. That God had placed her in that very spot, to fly free for one glorious moment in her life.

She dedicated the moment to the remarkable woman who had changed both her life and Colin's.

They flew through the act, Colin directing their mastery of the ring with his bow.

Ingénue glided with hooves that danced on air, Rosamund feeling the memory of every turn and start and stop with her hands and heart in unison. She thought of Mable, how time had drawn too short too fast. And of Bella and the Rossi family, how everything had changed in the blink of an eye. And of the rest, her family, Owen, Annaliese, and the ever-smiling Ward. And the animals, led by the kind-eyed Nora and her little Mitra, who had followed along behind his mama with trunk clinging to her tail.

Theirs was a story she wanted to tell that night, of the resiliency in the people's menagerie she'd found at the circus. She prayed always to look through life with a lens of love and kindness, just as Mable had.

To shed the mask and the costumes, to offer her best to the world in return.

The act came to an end, she and Ingénue flowing through their final backbend lift with precision. And she trusted Ingénue to edge over to the side of the ring, as always. She slipped down, waiting for the roar of the applause.

But it didn't come.

No sound permeated the air until Rosamund heard steps

crunching on sawdust and straw. She turned her face to it. And she felt a hand slip into hers. Colin stood at her side, and she needed no invitation to know what to do—they bowed together, receiving the ovation of their lives. Even with a faceless crowd. And even with a Big Top that was pitch-black all around her.

"Thank you for the new watch," he said, leaning close to her ear.

"You found it."

"Yes. You're smarter than Mable gave you credit for, slipping it into my violin case. Did you know I'd play for you tonight, that I had to do it one last time?"

"No," she answered truthfully. "But I hoped you would, for all of us. Mable wanted you to have your time back."

"I went to see her, you know. Yesterday. She wasn't awake, but I was able to speak to her. I thanked her for my life, and I didn't even know she'd thought of me in her last days. Not until you brought me this watch."

"She said you've given enough to your grief and it's time to live. So," Rosamund whispered, easing her hand from his and replacing it with Ingénue's reins, "live. And please—you and Ingénue take care of each other for me while you do."

CHAPTER 36

1929
Beacon, New York

The calendar was but a breath from turning the page to autumn.

Rosamund sat in a wicker deck chair in the expanse of fields beyond her aunt's estate, rolling Bella's golden thimble in her fingertips. She listened to the song of the birds in the trees and the wind that sifted through their branches, giving her just a bit of evidence to picture what their rustling must have looked like.

The early-morning hours were her favorite. She'd taken to sitting there each day, wondering what the New York fields looked like in comparison to the foggy mist painted in the fields at Easling Park.

The sounds around her were amplified with the limitations of sight. And though it often rained on the North Yorkshire mornings she'd spent outside, she could already feel the promise of the sun's late-summer warmth beginning to caress her face along with the wind. She could sense the memory of Ingénue's hooves, almost hearing the sound they made when connecting with the earth.

"Rose."

Her name came out on a breath of wind.

Colin.

She turned her head, shock freezing her hands in her lap. The breeze caught up wisps of hair around her brow, dancing them against the skin of her cheeks.

"Colin?"

"Yes," he said, his voice close to her ear. He was kneeling. She knew because she could feel his warmth at her side. "We didn't mean to startle you. Your aunt said we could find you here."

"We?"

"Yes. I come bearing gifts again."

She felt his fingertips slip over hers, opening her hand. If he was surprised to find a thimble there, he chose not to say. Instead, his fingertips connected with the skin of her palm, sweeping the golden trinket away and replacing it with a thick leather strap.

"Here," he said, easing her fingertips over the worn leather reins.

"Ingénue!" Rosamund's heart leapt, turning somersaults in her chest. "My friend." She heard the horse's soft neighs behind her.

"Yes. She's here. You brought me a gift, remember? Well, Mable wanted you to have one as well. Mr. Ringling said she was quite insistent that you two should be reunited. And that you know in this gift, Mable wanted *you* to have *your* time back. She said you've spent far too much of it grieving. That it was time to go home."

A tear slid down Rosamund's cheek, and Colin caught it softly, in a butterfly's kiss of a fingertip to skin.

"You told Ingénue and me to take care of each other," he whispered. "You couldn't have meant us to do that on our own. Without you, neither of us makes a lick of sense."

"Are you really here right now?"

She gripped the reins, pushing up against the chair's armrests to stand. She felt Colin stand too, offering a hand to brace under her elbow.

"Yes," Colin said, his voice soft and tipped with the Irish brogue she so loved. "Ingénue is right behind you. You can reach out and touch her if you want."

Rosamund shook her head, allowing the reins to drop from her fingertips. She raised an arm, feeling the soft touch of linen beneath her hand. She slid her hand up until it hooked around his neck. "I meant you. You're here."

He laughed softly, encircling her with strong arms.

"You left the show for me?"

"In the thick of the season," he confirmed.

She could hear the smile in his voice.

"We rolled into Decatur, Illinois, mid-June. I told Mr. Ringling then that I had no choice—I would be forced to trail after a bare-back rider who'd left his employ. But I couldn't desert him then. Not after we'd just lost Mable. It took some time, but we brought Owen and Jerry in to take over shared management. And when the train went west from Missoula, Ingénue and I caught our own train back east. And it brought us all the way here. To you."

Rosamund let a breath escape she hadn't realized she held. "Then you left for good?"

He chuckled, and she could picture him smiling. Just as he always had. She hoped his blue eyes were dancing, staring back at her.

"Yes, Rose. If you wanted me to, I'd walk away from the life. In a heartbeat."

"But you're circus, Colin. It's in your blood."

He paused. She listened, turning her face into the breeze, wishing she could see his face to know why he'd stopped.

"And you told me once that it's in yours too."

"But this might never change. I could be blind the rest of my life," Rosamund cried, raising her hands to his face, seeing only shades and shadow where his smile used to be. "I'll never see you."

"You've always seen me, Rose. That's the difference. I couldn't accept a new watch for a new life unless you're in it. And Mable knew that. Seeing isn't always with the eyes, love. But we can do that together too. I'll play for you like Hendrick once did. You can ride Ingénue and I'll be at your side, performing with you in the ring. And I'll describe everything, like it's the Cà d'Zan we're seeing all over again. We can even fish on every dock and dance in every tower in Florida if you want to."

"Mable would have expected nothing less. Somehow she knew I'd go out and perform too, didn't she?"

"I think she did," Colin said, chuckling ever so slightly. "Mable Ringling was a remarkable woman. Our friend. A blessing, I think, to see that both of us came back to one another."

"If you ever came back, I assumed it would be to say good-bye. I thought you'd only be able to see me as broken now."

"We're all broken, Rose. You told me that once, remember? That's the point," he whispered, his lips grazing hers. "Everyone has scars. Some you can see, like the one on your wrist. Others, like a watch, remain hidden in the pockets of our past. But to heal? We can't possibly do it on our own."

"I was never on my own. Not from that day I stepped onto the train at King's Cross Station. And I was wrong. My home was never the circus. It wasn't under the Big Top sky or turning circles in front of the crowds. I was on a circus train traveling from place to place, but my home has always been with you."

"Then why don't you marry me?" He leaned in, whispering in her ear. "Because my home is wherever you are too."

Rosamund stood on tiptoe, trusting her heart to connect her lips to his. She pressed in, feeling the strength of familiar arms come around her. Reveling in the presence of him once again in her life.

"Is that a yes then?" he asked, the smile of a happy Irishman alive in his voice.

"Aye. It's a yes," she teased, smiling back because he hadn't needed to ask. "Mable said we only see what we want to see, and I want to spend the rest of my life looking at you."

EPILOGUE

Camden Keary-Smith never heard her name called over the microphone.

A stage had been erected against the backdrop of the Cà d'Zan, with the crystal waters of the bay rolling beyond. She gazed out over the water, imagining what the yachts and the grand parties must have looked like in Mable Ringling's day.

Ruby nudged her shoulder. "Mom, it's time."

"Hmm?"

"They called your name . . ."

Her attention was drawn back and she remembered at once why they were there.

"Oh yes." Camden fluttered her hands, almost dropping her program in her haste to stand. "Yes, of course."

Ruby braced her at the elbow, helping her to her feet.

They took the steps slowly. Having waited for the moment for some time, she now wanted to savor it.

A young lad stepped up, adjusting the microphone in front of her.

338

She nodded in thanks, then looked out over the crowd for the first time. "I've never spoken in public before . . ."

The young man hopped up again, tapped the microphone.

"Right here, Mrs. Smith. Speak right here."

She exhaled, then smiled. "I've never spoken in public before," she said, trying again.

Her voice was loud this time. Crystal clear. Booming out from the speakers to mingle with the swaying palms and the roses in Mable's garden.

"But this is a very special occasion, and both my brother, Jack Keary, and I are delighted to be here for this historic day. The Cà d'Zan reopens today, after the greatest renovation in this property's history. We gather here now, in its shadow, proud to stand as two of many who represent the rich history of this place.

"Our parents, Colin and Rosamund Keary, traveled with the Ringling Brothers and Barnum & Bailey circus for over four decades. They held roles as manager, bareback rider, musician, and in 1957, with the Big Top no longer in use for the shows, they spent their final working year as ticket takers at the venue doors. Our parents not only spent time at this property, but they loved the family who owned it, and credited Mable Ringling in particular with bestowing compassion and kindness on all who entered this home.

"In the days when names such as May Wirth, Lou Jacobs, and Lillian Lietzel were known the world over, our father worked humbly behind the scenes, partnering with the Ringling Brothers to bring the circus to countless towns and cities all across the country. He retired in 1958, after faithfully serving for forty-six years.

"Our mother, Lady Rosamund Easling-Keary, received her paid passage from the Ringling Brothers in 1926 and traveled from England to Sarasota, where she began a bareback riding career that spanned decades. After an accident sustained in the years following her circus debut, she was declared legally blind, and believed her circus days were over. But it was the belief my father had in her abilities and the extraordinary friendship they shared with John and Mable Ringling that she credited for the career she had in the years that followed."

Camden stopped, overcome with emotion.

She turned, gazing at the Venetian palace that sparkled in the sun.

There was restored whimsy in every corner. A playfulness that combined with the rich artistry of a piece of history one couldn't read about in a book. It was so much more.

She brought her attention back to the crowd, searching for young faces to talk to. Her eyes sought out families—the ones who would make this place live on.

"I speak to you today, to the children of the next generation who will visit and truly cherish this place. Everything the Ringlings loved is here. *They* are here, and their story—waiting to be discovered anew. And so we leave you today with Mable's words, because what we see is a choice, as is what we offer the world in return. And it's only behind the costumes and the masks that we can be who we truly are. Embrace that today, and may we never be afraid to really live. Thank you."

Camden heard the applause as she walked back across the stage. But it didn't feel as though it was for her. She turned a half circle before stepping down again, catching a final view of the glorious Cà d'Zan—the House of John—before the Ringlings welcomed the world again.

CHRONOLOGY

1866—John Nicholas Ringling born May 31, in McGregor, IA, to August Frederich Rungeling (Ringling) (b. 1826, m. 1852, d. 1898) and Salome Marie Juliar (Ringling) (b. 1833, m. 1852, d. 1907).

1875—Armilda E. (Mable) Burton born March 14, in Moons, OH, to George Wesley Burton (b. 1848, m. 1869, d. 1919) and Mary Elizabeth Wilson (b. 1852, m. 1869, d. 1929).

1882—Ringlings move family, including seven sons and one daughter, Ida Lorina Wilhemina Ringling (b. 1874, d. 1950), to Baraboo, WI.

1882—Ringling brothers Albert Charles "Al" (b. 1852, d. 1916), August Albert "A.G." (b. 1854, d. 1907), William Henry Otto "Otto" (b. 1857, d. 1911), Alfred Theodore "Alf T." (b. 1863, d. 1919), Carl Edward "Charles" (b. 1864, d. 1926), John Nicholas (b. 1866, d. 1936), and Henry William George (b. 1868, d. 1918) organize first winter-season hall shows, performing in Wisconsin town halls.

1884—Circus formed in partnership with Yankee Robinson. Billed as Yankee Robinson and Ringling Bros. Double Show.

1885—Ringling Bros. established as sole proprietors.

1890—Circus travel ceases by wagon, converts to rail.

1893—World's Columbian Exposition (Chicago World's Fair) opens May 1, recognizing 400th anniversary of the New World's discovery by Europeans, spanning 600 acres, with 200 newly built structures and culture displays from 46 countries. Draws world record with more than 27 million in attendance through closing day, October 30.

1905—Mable Burton marries John Ringling December 29 in Hoboken, NJ.

1907—Ringling Bros. purchase Barnum & Bailey Circus from Bailey family heirs.

1918—John Ringling purchases summer home along Hudson River in Alpine, NJ.

1919—Ringling Bros. merge circus proprietorships to debut Ringling Bros. and Barnum & Bailey Combined Shows March 29 in New York City.

1923—Doge's Palace opens as museum in Venice, Italy. John and Mable Ringling spend year touring Italy, finding inspiration to build their new winter home in Sarasota, FL. Society architect Dwight James Baum commissioned as architect for Cà d'Zan ("House of John").

1924—Construction begins on 36,000-square-foot Cà d'Zan, winter home for John and Mable Ringling. Venetian-style mansion spans 20 acres of Sarasota Bay waterfront and includes $50K electric organ, 41 rooms and 15 bathrooms, waterfront dock with Venetian gondola, five-story belvedere tower (kept lit in evenings at Mable Ringling's request), and roof with antique Spanish barrel tiles salvaged in Granada by John Ringling.

1926—Cà d'Zan mansion completed at then-staggering cost of $1.5M. Charles "Mr. Charlie" Ringling dies December 3.

1927—John and Mable Ringling Museum of Art established in Sarasota, FL. In January, circus winter quarters move from Bridgeport, CT, to Sarasota, FL.

1929—Mable Burton Ringling dies, age 54, on June 8 in New York. John Ringling purchases American Circus Corporation, absorbing major circus shows Sells-Floto Circus, Al G. Barnes Circus, Sparks Circus, Hagenbeck-Wallace Circus, and John Robinson Circus at a cost of $1.7M.

1930—John Ringling marries Emily Haag Buck December 19 in Jersey City, NJ.

1932—John and Mable Ringling Museum of Art opens to public January 17 in Sarasota, FL. Circus partnership dissolves into corporation formed by Ringling creditors. John Ringling remains as president with no assigned duties.

1936—John Ringling and Emily Buck divorce July 6.

1936—John Ringling dies December 2 in New York City, with reported $311 in the bank. Estate is closed to public. Cà d'Zan, John and Mable Ringling Museum of Art, and estimated assets of $24M bequeathed to state of Florida. John Ringling North (nephew) and Ida Ringling North (sister) appointed estate executors.

1946—Cà d'Zan reopens to public. John and Mable Ringling Museum of Art and Cà d'Zan mansion ownership transferred to state of Florida, with final settlement between the state and Ringling's executors in 1947.

1996—Cà d'Zan falls into disrepair, serving as setting for Miss Havisham's dilapidated mansion in Hollywood remake of Dickens's classic *Great Expectations*. $15M restoration and conservation project begins on Cà d'Zan mansion. Full restoration is completed in April 2002.

AUTHOR'S NOTE

In a time when America saw a rise in wealth and prosperity, the Jazz Age became synonymous with the questioning of long-held societal rules, the boom of innovation, and the exodus of workers from rural to more urban-centered lives. Entertainment, industry, and culture saw great change in this post-WWI society. It's during this shift that English-born Rosamund Easling would have had to make the life-altering decision of whether to risk leaving her traditional world behind to embrace a new hope for her future.

The story in this novel underpins themes of faith and characters living out their true calling, both fictional, in Rosamund and Colin, and historical, in John and Mable Ringling. It mirrors the "world within a world" perspective of performers' nomadic lives in the late 1920s, steering the ripple effects of the circus's impact on the menagerie of people living and entertaining in that world.

Few details are known about Armilda (Mable) Burton's life prior to her marriage to John Ringling. Notoriously reticent with the press, Mable never agreed to be photographed and gave only one official media interview in her lifetime. Instead of basking in the limelight as the Ringling circus queen, she chose to place value in the relationships she fostered with close friends and family behind the scenes, hosting parties for the Sarasota Garden Club at the Cà d'Zan estate and staging social events in the surrounding community of Sarasota.

A woman said to possess both uncommon wisdom and kindness, Mable also exhibited a poise and warmth that were the perfect complement to John Ringling's more reserved and sometimes serious nature. Though it's uncertain how they first met, we imagine how a relationship might have begun and how their shared passion for the circus, travel, and fine art, and a matching sense of wit and humor, may have formed the foundation for the deep love and affection in their twenty-four years of marriage. Though much research went into telling this story, the account is fiction—one I hope helps readers discover the Ringlings' legacy anew.

Along with the intimate look at the lives of John and Mable Ringling, readers will find other familiar historical figures in this book: Dulcey Burton (Mable's sister), Charles Ringling (one of John's six brothers), Hollywood entertainer Florenz "Flo" Ziegfeld and his wife, actress Billie Burke (who were frequent guests at the Cà d'Zan), and William "Willy" Pogany (a celebrated Hungarian illustrator who contributed many playful designs to Mable's vision for the Cà d'Zan). There is also an implied appearance by creative genius Walt Disney himself, who was an acquaintance of Willy Pogany, though there is no evidence that he actually visited the Ringlings' winter home.

In addition, real-life vaudeville and circus performers May Wirth (equestrienne), Lillian Leitzel (acrobatics), Edith Burchett (tattooed woman), Rebecca Lyon (bearded lady), and even Mary, the Ringling Brothers' first rhinoceros, are all included as a part of this eclectic mix of characters.

Though the Ringling Brothers' winter lodgings (as seen in the 1952 Hollywood film *The Greatest Show on Earth*) no longer stand, guests can still tour circus sites in Peru, Indiana; Baraboo,

Wisconsin; and Sarasota, Florida. Just as our family did to research this novel, readers who want to learn more about the Ringlings' legacy can walk through the immaculately restored Cà d'Zan mansion and tour the treasury of art at the acclaimed John and Mable Ringling Museum of Art.

I've been enchanted by depictions of the circus in books and film since childhood. It is every storyteller's dream to fall in love with a story that includes this kind of nostalgia. Thank you, dear reader friends, for taking this journey with me.

Mable Ringling

Photo courtesy of the Ida Ringling North family archive

ACKNOWLEDGMENTS

Our Midwest landscape in September is one of transition: hills tall with corn, still green but beginning to burnish the horizon in autumn's gold. The mornings are cool and the afternoons steamy.

It was on one of those "almost autumn" mornings that I began editing this book. I sat down to coffee with Annie—a new friend from our sons' school. As we chatted about the usual things moms do, it surprised us when our conversation began to go deeper. Walls came down and authenticity edged in. We admitted honest struggles. Shed a few tears. Took sips of our lattes in between shared truths. And as we prayed together that day, hand in hand, I was overcome with the unexpected blessing of transitions.

Much like the landscape in our rural town or the blossoming of a new friendship, it's usually easier to define the beginning or ending points of a journey than it is to see clearly through the middle. This book had many of those "in between" moments—the transitional kind of experiences that can forever change a story. The heart of this book felt very much like Mable's real-life and Rosamund's fictional journeys; both women stepped out, daring to imagine a new life for themselves. Each braved the transition time in her own way, knowing that eventually, gold lay out on the horizon.

I wake each day astounded by my publishing family at

HarperCollins Christian Publishing. The team that guided the creation of this story! You are my heart: Daisy Hutton, Amanda Bostic, Becky Monds, Jodi Hughes, and Kristen "Goldie" Golden, who should claim the title of Inspiration-Yoda for bringing me the vintage soundtracks and classic movies that flavored the words penned in this book. To Kristen Ingebretson: Of you I remain in awe! This art history–loving gal never could have dreamt of such masterful cover art to call my own. I am officially your biggest fan. To editors Becky Monds (my heart!); my fellow *Once Upon a Time* fandom queen, Jodi Hughes; and LB Norton (who is an ever-patient joy to me), I owe a heaping debt of gratitude. Your editing instincts are spot-on, and this story enveloped my heart because of them. Thank you for your brilliance in cleaning up my literary "oopsies" and for your grace every time you have to. You're so posh, ladies.

To the mentors who counseled this writer-gal's heart along this storytelling journey, I'm so grateful for each of you. Our family is indebted to the investment you've made in us. Thank you, Katie Bond (who just *knew* Mable had a story to tell); Colleen Coble; Allen Arnold; and to my amazing agent, Rachelle Gardner, for leading with integrity, wisdom, and Christlike grace. You go above and beyond the job title to be a true friend. To dear friends Mary Weber, Joanna Politano, and my sweet author sisters on TheGroveStory.com: Katherine Reay, Beth Vogt, Cara Putman, Sarah Ladd, Courtney Walsh, Katie Ganshert, Melissa Tagg, Jeane Wynn, and Casey Herringshaw. You saved me this year. Love all around.

Many writers will attest to the fact that coffee and prayer play critical roles in any book that comes to market. It's true in this case. I have to thank my beloved Bible study sisters for the prayers, the laughs and support, and especially for keeping me caffeinated during the writing of this novel. My forever-hugs are yours: Kerry,

Carla, Denise, MJ, Katie, Diane, Leah, Jasmyne, Toni, Judy, Pam, Joyce, Sue Linn, Janet, and Alisa Roberts, our study sister whom we will fondly remember. A very special thanks goes to Coffee Crossings and Kölkin Coffee, for allowing me to take over hidden corners of your shops. Keep the coffee coming! And to Todd Mullins, Cami Gomez, and family: We thank you for welcoming our family of Ringling researchers into your home with such love and care. Your every kindness made this story possible.

To my pillars—besties Maggie Walker and Sharon Tavera; my almost-twin sis, Jenny Thompson; and my momma, Linda Wedge: I couldn't smile without your uplifting presence in my days. Thank you for your unconditional love. To Jeremy, husband and best friend: My heart is yours. You've supported and remained steadfast in my every corner. I'm humbled by the man God has given me to journey alongside in this life.

To the performers and professionals who tell the circus's story each day, I feel as much wide-eyed wonder in you as the children who packed the Big Top for generations. To the incredibly helpful staff at the John and Mable Ringling Museum of Art and the Cà d'Zan mansion in Sarasota, Florida, I send a most dedicated thank-you. And especially to curator Mr. Ron McCarty (whom readers will recognize as a character in this book): You made John and Mable come alive for this story. The time you spent touring every corner of the mansion and grounds with us has become one of the most vivid memories of our family's life. Thank you for your commitment to excellence and for framing the fictionalized story of a truly remarkable couple. It was a researcher's dream.

The photo in this book (page 347) was graciously donated by Lara Brightwell, Ida Ringling North's great-granddaughter, and her husband, Jim Dexheimer, from the family photo archive that Jim has collected over the last several years. It is to his credit we have this image of Mable today. To the Burton and Ringling-North families, who shared their rich family legacy with me, I extend my most sincere appreciation. You help us all imagine what the Ringlings' circus world must have been like—a world of enchantment I hope will live on in this book.

To Brady, Carson, and Colt: You are my world. I am so blessed to be your mom. And to the hearts of children and readers alike, this book belongs to you. To the nostalgia we hold in childhood memories, to the starry-eyed, laughter-filled, and silly, I dedicate this book. And for every adult out there (and those of us who secretly cling to the memory of youth), remember that we're never too old to be Someone's child.

And to my Savior—Jesus, You are my everything.

With joy,

Kristy

FOR FURTHER READING

Apps, Jerry. *Ringlingville USA*. Wisconsin Historical Society Press, 2005.

De Groft, Aaron H., and David C. Weeks. *Cà d'Zan: Inside the Ringling Mansion*. John and Mable Ringling Museum of Art, 2004.

John and Mable Ringling Museum of Art, Cà d'Zan: www.ringling. org/ca-dzan.

John and Mable Ringling Museum of Art, Education Center: www. ringling.org/education-center.

LaHurd, Jeff. *Hidden History of Sarasota*. The History Press, 2009.

Weeks, David C. *Ringling: The Florida Years*. University Press of Florida, 1993.

DISCUSSION QUESTIONS

1. Lady Rosamund Easling was born into a family heritage of wealth and opportunity. Armilda (Mable) Burton wasn't born with such advantages, but found them later in life. Though these two women began their journeys in very different places, both shared a longing for something more—the courage to step out and live the life they'd imagined. How would their lives have been different if Rosamund and Mable hadn't been willing to risk everything in order to pursue their calling? Would Rosamund have stayed with the circus if Mable hadn't been a mentor in her life?

2. The circus welcomed an eclectic mix of performers from varying ethnic and cultural backgrounds. This was eye-opening to Rosamund, whose relatively sheltered life was dramatically changed when she became a part of the Ringling Brothers' circus show. How does Rosamund's view of the world around her change through her first years as a performer?

3. Despite finding his niche as an agent for the circus, Colin Keary carried a pocket watch from his youth—a constant reminder that he was attempting to outrun the brokenness of his past. How can past brokenness affect our decision

making in the future? Would Colin have let go of his past and hoped for a future with Rosamund if Mable hadn't urged him to do so?

4. For all of the happiness John and Mable Ringling enjoyed in their life together, they had to overcome numerous obstacles. How did their shared interests, love, and faith in each other allow them to weather the difficulties in their marriage?

5. Rosamund's journey begins with her pursuit of a calling outside her family's strict expectations for her life. Though she did eventually find love with Colin, the journey wasn't without loss—she never fully regained her sight. When an unforeseen experience changes our expectations about life, can we still find contentment in new circumstances? How did Rosamund and Colin move on from great losses in their lives?

Also Available from Kristy Cambron, the

Hidden Masterpiece Novels!

A mysterious painting breathes hope and beauty into the darkest corners of Auschwitz—and the loneliest hearts of Manhattan.

Bound together across time, two women will discover a powerful connection through one survivor's story of hope in the darkest days of a war-torn world.

ABOUT THE AUTHOR

Photo by Danielle Mitchell Photography

Kristy Cambron fancies life as a vintage-inspired storyteller. Her novels have been named to Library Journal Reviews' list of Best Books of 2014 and 2015 and have received nominations for RT Reviewers' Choice Awards Best Inspirational Book of 2014 and 2015. She holds a degree in Art History from Indiana University and has fifteen years of training and communications experience for a Fortune 100 corporation. She lives in Indiana with her husband and three football-loving sons.

Visit her website: www.kristycambron.com
Twitter: @KCambronAuthor
Facebook: Kristy-Cambron